"Don't make this harder than it already is," she whispered.

Hurt seared Conall's insides. "If you think I'm going to walk away from you without an explanation, you don't know me very well. There's not a snowball's chance in hell, Bailey."

"I'll explain."

"Damn right you will. You would have let me make love to you last night."

"Don't you see? That's exactly why we have to break up."

"How is the fact that we're extremely sexually compatible a problem?"

"I'm not a casual affair girl. I can't make love to you and go our separate ways. And I can't fight temptation any longer."

Dear Reader,

Let April shower you with the most thrilling romances around—from Silhouette Intimate Moments, of course. We love Karen Templeton's engaging characters and page-turning prose. In her latest story, *Swept Away* (#1357), from her miniseries THE MEN OF MAYES COUNTY, a big-city heroine goes on a road trip and gets stranded in tiny Haven, Oklahoma…with a very handsome cowboy and his six kids. Can this rollicking group become a family? *New York Times* bestselling author Ana Leigh returns with another BISHOP'S HEROES romance, *Reconcilable Differences* (#1358), in which two lovers reunite as they play a deadly game to fight international terror.

You will love the action and heavy emotion of *Midnight Hero* (#1359) in Diana Duncan's new FOREVER IN A DAY miniseries. Here, a SWAT cop has to convince his sweetheart to marry him—while trying to survive a hostage situation! And get ready for Suzanne McMinn to take you by storm in *Cole Dempsey's Back in Town* (#1360), in which a rakish hero must clear his name and face the woman he's never forgotten.

Catch feverish passion and high stakes in Nina Bruhns's *Blue Jeans and a Badge* (#1361). This tale features a female bounty hunter who arrests a very exasperating—very sexy— chief of police! Can these two get along long enough to catch a dangerous criminal? And please join me in welcoming new author Beth Cornelison to the line. In *To Love, Honor and Defend* (#1362), a tormented beauty enters a marriage of convenience with an old flame…and hopes that he'll keep her safe from a stalker. Will their relationship deepen into true love? Don't miss this touching and gripping romance!

So, sit back, prop up your feet and enjoy the ride with Silhouette Intimate Moments. And be sure to join us next month for another stellar lineup.

Happy reading!

Patience Smith
Associate Senior Editor

Please address questions and book requests to:
Silhouette Reader Service
U.S.: 3010 Walden Ave., P.O. Box 1325, Buffalo, NY 14269
Canadian: P.O. Box 609, Fort Erie, Ont. L2A 5X3

Midnight Hero
DIANA DUNCAN

INTIMATE MOMENTS™
Published by Silhouette Books
America's Publisher of Contemporary Romance

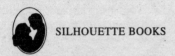 SILHOUETTE BOOKS

ISBN 0-373-27429-7

MIDNIGHT HERO

Books by Diana Duncan

Silhouette Intimate Moments

Bulletproof Bride #1284
*Midnight Hero #1359

*Forever in a Day

DIANA DUNCAN's

fascination with books started before she could walk, when her librarian grandmother toted her to work. Diana crafted her first tale at age four, a riveting account of Perky the Kitten, printed in orange crayon. The discovery of her mom's Harlequin Romance novels at age fourteen sparked a lifelong affection for plucky heroines and dashing heroes. She loves writing about complex, conflicted men and strong, intelligent women with the courage to dive into the biggest adventure of all—falling in love.

When not writing stories brimming with heart, humor and sizzling passion, Diana spends her time with her husband, two daughters and two cats in their Portland, Oregon, home. Diana loves to hear from her readers. She can be reached via e-mail at writedianaduncan@msn.com or snail mail at P.O. Box 33193, Portland, OR 97292-3193.

For my husband, Darol, who supported me, helped me,
dried countless tears, washed endless dishes
and put in over 7,000 hours of overtime
the past six years so I could follow my dream and write.
I love you, honey. You'll always be my hero.

"Yesterday is ashes; tomorrow is wood. Only today does the fire burn brightly."

~ Old Eskimo Proverb

Prologue

Riverside, Oregon
New Year's Eve, 8:00 p.m.

SWAT team door kicker Conall O'Rourke studied the blood under his fingernails. He'd scrubbed his hands, but blood under the nails was always a bitch to get out. How'd he end up butt-deep in bullets and blood anyway? He'd started the day off with a promotion, and had planned to cap it with a long-overdue marriage proposal. Today was supposed to be one of the happiest of his life. Instead, he was grimy, battered and exhausted.

Trapped like a rat in a maze.

His chest tight, he stared down at Bailey dozing beside him in the cold gloom of the canvas tent. She trusted him to keep her safe—enough to sleep in the middle of combat—and he wouldn't let her down. Her long, coppery eyelashes rested against her creamy cheeks, and delicate blue veins traced under her eyelids. Her pulse fluttered evenly in her throat. She was beautiful, but he'd never been big on dating women for their looks. He was far more intrigued by what went on inside them. What made them tick. And he'd chosen well. Bailey's tender emotions warmed his aching heart like flickering candlelight in a dark room. And without her quick intelligence, he might not be alive right now.

His girl only *looked* fragile. Only *thought* she was weak. Deep down, she was made of sturdy stuff. Otherwise, she wouldn't have triumphed over tragedy with her spirit intact.

Wouldn't have won freedom from her oppressive mother. Wouldn't be the caring woman he loved. He stroked her red-gold curls, and she breathed a soft sigh. If the worst happened, and Bailey had to live without him, he hoped he'd given her enough tonight to sustain her.

And if *she* died?

Wrenching pain stopped his heart. Then it resumed beating, steady and determined. He would do anything to make sure that didn't happen. Give everything.

Even his own life.

He was grateful she'd finally succumbed to fatigue. At least he didn't have to fake it anymore. It was damned hard to project strength when he was afraid clear to his bones. To stay upbeat, when the odds were so long against them, that even he, an incurable optimist, wouldn't bet on himself in the coming battle.

He could no longer pretend confidence, when every instinct he possessed screamed they were all going to die.

If it were only his life at stake, he wouldn't be worried. He'd launch a tactical assault, and accept the risk. But how was he supposed to keep the woman he loved and three hostages alive against six Uzi-toting bank robbers? With no way out, no backup and armed only with a baseball bat. Wait, make that five bank robbers. He'd taken one down earlier in hand-to-hand combat. Still, five Uzis against one Louisville Slugger wasn't such hot odds.

Eerie silence crept over him, prickling the hair on the back of his neck, and he glanced up, straining to hear the slightest noise. Being hunted had honed every sense to a razor's edge. Careful not to disturb Bailey, he tore open a pack of cinnamon gum. Chewing gum helped him focus on the way to an incident site, and in the midst of long sieges. During an assault, the spicy taste overrode the smell of gunpowder and gore. Right now, he needed the boost to his concentration. All his focus. Four other lives depended on him.

He needed every scrap of wits if they were to survive until dawn.

Chapter 1

Earlier that morning.

Conall O'Rourke was psyched to take the biggest risk of his risk-filled life. Determination and adrenaline pumped in his system as he strode across the parking lot toward the diner. Tucked into one pocket of his jacket were two dozen gold-shield condoms. In the other was the best platinum-and-diamond engagement ring a public servant's salary could buy.

The ring might be premature. The condoms were way overdue.

Winter clouds loomed on the rainy Oregon horizon like smoke over a battlefield. Con flipped up the collar of his black leather jacket to stave off the dropping temperature. A winter storm was in the forecast. But no matter what the weather threw at him, it was gonna be a beautiful day. And night.

He paused outside the door in the chilly gloom to automatically scan the interior, and brushed his hand across his thick black hair. The habitual gesture was one of the reasons he went for a short spiky cut. Women had dubbed his hair "adorably tousled, stylishly edgy and just-went-a-wild-round-between-the-sheets sexy." To him, it was convenient. When you could be called out any time to bash down doors and eat bullets, there was no time to screw around with your hair.

He rolled his wrist and consulted his watch. Ten in the morning, right on time. His girl's idea of punctuality was arriving everywhere five minutes early. Through the window, he caught a glimpse of her and smiled. As dependable as the sunrise, Bailey was sitting in their booth at the back. The familiar cocktail of lust and tenderness kicked him in the chest—as it had the first time he'd seen her, and every time after that.

His woman. His soul mate. His future.

Some guys might consider proposing after only six months moving too fast. He didn't. The average SWAT assault-and-rescue, from door breach to secure status, lasted four to nine seconds. His life and the lives of his teammates depended on his ability to devise a plan and act. Make quick decisions. Good decisions. Waffle, and you die. Worse, your buddies die because of you.

Fast was relative.

Bailey's early phone call requesting a breakfast meeting had been unexpected. They already had plans to ring in the New Year tonight at the Montrose Hotel. She knew about dinner and dancing. His bended knee proposal and the resulting night of passion in the Ambassador Suite would be a surprise.

He couldn't wait to see her face when she saw the ring. He'd scoured jewelry shops, hating the ice-cold stones and sterile settings. Discouraged, he'd stopped for a coffee break and spotted the ring in the window of an antique store next door. A one-carat emerald-cut diamond flanked with smaller heart-shaped diamonds. Vintage 1930s. Like the woman he'd purchased it for, the ring was unique. Old-fashioned yet stylish. Classic, yet romantic. Sparkling with warmth and personality. Like their love, it was timeless, and would last forever.

As he stepped inside, the smell of crisp bacon and fresh biscuits in the steamy air heightened his anticipation. Working up the nerve to propose cranked up a guy's appetite. A clanging brass bell over the door announced his arrival, and Bailey's head jerked up.

Her amazing blue eyes connected with his and his blood heated. He couldn't believe his good fortune. One breakfast a day for the next sixty years equaled…21,900 chances to sit across the table from this fascinating, intelligent, sexy woman. The rest of his life. He fingered the velvet ring box in his pocket and fought the urge to jump the gun and propose now. Timing was everything. He, of all people, knew that.

He grinned and waved. Her posture tense, she didn't return his smile. Instead, her wary stare watched him approach the booth. He blinked away a discomfiting mental flash of a hawk swooping down on a defenseless robin.

What the hell? He replayed their date last night. Had he said or done something to upset her? Where had he slipped up? They'd watched a chick flick. He hadn't minded too much, as long as he was with her. They'd consumed popcorn and soda, and then made out on her sofa until his pager beeped. A lucky interruption, considering how tough it was to fight his desire to make love to her. He chafed under the growing need for her to belong to him in every way. For him to belong to her.

"Mornin', darlin'. Switch with me?"

"Sure." Her agreement was too quiet. Foreboding itched between his shoulder blades. During a siege, things often got too quiet right before all hell broke loose. She rose, her usual graceful movements awkward. "Sorry, I'm distracted this morning. I forgot you like to sit where you can see the door."

As she passed, he breathed in her scent. Rose petals and peppermint. Warmth curled through him. "No biggie." He slid into the seat across from her and brought her hand to his lips. Her deathly cold fingers quivered. Not passion. Distress. What was up with that? "What's got you so upset, sweetheart?"

Before she could reply, the stocky, gray-haired waitress moseyed over with coffee for him and requested their orders. Con looked at Bailey. She nodded, and he ordered their usual breakfasts.

The waitress sauntered toward the kitchen and Con turned back to Bailey. The silver hummingbird charm he'd bought her on their first date nestled in the hollow of her throat. Right above where her pulse throbbed a shade too fast. The charm dangled from a black ribbon she'd tied around her neck. She never took off the trinket.

The pink ruffled blouse she wore normally complemented her creamy complexion. Today, her face was a wan contrast to her shoulder-length strawberry-blond curls. A barely touched mug of peppermint tea sat on the tabletop. That wasn't like her at all; his girl loved her tea. Something *was* wrong.

She tugged her hand free, and his muscles tensed in apprehension. "Bailey, what's wrong?"

"Nothing. Exactly." She shifted. Scrubbed her palms on her gray wool slacks. Wouldn't meet his eyes. All the nervous tells he'd seen in suspects sweating out an interrogation. His own tungsten nerves were taking a beating. If she didn't get to the point soon, he was going to start twitching.

"No, everything's wrong." Her teeth bit into her bottom lip. Last night, his teeth had teased and tempted that lush bottom lip until they'd both been gasping for breath. "I've agonized for a long time, and finally made a decision."

He relaxed. She'd had problems with her job for weeks and struggled with the options. Bailey gave every decision careful consideration. Loyalty to her customers and co-workers warred with her desire to escape an obnoxious boss. "Finally decided to tell Mole Man to stuff it, and take that management position in the other store, huh?" He lifted his mug in a salute before gulping the hot, rich coffee. "Way to go."

"This isn't about work." She absently sipped her peppermint tea. "Things nearly got out of control between us last night."

He switched gears without effort. Ah. Like him, she'd reached her sexual frustration limit. Unlike him, she was shy talking about it. They'd have as much rapport in the bedroom as they did elsewhere. "Now, darlin', just because I scorched your sofa..."

"If you hadn't been called up, we'd have ended up in bed."

He shook his head. "I was pretty far gone, but not out of control." Perilously close, he'd clung to the razor's edge. She'd want commitment first, because that's the woman she was. Her utter commitment was one of the qualities he admired about her. But asking him for it had her tied up in knots. She was probably afraid he'd run—the typical male response.

He'd never been typical. Falling in love with quiet, intense Bailey was a prime example. His previous women had been blatant extroverts. Good-time girls. Fun, but as shallow as a politician's promise. He hadn't known he was missing a soul-deep emotional connection until he'd met Bailey Chambers.

Con again brushed his fingers over the velvet ring box. Hoo boy, was she in for a surprise. "Baby, I wouldn't have taken you any farther than you wanted to go."

"That's the problem. I wanted to go farther—" She swallowed hard. "My decision is about us."

He grinned, deciding to end her misery. Give her the commitment she needed to take the next step. What the hell. In his line of work, he'd learned to improvise when things changed without warning. He'd propose now and they'd celebrate later.

"What a coincidence. I've also made a decision about us." In spite of himself, nerves jittered up his spine. Damn, this was more intimidating than eating bullets. His mom would call it a "life-defining moment" and caution him to remember it. He would. Every detail. Someday, he'd tell their children the story, and if he was very lucky, their grandchildren.

The atmosphere wasn't moonlight and roses like he'd planned, but at least he would go down on one knee and do that part right. Con slid toward the edge of the seat. "Bailey—"

She stopped him with a shaky grip on his arm. "Please let me say this before I lose my nerve." She inhaled, shuddered. "I'm sorry, Con. So sorry. We have to break up. It's over."

He froze. Impossible. He'd misunderstood, that's all. It was hard to hear over the roaring in his ears. "What?"

The waitress reappeared, bearing a loaded tray. Bailey's heart-shaped face crumpled in silent misery while the woman placed steaming plates in front of them. The fine tendrils curling at her temple made Bailey appear delicate. Like one of the china dolls his mom kept in a sturdy, locked cabinet safely out of reach of her four rambunctious sons.

The waitress strolled off, and Con shoved away his breakfast. He couldn't force a single shred of food past the burning lump in his throat. Not even if someone held a loaded AK-47 to his head. "What did you say?"

Bailey pushed aside her veggie omelet. Apparently she didn't have an appetite for this, either. "We have to break up. I can't see you anymore."

Con's heart tried to slam out of his rib cage, and he fought to keep his voice level. There had to be a logical explanation for her sudden change of heart. Or was it sudden? Had he misread the situation? "What's going on? I love you. You love me."

"Please," she whispered. "Don't make this harder than it already is."

Hurt seared his insides. "If you think I'm going to walk away from you without an explanation, you don't know me very well. There's not a snowball's chance in hell, Bailey."

"I'll explain."

"Damn right you will. You would have let me make love to you last night."

"Don't you see? That's exactly *why* we have to break up."

Was she implying that he'd forced her? He swallowed a surge of nausea. No. Her soft lips had parted willingly for his kisses. Her eager hands had sought his body, and her hips had arched as he'd rocked against her. "How is the fact that we're extremely sexually compatible a problem?"

"I'm not a casual affair girl. I can't make love to you and go our separate ways. And I can't fight temptation any longer."

Did she think he was a jerk who would use her and dump her? Maybe she *didn't* know him. Funny, he felt as if he'd known *her* forever. "I realize that, sweetheart." He thrust his hand in his pocket, and his fingers clenched on the ring box. "That's why—"

Panic skittered across her face. "Please, wait, and hear me out. I've thought about our relationship, agonized over all the angles. My mother suggested I carefully weigh the pros and cons of staying together."

The picture morphed into painful focus. Dr. Ellen Chambers hadn't bothered to hide her icy disapproval of him. The chilly polar opposite of her vibrant daughter, Dr. Chambers was a renowned cardiac surgeon. He could see why. She'd have no problem cutting out hearts. At their first meeting, the austere brunette had cornered him in her kitchen after an uncomfortable dinner filled with too-long silences. In a voice that could have flash-frozen his gonads, she'd told him he wasn't a good influence on her child.

He'd just as bluntly reminded Dr. Chambers that her daughter was an adult. And what Bailey did with her life, and who she spent time with, was her decision.

Bailey was her own woman, but even the toughest barricade eventually collapsed under relentless pressure. He was in for serious damage containment. He leaned back and crossed his arms.

"My brothers have pointed out I'm far from perfect, many times. I'm open to new ideas. Go ahead. Let's hear all my faults."

She shook her head. "There's nothing wrong with you. Nothing wrong with me. We're both good people. We simply aren't right for each other. I'm not trying to hurt you, just trying to explain. We're too different. There's no need to hash out—"

"There's every need."

"All right." She paused. "You're quick and decisive, I'm deliberate. You kick down doors and nail bad guys to the wall, I sell books and visit sick kids in hospitals."

"So, we have some differences. Enough differences to clash—in a positive way—and enough similarities to click. We complement one another."

"We don't have *any* similarities."

"Don't we?" He smiled at her. "We're both intense. Both dedicated to our jobs. Loyal to our loved ones. We care about people and their welfare. You educate, enlighten and entertain them, I protect them." He grew serious, leaned forward. "Most importantly, we love each other."

She hesitated. "Where do you see us in five years?"

He held her gaze, his thoughts tender. Five years? He could see them in fifty-five years. "Married. Happy."

She gulped and looked down at their uneaten food, breaking the connection. "Where do we live? How many kids do we have? Are you still in the same job? Am I? What kind of shape are we in financially? What are our interests, who are our friends?"

He'd known her propensity for planning, but this was overkill. And smelled like more of Ellen Chambers's influence. "Darlin' there are unanswerable questions in life. Some things can't be scheduled. Sometimes it's better to keep things simple. Ad-lib."

"It's not. The only way to be secure, have peace of mind, is to be organized and prepared. Keep things under control."

"Life isn't in our control. Crap happens. You deal with it." He shrugged. "We'll handle whatever comes, as it comes. Together."

"You can't know that. We've only been dating six months."

He used his index finger to tip up her chin until her gaze again met his. "I fell in love with you in six seconds."

Stark misery shadowed her blue eyes. But there was no mistaking the resolve in her gaze. His gut clenched. For the first time since she'd ambushed him with the breakup, he questioned his ability to assault-and-rescue her doubts. He squared his shoulders. He never accepted defeat. On any level.

Tears pooled in her eyes. "Sometimes love isn't enough. It boils down to who we are. You shake hands with violence and death on a daily basis. I don't understand violence, can't be a part of it." She gave him a sad, tremulous smile. "I can't even kill the mice that get into the storage room at the shop, even though they chew the books. I use humane traps and let them go."

Trap and release didn't work with criminals. He'd arrested too many perps already on parole for prior crimes. The minute the vermin got out, they crawled right back into your house. But his sensitive girl wouldn't buy that—she was determined to see the best in everyone. He shrugged. "I don't have a problem with humane mousetraps."

"This isn't about mice, and you know it. It's your job."

"Why now? You've known what I do since our first date."

"And lived in denial. Knowing and seeing are two very different things. The morning news forced me to face it."

Understanding dawned. "Ah. Well, you know the media maggots. They always blow everything out of proportion. Sensationalize every detail. Juice it up to increase ratings."

"I saw the raging fire and the SWAT team dodging exploding gunshots. Saw the burnt-out meth lab your team was called up to serve a high-risk warrant on. Saw the medical examiners carrying out body bags." Tears streaked her face with crystal rivers of sorrow. "Four body bags. Three suspects and one SWAT officer." Her voice broke. "They didn't say who the officer was."

He cradled her hand in his. "I'm sorry, sweetheart. I had no idea they broadcast that. The casualty was from another team. I was going to call you this morning as soon as I was sure you were awake and let you know I was okay. You called me instead."

Her fingers trembled in his grasp. "You can't help wanting to be first in line to catch bullets between your teeth. You can't help being a hero, because that's what you are. Who you are. And I'd never ask you to give it up. Ever."

"I'm no hero." Ice slinked up his spine. This was no mere case of commitment jitters. The survival of their relationship was in serious jeopardy. "I'm just doing my damn job."

"Accountants are just doing their jobs. Shoe salesmen are just doing their jobs. You're risking your life every minute. My father was a hero, and he came home in a body bag. After what that did to my mother, to me, I can't go through it again." Her entire body was shaking violently.

He studied her stricken face. The decision was tearing her apart. If she really wanted to break off with him, she wouldn't be so heartbroken. "You can't seriously tell me this is what you really want."

"What I *want* doesn't matter. I can't make this choice with my heart. I have to make it with my head."

"The *only* way to make this choice is with your heart."

"No. I have to do what's best. For your sake."

Bewilderment snaked through him. "What does that mean?"

"I'm not the kind of woman you need. Or deserve. I don't have the strength to support you." She was openly crying now. "I've seen the consequences. With my parents."

"We are not our parents." He cupped her face. Hot, wet tears dripped onto his hand, making his throat ache. "Bailey, listen. You're exactly the kind of woman I need. You're the only woman I want. We can work this out."

"We can't. I was drawn to your vitality, your heat—tempted to dance too close to the fire. I'm more like my father than I thought. My mother warned him, and he didn't listen. He died. She might as well have, too, and I refuse to end up like her."

"You need some space. I respect that. We'll spend time together and work it out. We won't get physical. No pressure."

"Con, the more we're together, the closer we get, and the harder it will be to end it. I'm just not cut out for your brand of adventure."

"*Life* is an adventure, darlin'."

"Not my life. I like my life steady. Predictable. Safe. No matter how much attraction sizzles between us, no matter how much I…I c-care about you—" She choked and blew her nose on a paper napkin. "In the end, my fears will destroy you."

"You're upset, understandably so." He stroked her cheek with his thumb. "Last night was an ugly business. On TV, the incident probably looked scary and chaotic, but my team had everything under control. Once you get used to it—"

She shuddered. "A daily dose of violence and death, and you grow immune? I could never get used to it. I *refuse.*"

"That's not what I meant."

"I could never do what you do."

"Nobody expects you to." Frustrated, he scrubbed a hand over his jaw. "Let's go somewhere private and I'll explain—"

"I'm sorry, I'm simply not brave enough." She tugged her hand from his and grabbed her purse. "No matter how thrilling the ride, I won't buy a ticket on a runaway train to heartbreak."

"Bailey—"

She leaped to her feet. "Goodbye, Con." Sobbing, she fled.

Con sat unmoving in the tomb-silent booth, as stunned and shaken as if a flash-bang grenade had exploded in his face. What the hell had just happened? He'd walked in pumped to ask Bailey to marry him. And here he sat. Alone.

She'd left her coat on the seat when they'd switched places, and then run out without it. He picked it up and buried his nose in the soft beige wool. Like the woman, the disparate scents of rose petals and peppermint mingled into an intriguing combination. Soft and sweet, yet fresh and invigorating.

The world went gray. For a few moments he thought the lights had gone out, then realized the clouds outside were massing overhead. The sky darkened, until morning looked like midnight. Then again, maybe it was the haze over his vision.

What was he supposed to do now? He'd unblinkingly faced down gangbangers bearing Uzis. Been stabbed in the forearm by a crazed crack addict during a raid and kept shooting. Rappelled out of a chopper without hesitation into a line of gunfire so heavy the smoke obliterated his sight. In five years on the force, he'd never frozen in the line of duty. But none of his combat training had prepared him for a direct assault on his heart.

A cold shot to the heart hurt more than he'd ever imagined.

Fighting the urge to run inside and snatch back her fateful words, Bailey choked back sobs as she drove out of the parking lot. Con wasn't the type to surrender. He'd come charging out the diner's doorway any minute, determined to batter down her barricades. She had to get away. Before he got her alone and her resolve crumbled under the hurt in his beautiful brown eyes. Wounds she'd inflicted.

Trembling all over, she resisted the need to look back as the diner shrank in her rearview mirror. To watch her future fade along with the place that held so many happy memories. Streaming tears blurred her vision. Driving in this condition was as dangerous as driving drunk.

She pulled into Riverbend Park. Twisted branches formed a skeletal canopy overhead. A fountain in the park's center spewed icy cascades into the air. The park was deserted, the fountain lonely. As cold and empty as her soul. She shivered under the morning's damp bite. She'd accidentally left her coat in the diner, but there was no going back. Not now. Tears flooded her eyes and she swiped them away. The coat was the least valuable thing she'd left behind.

This was the second-worst day of her life. Only her father's funeral had been more painful. Her chest hurt, and misery churned in her stomach. Bailey clutched the wheel so hard her hands ached. She wanted to cling as tightly to Con as she was to the steering wheel. She never wanted to hurt him in any way.

Which is why she had to leave him.

She watched the fountain and prayed for peace. The rushing water created miniature waterfalls, which brought to mind her and Con's first real date. When he discovered she loved bird-watching and being near the water, he'd asked her to hike the waterfall trail in the Columbia River Gorge. On a gorgeous summer day in July, they had walked the circular trail through the green woods, stopping at five waterfalls scattered along the loop.

Thrilled to her toes, she'd stood hand in hand with him on a
bluff over a shimmering waterfall as they'd watched a pair of bald
eagles wheeling and dipping over the shining water.

Afterward, they ate on an outdoor deck at an inn overlooking
the river. Sun glinted off the choppy waves, and the breeze tousled her curls. Con reached out and brushed a strand of hair off
her cheek, and the high-voltage connection that arced between
them shook them both. Breathless, she turned her head and
watched the dozens of windsurfers on the river. Their sailboards
danced across the waves like bright butterflies.

Con asked if she wanted to windsurf. She declined. But she
couldn't hold out against his enthusiasm, and five minutes later,
found herself in the inn's gift shop renting a wetsuit. Con had
been windsurfing the day before and still had his board and wetsuit in the back of his truck. They spent a sparkling afternoon on
the river. Con's warm, solid body behind her, his protective
stance around her as he steadied her on the board felt so right.
Like she belonged in his arms.

A patient tutor, he good-naturedly hauled them both out of the
water when she repeatedly overbalanced and upended them. She
laughed more that day than she had in a lifetime.

When they returned her wetsuit, they bought ice cream
stacked inside waffle cones. Peppermint for her, huckleberry for
him. Con noticed her admiring glance snag on a tiny silver hummingbird charm in the gift shop, and insisted on buying it for her.
They drove home engrossed in conversation.

At her door, she'd longed for him to kiss her. Instead, he'd
tugged a lock of her hair and flashed his mischievous grin. The
sexy cop's killer grin should be a felony. It sure assassinated all
her inhibitions. He'd extracted a promise from her to have dinner with him that weekend, then sauntered to his truck.

Intoxicated by happiness, she'd waltzed into her apartment
with a sun-kissed complexion and soaring spirits. Her sense of
wonder and rightness had confirmed their initial whammo attraction. The connection wasn't merely chemistry.

It was destiny.

An hour after Con left, her mom had dropped by and delivered a stern lecture about skin cancer from sun exposure and the dangers of windsurfing, along with a dire warning about risk-taking men. Bailey had let her mother voice her worries, while silently holding her own joy close to her heart.

Outside, the wind howled, rocking the car in its frigid teeth, as if trying to tear away her warm memories. Her mom used to be different. Her parents had started out happy. Bailey remembered sunny, laughter-filled family outings. Affectionate glances between her mom and dad. Loving embraces. As time had passed though, the silences lengthened and grew cold. Angry words screamed in the darkness as she huddled, scared and shaking, in her bed.

She'd been too young to understand what the fights were about, or why her mom wanted her dad to quit his job. How could he? When his job was such an important part of him. A firefighter. A brave knight in Nomex armor who battled fire-breathing dragons and rescued the innocent. A hero.

When Bailey was fourteen, he'd died being a hero.

Her mom had frozen into a glacier. She'd grown overprotective, smothering her daughter. Bailey hadn't had the heart to fight her after the trauma they'd suffered. In self-defense, she'd retreated more deeply into her beloved books, becoming subdued and withdrawn.

The wind howled louder. A pinecone slammed into the windshield, and Bailey crashed back to the present. Nothing lasted forever. Carefree summer days were over. Summer was dead and winter's cold fingers held the world in an icy grip.

She clutched the hummingbird charm. She couldn't suppress her fears and be the wife Con needed. She'd make him unhappy. Bitter. They'd both be unhappy. She was a Pisces, a water sign. Con was as bright and hot and appealing to her quiet nature as the fire sign that marked his birth date. Aries, the god of war.

In the end, water would quench the fire. Leaving ashes.

Giving in to sorrow, she sobbed out her heartbreak. In the end, love wasn't enough. Yet love would give her the strength to do what she must. She loved Con too much to destroy him.

She had to let him go.

Chapter 2

For a woman who'd suffered an emotional meltdown, Bailey put on a pretty good front. She turned from the refreshment bar in the reading corner of Bookworm's bookstore carrying a bag holding three warm chocolate chip cookies. Today, the sweet smell made her stomach churn. "Here you go, Nan. Anything else?"

Nan Thompson's green eyes sparkled as she patted her distended abdomen. "I'd like a baby to go, please." The young brunette giggled. "The ultrasound said it was a boy and it must be right. Men are perpetually late. He's probably in there refusing to ask for directions."

Bailey's heart contracted. Con had never once been late. *Con.* The man she'd left dazed and wounded. Thinking of him hurt so badly she could barely breathe. So much for a pretty good front. "You should be home, resting." Nan had insisted on staying in her position at the mall's bank right up to her due date. "I'm surprised the bank manager hasn't booted you out, for fear you'll have that baby in the lobby."

"He's already griping about my maternity leave."

Bailey lowered her head to hide her roiling emotions. "Seems bosses are all the same."

"Seems like." Nan's sharp gaze fastened on Bailey's face. After years of lunchtime heart-to-hearts, Bailey's shaky facade probably hadn't fooled her friend. She'd done her best to repair the wreckage, but she wasn't a pretty crier. No surprise considering how splintered and torn she was inside.

Nan frowned. "Is that what's bothering you? Mole Man up to his usual tricks?"

Bailey focused on Nan's watermelon shape. Big mistake. She'd dreamed about some day having Con's children. Had pictured them cradled in her arms. Long-lashed, starry brown eyes and irresistible smiles, just like their daddy. That wouldn't happen now. Another woman would carry Con's babies. Scalding air jammed her lungs. She fumbled for a cup of water and tried to douse the anguish with icy liquid. It didn't work. "I'm fine."

Nan's voice gentled. "You're anything but fine. Business is dead-slow today." She patted an overstuffed navy chair in the cozy reading nook. "Did you decide to leave us and take that other job after all?"

Business *was* slow. A combination of New Year's Eve and the nasty weather forecast. Too much time to think. To remember. Bailey couldn't get Con's bewildered face out of her mind. His devastated brown eyes. The hurt bracketing his mouth. Pain lanced through her. She couldn't bear to think about him. Or talk about him without losing it completely. "I can't discuss it. Not now."

"Okay but—" Nan's eyes widened. "Yikes! Monster spider!" She grabbed a newspaper, rapidly rolled it and raised the weapon.

Bailey grabbed her arm. "Don't kill it!"

"What, you want to take it home on a leash?" The big gray-brown spider meandered along the brick-red counter and Nan edged back. "That sucker is big enough to wrestle my cat."

"It's a wolf spider. They usually stay in their burrows in winter. Poor lost soul." Bailey snatched the paper and scooped up the lethargic arachnid. Her gaze traveled around the deserted room. "Watch the store for me? I'll be right back."

"Yeah, if Franken-Spider doesn't eat you."

Bailey carefully balanced the newspaper as she strode down the mall's quiet corridor and out the main doors. Dark clouds overhead wept icy drizzle, a dreary reflection of her sorrow.

A barrel-chested man with salt-and-pepper hair lounged outside under the entryway, smoking. He was turned aside so she couldn't see his face, but she felt his eyes watching from the shadows.

As she gently dumped the spider beneath the sheltered bushes beside the building, he took a drag on his cigarette. "Most women have screaming fits over anything that big and ugly." His speech bore a hint of the Bronx.

The spider scurried under a leaf. Bailey empathized with the arachnid's relief at being returned to her environment, away from threatening predators. The spider would burrow under the dirt, safe from the storm. A pointed lesson from nature. Don't wander from where you belong. Adventure often has a lethal ending. "She's a wolf spider. They live in underground burrows and eat damaging insects. There's no reason to kill her simply because she got lost and wandered into the wrong territory."

His broad shoulders covered by a black wool peacoat hunched against the cold. "A smart babe with a soft heart." He laughed, but the deep, graveled bark wasn't humorous. "You remind me of someone I knew a long time ago."

Bailey sensed his gaze assessing her, a hawk watching his prey. The back of her neck prickled and she shivered. Chill or warning? Mom had always forbidden her to talk to strangers. Of course, Mom was paranoid. Still, it was good advice. Without another word, she spun on her heel and hurried inside.

Syrone Spencer, the hulking security guard, stood by the one-hour photo booth. People would never guess the intimidating man was an avid chess player. A week after Con had started dating Bailey, Syrone had shown up at the bookstore at closing. Under the guise of a chess match, Syrone had checked him out as expertly and thoroughly as any wary father. Con had passed muster, and the two men had become close friends over the past six months. He and Con often amused themselves with competitive matches while he waited for her to close up the bookstore.

Con. Nothing in her life was untouched by memories of him. She'd have to live with the throbbing echoes forever. Just penance for hurting him.

Syrone's ebony face broke into a smile as she approached. "Hey, Bailey. What's up?"

"Hey, big guy. Not much, it's slow." She hesitated. Maybe the man outside was simply indulging a nicotine fit. The mall was a public place, frequented by all kinds. Maybe the menace she'd felt wasn't real. Her traumatic morning had thrown her off balance. However, her creep radar was usually right on target. "There's a guy smoking outside the main entrance. Black peacoat, gray-streaked hair. He seemed…spooky. Out of place."

Syrone's expression grew serious. "I'm all over it."

"I feel safer knowing you're on the job. Be careful, okay?"

Syrone nodded. "I'm always careful. I've got a beautiful wife and four munchkins who depend on me."

She hurried back to the bookstore, where Nan leaned against the counter. The store's cheerful warmth did nothing to ease the chill that had seeped into Bailey's bones. She shivered again.

Nan pointed to the picture tucked on the far side of the cash register. "You take that?"

Bailey glanced at the snapshot of Con and his three brothers, and sorrow slammed into her. "Yes, Christmas Day." Christmas at the O'Rourkes' was an event. Unlike the quiet holidays spent alone with her mom, the O'Rourke home had been a rowdy whirlwind of bright wrapping paper, bountiful food, nonstop teasing and masculine laughter. An event she'd never again be part of. The picture showcased how much Con, Aidan, Liam and Grady, all SWAT officers, looked alike. Yet each man's unique, vibrant personality shone through.

Their irrepressible mom called the boys her four "S" men. Not just because they stair-stepped in age from twenty-seven to thirty. Or because they were all SWAT. She had her own special handle for each of them. Aidan, the strong. Con, the sensitive. Liam, the scamp. Grady, the searcher. As if Maureen O'Rourke had room to talk. The vibrant, sixty-year-old redhead was as strong and stubborn and capable in her own way as any of her sons. Maybe more than all four of 'em put together. Tears she'd thought cried out crowded behind Bailey's eyelids.

"Verra nice, girlfriend. A woman would have to be a hopeless idiot to turn down a dip in that gene pool."

So what did that make her? Bailey blinked rapidly, nearly unable to speak around the choking lump in her throat. Had she ever been as young and exuberant as Nan? She hadn't felt young since she was fourteen. She'd been forced to grow up over-night—between her dad's death and his funeral. "The weather's getting dicey. Maybe you should go home early."

Nan's face lit up. "Great idea! Maybe I can throw together an impromptu New Year's Eve party. You and Con want to come?"

Con had planned a candlelight dinner, followed by dancing at the Montrose Hotel. Instead of spending New Year's Eve with the man she loved, Bailey would be home crying her eyes out. *Your choice.* No. Her responsibility. She cleared the tightness from her throat. "I'm not really in a party mood, thanks."

"Okay. Try to have a Happy New Year." Nan patted her arm. "I've got to scoot. When you want to talk, look me up."

Happy New Year? Not a chance. Heaviness weighed on Bailey's chest like a sodden blanket. How long did a broken heart take to mend? She suspected healing would take a very long time.

Letty Jacobson scurried into the store, bundled in a red parka with black fur trim. Eiffel Tower earrings and a zebra bag completed the colorful ensemble. Claiming she needed some stud muffins to keep her warm if the power went out, Bailey's favorite senior citizen quickly selected a stack of romance novels. The O'Rourke family's lifelong neighbor, Letty possessed an abundance of grandmotherly interest and a serious case of matchmaking fever.

When Bailey slotted Letty's debit card, the lights flickered and the cash register didn't respond. Neither did the debit authorization center, and Letty had to make out a check. The weather must have worsened enough to affect the power and slow the phone lines.

While Letty wrote, the lively octogenarian waxed lyrical about a new generation of O'Rourke scamps, and how she couldn't wait to hold Bailey and Con's future babies.

Keeping her face averted, Bailey bagged the books and battled for composure. *Get a grip. You can cry at home.* Once she started, she wouldn't be able to stop. By the time she turned and passed the purchase over the counter, her expression was under control.

Letty patted Bailey's arm. "Honey, whatever has happened be-tween you and your young man, talk it out. Don't let the sun set on your troubles."

The woman bustled out toward the bank, and Bailey slumped against the counter. How had Letty guessed the reason she was so upset? Sometimes, the older woman's perception was downright scary. Much more of this and she'd be on the floor. She needed to go home, curl up in her favorite raspberry-plaid fleece blanket and sip a comforting cup of tea.

The lights flickered again, and the mall's PA system crackled. "Attention River View Mall customers. Due to a computer malfunction, our registers are not working. The mall is closing. All outer doors and freight doors have been automatically locked for your safety. Please proceed to the three main exits on the ground floor, where a security guard will escort you out. We are sorry for the inconvenience, and hope you will shop with us again."

Safety, right. The doors automatically locked down during emergencies to prevent widespread five-finger discounts. Theft by both customers and certain employees was a constant problem. But the computer glitch explained the cash register's constipation.

Bailey checked her marcasite watch. Nearly one o'clock. They weren't due to close for five hours. The several ice storms Riverside experienced each winter usually started farther east and moved in fast. Mild storms caused slippery inconveniences that melted overnight. Severe storms entombed everything in a thick layer of ice for days and brought trees and power lines crashing down. Widespread destruction. She shivered and wondered what kind of storm was headed their way.

She strode to the back of the store to begin the pre-closing routine. She unplugged the Christmas tree, using the arm of the navy chair beside it to rise. When Con wasn't playing chess with Syrone, he'd often settle into the chair and read a magazine while Bailey closed up. At least he'd start out reading. Then she'd glance up and find him courting her with his eyes. Sending silent messages her heart didn't have any trouble interpreting. He didn't have to touch her. Her skin would heat, her cheeks flush, her body tingle. By the time they arrived home, she'd be longing for his kisses. Aching for his caresses.

She bit the inside of her cheek. Memories of Con were every-

where. Healing was impossible here. She would have to accept
the other position offered by a store across town. Leave her beloved regular customers, familiar routine and mall-employee
friends. Start over. Where reminders of the man she'd given up
wouldn't haunt her every waking moment.

The PA system crackled again. "Attention employees. The
mall is now closed. Because of the electrical instability, security
gates for individual stores may not operate. Follow emergency
procedure code yellow. Your key cards will not open any doors,
including freight doors. When you complete cleanup and cash
tallies, proceed to the main mall exit B on the ground floor,
where a uniformed security guard will escort you out."

Emergency procedure code yellow? Bailey hurried to the
storeroom to locate a handbook. It instructed her to tally her register and deposit the contents at the mall's bank. Included was a
notation that no funds would be disbursed until the following day.

No funds disbursed. She groaned. She'd forgotten it was pay-
day. She'd have to wait until tomorrow for her money. Oh well.
She wasn't going anywhere except home. A hot bath and a good
cry were the only items on her agenda.

Her decision to let Con go had cost her everything. But grief
was free.

Carrying the cash bag stamped with the store's name and account number, she exited the storeroom. A gasp punched out of
her and she jerked to a halt. Con stood beside the counter, his
face solemn, hands clasped behind his back.

Memories of the first time she'd seen him flooded her. He'd
strolled into the store, a modern Lancelot exuding confident
grace and power. He'd asked for an antique book of Celtic verse,
a birthday gift for his mother. Bailey had been struck by lightning. It was the only explanation for the flash of blinding sparks
and overwhelming heat. She'd fumbled through the special order
in a daze. She'd spent the following week thinking of nothing
but Conall O'Rourke and his breath-stealing grin. And counting
the minutes until he returned to pick up the book.

He'd accepted the volume with a smile that had kicked her
pulse into the stratosphere. Cradling the book in his big, capa-

ble hands, he'd flipped through the pages. Then, his gaze holding hers, his eyes as warm and lustrous as polished mahogany,
he'd recited:

> "Read these faint runes of Mystery,
> O Celt, at home and o'er the sea.
> The bond is loosed; the poor are free.
> The world's great future rests with thee!

> "Till the soil; bid cities rise.
> Be strong, O Celt, be rich, be wise.
> But still, with those divine grave eyes,
> Respect the realm of Mysteries.

"Would you like to know the realm of mysteries, Bailey?"
he'd asked in a voice as rich and tempting as a caramel sundae.

The most contagious case of charisma she'd ever seen. She'd
succumbed. Fallen hard and fast, with no known cure. She'd accepted his invitation to the mall's coffee shop after her shift. Two
hours and three cups of peppermint tea later, her heart was irrevocably under his spell.

"Bailey?" Con said gently. The past merged into the present
and she jolted back. He had on the snug, faded jeans, work boots
and long-sleeved dark blue T-shirt under the black leather jacket
he'd worn at breakfast. But his dark spiky hair was sleek and wet,
as if he'd just come from the shower. He must have been working out. He hit the gym whenever he was troubled.

She'd caused his troubles today. Bailey steeled her resolve.
She would *not* go there. She had to stay strong. For both their
sakes. "How did you get in? The mall is closed."

"Syrone let me in." He inclined his head toward the counter,
where her coat rested. "You forgot your coat this morning. I
didn't want you to be cold."

She *was* cold, clear to her soul. However, the coat wouldn't
help. She'd never be warm again.

"And these." He produced two dozen pink roses from behind
his back. "You're a fair woman. Let me have my say."

Her favorite flowers. "Oh, *that's* not fair." A suffocating lump wedged in her throat. "Con, please don't do this."

"All's fair in love and war, sweetheart. This is both." He held out the vibrant bouquet.

Afraid she was already losing the battle, she accepted the flowers and walked to the storeroom. Con followed as she found a pitcher used to water the store's plants and shakily filled it at the sink. She nestled the fragrant blooms inside, set them on the storeroom counter and then snatched up a paper towel. She blotted the water she'd spilled with nervous, jerky movements.

Con took the towel and settled gentle hands on her shoulders. He turned her to face him. "Talk to me, Bailey."

His touch was as electric as it had been the first time. As it was every time he touched her. A startling connection of mind, body and soul. She should pull away, but her ravaged heart craved his hands on her, no matter how brief. "Okay."

His shoulders hitched, the barest movement, and he exhaled a quiet, relieved sigh.

The small, vulnerable gesture nearly destroyed her. Bailey couldn't meet his eyes. Instead, she glanced around the dim storeroom, crowded with boxes. The room seemed too tiny to contain Con's formidable energy. Though the words stung like acid in her mouth, she'd say them as many times as necessary. "We have to break up. We're too different—"

He cut her off. "Not the rehearsed version. You sound like a politician stumping on the campaign trail." His hands tightened on her shoulders. "Look at me. Speak to me from your heart."

She forced herself to meet his gaze and saw determined steel in the dark pools. Her fingers curled into fists, nails cutting into her palms as she summoned resolve. "I told you, I'm trying to make this decision with my head, not my heart."

"Is that why you chose to break it off with me in the diner? You wanted a clean, surgical strike, right? No arguments, no emotional fallout." The hurt swimming in his eyes burrowed into her chest. He shook his head. "Did you actually believe you could drop a bomb like that and then walk away?"

How could she possibly speak from her heart when it ached

so badly she could hardly talk? "A clean, fast incision is less pain-ful, and heals better."

"Those are your mother's words, not yours."

The world stopped. *Oh no!* Was it too late? Had her mother succeeded in making Bailey over into her image? *No.* That's what Bailey was trying to prevent. She refused to amputate her feel-ings. She would feel every stab of pain, be completely honest with Con. She owed him that. Owed herself. "I chose a public place because I knew if we were alone, you'd use your talent for blar-ney, and if necessary, those agile hands to charm and sway me."

Needing distance, she stepped back, breaking his hold, and he released her. Why couldn't it be that easy to break his emo-tional hold on her? "I can't resist you when you're in persuasive mode, Con."

"If you could, I would let you go. It's the same for me, sweet-heart—I can't resist you, either. We belong together."

"We'd start out happy. But I'll end up bitter and angry and you'll be cold and resentful. I've seen it before."

"Like your parents, you said. You've never talked about them until now."

Maybe if she explained, he'd accept her decision. "I've never talked about them before because it hurt too much."

"I don't want to dredge up bad memories, but if it affects us, you need to tell me."

"Yes. You *should* know." She braced herself against the pain and dove in. "My parents met at a ball for the children's burn ward at Mercy Hospital. He was a fireman, she was in her last year of residency. The attraction was instantaneous for them, too. He was a handsome, risk-taking adrenaline junkie, and Mom fell hard. They dated for six exciting, romantic months, then married. I was born two years later. At first, everything was wonderful."

"What happened?"

"When I was eight, Dad got trapped in a warehouse fire and received second- and third-degree burns on his arms and face."

Empathy softened his eyes to brown velvet. He reached for her hand, held it in both of his big, warm ones. "That's why you volunteer at the children's burn ward."

"Yes. As a tribute to his courage and devotion."

He squeezed her hand. "He…didn't recover?"

"He did. His recovery was painful, but he was back on the job in a year. With major facial scarring. Not that it mattered. I could see past the scars to the man underneath." Pulled by need stronger than will, she edged nearer to Con. The heat and strength of his lean body compelled her, comforted her.

"But the injury changed more than his face."

She nodded. "He had scars on the outside, but Mom had scars on the inside. They argued about him returning to active duty. Between disputes, they were silent for days. He said firefighting was his calling, just as healing was hers. The arguments escalated. Screaming recriminations. Tears. Ultimatums."

"That must have been terrifying for you."

She gazed at the compassionate face of the man she loved and her heart shattered for the second time that day. "You're just like him. Brave and dedicated, one hundred percent committed. The chances you take scare me beyond belief." She was trembling all over. "The same thing would happen to us. We'd fight. You'd go to work distracted, and—"

"And what?"

"You'd die."

He tugged her closer, a mere breath away. "Is that what happened?" She watched the light shimmer in shiny water droplets in his hair, smelled the fresh, tangy soap he'd used. Longed to be held in his arms. But she'd relinquished that privilege.

"They had a terrible argument—the worst. He got called up for a five-alarm fire. Mom said if he walked out the door, she was taking me and divorcing him. He kissed me with tears in his eyes, and told me he had to do his job." Living it again, tears pooled in her own eyes. "The look of resignation on his face as he left…" She struggled for control. "He knew by choosing duty, he'd lost us."

He drew her into his arms, held her close. "And a man with no hope is a man with no fear. I'm sorry, darlin'."

Weary beyond bearing, she rested her cheek on his chest and sought comfort she had no right to accept. Listened to the steady thud of his heart under his soft cotton shirt. "Dad was attempting to rescue a family of five from the top floor. The captain radioed him, warning the roof was about to collapse and ordered him out. The family made it out, with his help." Her voice broke. "He didn't."

"I'm so sorry. Grief and guilt, a two g-force." Con rocked her in a soothing rhythm. "Do you blame your mom for your father's death? Is that why things are strained between you?"

"No." She got a grip on her faltering composure. She couldn't afford to fall apart. "Mom couldn't help being terrified for his safety. His scars were a constant reminder of the danger he faced every day. I'm sure she blames herself, though. She wasn't always the Ice Queen. After Dad's death, she shut off her emotions. Almost like she died, too. She became obsessed over something happening to me, and got so overprotective I could barely breathe."

He tipped up her chin. Understanding softened his handsome face. "I wish you'd told me before. It explains a lot."

"I wish I'd thought it through before I got involved with you, and spared us both. You're fire, Con. Hot, bright, and so tempting, I couldn't resist. Like my dad, I thought I could slay the dragon." She stared into his eyes, willing him to accept, to walk away from her. "I couldn't. And burned us both. I'm sorry."

"I'm not. I'll never regret loving you."

She couldn't stop shaking. "You're wrong. I'll quench your spirit. Mix water and fire and you get nothing but ashes." She hated herself for being unable to stop another rush of tears. "Cold ashes in a body bag."

He cupped her face and wiped away the tears with his thumbs. "Please, don't. When you cry, it rips my guts out."

"There will only be more tears. More sorrow. Regrets are inevitable. I never want to hurt you, in any way." She swallowed, trying to hold in her grief. She dug deep, summoned the fortitude to pull away, but this time, he didn't release her. "I'm not good for you. Which is why I have to let you go."

"Sweetheart, *you're* wrong. You aren't bad for me." He lifted her hand to his lips and pressed a kiss into her palm. "You make me whole." His steady gaze held hers. "Trust what we have together."

She inhaled sharply. How could she stand up to his steadfast faith? How could she make him see it wouldn't work? "Con—"

He lowered his head and his lips touched hers in a sensual whisper. "Believe in the realm of mysteries. Believe in *us*." His soft, warm lips brushed hers in a feathered caress.

"I can't." She nearly choked on the words.

"You can. I'll help you." His hand slid to her nape, steadying her, and he covered her mouth with his. She was so cold…and his warmth surrounded her. So empty…and his faith filled her. Her heart ached…and his light, tender kiss comforted her. She'd hurt him, yet his gentle lips forgave her.

Absolution.

Rational thought fled. Her fears and objections seemed foolish, evaporating like morning dew in the sun. She slid her arms around his neck, urging him closer. Body to body, soul to soul. His heartbeat thundered in his chest, his heart calling to hers. A cry she could not ignore if her life depended on it. He deepened the kiss, and his dauntless love filled her.

Completion.

His tongue swept inside, and she tasted her own salty tears, spicy sweet cinnamon gum, and Con. Clean, warm, male. Her mate. On fire—for her. The taste and scent of him raced through her system like molten silver. Hot, bright and dangerous, luring her in. Breaching all her defenses. His gallant soul wooed her.

Seduction.

He drank her in as if he'd been wandering scorched and blinded in a desert. He was shaking now, too. She reveled in his awe, absorbed his reverence. Making her feel as if she were his own personal miracle, he made love to her mouth. He ravished her senses, consumed her with his heat. She fell into the spiraling pleasure, into the inferno. Searing connection arced between them, fused them into one mind, one body.

One spirit.

His fingers threaded into her hair, kneading her scalp, and she melted against him. They touched and tasted. Took and gave back. This strange phenomenon happened every time he touched her. He scrambled her brains, ignited her body. Satisfied her heart. She'd never needed, wanted anything like she needed him. Weightless, she floated in hot, bubbling delight.

One broad hand slid down her spine to the small of her back, both soothing and inciting. He pressed her closer, and his arousal pulsed hard and insistent against her. Heartbeat slammed against heartbeat. Desire sparked in her veins, sizzled through her limbs. His passion fueled hers and she moaned into his mouth. Liquid, shattering intimacy that was so much more than physical welled inside her. Nothing, no one existed but Con.

He broke the kiss, and his essence ebbed away, leaving her empty and aching. He took a half step back and loss punched into her heart like a fist, leaving it bruised and lonely.

His chest heaved with ragged breaths, and his pulse pistoned in his throat like a jackhammer. Desire smoked his gaze. "You know what you get when you mix fire and water, Bailey?"

Dazed, she looked up at him, unable to think. To speak. She shook her head.

He gave her a shaky grin. "Steam."

Chapter 3

Panting, Con wrestled for self-control, which had incinerated in the vicinity of his kibbles and bits. Breaking the connection between them and stepping back had taken every ounce of will-power. As much as he wanted to make love to Bailey until she forgot every objection, they both needed clear heads.

He looked at the woman who owned him, body and soul. Her cheeks were flushed pinker than the roses he'd brought, her lips swollen from his kisses and her eyes sparks of blue flame. His heart jolted. He'd rather chop off his right arm than lose her. Which would damn well wreak havoc on his status as the team's best shooter.

Bailey leaned against the counter, her uneven breathing loud in the small space. "Kissing doesn't solve anything."

When his breathing slowed, he brushed back a red-gold curl that had strayed over her temple. He couldn't stop a grin. "Very good kissing. Set-my-tighty-whities-on-fire kissing."

"We need results, here."

"Believe me, sweetheart, you got plenty of results." Pressed body to body mere seconds ago, she couldn't have any doubts about what he meant.

She smiled, but worried her lower lip with her teeth, drawing his focus to where his mouth had sipped her minty sweetness. His gut clutched on a rush of heat, and he battled the impulse to kiss her again. As if she read his thoughts, her smile wobbled. "We're complicating things even more."

"I hate to admit it, but I agree. Come home with me where we can discuss this in private."

She hesitated and he held his breath, waiting. Finally, she shook her head. "I can't be alone with you."

"You're not afraid of me." Not a question—a challenge.

"Of course not." Her glance flitted around the room, her posture as tense and wary as a cornered suspect's. "I'm afraid of myself. I don't have any willpower where you're concerned. You're a dangerous narcotic, and I can't 'just say no.'"

"Don't feel like the Lone Ranger, darlin'. I could stand to attend a few Bailey-Anonymous meetings myself."

Her gaze collided with his and her eyes widened with anxiety. "This is impossible. What are we going to do?"

"Sit with me." Holding her hand, he led her to the reading area. One night she'd confessed she'd volunteered three weeks of her own time last year during the remodeling to choose the store's decor. A natural-born nester, she would create a warm, cozy home for their family. All he had to do was convince *her.*

When they moved to the love seat, she tried to scoot to the opposite corner. He pulled her down beside him. "You're not running away from me that easily." *Physically or emotionally.*

"We're here to talk, remember?"

"I remember. However, if you have a more prone scenario in mind, sing out." He patted the cushion. "It's a tad small, but will get the job done." He wiggled his eyebrows, hoping his teasing would lighten the mood. "I meant the love seat."

Her lips twitched. It was working. "I'm well aware of your… arsenal, Officer. There's no need for shameless bragging."

"A woman who appreciates a double-action, wide-barrel shotgun."

A reluctant grin bloomed. "Behave, Conall Patrick O'Rourke."

"Uh-oh. The full name, I'm in trouble now."

Her grin disappeared. "We're both in trouble." The distress in her low reply made his stomach clench again, for a different reason.

"All right. Let's talk about the realities of my job. I admit some cops are hooked on the adrenaline rush. I'm not a hotdogger." He took her hand, held her gaze. "I stand between you and the bad guys. I stand for every innocent victim. I take the bad guys down, get them off the streets. I make a difference."

"Yes, you do. Don't get me wrong, Con. I admire that."

He stroked his thumb in a circular caress over her palm, and her hand trembled. "SWAT officers don't take stupid chances, despite the creatively edited, sensationalized crap they show on TV. Every op is planned and rehearsed for hours, sometimes days. As thoroughly as possible. No detail is left to chance. We don't bash down doors, charge in and hope nobody dies."

The lights flickered again and then went out. Con snatched his hand from hers and thrust it inside his jacket for the Glock that normally rode in a holster over his rib cage. Dammit! The Glock that he'd dropped off at the gun cage to have adjusted on his way out of the station. Riverside PD officers were not required to carry a weapon when off-duty, though he usually did. He'd pick up his weapon on the way home, but right now, he felt naked without it.

Seconds later, the mall's amber emergency backup lights blinked on. The security cage dropped a third of the way and then ground to a halt. "What's up with that?"

"During the remodel, all the security cages were automated, so we can push a button instead of cranking them down manually. Those manual gates were heavy, awkward and downright dangerous. In the event of a power failure, the emergency backup is supposed to provide enough current to operate them. Looks like it doesn't. Unfortunately, higher technology equals more glitches."

His internal red alert stood down and he withdrew his hand from his jacket. "The power surge must have made them malfunction. Lucky for us the gate didn't drop all the way, or we'd have to bust our way out."

Bailey looked at his hand and sadness shadowed her face. "That says it all. When the power fails, most guys reach for a flashlight. You go for your gun."

He despised being responsible for dimming the glow inside her. "That reflex keeps me alive, darlin'."

"Exactly my point. No matter how thorough your plans, people *die.*"

"People die every day, just driving to the grocery store. Hell, you can buy it slipping in the shower."

"But they don't purposely put themselves in harm's way. The fact that you do is horrifying." She swallowed hard. "Factor in the violence and I...I'm sorry, Con. I can't live with it."

He lifted her chin to stare into her eyes, dark with distress. "There's no possible way we can compromise here?"

Her chin quivered, and she firmed it. "I'm afraid not."

"That's it, then? Your final decision?"

"I lo—love you." She stumbled over the word. "I admire you. More than you'll ever know. I'm in awe of your strength, courage and dedication. And *yes,* that is my final decision."

"I love you, too. We *can* make this work."

"Your job is incomprehensible to me. I'd drag you down." She gripped his arm. "We do not have a future together."

They did, and he knew exactly how to prove it. He tugged a set of papers from the inside pocket of his leather jacket and showed them to her. "Promotion to team leader." Awe welled in his throat. When his C.O. had given him the papers that morning after breakfast, he'd been stunned. *Team leader.* The ultimate dream—a SWAT team to command at thirty. A goal he'd worked toward since his first day on the force. Through hard work and good choices, by doing the right thing last night, he'd earned his heart's desire. Pop would have been proud of him.

"Congratulations," she murmured. "I know how long you've wanted that."

One look at her face told him differently. By doing the right thing last night, he'd lost the woman he loved.

Awe sank under dread's cold weight. His ultimate dream was Bailey's ultimate nightmare. Accepting the position would be the kill shot that doomed their relationship. Fate, that unpredictable son of a bitch, had thrown a sadistic twist his way. He had the devil's own choice to make.

Light glinted off the hummingbird charm at her throat, and realization whammed into him. If she was serious about the breakup, she wouldn't be wearing it. Any lingering doubts dissolved. She loved him. She was just scared. They shared the key ingredients of a lasting relationship. Friendship, fidelity and faith. Her faith was a little shaky right now, but he had enough for both of them. He hoped.

Deadly calm settled, displacing hurt and anger. His thoughts crystallized, painfully clear. He knew what he had to do. Had suspected since breakfast this morning. He made his decision as he'd made every other in his life. Quickly. With his eyes wide open and fully aware of his options. Which didn't mean it didn't hurt. He opened his hand and let go of his dream, and the papers dropped into the garbage can beside him.

"What are you doing?"

Burying one future so he could have another. She was worth any cost. "I quit."

She gasped. "No! You can't! I won't let you!"

"I want a life, a future with you. And if it means giving up SWAT for a desk job, I can deal with that."

"What about the knight in shining armor, standing for the innocents? That wasn't just talk. That was from your heart."

"My heart chooses you."

Her face paled. "Get out."

"Come again?"

She pointed with a trembling finger. "Get out. Leave."

Whoa! Where were her happy squeals, the jumping for joy? Bewildered, he frowned. "What the hell?"

The outrage clouding her angelic features was anything but joyous. "Your father lost his career and never recovered. He died before realizing his dream. I *refuse* to be the reason you lose yours."

"Pop's career was snatched out from under him. I'm making a choice. Entirely different."

"You think this is what you want now." Even her lips were white with strain, stark contrast to the dark sorrow in her eyes. "What happens a few years down the road? When resentment kicks down love's door and bitterness barges in?"

"We are not our parents, sweetheart. I promise I won't resent you. Ever."

"Dad promised he'd never leave me." She shoved to her feet.

"But promises walk away. They get burned up." Her voice dropped to a whisper. "They die."

He swore under his breath. He was a moron. He should have figured it out the minute she'd told him. He rose and drew her into his arms. "Oh, baby. Your mom and dad weren't the only ones scarred by his accident and death."

She snatched in a breath. "What are you talking about?"

"Danger, violence are valid worries. But what you're really afraid of is when the going gets tough, I'll pick the job over you. And walk...like your dad."

Her body shook. "He did what he had to do. I don't blame him." She gritted her teeth and squared her shoulders. "He saved five lives that night. He was a brave hero."

"He did what he thought best. But he was just a man, sweetheart. Sometimes people do the wrong thing for all the right reasons."

She dropped her head into her hands and covered her face. "How does a person know? I'm struggling to do what's best for you, Con."

"So, instead, you're doing what you believe is the right thing—leaving me—for all the wrong reasons, darlin'?"

"They don't seem wrong to me."

"That's the hell of it. Trying to discern which decisions are right, and which are fear-driven. Look at me." She complied, and he continued. "I understand you've been hurt. You're scared, and I don't blame you. I wish I could protect you, make it all go away. But only you can slay that dragon."

Torment burned like a blue flame in her eyes. "I'm so confused. I don't even know which way is up anymore."

He wanted to ease her pain, and couldn't. Hated feeling helpless, hated the uncertainty that was tearing her apart. Tearing them apart. For the first time in his life, he faced an enemy he couldn't bring down with force. He could not conquer her fear with fists or weapons.

So Con charged into combat with the only ammo he had. Faith. Integrity. Trust. He placed her palm over his heart and covered her hand with his. "I swear on my life, nothing you do will ever make me walk. Nothing will ever make me stop loving you. I've made my choice. I'm off the streets, off SWAT."

She jerked. "Con, no!"

"Think it over and make a logic-based decision. If you still want to end it, I'll accept that." Though losing her would rip out his heart. "But I won't let you push me away because of fear." He brushed his knuckles over her cheek. "Look past the scars, see what the woman inside you really wants."

He cupped her head and kissed her soft mouth. Her rosy fragrance surrounded him, filled him. An exhilarating, too-brief taste. He stepped back and thrust his hands in his jacket pockets before he was tempted to do more. He'd just committed to riding a desk for the next twenty-five years. He shuddered. His fingers brushed velvet and he closed his fist over the ring box, holding it tight. When push came to shove, she mattered most. With her by his side, he'd be content painting houses.

"Now *you* have a choice to make." He turned and strode out of the store.

Stunned, Bailey stared at the empty doorway. Of all the reactions she'd envisioned, Con giving up active duty wasn't even on the list. No way would she let him do it. He'd never be happy strangled in a suit and tie. Wielding a pen against reams of papers instead of wielding weapons against bad guys. Mediating political squabbles instead of protecting innocents. And the worst slap in the face, approving ops—sending other men into harm's way—without taking part.

She reached down and plucked the team leader application from the garbage. As she straightened the sheets crumpled by Con's lean, capable hands, she read: *Qualities demonstrated in the field by Officer C. O'Rourke. Above average intelligence. Can assess a situation, review possible alternatives and come to a sound decision, all while under tremendous stress. Maintains emotional control, whether in traumatic situations or with suspects who may have perpetrated heinous acts upon hostages. Well-disciplined team member who looks out for other mem-*

bers. Quickly and flexibly adapts when the unexpected event occurs that throws the plan into disarray. Suppression of fear—cool head and high function under fire. Highly motivated and patient. Does not rush into incidents without thinking.

She knew Con's depth, intelligence and dedication. The report confirmed everything he'd stressed about preparation. A SWAT officer's job was much more than bashing in doors and eating bullets.

The words *commendation for bravery* jumped out at her. With growing dread, she read on. Last night, Con had apparently spotted and neutralized a series of deadly traps hidden in the path of his brother Liam and Liam's K-9 partner, Murphy. He'd saved two lives. At considerable risk to himself. He would always be a dragon slayer.

Just like her father.

Sick inside, she stumbled to the counter to get her purse and tucked the folded papers away. She'd make sure he got the application back before he missed the deadline.

Bailey stared at the register, trying to sort her thoughts. Deadline. She had to count the money and deliver it to the bank. She glanced into the murky, deserted mall, and her stomach sank. She might already be too late. Getting fired for negligence would make this horrible day intolerable.

The key opened the register and she separated bills into neat piles. Con had told her to think through the problem logically, without emotion. She tried to push emotion aside. There was no doubt in her mind Con loved her, and she loved him. Logically, how strong was love? Stronger than duty? Stronger than sorrow? Stronger than fear?

Not in her experience.

If love were strong enough to overcome all those things, the divorce rate wouldn't be so high. And the divorce rate for cops was astronomical. Thank goodness the news broadcast this morning had jolted her to her senses in time.

She unzipped the bag and stuffed the bills and deposit slip inside. Logically, if someone listed her suitability to be a SWAT wife, she'd fail miserably. Unlike Con, she wasn't cut out for the job. She'd suspected that when he'd taken her to the department's Halloween party.

The officers' wives hadn't noticed her floundering out of her depth. They'd welcomed her, appearing no different from other engaging, friendly women she'd known. Until the call-out came. The women of Alpha Squad had kissed their men—maybe for the last time—without tears. Had sent them off to war with smiles on their faces and no traces of fear in their eyes. Instead of rushing home and worrying…waiting in dread…those women had stayed at the party and managed to have a good time.

She didn't have the strength or courage. So what if she spoke Latin, French, Spanish and Italian and could recite both positive and negative effects of theobromine? Romance languages and the chemical breakdown of chocolate were of no use to Con.

Bailey sighed in longing. Con wanted her, she wanted him. Giving in to her need would be easy. They'd be happy for a while. She scooped the change from the tray into the bag with the bills, then stared at the money. But at what cost? Logically, as time passed, they would pick and tear each other apart until one of them couldn't take it. The price was just too high.

The unvarnished truth—Con possessed a poet's heart and a warrior's spirit. Logically, in the final battle, the poet didn't stand a chance. The warrior would choose duty over love. Sacrifice his personal feelings for the greater good. He would leave her. Either by desertion or death.

Just like her father.

She zipped the canvas bag closed. Finished. Shoulders slumped in defeat, she stepped into the gloomy, eerily silent mall. River View Mall had been remodeled last year. Rather than a long, corridor-type layout, it spiraled three stories upward, with intricate columns of escalators at its center. During the holiday season, a towering Christmas tree stood on one side of the escalators, reaching almost to the third floor.

A glass-walled sky bridge connected to the food court on the third floor offered panoramic city views. Beautiful fountains, imaginative sculptures and eclectic art drew browsers as well as shoppers. At the moment, some stores were dimly lit by emergency lights, some cloaked in shadow. Christmas displays that had looked cheerful an hour ago now seemed spooky. She shivered. She preferred the mall warmly lit and bustling with interesting people to this eerie emptiness. The cold, deserted space echoed the barren desolation inside her.

As she trudged past Beautiful Brides next door, she looked away from the wedding gown displayed in the window. Every cell of her being recognized Con as her mate, yearned to be with him.

Why did it have to be so complicated? So impossible. So cruel.

Would she ever remember him without the pain, the longing? She touched the hummingbird charm nestled at her throat. She didn't think so. More scars for her to bear. He was stronger, more resilient. He was hurt now, but in time, he'd be okay. He was better off without her. She had to believe that.

She cut kitty-corner across the mall's imitation marble floor. Why couldn't she be the woman he needed? The woman he deserved? Why had she been given the desire, but not the courage? She didn't want to give him up.

She jerked to a halt in front of Santa's workshop. Everything in her roiled in hot rebellion at surrendering. She clenched her jaw. She descended from hardy, dauntless pioneer stock. Her past might have left scars, but she wasn't a coward. If there was any way for her to overcome her fears and not let Con down, she'd grab it in a heartbeat.

Bailey stared morosely at Candy Cane Lane. During the past month, excited kidlets had traipsed past reindeer and elves to sit on Santa's lap and request their hearts' desire. But Santa was gone, and Bailey's childish faith had burned to cinders.

She turned her back on the sight. The wishing-well fountain loomed in front of her. Visitors had thrown coins into the pool, each representing a wish, a dream. Hope for a miracle. The money glittered in the fountain's soft, rose-colored lights.

Con's smooth, deep voice floated through her memory. *Believe in the realm of mysteries. Believe in us.*

She hadn't believed in miracles for a very long time. Maybe that was the problem. It was the Christmas season. A time of miracles. On impulse, she unzipped the canvas cash bag and fished through the coins inside until she found three pennies. One with Con's birth year, one with hers, and a new, shiny copper with the current year. She'd repay them from her purse.

She turned away from the fountain and gripped the coins. "I want to be with Con, forever." She tossed the penny with his birth year over her shoulder. The coin plopped into the water.

"I need courage to be the woman he needs." She threw the second penny, with her birth year, and waited for the plop.

"I'll do anything. Pay any price." Holding her breath, she tossed the third coin. The splash sent hope streaming through her.

Silly, ridiculous and nothing more than superstition. She was the first to admit it. But stating her determination to try had given her resolve. Like a timid wren pushed out of the nest expecting to fall, but discovering she could fly instead, sorrow's unrelenting weight soared from her shoulders.

She zipped the bag and her footsteps were light as she approached the bank. She'd find an answer. Counseling. Assertiveness classes. A police family support group.

She paused outside the wide glass doorway and clutched the bag to her chest. Why *not* believe in the realm of mysteries? Con did. And she believed in him. It was about time she took control of her life. Went after what she wanted with everything she had.

She couldn't see anyone inside the bank, but amber lights illuminated the lobby and the doors were open. Relief streamed through her. Mike Hayes, the manager, often stayed late. He was probably at his desk, or in the vault. Surely, he'd accept her deposit. Especially since this was an emergency situation.

She started to take a step forward, opened her mouth to call out, then hesitated. The hair rose on the back of her neck and prickles crawled up her spine. The sense of menace she'd felt earlier, when she'd taken the spider outside slithered over her. Something was wrong.

She rose on tiptoe and peered inside. The teller cages were deserted. As were the desks. She glanced farther down the lobby, and horror punched into her chest. Nan and Letty cowered on the beige carpet, along with Mike Hayes. A stocky man dressed all in black, wearing a black hood, stood with his back to Bailey, pointing a gun at her friends. A big, deadly looking machine gun.

As if sensing her presence, the man started to turn. Bailey's heart slammed into her ribs. She froze. Ice-cold terror pumped through her veins and a scream swelled in her throat.

Chapter 4

An iron hand clamped over Bailey's mouth. Aborting her scream before it was born. Cutting off her air. A thickly muscled male arm snaked around her waist and brutally yanked her to the floor.

Pinned facedown in the dark, crushed between the cold floor and a hard male body, panic ripped through her. Primitive, animal instinct for survival drove her to struggle, futile against her assailant's strength. She bit into the smothering fingers. The attacker grunted, but his ruthless hand clamped like a vise. Desperate, she clawed at the air. His forearms tightened, shackling her arms to her sides. She bucked, but he was too heavy to dislodge. Caught helplessly in his grip, she fought for freedom, her murdered scream ricocheting through her brain.

A low growl rumbled in her ear. "It's Con. Stop fighting."

Relief deflated her like an empty balloon and she went limp.

"Nod if you recognize me, sweetheart." His voice was a near soundless whisper. If she hadn't freaked out, she would have immediately known his unique, masculine scent mingled with cinnamon. She nodded and his grip loosened a fraction. "Keep quiet, and do exactly what I tell you. If you understand, nod again." She managed another nod and his hand released her mouth.

Trembling, paralyzed by shock, she gasped in shallow gulps.

Con tugged her to a sitting position, crouched under the solid half wall under the bank's windows. "We need to move fast and quiet. Can you run?"

Her muscles were as weak and useless as cooked noodles. Even shaking her head *no* was an effort.

He caught her face between his hands. They were warm, solid and steady. "I know you're scared. But you've got to focus."

She couldn't seem to suck in any air. Her vision fogged around the edges. A vast, echoing pit opened beneath her.

"Look at me." Con's tender gaze held hers, kept her from falling into the abyss. His hands clasped her shoulders and he shook her. "Bailey, *breathe.*"

With extreme effort, she forced her lungs to inhale.

"Hold it to a four-count. Let it out slowly, to a six-count."

He made her repeat the soothing pattern until her vision cleared and the numbness receded from her trembling limbs. She turned and flung her arms around his neck, clinging to his sure strength. "Con! I thought you'd left."

"Everything will be okay." His confidence seeped through her terror, slowing her trembling. "We've got to get out of here."

As appealing as escape was, she couldn't leave her friends at the mercy of a gun-toting criminal. "What about Nan, Letty and Mike?"

"We're their only hope. If we're neutralized, the hostages are screwed."

She couldn't think straight. "What are we going to do?"

"We have to reach the main doors. Syrone will let us out, and we can call for backup."

Backup sounded like a fine idea. Lots and lots of cops. The more cops, the better. "O-okay."

"Can you run now that you've got some oxygen in you?" At her nod, he flashed a reassuring smile. "That's my girl. First, we're going to crawl along this wall. Without a sound." He eased his head up for a peek into the bank, and then jerked back down. "Go!"

What seemed like forever in reality probably took minutes. Crawling with Con's staunch presence behind her, she arrived at the corner of the building and stopped. A huge space in front of the back doors loomed ahead. An empty void affording no shelter to the hunted. They had to cross yards of exposed fake marble to reach the main doors. To Syrone and safety.

Con's hands settled on her shoulder. "When I give you the green light, I want you to run across," he murmured. "Stay low. Then hit the floor by the front corner of the shoe store."

Her nerves jittered. Surely he wasn't sending her into the open alone. After all, he had the training, the experience. The gun. "Where will you be?"

"Right behind you." He bobbed up and took another fast peek inside the bank. "Go!"

Exposed, vulnerable and expecting to feel a bullet slam between her shoulder blades any second, she ran. For the first time since the lights failed, she was grateful. Semi-darkness hindered predators and helped prey. She'd once picked up a fallen baby sparrow whose frantic pulse had raced in her cupped hands. Empathy for the tiny bird's terror thundered through her veins as she huddled in front of the shoe store.

She turned, glancing in trepidation at the bank windows behind Con. Dreading to see the dark silhouette of a man with a machine gun who would snuff out his precious life in a hail of bullets and blood.

Con prowled across the void, his body low, his fluid stride as graceful as a tiger's. He wasn't even breathing hard when he reached her side. "All right?" She nodded, and he smoothed back her hair. "We're gonna be fine. I promise."

"You can't promise. You have no control over this situation."

"The hell I don't. Those slimeballs just hit the wrong bank. Their last bank."

"I only saw one slimeball."

"I saw three, and my guess is there are least three more. I'm betting the power failure isn't due to the weather. For a job this size, you need a full crew."

She gulped. Six—or more—against two. The odds against them had tripled. "How come you're not scared?"

His teeth gleamed in a dangerous smile. "I know what I'm capable of. This little adversity is a chance to learn and grow. Find out what *you're* capable of."

At the moment, not wetting her pants was a major accomplishment. In spite of her abhorrence to violence, admiration washed over her. Instead of wigging out, he saw facing his greatest fears as challenges. Growth opportunities, for Pete's sake. "You are some piece of work, Conall Patrick O'Rourke."

His lightning grin flashed for the second time. "Am I in trouble again?"

God, she loved him. Every gorgeous, mischievous, courageous molecule. "Con, if we get out of here—"

"Not if. *When.*"

She wasn't so sure. Wouldn't that be one of fate's nasty ironies? To die just when she'd decided to really live? "If we get out of here, I'm going to try—"

"*Shh.*" His hand again covered her mouth as the sinister silhouette she'd dreaded appeared in the bank's windows. "*Freeze.*"

No problem. Her blood froze in her veins, her heart stopped.

Another silhouette joined the first, and she held her breath. Though she couldn't see their faces, like all hunted things, she felt their probing gazes piercing their hiding place.

The silhouettes shrank, disappeared. Con's hand slid from her mouth, and she sucked in a quivering breath. "Did they see us?"

"No."

"How do you know?"

He grinned again. "Because there aren't any bullets screaming past our heads."

"Could you possibly be any more audacious?"

"This is combat, sweetheart. If I lose my head, we both die. The hostages die. And that isn't going to happen."

Her gaze snagged on his. Sharp wariness underlying the resolve in his eyes told her he wasn't nearly as unaffected as she'd believed. High-alert vibrations emanated from his tense muscles. His words might be cavalier, but his mind and body were taut and ready for action. The thought whammed her like a sledgehammer to the skull. He was scared, too. A phrase from the SWAT evaluation report replayed in her mind. *Suppression of fear.* How much of his bravado was a front for her sake and how much was real? Did it matter? Either way, she trusted him with her life.

"What now?"

"Keep advancing, fast and quiet. Stay on this side until we're even with the One Hour Photo booth." He flicked a glance at the empty bank windows. "Go!"

She sprinted past CD Palace. Past Quality Leather Goods. Her breathing loud and raspy in the tomb-quiet mall, she hunkered outside Death by Chocolate. She'd worked at River View five years and this was the first time it had seemed threatening. Running from criminals past windows full of fudge lent an aura of unreality. The smell of chocolate lingered in the air, the rich scent incongruous in the frightening dark void. Her stomach grumbled.

Con's arm slid around her waist. "Hungry?"

She leaned against him, taking comfort in his unshakable warmth. "I don't feel hungry." Terror tended to squelch her appetite. "I guess my stomach is complaining because I didn't eat breakfast or lunch." She'd been too upset to manage either.

"After this is over, I'll take you wherever you want. Deal?"

A line from every B movie she'd ever seen popped into her head. "How can you think of food at a time like this? I just want out of here. Intact."

He gave her a hug. "Almost there. Next stop, One Hour Photo."

The fifteen-foot-square booth perched in the middle of no-man's-land, between them and the main doors. Con scanned the walkway in all directions, and again commanded her to run.

Gasping, she clung to the orange cabana, and rested her forehead on the cool vinyl. The main doors reflected muted interior lights. Outside, black storm clouds and pounding sleet crowded the glass, thick and impenetrable. Freedom. Safety. A few hundred yards away.

"There's Syrone," Con whispered in her ear.

The big, uniformed, African-American man had his back to them, staring into the storm. "I wonder why he's still here?"

"Probably waiting for you. You know Syrone. He won't leave until every last person is accounted for."

Guilt assailed her. If she hadn't spent all that time agonizing over her decision about Con, she'd be long gone. Home. Safe. And so would Con and Syrone. But what about Nan, Letty and Mike? "Con? I'd thought you'd gone home. Why did you come back?"

He hesitated. "The roads are icing up. I planned to follow you at a distance to ensure you got home okay. I hung out in my truck

for a while, and finally came to find out what was taking so long."
His smooth, deep voice was low, intimate. "I wasn't going to let
you see me, because you needed time alone. Until our friendly
neighborhood bank robbers threw a monkey wrench into the
works."

Another phrase from his evaluation popped into her head.
Sometimes, a photographic memory was a pain. Sometimes, a
comfort. *Quickly adapts when an unexpected event throws the
plan into disarray.* Thank goodness. Otherwise, she'd be cowering in the bank with her friends. With a gun pointed at her head.
And nobody would know they were being held hostage. Maybe
until it was too late.

Con's nudge derailed that awful train of thought. "Looks clear.
Tell Syrone what happened. Call 9-1-1. You have your cell?"

"No, it's in my purse, in the bookstore."

"Syrone has a radio, but just in case, take my phone. Cell
phones don't work in this blasted mall anyway." For some reason, maybe the tall, cylindrical structure, or the steel girders
supporting the sky bridge, cell reception wasn't clear inside the
mall. The remodeling was supposed to correct the problem, but
hadn't. He passed the phone over her shoulder. "Here."

Like his camera, the cell phone was an up-to-the-minute,
complicated technological marvel. The man did love his gadgets.
007 had nothing on him. "If I can figure out how to work it."

He chuckled. "When you and Syrone get out, dial 9-1-1 and
press Send. Have dispatch call up Alpha Squad. Tell 'em I'm inside with a confirmed visual on three hostages and three suspects,
with a probability of a crew of six or more. I'll signal from the
third floor east windows when they arrive."

As she slid the phone into her pants pocket, his words hit
home. Shock collided with disbelief. She spun to face him.
"You're not coming with me?"

"I need to gather intel and scope out the inner perimeter."

"Are you insane? Those guys have Uzis, all you have is a
handgun!"

His impassive gaze flicked away from hers. Not fast enough.
The memory of him withdrawing his hand from his jacket in

the bookstore rose like a specter in her mind. *His empty hand.*
"Where's your gun?"

"Don't worry about me, I can take care of myself."

"Where. Is. Your. Gun."

"At the armorer's," he admitted. "Needed an adjustment."

Sick fear roiled in her stomach. "There is no way I'm aban-
doning you to those maniacs alone and unarmed!"

"Baby, this is what I do. I'm damn good at it."

"I am not leaving without you."

"We want all the hostages to go home safe and sound. In
order for that to happen, I need to do my job."

"Taking on six armed bank robbers with your bare hands? No!"

"I'm not about to pull anything stupid." The determined look
in his eyes said *unless I have to.* If hostages were threatened, he
wouldn't hesitate to dive into the line of fire. "Trust me."

"Con—"

"Sweetheart, we don't have time to debate." He backed her
against the wall. His hard body pressed into hers as he lowered
his head and kissed her. Hot and silky, his tongue thrust into her
mouth, giving and taking. Reassuring and seeking reassurance.

She tasted love. Longing. And an edge of desperation that
scared her more than anything that had happened in the past
thirty minutes. She clung to him, kissing him with recklessness
born of fear. She could not lose this man she loved with all her
being. Not before she had a chance to show him how much he
meant to her. If she left and anything happened to him, he'd
never know.

He ended the kiss. The steely resolve in his eyes terrified her.
The wistful hope wrenched her heart. "Go. I'll see you soon."

"I'm not going anywhere. I love you."

"Then let me do what I'm trained for." His face was resolute,
his gaze tender. "You're a liability I can't afford. Now go."

Scalding tears stung her eyelids and she blinked them into
submission. He was right. She'd only be in his way. Clutching
and whining would get him hurt. She had to be strong, for his
sake. Bailey straightened her spine. Kissed him one last time,

with her heart beating so painfully in her throat it nearly choked her. "I'll see you soon. And no heroics. Promise me."

He cupped her face and stroked his thumb over her lower lip. Her crazy mixed-up insides did a slow loop-de-loop. He smiled. "Men make promises, darlin'. Heroes keep them."

Walking away from him was the hardest thing she'd ever done. Halfway to Syrone, she looked over her shoulder. Silent, graceful, Con loped up the stilled escalator to the second floor and glided alongside the balcony railing above her head. He offered a jaunty salute followed by a "get your butt moving" gesture before continuing.

"Syrone," she whispered, creeping forward.

The guard turned and Bailey froze. He was big. African-American. Wearing a guard's uniform. But he wasn't Syrone.

"Who are—"

The behemoth scowled and strode toward her. "How did you escape?"

"Bailey!" Con's hoarse cry echoed from above. "Run!"

His urgent command mobilized her. Instinctively obeying, she did an about-face and sprinted down the mall.

"This way," Con shouted, pivoting and running along the balcony parallel to her frantic flight.

Beneath him, she followed his fluid stride. He veered off and disappeared. Where was he going?

Panting, she risked a glance behind her. The guard was closing fast. For a big dude, he could move. Terror sank cold claws into the base of her neck. She poured on the speed, her pursuer's footsteps thudding behind her. Daily yoga kept her limber and toned, but not trained for a three-hundred-yard dash.

"Bailey, here!" She jerked her gaze up and saw Con leaning over the railing ahead, dangling a baseball bat. "Catch!"

Fleeing toward him, she caught the bat as it dropped. With the solid, heavy weight gripped in her hands, she ran on.

"Kneecap him, baby," Con ordered. "I'm coming down." He pivoted again and tore back toward the escalators.

She looked behind her. The guard was much nearer than she'd expected. Kneecap him? She glanced at the bat clutched in her sweaty palms. Imagined the crack of wood against bone. Torn tendons. Bloody splinters. Incapacitating injury. Bile stung the back of her throat. She could not do that to another human being.

She increased her speed, so did he. She tried swerving side to side like a blitzed quarterback on Super Bowl Sunday. Didn't work. His coarse breathing rasped loudly in her ears. Too loud. She wasn't going to be able to outrun him.

Again, she looked back. The giant was too close. Almost close enough to grab her. In the distance, Con raced toward them, another bat gripped in his hand. Fast, but not fast enough. Harsh breaths rasped her throat, her heart slammed into her ribs.

Con wouldn't make it in time.

Saving her hide was up to her.

Her frantic gaze spun down the mall. If she ran into a store, the behemoth would have her cornered. Nowhere to hide. What to do? *Please, God, what should I do?*

The answer flashed by in a blurry rainbow. One desperate chance. Stiff with fear, she lurched to a stop. Whirled. Hitched the bat over her shoulder and swung with all her might. Not at her pursuer—at the gumball machines lined up in colorful rows outside Toys Galore. Metal support poles clanged. Her hands stung. Glass shattered, smashed to the floor. Large, colorful jawbreakers exploded in every direction, bouncing across the faux marble.

Her pursuer treadmilled on the rolling projectiles. His feet flew out from beneath him. He grunted, swore and flopped down with a resounding crash as his skull banged against the floor.

He didn't move.

Holding her breath, she edged toward him.

"Stay back," Con shouted. Skidding on jawbreakers, he managed to keep his footing and slid to a halt. He went to his knees beside the fallen guard and dropped his bat. "Hells bells, slugger. I said kneecap him."

Her vocal cords didn't seem to want to work, and her lips were numb. "Is h-he d-dead? D-did I k-kill him?"

He shot a grin at her. "Nah. He's out cold." He sobered. "Unfortunately, we don't know if this commotion carried to the other end of the mall. We might be having company shortly."

"I'm s-sorry."

"We'll handle it." He patted the man down and tugged a two-way radio from beneath him, a smashed jumble of plastic and wires. "Well, that's useless. Bluto must have landed on it." He continued the search. "No gun. Obviously, they wanted him to look like Syrone to passersby. They weren't expecting trouble." He shook his head and swore softly. "No key card for the door, either. Probably planned on leaving with his buddies."

"I c-couldn't hit him. I j-just couldn't."

"You took him out, that's the most important thing. You did good." He rose and embraced her in a quick, hard, comforting hug. "Get it together. There's no time to fall apart."

She nodded. Sucked in a steadying breath. "What should I do?"

"Leaving an unarmed man at the door…these guys are arrogant, sure of success. We can turn it back on them." He strode toward the toy store. Like many of the other stores, the security cage hadn't descended because of the power failure. "Hang on."

He disappeared, and she glanced down the mall. They were a long way from the bank. Had the robbers heard the noise? Would she and Con soon have to face loaded Uzis? Anxiety gnawed her insides. Because she couldn't bring herself to injure a fellow human being, she might have put them in jeopardy. Traded their welfare for a criminal's. Endangering herself was one thing, but putting Con's life at risk…inexcusable.

She looked at the unconscious man. Confusion and slivers of hot shame splintered inside her. She felt horrible about knocking him out. Shaky, sweaty and like she might upchuck any second. Yet part of her regretted not following Con's orders and doing the deed quietly. Thus hurting the guy worse.

Had she just done the wrong thing, for all the right reasons?

How was a person supposed to know? How did Con deal with the moral dilemma? He disabled bad guys every day without his conscience making him queasy.

Con reappeared with jump ropes and bandanas in neon colors. "The landline phone is dead." He shrugged. "No surprise. The robbers would have been stupid not to pop the phone lines along with all the other mall systems." His calm, matter-of-fact demeanor eased her ragged nerves a fraction. No matter what happened, no matter how badly she crumbled, he'd be there to pull her out of the pit. "Tie his ankles. Take his boots off, first. If by some strange phenomenon he escapes, stockinged feet will slow him down. I'll tie his hands and gag him."

When the man was secure, Con hefted him over his shoulder. "Oof. This sucker eats his Wheaties."

"What are you going to do with him?"

"Make him feel at home in a nice, quiet stall in the ladies' room. Go hide in the toy store until I'm done."

"Actually, I kind of need to…um…when I get nervous…"

He chuckled. "Come with, then. Let's roll. We need to move."

She accomplished her business while Con dealt with their nemesis in the large handicapped stall at the end of the room. He must have locked the stall from the inside, because his head appeared over the top of the partition, and then he jumped down.

Con eased the restroom door open. "No sign of company. We might have lucked out." Outside, he used a tool on his Swiss Army Knife to trip the bolt. Then he pulled a small tube from his pocket. "Superglue from the toy store. It'll freeze the tumblers. The robbers will have to break down the door to spring him."

They returned to Toys Galore. He strode inside, unhooked two backpacks and tossed one to her. "Grab anything useful."

Bailey found four flashlights and inserted batteries. She set two on the counter to illuminate the store, tucked one into her pack and handed the other to Con. She lifted two more jump ropes off a rack, and picked up a plastic egg filled with Silly Putty.

He arched a brow. "Silly Putty?"

"You never know. It could come in handy."

"If you say so." Con palmed a black plastic squirt gun and whistled. "Looks real. Too real. Some kid got shot last year in the third precinct waving one of these puppies around. It might work. As long as nobody calls my bluff."

The thought of him facing loaded Uzis with an empty toy pistol increased her nausea. She picked up a package of markers. Stared at the picture of innocent, smiling children on the box before stuffing it in her pack. *Pictures.* "Acetic acid!"

"Did you call me a pathetic ass? An empty squirt gun isn't too impressive, but we have to work with what we've got, darlin'."

She laughed. "Acetic acid. A chemical used in the stop bath during photo developing. One Hour Photo would have some. It's a powerful skin irritant, and if shot into someone's eyes, would sure slow them down."

"Have I mentioned lately how much I admire your brilliant brain? You're a better soldier than you think." He handed her two toy guns. "We'll each take two. We'll fill 'em when we're done."

They continued loading items into their packs. Bailey picked up a small notebook and retractable pen from a cartoon stationery display, and began to make meticulous notes.

He peeked over her shoulder, his face inches from hers. Supercharged energy radiated from his muscled body. His warm lips brushed her cheek in a soft kiss and her nerve endings quivered. "Gonna write a book about our adventures later? How I Spent A Boring New Year's Eve at the Mall."

"Ha, ha, funny man. I'm logging what we take and how much it costs. The toy store shouldn't lose money, just because—" *Money.* She went rigid. The blood drained from her head leaving her dizzy.

"Hey." He turned her to face him. "What's wrong? You just went lily-white, sweetheart."

"The money. From the bookstore," she whispered. "When you tackled me outside the bank, I was carrying the deposit bag. I left it there. The store's name and account number are stamped on the front. If the robbers see it lying in front of the doorway, they'll know someone was out there and saw them. They'll know someone else is in the mall."

He frowned. "Low odds, but I don't like it. I need to circle back and do a thorough recon anyway. I'll retrieve it."

She grabbed his sleeve, clung. "No!"

He sighed. "Since we're in this for the long haul, let's get something straight." He grasped her forearms in a gentle but ironclad grip. His gaze held hers, steady and implacable. "I am in charge of this operation. The objective is to go home with the same amount of holes in our body that we came with. And to get our friends out of that bank alive. Understand?"

"Y-yes." She'd never seen this side of him before. Hard. Serious. All business. All cop. This Con was intimidating. Centering. And in an odd, unexpected twist, exciting. She'd always been attracted to his easygoing charm. Aroused by his sexy humor. Yet, this dangerous side of him turned her on. A lot. What was the matter with her? Had terror sent her round the bend? Was she stark-raving nuts? She was a pacifist, for heaven's sake.

"You cannot question every detail or balk at decisions. You do what I say, when I say. Otherwise, someone could die. Got it?"

Mr. Large-and-In-Charge had a point. She already had two potentially deadly mistakes on her account. Which didn't mean his drill-sergeant attitude rankled any less. She wasn't a complete moron. After all, she'd taken out a bad guy *and* given Con an idea for an effective weapon. Bailey Chambers could carry her weight. Straightening, she snapped off a crisp salute. "Aye, aye, sir."

"This isn't the navy. Make that, 'Yes, sir, Officer O'Rourke.'"

She stared into the twin lasers of his lethal brown gaze. Was he joking or serious? "Kiss my what? Officer O'Rourke. *Sir.*"

His sensual lips twitched. Then he burst into laughter. "Baby, I'll kiss any thing you want. Any time. Any where."

Whoo. "I appreciate the offer." Was it normal to indulge in a brief erotic fantasy in the middle of a life-or-death situation? For her pulse to throb, her skin heat, awareness tingle over her? She *was* going insane.

As if he'd read her naughty thoughts, his eyes grew dark and smoky. "It's not an offer, it's a promise. But if it makes you feel better, you can tally it in your notebook."

A guilty flush stole up her neck. What would he say if he knew over the past six months, she'd compiled a mental roster of intimate activities she'd like to indulge in with him?

"You're not pale now." He trailed a finger down her cheek. Studied her. Grinned with sudden enlightenment. "I'll be damned. You and your lists. I'd love to get an eyes-on assessment of that one, darlin'. How much am I into you for?"

Busted by Officer Sexy. Her flush burned hotter. "About twenty items."

Amusement and desire glittered in his dark eyes, danced around his mouth. "I'll pay up in full."

They had to live through the night first. Jolted to reality, she swallowed hard. "Let's table this discussion until later."

"Count on it." He sobered. "Enjoyable as this is, I've got a recon to perform."

"Right. What do you want me to do?"

He glanced around. "Most hunted animals, including humans, go to ground. If anyone comes looking, they'll search low." He pointed. "Up there."

A trampoline hung suspended from the ceiling. He lifted her onto the counter and levered up beside her. His cupped hands boosted her onto the trampoline's taut surface, and then he jumped to the floor. He extinguished the flashlights. "If you don't move, I can't see you at all in the dark. Stay put. Don't budge. Don't make a sound until I return and you know for sure it's me."

She scooted to the edge of the trampoline. "Be careful." She blew him a kiss.

He pretended to tuck the kiss into his jacket pocket. "For later." He gave her a roguish wink, turned and strode out.

Bailey lay spread-eagled on the trampoline and waited. Waited. And waited. Eerie silence smothered the room. How long did a recon take? She mentally skulked up the dark mall with Con, picturing every cautious step, every heart-shaking pause. Fear thrummed inside her. *Stop it.*

Seeking a diversion, she glanced around the store. A tiny pair of ice skates caught her gaze. She smiled. The mall held a lot of good memories. She and Con had gone ice-skating at the mall's rink on their third date. On a weekday, the rink was sparsely populated. She'd stroked the ice to pop songs blaring from the loudspeakers. A natural-born athlete, Con had tossed cinnamon gum into his mouth, skated backward and teased her to go faster. His joie de vivre was contagious. They'd danced across the ice, engaged in a breathless, daring one-upmanship that he'd won by executing a back flip.

She'd jokingly called him a show-off and pushed him down on his backside. Laughing, he'd tugged her on top of him, and kissed her for the first time. The instant their lips touched, she'd felt as if she'd belonged to him forever. Lost in the kiss, all awareness had faded. Until he'd gently reminded her they were in a public arena. He'd helped her up, wiggled his eyebrows and offered to kiss her thoroughly later, in a more private place. She'd blushed crimson from forehead to toenails.

More flushed and breathless from the kiss than the exercise, they'd sat at a cozy table in the back of the concession area and sipped cocoa dotted with marshmallows. Later, at her front door, when his hard body had brushed hers and he'd kissed her good-bye, he'd tasted of sweet, dark chocolate and cinnamon...and oh-so-tempting sin.

The desire to take their relationship to the next level both physically and emotionally had grown each time they were together. Each touch, each kiss, every beat of his heart had made her long to be his. Until her doubts and fears had begun to choke off her feelings.

Tingling in her fingers tugged her back to the present. Her hand was going numb from inactivity, and she shook it. How long had it been? She retrieved a flashlight from her pack and checked her watch. Twenty-two minutes. Twenty-two minutes was plenty of time. Waiting turned into worrying. What if he'd been caught? What if—?

No. She wouldn't wander down that horrifying road.

Con was smart, tough and capable. He'd be back. She rested her cheek against the trampoline's textured surface. The pebbled rubber smelled like new sneakers. Strange how insignificant details sharpened when every sense was on edge. Worrying turned into praying. *Please, keep him safe.*

She again consulted her watch. Thirty-five minutes. Praying turned into planning. Stay put and don't budge, my Aunt Fanny. In fifteen minutes, she'd go looking for him.

Ten more of the longest minutes of her life ticked by. Six hundred endless seconds before Con crept into the store. Relief made her giddy as she slithered to the edge of the trampoline, hung from the rim and dropped. She met him at the doorway. "Thank goodness! I was nearly frantic—"

Relief morphed into confusion. His face was sickly pale, his forehead and upper lip beaded with sweat. "What's wrong?"

He looked at her, his eyes stunned, bewildered.

Her anxious gaze spun over him. No blood. But in the gloom, she couldn't be sure. "Are you hurt?"

He blinked, as if he could not process her question.

She grabbed his shoulders. He was shaking. Her confusion blasted into fear. Steady, reliable, unshakable Con was trembling. "Con? What happened out there?"

A horrifying possibility speared into her. "Is it the hostages?" Even as her appalled mind rejected the thought, she blurted out, "My God, did the robbers kill Nan, Mike and Letty?"

Chapter 5

Bailey was waiting for him. Depending on him. The thought had speared the painful haze clouding Con's vision and forced him to keep moving. He couldn't remember finding his way back. Now that he'd reached her, his legs collapsed, and he slid down the wall.

"Con, are you hurt?" She dropped to her knees in front of him. Her hands reached inside his jacket, gingerly feeling along his ribs and over his abdomen. *"Answer me!"*

It hurts like a bitch. He nodded, then shook his head *no.*

"Which is it, yes or no?" she demanded.

He shook his head no again.

She left and he heard rummaging noises before she returned. "Open." Her fingers pressed his jaw and his mouth opened. Liquid poured over his tongue. He swallowed. Sticky, and far too sweet. "Gack!" He shuddered and the fog receded.

"Do you want more?"

He coughed. "Hell, no. What *was* that?"

"Instant glucose. Toy stores don't sell brandy."

"Huh?" He swiped his hand across his mouth and shuddered again.

"Candy syrup in a miniature wax bottle. Little kids drink it all the time with no ill effects. Well, except maybe excess energy. Better now?"

"Yeah." His reply emerged graveled and raw, like his insides.

She cupped his face in her chilled hands, her eyes wide with fear. "Con, is it the hostages? Are they—"

"No. They're okay, for now."

"Tell me what happened."

He still couldn't believe what he'd seen. The past thirty minutes were a disjointed nightmare. "The head honcho, the robber giving all the orders—" He swallowed again, the sweet aftertaste turning bitter in his mouth. "He's wearing my father's watch."

She gasped. "What? Con...he's been dead for nine years. How can you be sure?"

"My brothers and I gave the watch to Pop for Father's Day, the year I was ten. Liam and Grady did chores to buy the face from a thrift store, and Aidan and I tooled a leather band with Celtic symbols and attached a new buckle in shop class. It's one of a kind. Unmistakable. And that criminal is wearing it."

She gripped his shoulders and held his gaze, her expression troubled. "Did you see his face?"

"No, he still has on the Kevlar hood."

She frowned. "He couldn't possibly be your father?"

For a few horrible, sick moments, he'd wondered. The ugly rumors had sunk their claws into his chest and ripped out his memories...held them up, torn and bleeding for examination. Uncertainty had shredded his confidence. Doubt had lacerated his faith. The O'Rourke boys had endured scorn for nearly nine years, along with whispered speculation, not-so-subtle innuendos and outright insults.

Ever since their father had been investigated by Internal Affairs for being dirty. A cop on the take.

Not everyone swallowed the accusations. Veteran cops who had known Brian O'Rourke defended his integrity to this day. His wife and four sons believed in his innocence. Internal Affairs had never proven he'd taken the half million dollars missing from the armored car robbery.

Unfortunately, Brian O'Rourke had never proven he hadn't.

He'd been quietly shuffled off to ride a desk. Bitterly unhappy, he'd accepted the undeserved punishment with stoic fortitude inherited from ancestors who emigrated from famine-riddled Ireland. Maintained his dignity with tenacious Celtic warrior's blood that never gave up the fight, that enabled him to hang on to hope for future exoneration.

The same fighter's blood that flowed in Con's veins. That gave him the determination not to give up on Bailey and their future. Con swiped the back of his hand over the moisture trickling into his eyes. He wasn't getting teary-eyed, dammit. It was sweat from the exertion.

Their dad had died before he could clear his name. Assumed dead during the invasion robbery of his own house.

They'd never found his body. Or his killer.

The resulting court hearing had declared him legally dead. Murdered. There were still hard-line cops who thought he'd faked the crime scene. Rumor had him living the high life on a remote tropical island with his hot half million and a hot mistress.

Nobody who'd known Brian bought that garbage any more than they believed he'd stolen the money. But it hurt like hell.

Con cleared his throat. "Is the man in the bank my dad? No. No way."

"No wonder you're upset. It must have been an awful shock."

The understatement of the millennium. "You believe me, don't you—the man holding up the bank is not my dad?" Because he'd wavered, it seemed very, very important she did not.

She held him tight. "Absolutely. Your mom is too intelligent and principled to marry a dirty cop. And an unscrupulous man could never have raised four sons with such deeply rooted integrity."

He wrapped his arms around her and buried his face in her silky curls. If he hadn't known before she was the woman he wanted to spend the rest of his life with, her loyalty would have sealed the deal. He breathed in her flowery fragrance. "Thank you."

She drew away to look at him. "How did a criminal get your father's watch? Why would he wear it? It has no monetary value."

"One possibility." When the first stunned, frozen moments had passed, and he'd assured himself the man wearing the watch was not his father, the answer had wrenched his guts. "Pop died when robbers invaded our home. Those men are robbers. The math adds up."

"You think the criminal in the bank is responsible for your father's murder, and the watch is a...sick souvenir?"

"Yes. And I intend to prove it." He leaned his head against the wall. "The day he died, we'd been to a soccer game, did I tell you that?"

"No." She stroked his hair. "Go ahead. Talking will help."

"Grady was a senior in high school. It was the state championship. We'd planned a family outing, but Dad caught the flu. He was really torqued about missing out. He insisted on going, but Mom wouldn't let him. You know Mom, she prevailed."

Her lips curved in a tender smile. "I imagine she did."

"Pop went to every game, every school event, every Boy Scout activity when work permitted. He was a great dad."

"He was. You've got some wonderful memories."

Yeah, but this wasn't one of them. "Grady's alma mater won. The three of us carried him into the house on our shoulders, with Mom brandishing his MVP award. We were chanting some stupid cheer at the top of our lungs. We got halfway across the living room before we noticed the place was trashed. Stuff was missing." Staring over her shoulder into the gloomy store, he felt the blow all over again as he relived that awful night.

"Mom tore upstairs to the master bedroom. Grady and I hit the kitchen, Aidan and Liam rushed into the family room, calling for Pop. Then they went dead quiet. A tangible wall of silence rolled out. I don't know how to explain, but the shock hung in the air."

"You don't have to. I've experienced that feeling."

"Grady and I looked at one another, and knew bone deep it was bad. We ran into the family room. It was worse than anything we could have imagined. Sick and weak as he'd been, Pop must have put up a hell of a fight. Blood was everywhere. Enough blood…" He faltered, then soldiered on. "For the ME to testify Pop couldn't have survived. They never found his body."

"I'm sorry. Losing your father is hard enough when you've got closure."

They'd been forced to hold a memorial service instead of a funeral. There was no coffin to drape the flag over. After the mournful echo of "Taps" faded, the honor guard had simply handed the folded flag to his mother. "We didn't want Mom to see the carnage. It took both Aidan and me to keep her out. We brought her to Letty's. Grady was the most visibly upset and least functional, so he stayed with her while the CSI team worked. Hours later, when they'd finished and taken the evidence they wanted, Grady showed up. The four of us cleaned up the mess. Scrubbed away the gore."

"Oh, Con." She hugged him again, and her slender body trembled in his arms.

He held her, comforted by her presence. "Took us all night. We ripped out what was left of the carpet and took it and Pop's chair to the dump. Nobody except Grady showed any emotion." Pop's death had hit his youngest brother the hardest. "Until we threw that torn, lumpy recliner out of my truck. We stood there, looking at Dad's chair amongst the garbage, bloody and battered. Then we lost it. Four grown men. Put our arms around one another and cried like babies."

She drew back and touched his face. Tears spilled down her cheeks. "It's understandable. No wonder you're all so close."

He trailed a fingertip over her wet face. She shared his pain, just as he shared hers. Her empathy made the hurt more bearable. "Mom was devastated. But when we suggested she move, she got royally pissed off. She said—" An unsteady chuckle dislodged the aching lump in his throat. "Well, I won't repeat it. The gist was that criminals were not going to drive her out of her home and destroy her memories."

Bailey captured his hand in both of hers. "Your mom is incredible."

Anger crackled, burning away sorrow. He'd watched his mom fall to her knees after the death of her soul mate, then struggle to her feet and get on with living. "She should have had the privilege of growing old with the man she loved by her side."

"We can't change what's done, I know that better than anyone." Her eyes softened, deep blue pools of sympathy. "Dwelling on it will only hurt you more." She placed a tender kiss in the center of his palm. "Are you going to be all right?"

"Yeah." He'd stood outside the bank racked by grief, and battled the urge to rush in and confiscate the robber's Uzi. To turn the weapon on him and force a confession. To finally find justice. Only the thought of Bailey, alone and defenseless, hunted down by those ruthless men, had made him walk away. Each step had taken every ounce of stubborn Irish will he possessed.

Con sucked in a deep breath and yanked his thoughts out of the past. He would be fine. After he finished it.

"What do we do now?"

He looked at the woman he loved beyond all reason. Her eyes were dark with sadness. Her delicate face white with strain. Her sweet lips creased with worry. Those men had killed his father and now they were a threat to Bailey's life. And the lives of innocent hostages. Anger boiled into rage. "I'm going to stash you somewhere safe, go back to the bank and clean house. Exterminate the vermin. No catch and release."

She went rigid. "No! You can't!"

"Hide and watch me, Bailey." Years of anguish. His mother's quiet suffering. His brothers' pain. Tears. Loss. The ragged, empty hole in their lives that no one would ever be able to fill. No more. *Never again.* "They aren't getting away without a trace this time. I'm going to stop them before they hurt anyone else."

"Is that what you've been trained to do? Would your father want you to charge out there, hell-bent on revenge? I think not."

He clenched his jaw. "That bastard has no right to wear my father's watch like some kind of grisly trophy."

She shook him. Hard. "Focus, Con. Those hostages need you. I need you. If you lose it, we will all die."

She was right. Blind fury had overtaken him, pushed him too close to losing his head. To doing the wrong thing for all the right reasons. He'd come within a heartbeat of blowing off his training and throwing away his life to annihilate a criminal SOB who might very well have murdered his father. He'd nearly risked Bailey's safety and the welfare of innocent hostages. Shame washed over him, cooling his rage. He swore.

The seesawing emotions combined with loss of control rattled him to the core. He dropped his head into his hands. He'd been in scary, unpredictable situations before, but never like this. This time, his family was at stake. The woman he loved was at stake.

This time, it was personal.

Bailey shook him again. "Look at me."

Resolve steeled her gaze. "Conall O'Rourke is a dedicated police officer, not a vigilante. He upholds the law, does not take it into his own hands." The conviction in her voice yanked him back from the edge of no-man's-land. "Our objective is to go home with the same number of holes in our bodies we came with. And to get our friends out of that bank."

He gritted his teeth. Shoved his grief and anger deep inside. Right again. His priority was to keep them both alive. He rested his forehead against hers until the confusion and pain receded and he regained control. "What would I do without you?"

She kissed him, her soft, gentle mouth reviving his strength, her sweet, fresh taste restoring his purpose. "We're in this together, for now. So, I guess we need a…what do you call it? Tactical plan. Your forte, Officer Sexy. What's our next step?"

He managed a shaky grin. This woman amazed him more every second. "Communication. Get word out there's an incident going down in here." He hesitated. Could she handle the truth?

He should have known better. She read him as easily as one of the books she always had her nose stuck in. She frowned. "What aren't you telling me?"

Trying to hide it from her was futile. He might as well come clean. "If my suspicions are correct, this crew has been doing bank jobs and home invasions for years. They seem to fit the profile on a number of unsolved cases. They don't leave any witnesses. Once they crack the vault…" He didn't finish. Didn't need to.

She closed her eyes and inhaled sharply. "Oh no!" When she opened her eyes, panic laced her expression and her voice quivered. She grabbed his arm. "What can we do, Con?"

"Mike bought some time by slamming the vault door when the robbers stormed in. Calling out SWAT will buy more. The suspects won't kill the hostages if they need bargaining chips. I wish we had access to a phone or radio. We can hardly send smoke signals."

"Wait!" She jerked upright. "We can! What about the fire alarm?"

"The crooks disabled the electricity, phone and computer systems. Thus the earlier 'malfunction' announcement."

"But they might not know the alarms and sprinklers are on an independent, protected circuit…with battery backup. I saw the schematics when I chose the layout for the bookstore's electrical fixtures during the remodeling."

"That photographic memory of yours comes in mighty handy at times." He tugged a bright curl that had fallen over her shoulder. "So, we start a contained blaze, and summon the trucks. Then we have to signal the firefighters without putting their lives in danger." He pursed his lips. "It could work."

"The third-story windows on the sky bridge facing south are visible from the parking lot. What if we get a sheet, write SOS on it and hang it in the window?"

"Great idea." He grinned, steady and sure, his feet again on solid ground. "Only we'll write the police code for armed robbery in progress, with hostages involved. And add my badge number."

She surged shakily to her feet. "Let's go!"

"Not so fast, slugger." He rose and flexed his cramped muscles. "First, we train."

"But we have to hurry!"

"When you hurry, people die. We do this by the book." He glanced around the murky store and grabbed his pack and the baseball bat he'd snatched from the sports outlet upstairs. "Let's change locations."

"Okay." She picked up her pack and baseball bat. "How come?"

"Not smart to stay in one place when you're being hunted."

She froze with her pack dangling from one shoulder. "Are we being hunted?"

"Odds are good. The bookstore's deposit bag wasn't on the floor outside the bank. The robbers must have found it."

"I'm sorry, Con." Her delicate red-gold brows scrunched together in an anxious frown. "It's all my fault."

"It is *not* your fault. I grabbed you and scared you. Besides, we have an advantage. The bad guys don't know about me. They think they're after a terrified bookstore clerk. They'll search the

other end of the mall first." He left out the fact that the criminals
who were after them seemed as disciplined and heavily armed
as any SWAT team. Professionals with the precise teamwork of
ex-military men.

Con welcomed the sharp slap of adrenaline in his bloodstream as he shrugged into his pack. He'd need every ounce of
strength, courage and wits he possessed. Every moment of training. He and Bailey were in for the fight of their lives.

Bailey followed Con to the doorway. He motioned her to a
stop and then sidled out.

An instant later, he returned. "We're headed for the Bedroom
Furniture Emporium at the far end, across the way. We'll move
independently, in stages. I'll watch your back, you watch mine.
Stay low and close to the wall."

Relief trickled through her. He was back to normal. When his
composure had fractured, she'd wondered if he would recover.
Or if shock and pain would send him hurtling into a suicide mission. His evaluation report again appeared in her mind's eye.
Maintains emotional control. Con's CO knew him better than she
did. However, she was learning more by the second. And the
more she discovered about Con's true character, the more she admired him. The more she trusted him. The more she loved him.
The more bewildered she felt. After tonight's events, would she
still be able to walk away from him? Did she want to?

"Go!" His whisper mobilized her, and she crept into the oppressive silence. Confusion churned inside her as quickly and
quietly, they took turns scuttling toward their goal. She hurried
past the import store. The security gate had lowered all the way
down there and at Harry's Cigars next door. More had randomly
lowered at this end of the mall.

Bedroom Furniture Emporium was open, and she ducked inside, followed by Con.

Darkness shrouded the store. She studied the spooky space,
filled with towering silhouettes. Odd how everyday objects like
dressers and beds looked menacing in the dark. Amber security
lights broke the gloom toward the back, by the sales counter.

Con nodded in satisfaction. "Good. Lots of heavy cover."

They rearranged the sturdy furniture until a maze of barricades led to the mall opening. That way, they wouldn't get trapped inside. Con then taught her basic hand signals so they could communicate across distances or without speaking. He showed the same qualities as a teacher she suspected he would exhibit as a lover—focused, patient and extremely thorough.

Though he didn't say so, she realized he was also equipping her to communicate with the SWAT team in case something happened to him. At the thought of him hurt, or worse, a giant fist squeezed her heart. She shoved the horrible image aside. *Focus on the task at hand.*

Every instinct screamed to hurry. Get the SWAT team on site fast. "How much time do we have? Shouldn't we go upstairs?"

He rolled his wrist to consult his watch. "We're okay. Breaching the vault door is gonna take a while."

"How many white sheets do you want?" Tamping down her apprehension, she headed for the shelves on the back wall. Con had experience and training. He wouldn't put the hostages in danger.

He carried their knapsacks to the open floor space in the rear of the store. "Two should do it."

Amongst the rainbow of patterns and colors, plain white cotton was as rare as a missionary in a brothel. But she finally located some. She ripped open packages, unfolded the linens and shook them out, then knelt on the oak parquet floor beside Con.

He extracted the markers and passed her a red one. "Glad you picked these up. Make the letters and numbers as big as possible."

He outlined his sign with a black marker. She knelt and logged the bedding's cost in her notebook. That done, she wrote *10-23, code 2* on her bedsheet, and then began to fill in the spaces.

His warm butterscotch voice broke her concentration. "What kind of sheets do you have on your bed, darlin'?"

Startled, she glanced up and met his speculative gaze. He'd never been in her bedroom, nor she in his. She wanted commitment before investing her body, heart and soul in a physical relationship. He'd respected her wishes and hadn't pushed.

Resisting temptation hadn't been easy, however. Their sexual appetites were well matched, each ravenous for the other.

"Mauve satin with cream lace." A bewitching picture shimmered into her mind. Con, naked in her bed, his hard-muscled body tantalizingly draped in satin sheets. Warmth tingled over her skin.

A slow, lazy smile slid over his mouth, and the warmth blossomed into heat. "Ah, my girl is a sensualist. No surprise."

Jeez, his killer smile should definitely be a felony. She swallowed hard, struggling to formulate a coherent sentence. "What about you? What kind of sheets are on your bed?"

"Dark green cotton jersey. It's like sleeping on a favorite T shirt." His gaze darkened, grew intense. Desire smoldered in the rich brown depths. She read his thoughts as clearly as her own. Obviously, he had no trouble picturing her in his bed, either.

Her abdominal muscles clenched and heaviness pooled low in her belly. Had not making love been a mistake? They were fighting for their lives. If they didn't escape, she'd never know the wonder of being in his arms, the joy of belonging to him.

No. She again squelched her worry. Negativity devoured precious resources. She needed energy, focus and every smidgen of creativity to help them escape.

Bailey gave herself a mental shake and put renewed effort into the banner. Forming each letter carefully and precisely, she recalled a recent Scrabble match. She'd concentrated on beating Con, not an easy task, and hadn't realized what he was up to until well into the game. Until she'd really looked at what his tiles spelled. Passion. Desire. Arousal. Caress. Kiss.

When she'd glanced up, he'd arched a teasing brow. She'd lunged and kissed him soundly. They'd ended up locked in an embrace, rolling across the board and scattering tiles. How did he electrify her without uttering a sound? Without a touch? *Like now.*

Awareness hummed between them. His heat, his scent beckoned her. Her senses responded to every shift of his lithe body, every movement. Her tension escalated with his every quiet breath.

When the sign was nearly finished, she hesitated, the marker hovering over white cotton. "Con?"

"Yeah?" His husky reply had her stomach jumping again.

"Is it…? I'm…um…" Unable to meet his gaze, she swallowed again. "Is it normal to be sort of…turned on in the middle of a dangerous situation?"

Chuckling, he stretched, set down his marker, and then settled cross-legged on the floor. "Feeling a bit wired, are you?"

"Yes. Am I a pervert?"

He barked out a laugh. "No, sweetheart." He tugged her into his lap. "Adrenaline sings through your veins, doesn't it?"

"You can say that again."

"Every sense sharpens to hypersensitive. Colors look brighter, objects more clearly focused." He feathered his fingertips over her eyelids and she caught her breath.

"Every nerve ending quivers at the slightest touch." He cupped her face in his hands. His soft, moist lips grazed her jawline and she shivered.

"Your hearing grows keener," he murmured into her ear, his warm, moist breath prickling goose bumps along her skin.

"Smells become dizzyingly acute." His mouth a whisper from hers, he held her gaze. His scent—aroused male, tangy soap and cinnamon—wove an enticing spell, and she breathed him in.

Passion flared in his eyes. "Flavors flood your palate, are more vivid, more delectable."

She turned her body into his, and his lips touched hers. Rising on her knees, she tangled her fingers in his hair. Her lips parted and his tongue drove deep, kissing her hard. His taste jolted her system. Intense, hot, spicy. If she lived to be a thousand, she would never get enough of him.

He'd kissed her before with tender seduction. Undisguised hunger. Even nerve-jangling desire. But nothing had ever sent her pulse hurtling into a gallop, made her limbs tremble like this rapid-fire assault on her senses. The air punched out of her lungs. Her brain puddled.

Pounding heartbeat against pounding heartbeat, the fiery, shocking clash of lips, tongues, teeth flashed through her body. The heady, erotic explosion ignited her blood. Emotions blitzed her heart and lodged in her soul. Need. Love.

Possession.

Con was hers, and she would never give him up.

Someone moaned, deep and throaty. She didn't know if it was him or her.

She jerked back, breaking the kiss. "This is a bad idea."

"Probably, yeah." Panting, he rested his forehead against hers. He blinked, and then shook his head. "What was I talking about? Oh. Adrenaline. Razor-sharp awareness is a survival mechanism. You need an edge in a crisis."

Stunned moments passed before her jellied brain could process thought. She inhaled much-needed oxygen. Stress must have sent her around the bend. She was living her worst nightmare. An up-close-and-personal look at the reason she'd broken off with him. Getting physical would only worsen the untenable situation. How could she still want him so much when their basic life philosophies were in total conflict? "That doesn't explain the outrageous desire."

He smiled. "Sure it does, when you factor in the primal instinct to mate in the face of death. To create life and preserve the species. A biological imperative hardwired into our genes since caveman days. One hundred percent normal, darlin'."

She eased backward, putting distance between them. A moment ago, she would have followed the kiss anywhere it led. Now, she was questioning her sanity. "Biological imperative or not, I wouldn't have felt…um…wired if I were trapped with Aidan, or even gorgeous, wild-man Hunter."

His smile widened. "Glad to hear it. I'd hate to have to pound my brother or teammate." He stroked a finger down her nose. "Our feelings are exploding because we're emotionally connected. Crisis is forging our existing bond into a stronger link."

She wasn't so sure. Was bonding supposed to be so scary? So painful?

He consulted his watch again. "C'mon, sweetheart. Time to go upstairs."

Ashamed of herself, she wrenched her attention back to the current dilemma. "How could we waste time kissing when the hostages are depending on us?"

"Don't beat yourself up over it." In one smooth movement, he stood and lifted her to her feet. "During an incident, timing is everything. Acting at exactly the right moment can mean the difference between live hostages and dead ones." He glanced around the store. "I've got the situation under control. Now, we need to find something to start a fire."

Her shame faded. She may have momentarily forgotten the hostages, but he hadn't. Obviously, he could compartmentalize. A perfect complement to her photographic memory. The two of them were becoming a formidable team. If they could only work out their differences, they'd be unbeatable. "Other than the one we just ignited, you mean? I'm surprised we didn't set off the sprinklers."

"Too bad, because the cage on Harry's Cigars lowered completely, and we can't commandeer a lighter. I recall from my Boy Scout days rubbing two sticks together takes a damnably long time to get results."

"Hmm." She tapped her chin with her forefinger. "This is a furniture store, they must have tung or linseed oil around."

They found several cans of linseed oil in the storeroom. She grinned at Con. "Great! This stuff will burn like crazy."

"We still need a source of ignition."

"Static electricity." She grabbed a metal trash can and headed to the linen section. "We need a polyester thermal blanket. Ah, like this one." She opened the package. "Watch and learn." She vigorously rubbed two halves of the blanket together until they stuck, then rapidly separated them. Sparks crackled in the darkened showroom. "If nothing else, this will do in a pinch."

Con laughed. "Ms. Wizard, I adore you."

Glowing inside from his open admiration, she handed him the supplies. "When we get upstairs, if we pour the oil into the garbage can and create static, it should ignite the oil. Even the fumes are highly flammable. Linseed oil-soaked rags often spontaneously combust. It might take persistence, and we'll have to be careful. It could flare up suddenly and burn us."

"Maybe there's a fire extinguisher." He hurried behind the counter. "Got one!" He rummaged on the shelves beneath. "I wonder if there's any duct tape? We'll need to hang the sheets."

She folded their SOS banners, and then collected their backpacks and the bats. "Is there?"

"Nope." He picked up the trash can.

"We can look upstairs. If we don't find any, I have an idea."

His grin flashed again. "I'll just bet you do."

When they reached the furniture store's mall entrance, he paused. "Getting up the escalators will be tricky. They're in the central core, visible from all sides, and we'll be vulnerable. Don't silhouette yourself against the horizon, or a doorway—what we call a vertical coffin." He shouldered his pack. "If it goes to hell, run, and don't look back. I'll make sure nobody follows you. Stick to the plan, summon help and then hide."

There he went again, preparing her for the worst. Preparing to stand between her and the bad guys. She fought down roiling fear and squared her shoulders. Nothing and no one would separate them. Over her dead body.

She prayed it wouldn't come to that.

The trip up the stilled escalators to the third floor was torturously long, agonizingly slow and the scariest experience of her life. But uneventful.

Con left her in a fabric store while he scouted out the sky bridge. She collected more items for her pack and waited anxiously for his return.

Mere minutes seemed like hours. Finally, he prowled into the store and gave her the *all clear* sign.

She hurried to his side. "Any trouble?"

"Nope. Did you find tape?"

"Only the craft type, and that won't adhere to glass, at least not for long. Not with the temperature difference between outside and inside creating condensation."

"You mentioned an idea?"

"Silly Putty will stick to both the glass and the sheet. Moisture won't affect it."

"The way your brain works floors me."

"Is that good or bad?"

"Good." He winked. "You definitely trip my trigger, baby."

She batted her lashes at him in mock flirtation. Teasing him was a good way to relieve the tension. "I'd love to trip the trigger on your big gun, Officer Sexy."

He laughed. "I thought you didn't like guns."

"Depends on what kind of ammo they're shooting. And if they're rapid-fire repeaters or not."

"Whoa! Keep talking and you'll find yourself on the counter over there. Flat on your back and minus your clothes."

The idea had appeal. She smiled at him. "Maybe later."

"You want a championship marksman, I'm your guy. You'd better start me an IOU column in that notebook of yours."

They ventured onto the sky bridge and hung the sheets. The putty worked great. They lit the signs with flashlights. Then Con stashed her in Sears while he went to initiate phase two. She found a large plastic tarp in the automotive department and draped it over two end displays for a makeshift tent. She added more items to her pack, making detailed notations about what she borrowed.

What was taking Con so long? Had he run into one of the robbers? Was he having trouble igniting the oil? Or maybe he hadn't had trouble starting the fire, but with controlling it. Her stomach tightened. *Please, don't let him have been burned!*

Seeking distraction from her distress, she started an IOU column. She wrote *trip your trigger* in Con's column. *Kiss any thing, any time any where* was listed as owed to her, plus more inventive ideas about what he could do when she was flat on her back on a counter. Then suddenly the fire alarm clanged, and she jumped. *Success!*

Grinning, she sprinted for her shelter and arrived as the sprinkler system hissed on. Water rained everywhere, plopping onto the tarp and bouncing off the linoleum. The space between sprinklers meant that not everything on the shelves got soaked, but close enough. Hoo boy, the floor was a sodden mess.

Sirens wailed in the distance and grew louder. *Yes!* The sirens screamed into the parking lot, and then abruptly died. Had the firefighters seen the banners? She didn't know if the sprinklers were on a timer, set to react to smoke or flames, or if the fire department had a remote shutoff, but after about ten minutes, water stopped pouring out of the ceiling.

"Yo, darlin'."

At the sound of Con's low hail behind her, she squeaked. "Ack! Cardiac arrest! I didn't hear you come up behind me."

His clothes were soaked, his short, sleek hair glistening. He hadn't had the luxury of seeking shelter when the sprinklers erupted. Amusement flitted across his handsome face. "You aren't supposed to. Goes double for the bad guys."

"Did the fire trucks see the message?"

"Ten-four. SWAT should be scrambling as we speak."

She breathed a quiet sigh of relief. She and Con had bought Letty, Mike and Nan a fighting chance. "Do we hide and wait for the cavalry?"

"No. We load our squirt guns. I don't suppose we could use the linseed oil? It would sting like a mother, too."

"It's pretty thick. It probably wouldn't shoot very far, and might clog."

"Okay, so we go after the acetic acid."

"You'd better change into dry clothes. The temperature is getting chillier by the minute."

"I want those guns loaded first. And I have to do another recon on the bank to see how the suspects reacted to the alarm and sprinklers. When SWAT gets here, I need up-to-the-minute intel."

Her relief died a premature death. Back downstairs? Back into the jaws of danger. Another risk to Con's life. Cursing her jangling nerves, she picked up her pack and bat. She forced confidence she didn't feel into her words. "Let's go."

"Be extra vigilant. Because of the alarm, the robbers are going to wonder who's out here and what we're up to. These guys aren't stupid, they'll be surveilling the area. After the way the fire trucks responded, then took off like bats out of hell, they've got to suspect the cops are on the way and be uptight. Likely to shoot first and ask questions later."

"Great. Got any more good news?"

"Yeah, the floor is slippery as a greased guinea pig. Watch your step."

"And you'd know how slippery a greased guinea pig is?"

He didn't say anything as they strode toward the front of the store, but his lips twitched.

"Oh, no. You didn't!"

"Aidan and I thought Grady's Mr. Peepers needed a slick hairstyle, like Fonzie's. Neither Mr. Peepers nor Grady was too enthusiastic about the new do." He chuckled. "Hey, give me a break. We were five and six. The ultra cool Fonz was our hero."

"It's a miracle your mother doesn't chug antacid directly out of the bottle and toss back ibuprofen like M&Ms."

"That's why she took up rowing, to work off stress."

"She must have had to row to the Pacific Ocean and back."

He hesitated at the entrance to the mall and checked both directions. "Have you ever thought about how many kids you might eventually want?" The question was casual, his tone and body language anything but.

Con's babies. She'd dreamed of them. Thought they were out of her reach. Longing twisted deep inside. "I always hated being an only child. Too lonely. I wouldn't mind three or four."

He smiled. "Four is a nice, even number. Like my brothers and me."

"Unleashing more male O'Rourkes on an unsuspecting world…what a terrifying thought!" She wrinkled her nose at him. "I think you'd better hope for four girls."

"Little girls are a different kind of trouble." He trailed a callused fingertip along her ear, sending tingles racing down her spine. "So are big girls."

"Not nearly as much trouble as big boys."

"That's the fourth time you've mentioned size. Have a fixation, darlin'?"

Warmth surged into her cheeks. "Guess you didn't get the memo. Size doesn't matter."

"Whew." He put his hand over his heart and heaved an exaggerated sigh. "Wouldn't want to disappoint."

She snorted. "Stop fishing for compliments. I've got eyes."

He arched a brow, and her cheeks blazed. Gad. How did they end up in these impossible discussions? In the midst of sneaking around trying to avoid bank robbers, yet. "Never mind. Let's go."

As they made their way down the dead escalators, dread inched up her spine. Just like when she'd walked toward the bank, her senses shrieked unease. By the time they arrived at the One Hour Photo booth, every muscle screamed with tension, and the hair on the back of her neck was standing on end.

"Con," she whispered. "Something's wrong."

"I know. I feel it, too."

Were the robbers waiting to ambush them? She peered around the corner into the shadows, but didn't see any movement. She propped her hand on the wall to steady herself and connected with something wet and sticky. The overhanging eaves had protected the booth's vinyl walls from the sprinklers. Whatever she'd planted her palm in wasn't water. Some kid's leftover slushy? Ugh!

She stared at her hand in the murky light. The wet, sticky goo was thick and dark. Chocolate? She took an experimental sniff. The sharp, metallic smell could never be confused with chocolate. Her stomach lurched.

Her palm was covered with blood!

Chapter 6

4:00 p.m.

"**C**on!" Bailey's frantic whisper jolted Con's thrumming senses into overdrive. "Blood!"

He whipped around. She held up her red-streaked palm, and his lungs constricted. He grabbed her wrist. "What happened?"

"It's not mine."

The weight lifted from his chest. "Where did it come from?"

"It's all over the side of the kiosk. Look."

His gaze followed a trail of droplets splattered across the floor. The sprinklers hadn't completely erased the watery red marks from the pale gray fake marble. Where the water hadn't reached, the trail was dark and deadly. "We'd—" Movement registered in his peripheral vision. Someone was out there! He flashed her the hand signal for *silence,* followed by *down.*

An armed man wearing camouflage slunk into view. Without taking his gaze off the guy, Con eased his pack to the floor. His jacket followed. The robber hadn't seen them.

Yet.

The photo booth was centrally located in the main hall. The man was searching store by store, Uzi at the ready. They were trapped. Con gripped his bat and formulated a plan. Flight wasn't an option. He had no choice but to fight.

His muscles tensed, ready for combat. Balanced on the balls of his feet, he concentrated on breathing evenly and visually tracking the robber's progress. Learning his enemy's body language. Gauging his experience. Waiting for exactly the right moment.

As he'd told Bailey, timing was everything.

The sucker was at least a head taller than he. And ripped. The second Incredible Hulk of the day. What kind of vitamins were these dudes chugging? Gigantor wore a Kevlar vest, Kevlar hood and carried an Uzi. Con had a baseball bat, determination and the element of surprise.

Behind him, palpable waves of terror rolled off Bailey. She vibrated with fear. He wanted to hold her, reassure her, but couldn't. He didn't blame her for being afraid. If he failed, she'd be on her own. At the robber's mercy.

There was nothing he could do to ease her distress. Still watching the approaching man, his grip on the bat tightened. *Focus.*

Failure was not an option.

He ruthlessly shoved everything from his mind except the approaching battle. Bailey's survival, as well as his own, depended on his actions in the next few minutes.

Gigantor skulked closer to their meager cover. Con kept his gaze on the suspect's hands, as he'd been taught. Broad and scarred, with prominent veins. Hand movement nearly always revealed intentions, even in the most disciplined combatants. A mere split-second warning could give him an advantage.

Almost there. *C'mon, big boy. Come to Papa.* Closer. Closer. Con tensed. There was no strap connecting the Uzi to the man's body, a lucky break. The hulk reached the corner of the booth.

Batter up!

Gigantor saw him a heartbeat before Con stepped and swung. The man jerked the Uzi up, and Con slammed the weapon out of his hands. Home run! The Uzi sailed into the air and clattered across the floor. Con swung again, aiming for his opponent's unprotected pelvis. Gigantor pivoted, crouched, and the bat thudded on Kevlar.

Gigantor took advantage of Con's open position to ram his fist into Con's gut. The breath burst from Con's lungs and he reeled. The hulk spun into a roundhouse turn and kicked the bat loose. It too, clattered to the floor.

Great. Gigantor was also trained in martial arts.

A meaty fist rocketed toward his face, and Con feinted left. Attacking fast and low, he tackled Gigantor, head-butting his stomach. Using the man's bulk and momentum against him, Con bulldozed him up and flipped him over his back. Being a giant had its disadvantages. Con had a much lower center of gravity, and it was harder for the big man to knock him off balance.

The guy hit the floor with a thud that rattled the rafters. Con lunged for the bat, four feet to his right. Steely fingers snagged his ankle, yanked him to the floor, facedown. He rolled onto his back, flexed his legs and used his feet as a battering ram. Both boots connected with Gigantor's knee. Bone crunched and the big man grunted in pain. Con gave him tough-guy points. Most dudes screamed when you broke their kneecaps.

His opponent's massive torso slammed across him, pinning him down, and Con again lost his breath. Gigantor sat on him, and his hands constricted Con's windpipe. Black spots swirled in his vision and the world grayed at the edges. He wedged his forearms between the heavily muscled, strangling arms and tried to loosen the iron grip. When that failed, he used his thumbs to gouge Gigantor's eyes. Bloodied, Gigantor let go. Gasping oxygen into his burning lungs, Con drove the heel of his hand into the man's nose. Another grunt of pain, another gush of blood.

Gigantor reared back in reflex. Con bucked and hammered his knee into the hulk's kidneys, and he collapsed like a pitching net in a windstorm. Con rolled, holding his opponent down. Gigantor wasn't out for the count. His fist smashed into the side of Con's head, and stars exploded in his line of sight. The hulk scissored his legs and twisted. Locked in a deadly embrace, the men rolled across the cold, wet marble, grappling for superior position.

Con threw punches, left, right. A few grazed the target, several landed on the Kevlar, bruising his knuckles. Punches flew toward him. His head snapped back, absorbing a nasty blow to the jaw. *Ouch!* That was gonna leave a mark.

Time to close up the ballpark. He shoved away from his opponent and maneuvered behind him. Crouching, he flung his arm around the man's neck and wedged it in the crook of his elbow. Using his body as a lever against Gigantor's weight, Con pulled back and squeezed, compressing the carotid artery.

Gigantor thrashed, and the battle went into extra innings.

Bruising elbows pummeled Con's ribs, but he hung on. The sleeper hold did its job. Gradually, the fight went out of the hulk. He went limp, and Con lowered the unconscious man to the floor.

Three strikes and you're out, pal.

Panting, sweating, aching from multiple blows, and soaked from rolling on the wet floor, he crawled to the Uzi and scooped it up.

He pushed to his feet and staggered to Bailey. Pale and shaking, she huddled on the floor at the corner of the booth.

He reached to help her up, and she flinched away. "Don't."

What the hell? "Don't be afraid. It's me, baby."

Her blue eyes regarded him warily. "I've never seen anything so brutal."

He clenched his jaw, ignoring the twinge of pain. "I did what I had to do."

She swallowed hard. "You gouged that man's eyes. You broke his kneecap. And his nose."

"Those weren't love taps he dished out. He was playing for keeps. If I hadn't done the same, you'd be answering to him right now."

"I realize that, and I'm…" She swallowed again. "Grateful. Are you all right? You're not hurt?"

Other than the fact that she seemed to have a major problem with him all of a sudden? "I'm okay."

"He's not…" She pressed white lips together as if she were struggling not to be sick. "Is he…d-dead?"

"No. I choked him out, he's unconscious." He tucked the Uzi under his arm and offered her his hand. A challenge. *Believe in me. Accept me.* "We were too far away for the guy to yell for backup, and the fight wasn't overly loud, but in case anyone heard, we need to haul butt."

Ignoring his hand, she used the kiosk wall for support and clambered unsteadily to her feet. Her expression uncertain, she stared at him like a coiled rattlesnake in her path. As if he were a stranger. A man she didn't know and wasn't sure she could trust.

Hurt seared his insides and his stomach lurched. "Dammit, Bailey don't judge me for saving your life."

"I'm not."

At his blatant look of disbelief, she reiterated, "I'm not judging you."

"The hell you're not. You can't bear for me to touch you."

"I just…need some time, that's all." She shuddered. "I've never seen a real fight. The savagery was a shock."

"Time's in short supply." No time to banish her apprehension. Soothe her fears. Discuss and overcome her sudden, unexpected aversion to him. Frustrated and upset, Con scrubbed a hand over his sore jaw. He'd had no choice. He had to protect her, whether or not she approved of his methods. Neither of them could afford for him to pussyfoot around and get hurt. To lose.

Now she resented him for it?

He didn't look for trouble, but when trouble arrived, he didn't turn the other cheek and let the bad guys win. Surrender wasn't in his vocabulary. You could not negotiate with evil.

Was this chasm too big for them to bridge? Had he just saved her life and at the same time doomed his chance to spend it with her? Perhaps fate had shoved a blatant message in his face.

Con slammed the door on hurt. Barricaded out doubt and fear. He'd deal with it later. How, he had no idea. He gestured at her pack. "Pull out the other jump ropes and bandanas."

He stripped off Gigantor's Kevlar hood and vest. Under the gear, the blunt features belonged to a big, tough-faced blonde Con didn't recognize from any wanted bulletins. Still trembling, Bailey handed him several jump ropes.

He scanned her in a fast visual assessment. Pale and withdrawn, her breathing was too fast, her movements uncoordinated. Maybe she was suffering battle shock. It would explain her reaction. Even some combat-trained soldiers shut down when they witnessed brutality, especially the first time. For Bailey, who'd been sheltered all her life, the fight would have been terrifying. He gentled his voice. "Sweetheart, everything will be all right. We *will* get out of here, and save our friends."

She nodded, but said nothing. Strained silence loomed between them as they tied and gagged their captive. Hefting the behemoth over his shoulder, Con carried him into the men's room.

He popped the outer door lock and filled it with the remaining super glue.

Two down, four—or more—to go.

After the first two didn't return, more would come looking. Guerrilla tactics, picking off the bad guys individually, was his only viable option. Six to one were lousy odds, and storming the bank would only get the hostages killed. Before long, the guy in charge would figure out he wasn't up against just a bookstore clerk. Until then, Con had the advantage.

He exited the bathroom and strode to Bailey's side. He scooped up the vest. "Put this on."

She bit her lip. "You should wear it. You're most at risk."

"Don't argue. Do it."

Her shaky fingers fumbled with unfamiliar straps, but her remote, guarded expression warned him not to help. Instead, he jammed the hood into his pack. He wanted unobstructed vision for now, but the extra protection might come in handy later.

She shifted, having trouble with her balance. "It's heavy."

"It's an older model. Weighs twenty-five pounds. New ones weigh sixteen."

"I don't know how you function in one of these things."

He snorted as he shrugged on his pack, picked up his jacket, and then checked the Uzi's magazine. His baseball bat had shattered under Gigantor's kick, but they still had hers. They also had the vest, hood and a decent amount of ammo. That leveled the rocky odds some. "Add in the other gear, and SWAT officers pack about forty pounds into combat."

Her uneasy gaze slid away from his, and he fisted his hands. Right. Don't mention combat around the lady. "Let's move."

She shivered. "You should change into dry clothes. It's getting awfully cold. And you're even wetter now."

He rolled his taut shoulders. The soggy clothes were uncomfortable, but comfort wasn't a top priority. "I'm plenty warm after all the exercise. First things first. We need to find out who used to own all this blood."

"You don't think…could it be a hostage?"

He hoped not. Had the alarm spooked the robbers into shooting a hostage? His throat tightened as he slowly followed the splotches along the fake marble. "Way down here, so far from the bank? Unlikely."

"Maybe someone escaped and was shot in the process. Maybe that's who the robber was looking for."

He'd rather believe the crooks had a falling out over what to do after the fire alarm sounded and had gone their separate ways. Violently. That scenario would sure make them easier to neutralize. "Maybe. We'll soon see."

Watching for more gun-toting suspects, he tracked the grisly markers. The watery, yet unmistakable trail meandered into stores and out, seemingly at random. Larger pools showed where the victim had stopped to rest. At one point, the path made a wobbly loop toward the bank, then turned and wove toward the end of the mall.

Finally, the trail stopped at a rock-and-gem shop. Con signaled Bailey to wait in a sheltered alcove inside the entrance while he followed the blood to the back. Her safety was his number-one concern. However, if he had to subdue a suspect, he'd rather she didn't witness it again. He already had enough opponents. He didn't want to fight her disapproval, as well.

Uzi at the ready, he edged around a glass display case. And came face-to-face with a man sitting on the floor, propped against the oak paneling. Con's finger slid to the trigger of his weapon; then the man's identity registered. Syrone! A bloody bullet hole marred the upper left shoulder of his pale blue uniform jacket. More blood soaked the front. Way too much blood.

Syrone raised his fist, wrapped around a huge, sharp chunk of unpolished agate. "Come and get me, jerkwad." His voice was weak and shaky.

"Whoa!" Con whispered, lowering the Uzi toward the floor. "I'm on your side."

Syrone dropped his head back against the paneling. "Irish! Am I glad to see you."

"Can't exactly say likewise. Looks like you're in a jam here." He half rose. "Bailey," he called softly. "C'mon back."

She rushed in. "Who—" She stopped, gasped. "*Syrone!* You're hurt!"

"Bailey, you tangled in this mess, too?" Syrone shook his head. "I didn't see you leave before they jumped me, but I'd hoped you made it out okay."

Con pressed two fingers to Syrone's wrist.

"You trying to hold hands with me, O'Rourke?"

"Not on the first date. Maybe the second, though." The big man's pulse was weak and thready. Con squeezed his uninjured shoulder. "Can you stand?"

"Don't think so. My arms and legs feel disconnected." Syrone shook his head. "Took everything I had to stay on the move, keep two steps ahead. I'm about tapped out. Those bastards are hunting me."

"They won't get you." Con glanced up at Bailey. "Run to the bedding store and get sheets and quilts. Then find first-aid supplies. Move in the zigzag pattern I taught you, and watch your back. Hurry. He's shocky."

"They *shot* him? In cold blood?" Incredulity pitched in her voice. "He doesn't even carry a gun."

The truth sucks, sweetheart. It's a cold, hard world. "Probably without a second thought. No witnesses for this crew, remember?"

Horror skittered through her eyes, and he watched understanding dawn. *Life or death—in-your-face brutality.* Without another word, she pivoted and hurried away.

His heart ached at her grief and bewilderment. Losing your illusions was never pretty. He'd learned that lesson firsthand. Maybe now she'd accept what had to be done. He said a silent prayer for her mental and physical safety. Sending the woman he loved out alone and unarmed against ruthless killers went against everything he was. But he could not go with her. He had to trust her protection to a power greater than his own. He clenched his teeth against the need to call her back. To keep her safely by his side.

Con found a stack of clean rags in the storeroom. He knelt, folded several into a makeshift pad and placed them on Syrone's back over the exit wound. Gently turning the big man, he leaned him against the display case so his weight would put pressure on the pad at the right spot. "The bullet went clean through."

"Well, isn't this just my lucky day?"

"Considering those scum decided to use you for target practice, yeah."

"Guess I should count my blessings that big SOB had lousy aim."

"Things could be worse." Con folded more towels and covered the entry hole in Syrone's shoulder.

"Things can always be worse, Irish."

"That they can." Hoping the statement wasn't prophetic, he took Syrone's hand and pressed it over the pad. "Hold this tight."

Syrone winced. "That hurts like a mother."

"I know. Sorry, buddy. I've got to leave you for a few minutes and clean up the blood trail."

"Hells bells, is that how you found me? I was so out of it, I didn't even think about that. Follow the bloody brick road."

Con chuckled. Syrone's body had taken a beating, but his spirit was intact. "You had other things on your mind, like survival. Be right back."

He grabbed more rags from the storeroom and then hurried out to the mall. Trying to block his worries for Bailey, he mopped up most of the blood except for the trail that backtracked toward the opposite end. The false lead might throw the bad guys off the scent. For a while.

Finished, he sprinted back to check Syrone. The guard was holding his own. Barely. Con couldn't relax until the bleeding was stopped, the shock under control and his friend safely hidden.

He tied the blood-soaked rags into a plastic garbage bag and threw it in the trash can in the storage room. "How'd you get away from them?"

"Once a Marine, always a Marine. Couldn't let some rat-bastard civilians take me down without breaking a sweat, could I?"

In spite of his anxiety about his friend's condition, Con grinned. "No, you couldn't."

Flushed and panting, Bailey hurried in. He'd never been so glad to see anyone in his life. He released the breath he hadn't realized he'd been holding. He looked up, embracing her in his gaze. *C'mon, sweetheart. Give me a sign we can work it out.*

Something. Anything. His feelings ran the gamut, yo-yoing from fear to anxiety to hope. "Have any trouble? See anybody?"

"No." Her glance slid away, and he squelched disappointment. The dragon still loomed between them. Dammit, he smashed down barricades for a living. Vanquished dragons daily. However, he could not fight this battle. She had to find the courage and strength inside her to slay the beast—her fear.

Standing on the sidelines awaiting the outcome while she fought alone was the hardest thing he'd ever done. He determinedly squelched his emotions. Top priority: concentrate on keeping everyone alive.

Con again took Syrone's pulse. It was faster, and his respiration had also increased. His ebony skin was clammy. Not good.

Bailey knelt beside Con and he extended his hand, palm up. "Scissors."

Syrone grabbed Con's wrist. "Hold the phone, Irish. What are you cutting off?"

He chuckled. "Your jacket. After today, Riverside Security better spring for a new one. Okay?"

"I dunno. You have a license to practice?"

Bailey patted Syrone's leg. "Don't worry. Con is trained in first aid."

Con frowned. "How do you know that?"

She still wouldn't meet his eyes. "You are, right?"

"Yes, but—"

She handed him the scissors. "Here."

The woman was a wealth of information. Had she been reading up on SWAT training? A small, positive sign. Hope flickered to the forefront. If she'd been researching his job, she was interested. In spite of her reservations, she cared. He cut away the bloody, wet uniform. "You must have been caught in the downpour."

"You, too, from the looks of you." Syrone attempted a grin, but it looked more like a grimace. "The rainstorm your doing?"

"Yeah. When the trucks arrived, we signaled them to call up SWAT. The boys in black should be on site any second."

"Smart, Irish."

"Bailey's idea. She's the mind behind the operation. I'm just the muscle." He unbuttoned Syrone's shirt, and again held out his hand. "Disinfectant."

Her movements jittery and distracted, Bailey hesitated. "Not true. We came up with the plan together."

Syrone gave a weak chuckle. "Awesome work, if you ask me. You two make a great dynamic duo."

Con looked at Bailey, and this time her gaze lingered on his. The hurt and bewilderment swimming in her eyes punched into his chest. He sent her a silent message. *We do make a great team. Believe. Trust.*

Internal tumult ravaged her face as she passed him a brown plastic bottle of hydrogen peroxide. His girl was hurt and confused. Lost. Sad.

His chest aching as if he were the one with the bullet hole, he poured bubbling liquid over the jagged wound, front and back.

Syrone howled. "Yow! You disinfecting with battery acid?"

"Sorry. I know it hurts." *I'm hurting right along with you, pal. For entirely different reasons.*

"You can say that again, Irish."

Con constructed a pressure bandage. "There. That's slowed the bleeding." Too damn bad he couldn't as easily keep his emotions from leaking out.

"Bailey, darlin', hand me a quilt." He swaddled Syrone as carefully as he would a baby while Bailey disposed of all evidence they'd been in the rock shop. "Okay, now shake out the others and layer them on the floor."

They helped the injured man move to the center of the heavy, padded blankets. Pulling the quilts by the top, they used them like a sled to drag him over the slick floors to the Bedroom Furniture Emporium.

Near the back of the store, Con shoved a bulky mahogany double dresser a few feet away from the wall. "Solid cover to hide him behind." He carried over a crib-size mattress and tore away the plastic wrapping. Bailey added four plump pillows.

They helped Syrone settle in. Con again checked the big man's vitals. His pulse was stronger, but still rapid, and his respiration too shallow. His skin was cool and slightly clammy, though a little better than before. But he'd lost a lot of blood and needed medical care ASAP. "Your pants are damp. Not as bad as your shirt, but you'd be warmer with them off."

"Nuh-uh. There's a good chance I'll be involved in another firefight before this is over. Marines don't get caught with their pants down."

"Your call. We'll layer on another blanket. That should help."

Bailey fetched an additional quilt and covered Syrone while Con barricaded one open side of the mattress with another dresser.

Syrone shifted restlessly. "I've got a powerful thirst."

Con stood back to survey his work. Even this close, the make-shift bunker wasn't obvious. For Syrone's sake, the less obvious, the better. "I know. It's common with severe injuries and shock. But you can't have anything by mouth. Grady will be transport-ing your butt to the hospital in the ambulance. I don't want baby brother ragging on me for breaking medical protocol."

"Lord forbid." Syrone succeeded in his attempt at a grin this time. "That boy does take his doctoring seriously."

Bailey smiled. "My sympathies. There's nothing Grady loves better than a patient to poke and prod."

Con hated to spoil the camaraderie, but they had to get mov-ing. "Do you have your key card?"

"Yeah, but it doesn't work. The robbers jammed the circuits. And they took my keys, including the manual override. Lifted my radio, too."

Con swore. There went his hopes for getting Bailey out and letting SWAT in.

Syrone shifted. "You need an escape route, I have an idea."

"I'm all ears."

"There's an access door at the bank end of the mall. It's hid-den behind a panel on the wall behind the fountain. We use it for bringing in equipment and pipes when the fountain needs clean-ing or repairs. It's locked, but not on an electrical circuit. A ham-mer and lock punch should do the trick."

"Or my Swiss Army Knife." Con nodded, his spirits rising. If he had to be trapped without his piece and a limited means of communication, a mall wasn't the worst place in the world. "I'm sorry, buddy. We're gonna have to park you here for a while." He despised leaving his friend in such a bad way, but had no choice.

Bailey gasped. "We can't leave him alone and defenseless!"

"Don't sweat it, Bailey. I already figured as much." Syrone hesitated. "If I…don't make it, tell Jazelle she's always been the only woman in the world for me. Make sure my Jazzy knows I loved her right to the end. And the rug rats. Tell 'em their daddy loved 'em, and did his best."

Bailey's chin wobbled. She gave Syrone a gentle hug. "Nothing will happen to you."

Con checked the injured man's vitals one last time. Again, slightly improved, but still far too weak. Without surgery, and maybe a transfusion, he might not last long. "You can personally deliver the message after we get you out of here."

Syrone's wise, dark eyes locked on his. "Don't blow sunshine up my skirt, Irish, I know I'm not doing all that great. Even if my injuries don't send me to the final roll call, the bad guys are hunting me. I'm as defenseless as a naked pawn on a chessboard. I can't run, can't evade. Can't fight. All I *can* do is pray SWAT reaches me before the hunters do. The odds aren't great."

"Remember, one pawn can still win the game," Bailey said softly.

"This will even the odds some." Con passed him the Uzi and the Kevlar hood.

Syrone tried to return the gun. "You can't give me your weapon!"

Con had known from the minute they'd discovered the wounded man he couldn't do anything else. If the robbers found Syrone defenseless, he was dead. At least Con had given him a fighting chance. Unlike his own dad, maybe Syrone would go home to his wife. Wouldn't leave devastated kids. "I have. I'll kill the emergency lights before we leave. Anyone who ventures in won't be able to see, and they'll be silhouetted against the doorway. Just look real carefully before you pull the trigger. My teammates will tear a strip off my ass if I armed the guy who shoots them."

"Will do." Syrone offered his right hand. "Don't get tagged and bagged, Conall."

Con shook the broad hand. "Likewise, Syrone."

Syrone gave him a broad wink. "Too bad you're a wimpy SWAT boy. You would have made one hell of a Marine."

Con chuckled. "We'll settle that on the shooting range after you're healed."

"Lord willing, it's a date. Our second. So I might let you hold my hand."

Bailey unfastened the straps on her vest. "He should have this, too."

Syrone's glance collided with Con's. Both combat experienced, each knew what the other was thinking. If the enemy got past the barricades and close enough for a body shot, Syrone was doomed anyway. Syrone offered a weak wave. "You're on the run, you need it more. Besides, it would make me look fat."

Bailey was too smart to miss the unspoken message. She planted a kiss on Syrone's cheek. "Stay safe."

"You too, Bailey." Syrone leaned into his pillows and propped the Uzi across his lap. "Look after one another."

Con glanced at Bailey. Sorrow and tenderness softened her face. He held her gaze, telling her without words he, too, found it unbearable to walk away from their injured friend. "Will do."

Con knelt and tugged the Kevlar hood over Syrone's head. He spread his leather jacket over the other man to add an extra layer of warmth. "Watch this for me," he whispered in Syrone's ear. "There's something special, something sparkly for my girl in the pocket. If they take me out, make sure she gets it."

Syrone's eyes widened. "You bet," he whispered back. "Guard it with my life." A frown creased his brow. "Like you told me, you'd better plan on giving your love to your woman personally."

"Always wise to have a backup plan." Con rose. He disabled the emergency lights, and then boxed in the open side of the mattress with a third dresser. Sealing Syrone inside what he sincerely prayed wasn't his final resting place. Swallowing the lump in his throat, he led Bailey out of the store and into the darkened mall.

Keeping to the shadows, they crept toward One Hour Photo,

intending to fill their squirt guns. He'd feel better when he had a weapon again.

Using the crowbar Bailey had added to her pack while she was waiting for him to set off the sprinklers, he broke into the booth and then the locked cabinet containing acetic acid.

"Careful not to get any of this stuff on you," Bailey cautioned. "It's extremely caustic."

They loaded the four squirt guns and then exited the booth.

Bailey swayed on her feet, and he grabbed her shoulders. "Steady, sweetheart."

She pressed her palm to her forehead. "I'm a bit lightheaded."

He rolled his wrist and consulted his watch. "No wonder. It's nearly seventeen hundred and you haven't had anything to eat or drink all day. Not to mention the toll of stress and trauma. Once I get you out the access door to safety, make them feed you, okay?"

"I don't have much of an appetite."

"You need to eat. Promise me you will."

"Okay." Still too listless, she glanced toward the mall's main doors. "I guess we head back toward the bank now."

Without warning, an enormous explosion shook the building. Grinding crashes rolled up the walkway from the bank end of the mall, and then a series of smaller crashes echoed in succession.

Bailey jumped. "What was that?"

He had to force his heart out of his throat and back into his chest before he could speak. He sidled around the booth, peering toward the sound, but didn't see anything. "I don't know. But it didn't sound good."

"Uh, Con? What is this?"

He circled back, and found her staring at a glowing red dot on her chest. He looked down, and a red dot appeared on his chest. "*Laser sights!* Someone has high-powered rifles trained on us!"

Bailey gasped. "They're going to shoot us!"

Chapter 7

Aidan O'Rourke shivered in the stormy winter night as he strode across River View Mall's south parking lot. Freezing rain pelted the top of his head, the backs of his hands. The murky rows of mall windows, backlit by emergency lamps, were barely visible in the icy gloom. He dismissed the storm, just as he dismissed the threatening emotional whirlwind inside.

He assigned uniformed patrol officers to positions on the outer perimeter by the headlights of a patrol car. Until Captain Greene arrived, Aidan was high-ranking officer. Team leader and incident commander by default. He was too busy to think about anything other than the job. Too busy to worry. Too busy to feel. That's what he kept telling himself.

Maybe, eventually, he'd believe it.

His exhaled breath fogged to white mist in the cold air as he studied the assembled Kevlar-suited SWAT team. The members of Alpha Squad...excluding himself and his younger brother Con. Con was trapped inside the mall with a crew of bank robbers. Unarmed and defenseless.

Aidan snorted. Unarmed, yes, but about as defenseless as a blowtorch in a dynamite factory. If there was any man in the world who could triumph over nasty odds, it was Conall Patrick O'Rourke. Aidan would bet his own life on it.

Con's life was resting on it. As well as Bailey's. And an undetermined number of hostages. Every man standing in front of him cared for and respected his brother. But Aidan loved him. With bone-deep, fierce, abiding loyalty. He and Con had forged a nearly inseparable bond since birth. A heart connection shared between all four O'Rourke boys that grew stronger by the day. No criminals were going to steal that from them. No matter the price, he would get his brother out alive.

Dozens of patrol cars poured into the parking lot. The massive war wagon rumbled across the asphalt, loaded with tactical weapons, specialized siege-and-breeching equipment and SWAT officers from other teams.

Aidan waited until the armored vehicle discharged its passengers before he continued giving orders. "Liam." He pointed at O'Rourke brother number three. "Work Murphy around the inner perimeter sniffing for explosives. Scout building access and report back with all available intel."

Liam and his ears-up German Shepherd hurried away. Baby brother Grady, part-time SWAT officer and part-time paramedic, was also present. Packing his MP5 submachine gun and his stethoscope, Grady was equally proficient with both. New Year's Eve at the mall had become a family affair.

Aidan turned back to his ready warriors. "We'll establish the command post…" He glanced across the street. The command post needed to be close in order to direct the action, but not close enough to endanger the occupants. A pink neon signed glowed above the door of one store, a small, cheerful beacon in the icy blackness. "At the Krispy Krunch doughnut shop."

A wry grin slanted his lips. Con would appreciate the irony. Never one to take himself too seriously, his brother loved cop humor.

Aidan pressed the vibration mic of his headset more firmly over his vocal chords and spoke. "Command to Alpha Five. Ten-twelve, prelim status check. Over."

"Alpha Five. Intel imminent." Hunter Garrett, the team's regular scout and sniper responded. Even after years living on the West Coast, a hint of North Carolina woods drawled in his slow, exact baritone. The tawny-haired man's trigger finger was as even as his cadence, his cool, gunfighter's eyes as precise. "Moving to high ground. Visual confirmation, ASAP. Over."

"Ten-four. Command standing by. Over and out." Aidan adjusted his earpiece and quelled his impatience. During an incident, not even the most minor detail could be rushed. Waiting the bad guys out was the one factor civilians, and sometimes even top brass, didn't comprehend. The public and upper echelons often demanded immediate results. But a hasty, aggressive assault only made people dead. Both hostages and cops.

"Cain, reporting in." The negotiator stepped forward, and gratitude trickled through chinks in Aidan's internal shield. Wyatt Cain was a shrewd negotiator, with uncanny instincts and a cool head under fire.

"Wyatt, the suspects have popped the phone lines. Attempt to establish communication. Try to determine hostage count and condition, and obtain a list of demands. Get them talking. Keep them talking." As long as they were talking, they weren't killing.

"Ten-four." Wyatt strode off.

"Excuse me." An authoritative female voice demanded his attention.

He spun around and came face-to-face with a woman. She appeared to be a few years younger than his mother, tall, regal, with blue eyes as icy as the freezing rain pummeling his head. "I assume you are the person in charge?"

Great, just what he needed. A curious bystander or, worse, an irate neighbor complaining about all the noise. "Yes. You need to vacate the premises immediately, ma'am."

The brunette clutched her fur coat more tightly to her chest, and fear slashed her arrogant mask. "I'm Dr. Ellen Chambers. My daughter Bailey works in the mall. I've been trying to reach her for hours." She paused to clear the tremor from her voice. "You just mentioned hostages. What's happened?"

She had his immediate attention and sincere empathy. They both had loved ones in the hot zone. "Dr. Chambers, I'm Officer Aidan O'Rourke. Let's move across the street to the command center. You look like you could use some hot coffee, and the family liaison officer will update you on what we know so far."

"O'Rourke?" Her voice frosted over, colder than her eyes, as she studied him. "The resemblance is unmistakable. You're related to Conall."

"Yes, ma'am. My brother Con is dating your daughter. He's also inside the mall."

"I might have known." Dislike hardened her sharp features. "Trouble sparks in that boy's wake. Along with a lot of dangerous pheromones. If I were a betting woman, I'd wager my Russian fox coat Conall O'Rourke got my daughter into this mess."

"Command, this is Alpha Five." Hunter's transmission broke over Aidan's headset. "Snipers in position. Ready with that ten-twelve. Over."

About damn time. Aidan held up a hand that wasn't as steady as he would have liked to Dr. Chambers. "Command. Go ahead, Alpha Five. Over."

"I have a confirmed visual. Alpha One is signaling for all he's worth." Aidan heard the grin of pride in Hunter's voice. "He might be flying solo, but he's already taken out two suspects. Over."

"Ten-four. Continue surveillance." Sweet relief streamed through Aidan. He closed his eyes and breathed a brief, silent prayer of thanks. Then he confronted Dr. Chambers's antagonistic gaze. "No, ma'am. Con did not get Bailey into this mess. But he *will* get her out."

Inside the mall, crouched behind the One Hour Photo booth, Bailey watched Con's capable hands begin to execute a graceful, complicated ballet. "What are you doing?"

"The red dots…the laser sights fixed on us? They're coming from the parking lot. Alpha Team's snipers can see us as well through their night vision scopes as if we were standing right in front of them. I'm telling them what's going on."

"How do you know it's them, and what they're doing?"

"For one thing, if bad guys were behind those rifles, we'd already be dead. As far as knowing what SWAT is up to, we've set up incident sites together so many times, we could all do it in our sleep." In response to Con's hand motion, the red dot on her chest bobbed back and forth, and he grinned. "Wave to Hunter, sweetheart."

Hunter Garrett. The wide-shouldered, soft-spoken cop with a golden mane of hair and the menacing grace of a stalking lion.

His sharp, blue-gray eyes didn't miss a trick, and his southern-bred manners were impeccable. He had a face as beautiful as an angel and the unerring trigger finger of the devil. If Hunter had his rifle trained on her, she had nothing to worry about. She sent him a wave, along with a wan smile.

"The boys in black are on site and ready to kick bank-robber butt."

Wild hope cut through the dulling edge of pain and terror. "Will they break down the door, storm in and rescue us now?"

He laughed. "Only on TV. When engaged in a standoff, usually the longer the scenario drags on, the better." He shook his head. "No, we're in for a wait."

"What about Syrone and the hostages? Syrone needs a hospital, and this kind of stress can't be good for Nan or the baby."

"We need time for the suspects to relax and climb off the razor edge of reactive behavior. Time for SWAT to plan and rehearse a dynamic entry if needed." Con rubbed his hand over his hair. "Time buys lives, darlin'."

Her emotions seesawed from high to low for the millionth time. "Feels like we've been trapped in here forever."

He moved as if to take her in his arms. His expression unreadable, he checked himself. "I know it's been tough, and you're feeling rocky. But the cavalry is here. We'll get you out to them, and then you can stand down."

Shame washed over her. She'd reacted badly to the fight, and Con was suffering the effects. Yet, as always, his thoughts were focused on her safety. If only they had time to work things out. "Con, listen…I—"

"No time to talk." He pivoted away from the doors. "Let's go."

Frustration and unhappiness churned inside her. No time for anything but endless flight, unceasing fear. Another crouching sprint up a gloomy corridor. Though the sinking pit in her stomach already told her the answer, she had to ask. "Are you coming out with me?"

"SWAT needs eyes and ears inside. I'm elected."

She couldn't leave with everything unresolved between them. What if the worst happened and she never saw Con again? She didn't want his last thoughts of her to hurt. She drew a shaky breath. "Too bad you can't decline the nomination."

"Other than the fact we won't be together, I don't want to. This is what I do."

Yes, it was. She'd learned in the last few hours exactly how capable he was at his job. And how hard and gritty the work. Bailey stomped down her roiling emotions. She could not, would not, think about how awful it would be walking out that door without him. She refused to be further hindrance. She'd have to snatch a few seconds to tell him her feelings before they separated. Once outside, she could indulge in a nice, quiet, private nervous breakdown. *For now, hold it together.* "What's the plan?"

"A couple of armed team members will be waiting for you outside the access door. The negotiator will create a distraction, and you'll be free before you know it. Run to them. Don't hesitate, don't stop and don't look back."

Another sprint up the mall, another fifty-yard dash toward freedom. Panting, she leaned against the shoe store. Running with the heavy vest on was exhausting her rapidly dwindling resources. The going was also slower and tougher now that the floor was wet. Behind her, Con was barely breathing hard.

She shivered and rubbed her arms through the thin silk blouse. The chill was growing more bone-rattling by the moment. She hoped the robbers spared a thought to Letty's age and were keeping her warm. Of course, if Con was right and they didn't plan to let her go, they wouldn't care. Bailey squelched the horrible thought. *Concentrate on here and now.*

"No talking from here on. We'll have to use hand signals."

In order to reach the hidden access panel, they again had to cross the wide open space by the back doors. Logically, one would think that after hours of constant terror, a person would get used to it. Maybe grow numb.

She could testify that wasn't the case.

Bailey in front, Con behind, they crawled on hands and knees under the bank windows. Rustling sounds, rapid footsteps and the sharp tang of cigarette smoke drifted out the open doorway.

"Filthy habit, smoking," Letty's calm soprano reprimanded. "It'll kill you one of these days, young man."

Bailey wanted to laugh and weep at the same time. Her friend was alive, and still very much in possession of her indomitable spirit.

"Pipe down, Grandma." The graveled Bronx accent belonged to the man she'd encountered in the parking lot. "I got enough problems, I don't need any more grief from you."

"I need to use the restroom." Nan's soft request was also calm.

"We're kinda busy at the moment, lady," Bronx snarled.

"I really can't wait very long."

"I can escort her," Mike supplied, sounding a lot shakier than the women.

"Oh, right. Like that's going to happen in this century."

"Hey, Tony, you were right about the C-4." A second man's voice, steeply pitched with excitement broke in. "Popped that vault slicker than snot on a banister. As soon as we get the dough loaded, we can finish it and get the hell out of here."

C-4? That must have been the explosion and first crash they'd heard. The robbers had grown desperate and blown the vault open. *Finish it?* Did that mean what she suspected? Bailey shivered again.

"Attention, in the bank!" Wyatt Cain, the hostage negotiator, shouted from outside. He must be using a megaphone because his mellow baritone echoed through the deserted mall, loud and clear. "This is Riverside PD. The SWAT team has the mall surrounded. There is no way out."

A chorus of vile epithets spat from the men inside the bank.

"Dammit! Doesn't it just figure?" the man identified as Tony swore. "My last, biggest and most brilliant job. My farewell bash, and there have to be mouse turds in the punch bowl."

"Put down your weapons and surrender," Wyatt continued. "Nobody will get hurt, and we'll all go home."

That was the signal. While the robbers were distracted by the announcement, Bailey and Con crawled around the corner of the bank.

"Surrender *this,* pig," a different man's voice challenged, and rough male laughter sounded.

Con and Bailey ran past the fountain to Santa's sleigh, which had tipped on its side. Water droplets beaded the intricate metal runners. Fallen reindeer lay drunkenly in the soggy cotton batting that was supposed to resemble snow. She peeked around the reindeer toward the access panel.

Oh no!

Stunned, she turned to Con, widening her eyes into a *what now?* look.

He peered around her. She watched disbelief, frustration and anger chase over his face as he saw the North Pole workshop had tumbled to the floor. The sides and roof of the twenty-foot cottage had split and collapsed. Giant shattered toys and dismembered elves littered the floor like war casualties. Candy Cane Lane leading to the cottage had fallen like dominoes, and ten-foot candy canes lay stacked across the end of the mall. A snarled fortress of cracked support platforms, torn, tangled strings of lights and wet, broken plaster. Sealing off the panel. Blocking their escape.

The display must have become unstable when soaked by the sprinklers, and then the concussion from the vault explosion had knocked everything down. That explained the smaller, secondary crashes. There was no way around the piled debris, no path through it, and no way to quietly move it aside.

They had no choice. Con signaled to backtrack.

Another long, cold and exhausting duck-and-run through the dark. The hunted feeling on the back of her neck was growing eerily familiar. With the heavy vest weighing her down, she barely made it up the escalators to the third floor. Con had to boost her with a hand in the small of her back the last ten steps.

"I have to catch my breath." Shivering with cold, and nearly too weary to stand, she leaned against the balcony railing.

"Hang on just a few seconds longer." He steered her into a craft store and behind the sales counter.

Her legs gave out and she sank to the damp floor.

"I need to go let the team know the number and position of hostages and suspects."

"You saw? How are Letty and Nan holding up, and Mike? How did they look? Are they scared? Are they hurt?"

"They looked tired and stressed, which is to be expected. But healthy and all in one piece, sweetheart. And nobody is freaking out. That's the most important thing right now."

She heaved a relieved sigh. "How many bad guys are there?"

"At least four in the lobby. There might have been some in the vault and one or two more could be out hunting us and Syrone." He stroked her hair. "I'll go signal SWAT from the sky bridge, scout around up here for unfriendlies and be back in ten minutes. Fifteen at the most. Okay?"

"Okay." He slipped out, and she stacked her forearms on her raised knees, pillowed her head on them and closed her eyes. The bleak, silent third floor felt far removed from the bank robbers, like a protective cocoon. An illusion Bailey willingly indulged. At the moment, she could not handle one more minute of fear, one more stint of running, one more dashed promise of rescue.

She might even have dozed off, because the next thing she heard was Con's gentle voice.

"Come here, sweetheart."

She looked up. Con stood with his muscled arms spread wide, and a wary yet hopeful expression on his handsome face.

She pushed to her feet and went willingly into his embrace. In spite of the fact that his clothes were soaked and his skin chilled, the hug was warm and reassuring. She rested against his broad chest, letting his solid strength restore her flagging spirits. "Con, I'm sorry for the way I acted after the fight."

"There's nobody on this floor but us. While we wait out the next phase of the plan, let's get some food into you. Then we can talk."

The brief nap had recharged her batteries slightly. "No, first you change into dry clothes, *then* we eat. You're going to catch pneumonia."

"You're wet, too, from crawling on the floor. We both need to change."

Figuratively speaking, she thought he was fine exactly as he was. She, on the other hand, was changing by the moment.

Keeping one arm around her, he guided her into JCPenney. He extracted a flashlight from his pack and shone the beam over racks of clothing. Cloaked in shadow, everything looked creepy and weirdly out of proportion.

She'd fantasized about being alone in the mall, able to shop at leisure with no crowds, noise or distractions. The real thing didn't quite pan out. She visually tracked the light, trying to get her bearings. "I'm disoriented."

"A combination of shock, hypothermia and lack of nourishment. When you're dry and fed, you'll bounce back." He grabbed unisex black jeans, black turtlenecks and black sweatshirts in his size and hers from a bottom row of wooden cubbies sheltered from the sprinklers. "We'll layer to stay warm."

He opened a bag of thick wool socks and retrieved women's lightweight lug-soled boots from a shoebox underneath the boot display to replace her sheer hose and feminine leather slip-ons. "You'll not only be warmer, but able to move faster in these."

Dry undergarments were also a necessity. Embarrassment tweaked her, but Con's matter of fact attitude in the men's department banished her self-consciousness. Until they headed to women's lingerie and he plucked a frothy, pink silk teddy from a rack. "It's your favorite color."

"That doesn't look very warm."

"Believe me, sweetheart, wearing this little number, you would not be cold. My personal guarantee."

"It's wet."

"In some cases, that's not considered a disadvantage."

She smirked at him. "Take my word for it, Irish. I doubt you'll need any help there."

"Ooh, I love it when you talk naughty, slugger." Laughing, he extracted a package from a bin, tore it open and brandished a pair of tiny black lace panties. He stretched them across his hands. "Hmm. These feel…comfortable. Look sexy, too. I can picture you wearing them. Great picture."

The erotic sparkle in his eyes made heat bloom in her cheeks. He caressed her with his glowing mahogany gaze and the heat spread, tingling through her limbs. The man smoldered. It was impossible to remain disheartened bathed in the light of his open appreciation. Not to mention the uplifting effect of his flying quips and flashing grins.

She snatched the underwear from him. "Get your hands out of my pants."

He laughed. "Spoilsport."

She found a packaged black stretch lace camisole to go with the panties, and Con expressed his enthusiastic approval.

Arms piled high, they entered a fitting room. Con propped the flashlight on a chair so it partially illuminated the first two cubicles. He shot her a mischievous grin. "Need any help?" He flexed his fingers. "All the better to undress you, my dear."

If only he knew how tempting his offer was. How overwhelming the desire to have his hands on her. "Remember what happened to that wolf."

"I'll huff and I'll puff and I'll blow—" He snorted. "Nuh-uh. I'm not touching that one with a ten-foot pole."

"Braggart. Anyway, you're mixing up your wolves. That was a whole other story."

"I'll reenact any story you want. I've always been partial to the *Kama Sutra*."

"Have you seen some of the impossible positions…" Flushing, she trailed off.

"So you *have* read it."

"I consider myself a well-read person in every area of life."

"Glad to hear it." He wiggled his eyebrows at her. "Now, about those positions…care to name your top five?"

She'd seen a few that looked intriguing. Had imagined her and Con entwined in intimate, exciting love play. Adventurous O'Rourke would take her anywhere she wanted to go. And then some. "I'm game if you are. I do yoga exercises every day, so I'm pretty flexible. Think you can keep up?"

"Just try and keep me down, darlin'," he drawled.

When Con looked at her like that, all sparkling mischief and smoky sex appeal, she wanted to pounce on him. Gobble him up like a hamster on a Cheeto. Unfortunately, this was the wrong time, wrong place. Arching a brow, she returned his grin. "Maybe you can show me that upstanding flexibility later."

He tweaked one of her curls. "You're racking up quite an account, you know."

"I'm good for it. I have excellent credit."

Chuckling, he strode into the second cubicle, leaving the first for her.

She struggled out of her damp clothing. With only a thin, three-quarter partition between them, she could hear the rustle of fabric as Con also stripped. Her stomach dipped and her knees went weak, and not from lack of food. The knowledge of him so near, naked, sent longing spiraling through her. If only they could escape. Talk things out. Laugh and love together like other couples on New Year's Eve.

Instead, they might die together.

A wave of dizziness washed over her and she staggered.

"Hey, you okay over there? I was teasing before, but if you really need help…"

If he joined her in the cubicle, she'd wrap her arms around him and never let go. The last thing he needed was a clingy, whiny woman. "I'm doing fine." She wiped off the vinyl bench with her blouse, then sat and tugged on the jeans, turtleneck and sweatshirt. She loosened the black velvet ribbon securing her hummingbird charm and retied it over the turtleneck, and then donned socks and boots. "What should we do with our wet stuff?"

"Leave it. We don't need anything else to haul around."

They exited the fitting room. "Except for these." Con grabbed three comforters sealed in vinyl bags on the way out of the store. "We need something dry to picnic on." He reached for her hand.

Her chilled fingers tucked securely in his big, already warm ones, she walked beside him toward the food court. "I feel so small and insignificant in this huge, eerie bubble of silence. Just the two of us, trapped inside, like caterpillars in a jar." A tremor shivered up her spine. "Only there are praying mantises on the loose."

Con squeezed her hand. "Don't worry. Dozens of patrol cars will respond to the call-out. They'll import an army of cops."

But up here, they were alone. At least she hoped they were.

The eerie thought sent goose bumps prickling along her skin. "Are you sure no one else is up here?"

To her left, a sudden movement, followed by a resounding crash sent her heart leaping into her throat.

Before she had time to form coherent thought, Con dropped the blankets, shoved her to the floor and flung himself on top of her. "Don't move!"

Chapter 8

Adrenaline rocketed from Bailey's toes to the top of her head, and her heartbeat exploded in her ears. "What was that?" she whispered.

"Stay put." Con eased off her and drew a squirt gun from the back waistband of his jeans. Appearing surprisingly deadly considering he was packing plastic instead of steel, he pivoted in a half crouch and pointed the makeshift weapon toward the crash.

Nothing happened. No movement. No sound. The taut moment stretched out, enveloped in heavy silence.

He noiselessly prowled across the floor toward Outdoor Outfitters. Squirt gun sweeping from side to side, he crept inside the store. Then he disappeared from sight.

She held her breath and prayed.

Suddenly, his laughter rolled out the doorway and over her. The low, husky chuckles undulated inside her, both stirring and confusing.

Laughter? "Con?" she called. "Who is it?"

"Maxwell Moose."

"What?"

"Outdoor Outfitters mascot, Maxwell Moose. There's a huge replica of him in here. Got wet in the sprinkler storm like everything else, and toppled over, taking a couple tents down with him. Looks like the collapsed tents have been holding up his considerable weight for a while. The fabric finally tore."

"Gad. Moose-induced heart attack. A unique cause of death for the coroner to list on my certificate." As the adrenaline tide swept out, she sat up and pressed her palm over her galloping heart. "So, other than Maxwell, we really are alone up here?"

He emerged from the store and returned to her side. "As reasonably sure as I can be. Three spread-out floors is a lot of territory for six or eight..." He grinned. "Now reduced to four or six...guys to track."

"I'd be happier if there were less."

"If I have anything to say about it, there will be. Eventually." He offered his hand and helped her up. "You okay? I didn't hurt you, did I?"

"No." She glanced at the floor. "Fortunately, I landed on the packaged comforters. Geez, Officer Sexy, I don't mind if you throw me down and leap on me, but issue a warning first."

"Sorry, no time for a warning. Or to cushion your fall. Good thing the blankets dropped where they did." His grin broadened, white and wicked in his beard-stubbled face. "I promise next time I jump you, it will be under more pleasant circumstances."

She'd give her right arm for Con's confidence. Armed only with a squirt gun and his wits, he was sure he could handle anything that came their way. Had no doubts they'd escape in one piece. At least no doubts he was sharing. She'd caught glimpses of the doubt he'd tried so hard to hide. After the fright, his good humor was appreciated...and contagious. She chuckled as her heart lightened. "Something else to look forward to."

"You know what I'm also looking forward to?" He squeezed her hand. "I'd barter one of my brothers to a tribe of Amazon women for a hot cup of coffee."

Relief and ebbing fight-or-flight response, combined with the prospect of food, made her giddy. "Mmm. Piping hot cocoa sounds heavenly. Maybe we can manage some, and without compromising your brothers' virtue."

He chuckled. "Not that they have any virtue to compromise. Or like they'd complain."

"A definite case of the lascivious pot calling the carnal kettles black."

"Hey, are you accusing me of being a hound dog?"

"If the flea collar fits..." she teased.

He growled at her, a low sexy rumble deep in his throat. Her bones melted and she nearly dissolved into a puddle at his feet. He tugged her close and gave her a quick love-nip on the earlobe.

Amazing how he could shoot her pulse into the stratosphere with a mere look, the barest touch. The scent of him—warm, lusty male—made her hormones break into a celebratory riot. "Yum. You want Milk-Bones with that coffee, Fido?"

He nuzzled his face into her neck. "I'd rather have you."

Her celebrating hormones kicked the party up a notch, and she eased back, breaking the contact. Not a good time to let desire run rampant over common sense. "Unfortunately, I'm not on the menu at the moment." If the man were any more compelling, they'd have to slap a warning on him like the ones on the MRI machines at the hospital. *Irresistible magnetic field. Please remove all metal objects before entering the vicinity.*

Breathless and distracted, she stared at the tent-jumbled doorway he'd exited. The lure of steaming, fragrant hot chocolate snapped her fuzzy thinking into focus. The only thing she wanted more badly than Con right now was food. "Outdoor Outfitters has tents and camping lanterns. And boy, does Maxwell Moose owe us one after scaring us half to death." Her empty stomach grumbled. "Do you know how to work a butane lantern? I don't."

"You bet. Having a former Boy Scout around comes in handy."

"Somehow, I have a hard time picturing you as a Boy Scout. I didn't know they gave merit badges for flippant flirting." Not to mention naughty double entendres and scorching intensity.

"I'll have you know I was top-notch." He winked. "At scouting, not flirting. Didn't make it to Eagle Scout like Aidan, but I had my strong suits."

"Starting fires, for instance?"

He held her gaze, his beautiful eyes smoky. "There are fires, and then there are fires."

Heat shimmered in her bloodstream. "Don't I know it."

"Let's scrounge up some grub, and come back." He tucked his pack and the blankets under a wooden bench inside Outdoor Outfitter's doorway. "Stash your stuff here."

The lure of sustenance drove them to the food court. The first restaurant in the loop was a fast-food outlet and offered raw frozen meat patties, frozen fries and packaged condiments.

Bailey shivered. The mall was growing so cold, if she didn't get something hot in her stomach, she'd end up as stiff as the white-frosted fries. She considered a foil ketchup packet. "I saw Lucy make tomato soup with ketchup and hot water on TV once, but I don't want to go that route unless we have no other choice."

"I'm hungry enough to eat just about anything, but that sounds as bad as Grady's Can-do Casserole."

"What is Can-do Casserole? I haven't had the pleasure."

"Lucky you." Con grimaced. "When it was Grady's turn to cook, what the rest of us called Desperation Casserole was his favorite dish. First, he'd dump random canned goods into a baking dish. Then baby bro would sprinkle the concoction with frozen Tater Tots, grated cheese, and cayenne pepper and bake it until he remembered to take it out, or his homework was done. Whichever came first." He shuddered. "Sometimes we renamed the crud Cajun Blackened Char-Tots."

"Blech." Grady's adventurous cooking didn't surprise her. Con had said that Grady was forever experimenting as a kid. Taking apart Con's alarm clock. Setting Con's bedspread on fire with wacky chemistry experiments. A reserve SWAT officer and part-time paramedic, Grady was the only medicine man in a long line of cops and soldiers, and was jokingly dubbed the black sheep of the family. Grady suffered from an incurable urge to fix everyone and everything. He was always hauling home stray dogs and birds with broken wings.

Con's mom had doled out age-appropriate household chores from the time her sons were knee-high. She'd told Bailey that no woman would need to look after one of her boys. Unlike Bailey, who hadn't been allowed near a stove, or "dangerous" household chemicals and appliances. After leaving home, she'd taught herself everything she needed to know from reading books.

"Can-Do Casserole sounds so Grady." Laughing, she pointed at the restaurant across from them. "Good Earth Café. Hopefully, we'll find something more palatable."

The refrigerator inside the café was loaded with treasure. Bailey stuffed bags with sourdough rolls, sliced cheddar, a big, moist chunk of carrot cake with cream cheese frosting for herself, and a generous piece of Con's favorite apple pie. Con used his Swiss Army Knife to coax open a vending machine. If he wasn't such a great cop, he could have a stellar career as a cat burglar. Vegetable soup, cocoa and coffee were still warm inside the insulated compartments.

Trying not to feel like a looter as they hurried back toward Outdoor Outfitters, Bailey mentally calculated the cost of the food to add to her notebook tally. She shifted her bag for better balance. "I love hearing about your adventures growing up. Your rowdy, dominantly male household was so different from mine."

"Life with your mom and Nanny Nightmare was suffocating, huh?"

Suffocating was the exact word to describe her stilted existence with her mom and the Wagnerian Valkyrie German nanny Ellen Chambers had insisted on hiring to ease the burden of being a single parent. When Bailey had protested she was too old for a live-in baby-sitter, the strict, humor-impaired woman had been dubbed her "tutor." Bailey had then been force-fed German.

She wrinkled her nose. "Oh yeah. Frau Herrman was about as cuddly as one of those frozen meat patties." Bailey had endured the dour woman's stranglehold until she had turned eighteen and determinedly struck out on her own.

Con's dark eyes warmed with sympathetic golden lights. "I'm sorry you had such a rough time, sweetheart."

"Hey, compared to kids with real problems, I had nothing to complain about. I was fed, healthy and cared for. Tell me more. When it was your turn to cook, what was your specialty?"

"Guess."

"Spaghetti and tossed salad with garlic bread?"

"Got it in one."

He'd cooked spaghetti dinners for her before. Served with Chianti and candlelight, the simple meal had become one of her favorites. The food was even more delicious because Con lovingly prepared it with his own hands. "What about Liam and Aidan?"

"Liam went for the preparation ease and one-pot cleanup of chili dogs. Aidan enjoyed mucking around with ingredients and recipes, and unlike Grady, actually possessed some talent. Other than Mom's cooking, which can't be beat, we got our most tasty meals from Aidan. His macaroni-and-cheese isn't half bad. And he makes a mean meatloaf."

She longingly pictured the O'Rourke clan gathered around Maureen's sturdy oak dining set. Teasing and laughter would have accompanied banter about the day's events over filling, homey foods. As she'd told Con, she had no reason to complain. She'd never gone hungry. However, after Bailey's dad died, meals at the Chambers' household became damask and china affairs with menus designed for sophisticated palates. With emphasis on intelligent conversation and using the proper fork.

Ellen Chambers had invested considerable energy into raising Bailey in preparation for what she called "marrying well." A serious, refined, Armani-clad financier or respected corporate lawyer would do nicely. Blech again. That kind of stiff sounded less appetizing than Grady's Can-Do Casserole.

Bailey, who'd escaped her rigid, no-nonsense home life through books and make-believe, had always had a thing for gallant knights in shining armor.

Con gestured with his bag. "Here we are."

He retrieved the packs and blankets from their hiding spots beneath a wooden bench inside the doorway. "Let's set up camp in one of the big tents in the back. It will be warm, dry and hidden." He piled the supplies on the bench and indicated for her to do the same. "Safety first. Come with me."

He strode out to the mall walkway and yanked down a length of fir swag from the balcony railing. He detached a handful of glass ball ornaments from the swag and passed them to her. Then he grabbed another handful and began throwing them to the floor outside the store. The shards tinkled musically over the faux marble. "Start chucking Christmas balls, darlin'."

She watched him, her brows knit in puzzlement. "You get a sudden, inexplicable urge to commit vandalism?"

"Listen." He stepped on the shards, and they made a distinct crunching sound under his boot soles. "Early warning system. We can cozy up in a tent in the back, and if anyone heads our way, we'll hear. To them, it will simply look like the swag fell under its own weight and the ornaments scattered and broke."

Amazed, she flung ornaments. "You are one smart cookie."

"Aidan gets credit for this maneuver. He knows damn near every survival trick in the book."

"Speaking of your capable, hard-headed-as-a-rock big brother, what are he and the SWAT team doing now?"

"First they'll secure the incident site and gather as much intel from as many different sources as possible. About the mall, suspects and hostages. Next, establish communication with the bad guys. Acquire a list of demands and bargain for hostage release."

They finished smashing ornaments and moved into the store. Inside, Maxwell Moose sprawled like a petrified hit-and-run victim across three collapsed tents, his hooves pointing straight up.

There were no emergency lights, and farther in, the hushed blackness was thick and inky. Bailey retrieved a flashlight from her pack and angled the beam in a slow circle. The store was huge. The vaulted ceiling was painted like a night sky, complete with glow-in-the-dark stars and northern lights. Wall murals gave the impression of a secluded Alaskan clearing surrounded by forest. Gave the perception of solitude. Safety. A fantasy she desperately wanted to buy into. Dripping fake trees sat around the room, along with water-beaded tents. Shelves bulged with camping and survival equipment. As a hiding place, it had merit.

"How will they contact the robbers? Yelling through a megaphone seems counterproductive to peace talks."

Con handed her the food bags and then picked up the packs and blankets. "The negotiator has a throw phone. A mobile unit he tosses out. The suspects retrieve it and take it inside. Meanwhile, armed officers have surrounded the building in both a tight inner and outer perimeter, and snipers are in position. They've got a miserable job. Lying on the ground, no matter the weather, waiting. Watching, staying alert, immobile for hours."

With him following, she walked to a large tent at the back of the store. She set the food on a dry spot on the carpet near the tent, and he did the same with the packs. While she and Con would be cozy inside their shelter, the men sent to rescue them would patiently endure hours of wet, freezing exposure in the storm. Worse, they could face gunfire. Sympathy, along with anxiety for the officers' welfare weighted her chest. She'd thought giving up her own time to help redecorate the bookstore was devotion to duty. "Are the snipers there to shoot the bank robbers?"

"Maybe, eventually." He got out the other flashlight and propped both to cast yellow circles in the immediate vicinity. "Right now, they're an important source of intel. They report everything they see through their scopes. They watch for a clear line of fire, but won't shoot without a green light from command. It's a last resort. With this many suspects, taking them all out with simultaneous cold shots is out of the question."

She shrugged off the heavy Kevlar vest and dumped it inside the tent. She rubbed her icy hands together. "What's a cold shot?"

"Depending on where in the body a person is shot, they can still function far too long. I've seen mortally wounded suspects run more than fifty yards. Continue shooting for nearly a minute. Plenty of time for them to inflict injury or death."

He folded back the tent flaps. The interior was protected from the sprinklers' devastation and would provide a barrier against the pervasive chill. "A cold shot is a bullet to the brain stem. It's a small target area, between the nose and upper lip, and takes considerable skill. Drops 'em instantly. Immediate neutralization."

She closed her eyes against the horrific mental picture, but it didn't help. His cool recitation about snipers severing brain stems might have been about the weather. How did Con block the disturbing images, the terrible memories day in, day out? She opened her eyes and focused on the shelves lining the store. As dangerous as their situation was, the worst thing she'd witnessed was a vicious fight and Syrone's bullet wound. She'd better prepare. As the night advanced, the risk of violence increased.

Dread churned in her empty stomach. If lethal force became necessary, could she handle watching Con kill someone? And how would she feel about him afterward?

He tore apart plastic envelopes containing the comforters and shook out the blankets, spreading one on the tent floor, folding the second into a bulky pillow and reserving the third in a crumpled pile inside the tent. "Shooting through wind, rain or glass changes the bullet's trajectory. One miscalculation and you've got dead officers and/or hostages. Which is why snipers spend hundreds of hours of their own time on the firing range. A lot of lives depend on them. They're carrying a huge responsibility on their shoulders."

"You all carry heavy responsibility." Her voice was thick with sadness for both the dead and the staunch officers who had to make the wrenching decisions. "Hold many lives in your hands."

He backed out of the tent and studied her somber face. "Ah, sorry, baby. More than you wanted to know."

"No, it's okay. I'm beginning to see the quandaries police officers face. Imagining what your job is like doesn't even begin to come close. It's important for me to know the truth. Knowing the circumstances helps me understand how you react to things. Helps me understand what you do and why you do it."

His considering gaze studied her. "A few hours ago, this conversation would have freaked you out."

"A few hours ago, I was living in la-la land. Reality got shoved in my face." She walked to the shelves and returned with a butane camping lantern, waterproof matches, insulated mugs and bottled water. "What else is happening out there?"

"Greene has probably called the birds for air support."

"You mean helicopters?"

"Yeah. And the war wagon, the armored transport truck, will be parked by the command center. It's jam-packed with battering rams, door breechers, flash-bangs, tear gas, grenades. Guns of every caliber. A shoulder-held missile launcher. Even a computer center. Everything needed for close-quarters urban combat."

He assembled a lantern with his usual efficient grace. "Now that I've signaled the position and condition of all involved, and command knows no lives are in immediate jeopardy, we can stand down for a while. We've done our jobs and we can let them do theirs."

"What will they do?"

"Wait. Negotiate. Wait some more. Cold, darkness, the long dragging hours all work in SWAT's favor. The suspects are under high tension. Uncertain of their position or tonight's outcome. The stressful conditions are wearing on their nerves by the minute. Hell, by the end of a siege, most suspects are happy to surrender and go to a nice, warm, well-lit jail cell."

"Most." She carried the supplies into the tent, and he followed with the lantern. "Not all."

"No." He scratched a match on the box and lit the lantern. "I could have used these earlier. Too bad we were at the opposite end of the third floor." He adjusted a knob and a soft glow permeated the tent. "There are always a few who insist on going down hard. Let's hope we don't come to that."

She removed cheese, rolls and napkins from the bag, and began to tear the rolls in half. "If we do?"

He retrieved the flashlights from outside. "No need to worry in advance. We'll handle it as it happens."

Anxiety quivered inside her. "I'll bet you've worried in advance, haven't you?"

"Worrying and planning are two different entities. I've run a couple mental scenarios, just in case."

"So, what are they? What's our next task?"

"At the moment, our priorities are eat, rest and recharge." He extracted the cardboard cups of soup, cocoa and coffee and transferred them to the insulated mugs she'd found. "The battle is far from over. We'll need every iota of energy, strength and wits to survive the night."

Busy stacking cheese on the rolls, she jerked, nearly dropping the food. "Will we survive the night?"

"Yeah. We will. One step at a time."

"How do you know?"

"Because I refuse to consider any other option."

Her Lancelot would never give up. Never surrender to evil. He'd fight to the last breath. Well, dang it, so would she. If, like the Cowardly Lion, she could only find her courage. She passed him a napkin holding two makeshift cheese sandwiches. "I owe you an apology."

He handed her a warm mug of soup and a plastic spoon. "Eat."

"But—"

"Baby, eat now. Apologize later. I insist."

"Only because you insist." She'd probably be more coherent after nourishment anyway.

Snuggled inside the tent, the lantern lending a soft glow, they feasted. The simple but hearty food and warm drinks lifted Bailey's spirits and restored her energy.

Con finished his pie and coffee, stretched, and gave a satisfied groan. "That hit the spot. My stomach was starting to think my throat had been cut."

He threw their trash into the trash can in the storeroom. Back inside the tent, he drew her down beside him, using the folded comforter as a pillow. Covering them with another comforter, he took her into his arms. "Now, the resting portion of the evening."

She yawned. Resting sounded wonderful. She glanced around the dimly lit tent, noticing he'd positioned himself where he could see the door. He'd put her behind him, shielding her with his body. An unsettling reminder of their situation and his determination to protect her. "It's dangerous for us to nap."

"I'm not going to sleep. You are. I've trained myself to rest yet remain alert. The broken ornaments will warn me if anyone ventures upstairs."

She nestled against his lean, warm strength and worried her lower lip between her teeth. "About that apology. I insist."

He sighed. "Only because you insist."

"I owe you. I reacted badly to the fight, and I'm sorry."

"It's okay. You were suffering battle shock."

"It's not okay. You saved my life, and I made you think your touch repulsed me. That's inexcusable."

He stroked his thumb across her lower lip, and the air hitched in her lungs. He chuckled. "I'd never think that."

"It's just…" It was tough to think with his glowing brown eyes so close, his intense gaze ensnaring hers. His muscled body, so solid, so warm, nestled against her. "Let me explain."

"Explain at will, darlin'."

"I've always believed that deep down, there's a shred of good in every person. Causing pain to anyone, or anything…hurts me. I imagine their suffering so vividly. Almost like their distress is my own. Inflicting hurt makes my heart ache."

"My sweet girl." He trailed a gentle fingertip down her cheek. "I can't fault you for having a tender heart."

"But I felt differently after we found Syrone, after I saw what they'd done to him. After he asked us to tell his wife and kids how much he loved them if he didn't make it…" Her voice wobbled. "I was sick at the thought they'd shot him in cold blood. I was furious. I wanted to hurt them back. Then *that* made me sick. I've never had vengeful feelings before. It was so confusing."

"I understand. I felt the same way. It's tough to stay objective when the pain is personal."

"I want to contribute something worthy to this difficult world we live in—make a difference."

"Getting mad at injustice doesn't make you a bad person, sweetheart. It makes you human. Don't be afraid of your feelings." The lantern's aura coaxed molten gold flecks from his dark eyes. "Now, acting on them is a different story."

"That's the worst part. How do you know when your motives are good and when they're not? I want to do the right thing."

"Since you're uncomfortable discussing my job, I've never shared the reason I became a cop. It's time I did."

"I didn't realize you avoided discussing your job." She sighed. "I'm sorry. I'd really like to hear why you became a cop."

"The story involves Letty, our irrepressible neighbor. When I was twelve, she was mugged. The attack happened in our neighborhood, in daylight. She was walking home from the drugstore around the corner. The guy knocked her down and stole her purse. She cracked two ribs and was in the hospital for a few days."

"Oh, no! How awful!"

"The physical injury wasn't the worst. After she got home, she was afraid to leave the house. She couldn't go shopping, stopped taking walks and wouldn't even work in her garden."

"She's so independent, I can imagine how traumatized she must have been for it to affect her that way."

"Pop's personal mission was to catch the creep. He worked the streets and pushed hard. He knew time was against him, and went without sleep for three days. Put in as many off-the-clock overtime hours as if the case had been a homicide."

A troubled expression creased her brows. "So your heroic tendencies are inherited—a second-generation warrior."

"Fourth. My grandpa and great-grandpa were cops."

She uttered another sad little sigh that made his chest ache. "I might have known. Did your dad catch the mugger?"

"Yeah." He snarled. "A junkie. Pop put him away for a string of smash-and-grabs on senior citizens."

"Did your father find Letty's purse?"

"Yep. He replaced her cash himself and told her he'd recovered it with the purse. He also started a neighborhood watch and a senior self-defense class." He grinned. "During the classes, Letty connected with her inner spunky woman. If any hapless mugger tried to victimize her now, she'd probably wallop him upside the head and give him a concussion."

She laughed again. "I don't doubt it. Your father was a good man. You inherited more than your profession from him."

"Thank you, darlin'." He smiled at her. "Dad didn't just recover Letty's stolen property. After he apprehended the jerk, she felt safe again. The arrest, neighborhood watch and classes restored the most valuable things the mugger stole—her confidence, independence and peace of mind. Dad returned those to her. That's when I knew for sure I wanted to be a cop."

"I can see why."

"Do you?" He held her gaze. "Like I said before, I stand between Letty and the bad guys. Between you and the bad guys. Between evil and the innocent."

"You're an incredible man, do you know that?"

"What I'm trying to explain is that when you know your priorities, and what you value most, the right decisions follow." His soft breath, smelling enticingly of apples and cinnamon, teased her lips. "Only you know your motives. Only you will know for certain you're doing the right thing."

"It's so complicated."

"If the right thing was easy, baby, more people would do it."
His beautiful mouth moved closer, and his soft lips touched hers.
"Don't worry," he whispered. "When the time comes, you'll know."

She slid her arms around his neck and deepened the kiss.
Empowered by the bond created by his mouth on hers, his body
pressed to hers, she poured out her pent-up feelings. Trying to
tell him without words how much she needed him. Valued him.
Cherished him.

In Con's embrace was exactly where she belonged.

He threaded his fingers into her hair, holding her as close as
two people could be. His silky tongue teased, danced, mated with
hers in a fierce, primitive rhythm only the two of them knew. His
taste, his scent flooded her senses. Nothing existed but him.
Nothing mattered except love. His for her, hers for him.

He lingered over her mouth, drinking her in. Cherishing her
in return. Nourishing and strengthening her more than the food.
The soul-deep connection thrummed like the heavy jungle beat
of drums between them.

His lips kissed a hot, moist path along her jaw, her earlobe,
the hollow of her neck. His ragged breaths teased her skin, raising goose bumps. The fine sandpaper brush of his beard rasped
in sensual accompaniment to his talented mouth. Pleasure raced
with gossamer wings over her nerve endings, dipping into every
curve and hollow, then settling, warm and liquid in her center.

Desire shimmered, arced into passion. Passion exploded into
aching need.

Fire burned inside her. Con's bright, hot fire that consumed
everything, yet gave back, tenfold. She slid her hands under
his turtleneck, her palms gliding over his smooth, heated skin.
Sculpted pecs bunched under her caress, and he groaned.

Pulse pounding, she arched against him, reveling in his
arousal. Her fingertips trailed down ridged abs and skimmed
along his taut belly. She unsnapped his jeans, his body hard and
ready under the rough denim. "Make love to me, Con. So a part
of me will always live in you, and you in me."

She struggled for breath, for hope. For life. "So that no matter what happens, we will always have this moment."

Chapter 9

Con's heart stumbled. *Oh, yeah.* The appeal he'd waited so long to hear. He grasped Bailey's shirts and tugged them upward. His mind's eye saw him strip them off, along with her jeans. Saw full breasts cupped by the black lace camisole. Milky white skin covered only by skimpy black panties. Her body bared to his stroking hands, arching under his eager mouth. He saw her eyes darken as he slid into her damp heat, her delicious lips part in a gasp of pleasure as she climaxed.

Saw the bad guys bursting in on them at the most inopportune moment, machine guns firing.

"Whoa!" He jerked back from the vision. From the warm, willing woman in his arms.

Fighting his way out of the passion-drugged high was like trying to stop a speeding getaway car by standing spread-eagled in the middle of the freeway. He was just as likely to get mowed down. His breathing as jagged as his composure, he gently grasped Bailey's hands and removed them from the hot zone. "As much as I want to make love to you, darlin'—" He sucked in a shaky breath and pulled down her rumpled shirts. "We can't."

She stared at him, dazed and vulnerable. "Why not?"

Damn, with her looking at him with her heart in her eyes, breaking it off wrenched his guts. When seconds ago, he'd felt her love and desire pouring into him in a heady rush. When her sweet taste still flooded his palate. Her flowery, feminine scent still tantalized his nostrils. When his need still roiled his senses.

When he did not know if he *would* survive the night.

In spite of reassuring Bailey to the contrary, in spite of his training, and SWAT on alert, nothing was certain. He'd seen incidents explode without warning—turn lethal between one breath and the next. Watched fellow officers die so quickly they didn't realize what was happening. He did not know if he would ever have a chance to make love to the woman who held his heart.

"Please, Con," she whispered. "I need you."

He groaned. "I *want* to." Tempted, he scrubbed an unsteady hand over his jaw. Battled the throbbing ache. There weren't enough baseball stats in the universe to distract him. Not enough icebergs in Antarctica to douse the volcano seething inside.

He silently counted to a hundred. "Baby, there is not enough blood in my body to make love to you *and* operate my brain. If the bad guys show up, I won't hear them until too late. I sure as hell won't be in any shape to fight."

She blinked. Blinked again. "I'm not...I didn't..."

"Not to mention," he continued in a gentle tone, "I don't want our first time together to be here, like this. Not under these circumstances. Rushed. Desperate."

The sensual haze cleared from her eyes like morning mist burned away by harsh daylight. Color flooded her cheeks. She buried her face in her hands. "I've lost my mind. I'm so sorry."

He heaved a silent sigh. For a few minutes, he'd wondered if he'd also hurtle over the cliff into a freefall. Now that both of them had stepped back from the brink of insanity, tumbling over the edge was impossible. "It's all right, sweetheart. You've ridden too many scary highs and rough lows today. It's bound to affect your equilibrium. Only natural to seek comfort." He'd experienced the same highs and lows, the same fears. But he couldn't afford to seek comfort. He had to stay strong—at least on the outside.

She squeaked like a stepped-on kitten. "*You* were comforting. *I* attacked you."

"Did you hear complaints?" He kissed the bright curls on top of her head. "I'll take a rain check on that tactical assault."

"How can you possibly even want me when I'm so...unworthy?" Her agonized question was muffled in his shirt.

"None of that. I'll always want you. Every minute of every day for the rest of my life."

"Self-control has never been my strong suit where you're concerned. I got caught up in the feelings and forgot where we are and the situation we're in. That's not like me at all."

He grinned. The all-male part of him loved knowing he could blow her mind with mere kisses. Just wait until he got her in his bed. He'd send her into nuclear meltdown. "That little confession makes me feel like the luckiest guy alive."

"I can feel you grinning. I'm such a doofus."

"I'm not laughing at you, baby. And you're anything but a doofus." He rubbed the taut, quivering muscles in her back, pleased when she relaxed. "For a civilian operating under incredibly stressful circumstances, you're doing great."

"I jeopardized your safety." She sounded near tears. "I'm sorry. I never want to hurt you. In any way."

"Hey, now." He tipped up her chin and forced her to meet his gaze. "Don't be so hard on yourself. You didn't do anything wrong, and you didn't hurt me. I wouldn't have let things get out of hand." Close, but he'd pulled out of the firing line in time.

Barely.

"I had this romanticized view of you…a valiant knight in shining armor. I didn't want to face the gritty truth, the blood, the violence, the death." She swallowed so hard it looked like it hurt. "But this job is what you're meant to do." She sighed. "I'm just not sure I can handle the day-to-day reality of it."

"That's your choice to make." And he prayed she would choose him.

"Yes." She gulped again. "Con, even if I find the courage to stay with you, it might not be the right choice. You might regret being with me if I can't support you the way I should."

So, they'd circled around to that again. Fear of abandonment was nipping at her heels. "You think even if you choose to stay, I'm going to suddenly decide you're not the woman I think you are? And walk out on you, like your father?" When she flinched, he gathered her close and kissed her eyelids, her cheeks, her warm, succulent lips. "When are you going to get it through your head that I know you, inside and out? That nothing you say or do will ever make me leave you?"

She sat up and folded her arms protectively across her body. "I wish I had your strength instead of being weak. I wish I could be an asset to you, instead of a liability."

The storm of shame in her gaze ripped out his heart. He'd been in the echoing, ultra-modern apartment she'd been moved to from her childhood home. She'd grown up with everything anyone could want. Everything but emotional support. Physical affection. Unconditional love. He was going to make that up to her. If it took until he was a hundred and she was ninety-five. "Come here." He sat up and tugged her close. "You've helped me numerous times tonight. You thought up the fire alarm. How to hang up the signal sheet. And alerted me to the criminal-stopping properties of acetic acid. You are not a weakling, or a liability."

Tears ran down her face. "I can't help thinking about my dad. I don't know what drove him, or why, but he spent his entire life trying to slay dragons. He was strong and brave, but in the end, it killed his marriage. Killed our family. Killed *him*. If he wasn't strong enough or brave enough to slay the dragon, how can I possibly be?"

"That might be the problem. You're a pacifist, darlin'. Maybe you shouldn't be trying to slay the dragon, but trying to figure out what it says when it roars. Come to terms with it."

"An approach I never considered." She frowned. "For a woman who doesn't believe in violence, I've been spending an awful lot of time trying to figure out how to assassinate an integral part of me. Talk about self-destructive."

"Don't be afraid to look deep inside and see what's there. Maybe you need to discover what you're made of and accept the woman you really are. Make peace with yourself."

"I'm a coward, that's who I am. I've been quaking in terror since this whole thing started. I wish I had your confidence."

He wished she did, too. He abhorred seeing her tortured by anxiety. Hated her self-doubt. Hurt at seeing her second-guess every thought, every action. She'd been so smothered, she didn't trust her instincts. "You think I haven't been scared?"

"You don't seem afraid."

"Only a fool wouldn't be scared. I know what kind of odds

we're up against: But I can't help anyone if I allow feelings to overrule logic. I've been trained to contain my emotions. You haven't. You have a lot more courage than you realize."

"How can you say that?"

"Courage is not lack of fear, Bailey. It's the ability to act in spite of it. You've been right beside me, pulling your weight through this entire ordeal. Believe me, you have courage."

"I'm not so sure."

"By the time we get out of here, you will be. We'll know each other more deeply than we ever thought possible. Who we are, what we are. As individuals and a couple."

"Maybe in the most horrible circumstances possible."

"You keep projecting the worst-case scenario, don't you?" He grabbed her hand and enfolded her small, cold fingers in his. "Okay. Let's drag out your biggest fear and stare it in the face. If one of us, or God forbid, both of us don't make it out of here, the survivors can cling to the knowledge that we did our damned-est. We fought the good fight. To the bitter end."

"What if I can't fight the good fight?" Her lips quivered and she pressed them together. "My worst fear is that I'll let you down. I'll fail. And you will die because of my shortcomings."

He squeezed her hand. "That is *not* going to happen."

"It could." Her face crumpled. "Because I'm not exactly a kick-ass kind of woman. I'm short on qualities like power and confidence and assertiveness."

Dammit. Con forced down the lump in his throat. She hadn't been abandoned only by her father, but her mother as well. Dr. Ellen Chambers had provided every material necessity, every social grace and educational opportunity. But what her daughter needed most, she'd been unable to give. She'd retreated into her own pain and left Bailey to struggle through the emotional minefield alone.

His father's death had given him and his family up-close-and-personal acquaintance with the crippling effects of sudden loss. The paralyzing properties of grief. They'd all slam danced with survivor's guilt. But they'd clung together. Navigated the murky waters as a team, throwing each other a lifeline when one of them sank under waves of despair.

He shook his head. Dr. Chambers had coped the best she could. He shouldn't blame, shouldn't judge. But when he saw the consequences to Bailey, he couldn't help but feel resentment and anger. "No, you aren't a kick-ass woman. You never had to be." He smiled at her terminology. "You got your point across without it. But you never know what you're made of until you're tested. Adversity is bringing out your true character."

She paled in the lantern light. "How can you possibly love me?" She snatched her hand away, scrambled up and out of the tent.

"Whoa! Wait a minute." He surged to his feet and followed her into the dark store. A painted full moon and luminescent stars overhead cast a faint shine, allowing him to see her standing rigid beside a grove of artificial trees. His senses scanned the area. The mall was deathly quiet, no signs of pursuers.

He strode to her, but she kept her back to him, her fists clenched. He rested his hands on her shoulders. "That wasn't criticism. I'm trying to help you see what I see."

Her shoulders hitched. "You need a powerful woman by your side. Like my mom. A powerful woman never lets anyone get the better of her."

"Which isn't always an asset." He stroked her tangled curls. "You've got something a lot more valuable than power. You walk into that burn ward every week with a spring in your step and a smile on your face."

She turned, her eyes wounded and wary. "That's no big deal."

"It's a very big deal. For two hours, you bring hope and laughter to those scarred, hurting, sometimes dying kids and make their lives better, make them forget their pain. You give them the rare and valuable gift of your very best. Do you know how much inner fortitude that takes?"

"It never seemed all that remarkable to me."

"Which is why you've got guts up the wazoo, baby."

She tugged on a water-dewed fir branch next to her. Droplets scattered across the carpet, the soft plops loud in the heavy silence. "I've never thought of giving to others as a strength."

"Well, it is. I don't have that kind of strength. I could never do what you do with those kids. It would hurt so much, I'd hold part of myself back from them. But you're not afraid to offer everything in your heart. To give until it hurts." He moved closer and cupped her face in his hands. She was shaking. "You wear mercy on your sweet face every hour of every day. For everyone but yourself. Cut yourself a break, darlin'."

"Well, when you put it that way…" She worried her lower lip between her teeth. "I guess I am stronger than I thought."

"You are. You refused to let your mother subjugate you, mold you into the image she wanted. Alone, you grew from a sheltered, broken-hearted teenager into a remarkable woman with a hell of a lot to offer. To me and the world."

Her breath caught, and her trembling increased with the force of her realization. "Oh, Con. You're right. Young and naive as I was, I fought for and won my independence. I was determined to carve out my own life, and I did." She stared up at him, hope glistening in her gaze. "I guess I need to recognize and have confidence in my abilities, huh?"

"You're smart and open-minded enough to admit your mistakes and learn from them." He brushed his thumbs over the smooth, baby-fine skin of her cheekbones. "Easy enough to take that conviction and turn it into confidence."

She swallowed hard, nodded. "I can do that."

He kissed the tip of her nose. "Of course you can."

"Which will help me become more assertive as well."

"There you go." Vindicated, he grinned at her. He hadn't misplaced his faith. "Insight. Another attribute you possess in spades. Too many people think they've already arrived. You realize life is a process and it's only during the trek that you grow."

Tears pooled in her eyes, huge shimmering pools of deep blue. "You honestly do believe in me."

"You bet I do." He kissed the tip of her nose. "All those incredible qualities are why fell in I love with you. The moment I saw you, I saw your heart."

The tears spilled over, shining silver streaks in the pale light. She choked. "Thank you."

He drew her into his embrace, holding her close. "You know, after Dad died, Mom hung a quote by Eleanor Roosevelt on the fridge. Something like, 'You gain strength and courage when you stare fear in the face.' You can say, 'I lived through this horror. I'll handle whatever comes along.'"

"So that's where you get the 'crap happens, I'll handle it' philosophy." She swiped at the tears with the back of her hand. "So, tonight is some kind of test? A trial by fire?"

"One way of looking at it, yeah. But you're not me, and you can't expect to respond like me." He swayed, rocking her gently. "I have to walk my road, and you, yours. We'll arrive at our destination in different ways. But we will do our damnedest. We will arrive. Exactly where, when and how we're supposed to."

She eased away to look up at him again. Understanding glinted in her gaze. "We're on the same path to a shared destiny."

If she escaped this situation believing in herself, then every moment of suffering was worth it. "We have been since we met. And no matter what happens, no matter how this turns out, hold on to one thought. Be at peace with it. We cannot control the universe. The Man Upstairs knows what he's doing. Though we may never know the reasons, tonight was meant to be."

"Even if…" She sucked in a breath. "The worst happens?"

"Especially then." Pressed body to body, her heart thundered against his. He breathed in her heady fragrance. "Believe in the realm of mysteries."

Her trembling slowed, then stopped as her inner storm subsided and calmness settled over her. Her heartbeat steadied. "With your words as my wings, your faith in me as my shield, how can I do anything but soar?"

He grinned as his heart soared along with her. "So, you'll keep the faith?"

"Yes. I have an obligation to the woman I *really* am."

"Just be yourself."

She gave him a wobbly smile that arrowed into his chest. "Have I mentioned lately how wonderful you are?"

They'd traveled a long way from breakfast, when she'd been determined to break up with him. To end their future before they had a chance to live it. Now they might have a shot, if only the bad guys didn't end it. "Never hurts to say it again."

"You are wonderful."

"Thank you, sweetheart." He glanced around. Still quiet. "You need to rest while the team outside tightens the web."

She touched his cheek. "There's a team inside, too. And we're getting better at working together by the minute."

"That we are." He led her back into the tent. "Now, close those man-killer blue eyes and sleep. I'll wake you when it's time."

Bailey's eyes drifted closed, and her breathing evened out. Her absolute trust warmed him, body and soul. He wouldn't let her down. Con rubbed the knotted muscles at the back of his neck. The strain of exuding unrelenting confidence had finally caught up with him. For hours, he'd been projecting assurance he didn't feel. But, for Bailey's sake, he had to pull it together and keep it together. Not to mention the hostages who were depending on him.

He extracted a tablet of cinnamon gum from his pocket and concentrated on taking slow, deep breaths. While Bailey slept, he silently battled the demons of doubt and terror.

Bailey opened her eyes and blinked in the dim light. "Where am I?" Panic pierced her grogginess and she struggled to throw off the thick comforter.

"Shh. It's okay, baby," Con's quiet voice soothed. "You're with me." His strong, warm hand stroked her forehead.

"Con?" She glanced over and saw him sitting beside her, watching her. Dark stubble shadowed his chiseled cheekbones and highlighted his gorgeous mouth. Puzzled, she frowned. He was normally smooth shaven. "What time is it?"

He glanced at his watch. "Nearly twenty-one hundred."

"Twenty-one hundred? Oh, almost nine." She studied the rumpled blankets. Drowsy and confused, a tingling memory of scorching kisses and soft caresses swirled in her muddled brain. "Did we sleep together?"

"Now that is *not* a flattering question." He laughed softly.

She sat up and rubbed her eyes. They were in a tent? The day's events hurtled back in a blurred rush of fear and running. "Rats. I thought I was having a really sensual dream about you."

A sexy smile quirked his lips. "Have those often, do you?"

"Not nearly often enough."

He laughed again, the husky sound making her belly clench. "Maybe sometime soon, you won't have to resort to dreams."

Bailey grinned at him. Boy, was he in for a surprise. He'd given her solid ground to stand on. Questions and answers that had made her decision so much easier than she ever imagined. Her knight lived in a violent world of blood and death. But he also possessed a tender heart, brimming with life and love. Steeped in loyalty and bone-deep integrity. He wouldn't let her down. How could she do anything less for him?

Their relationship, their love was special. Beautiful and rare as a flawless diamond. She refused to let her fears stop her. She'd find a way to be the woman he needed. To make their dreams come true a lot sooner than he expected. Once they escaped, she was going to leap on him and never let him go. They might not even make it out of the parking lot.

Being hunted down like an animal had given her a crash course in prioritizing. Being forced to face her own mortality had taught her not to put off important things. She'd never again worry about planning for every eventuality. If they made it out of here in one piece, she would forever live in the moment.

Don't worry, be happy.

She yawned and stretched. "The plan?"

"Find out how negotiations are faring. Check on Syrone."

"I'm coming with you." She glared at the Kevlar vest in the corner. "And I'm *not* wearing that. It's too heavy—I won't be able to run. You should wear it. You're the one always jumping in front of bullets."

He gave her a considering look. "Makes sense."

"Where do you want to contact the team?"

"From the sky bridge. I can use hand signals, they can send light signals back." He slipped on the vest, rapidly fastened the buckles. "It's on the opposite side from the bank, so the robbers shouldn't figure out what's happening."

She hated to leave their cozy nest. Wished they could simply curl up and hide until they were rescued. But that would be cowardly. And counterproductive. Unless they did their part, there might not *be* a rescue. For them or their friends downstairs.

They conducted a wary jog to the sky bridge. The night was growing colder, and her breath puffed out white in the chilly air. Beyond the glass, ominous darkness squeezed in on every side. Freezing rain sleeted the windowpanes, making her feel more sealed in. Creepy. Like they were entombed in a big, cold, glass coffin. Foreboding shivered over her.

Lights flashed, ripping holes in the heavy black blanket surrounding them. "Damn." Con turned from the window. "The suspects have refused to open the door and retrieve the throw phone. Not a good sign for the hostages if they won't negotiate. The robbers could be planning SBC."

"SBC?"

"Suicide by cop. Go out in a blaze of glory. It's more common than people realize."

Bile rose in her throat and she swallowed. "What now?"

"Same as we have been. Improvise, modify, adapt, overcome. We need to head downstairs and scope out the situation."

The PA system crackled and she jumped. "Yoo-hoo to the busy little mice running loose in the mall." The deep, graveled male voice was almost cordial. If you discounted the underlying hum of menace.

Bailey gasped. "That's the head bank robber! The one the other guy called Tony when we were crouched outside the bank."

Con's expression grew murderous. "The one wearing Dad's watch."

"FYI," Tony continued. "We've wired all the outside doors. If you attempt to open them, or blast through them…kaboom." He cleared his throat. "Obviously, you are able to communicate with the cops. Otherwise, they wouldn't be here, and attempting to discuss details they shouldn't know on the megaphone. So, here's the deal. You come and see me. Talk to me. Otherwise, these hostages…" He paused. "Have very short life expectancies."

Con swore viciously.

"You have twenty minutes. And so do they." The PA system went dead.

Her stomach dropped to her boots and her mouth went dry. "You're not...going down there and confront him?"

"No way. That's TV stuff again. Never lay down your weapon and never turn yourself into bait in an attempt to save hostages. It just makes more hostages. And/or dead cops." He slammed his fist into his palm. "I need a way to communicate with the suspects and still keep my distance. I wonder if the camping store carries walkie-talkies? That might fly."

"They do! I saw them when I got the lantern. Cell phones don't get reception in the mall, so would walkie-talkies work?"

"I don't know. Worth a shot. Different schematics, different operational modes, different frequencies. If we're lucky, I might even be able to contact SWAT. I can signal them with the frequency and channels, and they can patch in."

They sprinted to Outdoor Outfitters. Con read boxes by flashlight while Bailey located batteries. She stuffed packages of disposable hand warmers, two sets of foot-warmer heating pads and Polarshield emergency blankets in her pack. As cold as it was becoming, they might need them later. She also spotted a portable, retractable clothesline made of thin, black plastic-coated wire that might come in handy for tying up bad guys. She finished as he selected six walkie-talkies and laid them on the counter in the back of the store.

She inserted batteries into three red radios while he put them in three blue ones. He placed a hands-free headset and mic on her ears and clipped a blue receiver to her waistband. He then situated a headset and blue unit on himself. "I'm going to hook the robbers up with a modified two-way FRS system—family radio service—and lock in one channel. It's short range and they won't be able to hear or talk to anyone but us. SWAT will be able to tap into the transmissions, though. I'll be the go-between. The robbers will be on the blue set."

"And the red set?"

"The red set is a GMRS, or general mobile radio system. Transmits up to five miles, and to a greater range of frequencies." He clipped a red walkie-talkie to her waistband beside the blue unit and then one on his own. "If we switch the headset mic back and forth, we can talk to each other, and SWAT on the red unit, and the bad guys can't eavesdrop."

"Who is the third red radio for?"

"Syrone."

"Now for the million-dollar question. How are you going to deliver the radio to the robbers without getting caught?"

"I have a plan."

"Of course you do. Will I hate it?"

He didn't reply. "First things first. Back to the sky bridge."

They raced to the sky bridge, where Con performed another complicated hand dance, and more flashing lights replied. She switched on her red receiver and he showed her how to operate the radios. "These are both manual and VOX, voice activated. If VOX is on we don't have to key the mics. The receiving light will blink when someone transmits to us." He plugged the headset mic into his red unit, and she heard his voice in her earpiece. "SWAT Command, this is the Nutcracker, do you read? Over."

A few tense seconds of static buzz. Then a click echoed in her ears. The static disappeared. "Loud and clear," his big brother Aidan's smooth, deep cadence replied. "Nice to hear from you. This is SWAT Command. Is this channel secure? Over."

"Ten-four. As much as it can be."

"Got yourself into quite a conundrum there, eh? Over."

Con grinned. Close to all three of his brothers, Con was closest to Aidan. Aidan had always razzed Con without mercy. The two played pranks on one another, and on their younger brothers that usually landed the pranksters in major hot water. Aidan was always there when he needed an ear. Steady. Dependable. No better man to have at your back. On a tactical op or in an emotional shitstorm. "Nothing I can't handle. *You're* command? Over."

"That's a ten-four. I'm the senior ranking officer on site. Alpha Dog is ten-seven and out of communication."

"Oh, hell, we're all in deep shinola. Over."

"Nutcracker, what's your status?"

"Lead-free and rolling. About to visual hostages and contact suspects. Crew leader's name is Tony. He's issued a deadline and threatened the hostages' lives. Claims he's wired the doors. He blew the vault, so he's probably not bluffing. You have fifteen minutes to form an aggressive assault plan that doesn't involve the main doors. If you don't hear from me, green-light it. Over."

"Ten-four. Fifteen minutes. Make sure you're clear of the area."

"Roger that. And Command?" Con's voice cracked slightly. "He's wearing Dad's watch."

"*What?*" Shock echoed in Aidan's sharp question. "*Repeat. Over.*"

"Tony is wearing Dad's watch. The one he had on when he was killed. My gut says this crew has been pulling the string of unsolved bank jobs and home invasions. I know it's a long shot, but get somebody on the computers and see if the name and MO pops. Will advise next move. Stand by. Over."

"Ten-four." Aidan paused. "Nutcracker?" The low admonition belonged to the big brother, not the cop. "Watch your back."

"Always do." The emotion layered beneath the carefree words was the younger brother's. "Don't worry about me. Just nail this scumbag's butt to the wall. Over and out."

No matter how many times she witnessed it, the heart connection Con and his brothers shared never failed to awe her. "Why did you say you were the Nutcracker?"

"Never use names over the airwaves. You don't know who might be listening in." He studied her. "Think you can handle tossing a Molotov cocktail or three?"

"If I have to." Queasiness roiled her insides. "Do you want me to throw them at someone?" She wasn't sure she could force herself to do that.

"No, just create a diversion while I plant the walkie-talkie."

"I can manage a diversion."

"We've got to move. I'll fill you in on the details as we head downstairs."

One more quick trip to the camping store to fill emptied water bottles with kerosene. Torn strips of cammo pants twisted into fuses. A waterproof lighter completed the deadly kit.

They scuttled to the escalators, her rapid breaths loud in her ears.

Con rolled his wrist and checked the time. "Ten minutes. Ready?"

She nodded.

He kissed her, hard and fast. "Let's rock."

Chapter 10

Molotov cocktails at the ready, Bailey kept a nerve-racked vigil in front of Footloose Footwear. Her shaking hands were cold and clammy. Her blood beat fast and thick in her veins. She, who had never broken the law—heck, she hadn't received even a parking ticket—was about to bomb the shoe store.

Well, the six-foot tall 3-D advertising kiosk next to it, anyway. The acrylic triangle sat in the middle of murky no-man's-land between the bank and the shoe store, touting the multiplex's latest action flick. She muffled a nervous snort. When it came to action, Vin Diesel had nothing on Officer Sexy.

Who was, at this moment, a silent shadow, slipping up the corridor toward Santa's downed sleigh across from the bank.

He'd said the robbers would watch for their approach after issuing the ultimatum. His objective was to plant a walkie-talkie near the bank, without being caught. At least that was the plan.

They had eight minutes before Con had to contact the team and abort the dynamic entry. He'd explained on the jog down the escalator that an aggressive assault was the last thing they wanted. SWAT storming in, guns blazing, was a worst-case scenario, used only when hostages were in imminent danger. No matter how careful the team, no matter how fast they hit, loss of hostage lives was a huge risk. Con thought they could still bargain.

If they could establish contact in time.

She clutched the slippery bottles of kerosene and slick lighter, and tried to slow her ragged breaths. She couldn't afford to panic and miss Con's signal over the headset plugged into her left ear. His life and the lives of her friends depended on her.

Con had pinpointed the advertising triangle as a soft target. Isolated in the middle of acres of faux marble, the fire wouldn't spread. The kiosk wasn't tall enough for flames to reach the upper floors. Everything was still waterlogged, and the fire would probably die of its own accord. He didn't figure the crooks would stop to analyze that. They'd instinctively react to the threat, giving him enough time to plant the radio and hightail it out.

She watched the dim, backlit windows of the bank, thirty feet across no-man's-land. The robbers had pulled the shades. Bulky silhouettes moved back and forth, loading what she assumed were bundles of money into what looked like a cart. They'd picked a great time for a robbery—surely not by accident. On paydays, the bank carried plenty of extra dough. Since mall employees had been unable to cash their paychecks due to the electrical malfunction that she now knew the robbers had caused, all that money was sitting in the vault. Not to mention every store had deposited their tills for safekeeping, per emergency procedure. The crooks had done their homework, crippled the system and would net a small fortune.

Bailey's nervous glance roamed the desolate mall. If the robbers were busy loading money and—thanks to SWAT—revising their getaway, would they still be on the hunt? She hoped not.

"Sugarplum Fairy, this is the Nutcracker," Con's voice murmured in her earpiece. "In position?"

In spite of her anxiety, she grinned. Leave it to him to diffuse a terrifying situation. "Yes. I mean ten-four."

"About to deliver Santa's package. On three, light 'em up."

"Okay," she whispered back, mentally counting. *One.* Bailey shifted the lighter from left hand to right. *Two.* She thumbed the lighter and a tiny spark sprang to life. *Three.* She touched flame to wicks and fire flared along the kerosene-soaked rags. Holding her breath, she hurled the bottles at the base of the acrylic triangle. They exploded in a spectacular red fireball. Golden-red tongues licked up the sides of the kiosk. The charred smell of sizzling plastic stung her nostrils.

She stood mesmerized in horror. No wonder her father had dedicated his life to firefighting. Fire was a powerful, brutal foe.

She'd seen the toll the dragon took on humans…in her dad's scarred face, and in the disfigured bodies of the children on the burn ward. But she'd never had firsthand experience with the beast. Her heart stuttered. Her father had been braver than she knew, again riding into battle after being burned.

Shouting erupted from the bank. Bailey shook off the memories, pivoted and ran.

She sprinted past the shoe store, Quality Leather Goods and Death by Chocolate, then veered across the walkway. Gasping, she sped toward the Bedroom Furniture Emporium to meet Con. Was he behind her? She didn't hear him, but that didn't mean anything. His fluid movements were like a tiger's, silent and deadly. He could be directly on her heels and she wouldn't know.

Inside the store, she bent double, panting for air. Con didn't appear. Her pulse geared down from a gallop to a trot, and finally slowed to near normal. She peered anxiously around the doorway. Saw nothing but spooky shadows in the echoing gloom.

Fear clutched at her throat. Where was he? In spite of her successful distraction, had the robbers caught him?

"Yo, Bailey," Con said quietly from behind her.

She nearly leaped across the corridor. She whirled with her hand over her rocketing heart. "I'm either going to have to hang a bell around your neck or risk a coronary before the night is over. How did you get behind me?"

"I did a fast recon to the end of the mall and doubled back. Wanted to make sure none of the bad guys were around. All clear." His mischievous smile of approval made her tingle all over. "They're probably occupied battling the bonfire."

She squelched the relieved impulse to fling herself into his arms and never let go. Instead, she adjusted the heavy pack on her shoulders. "So, what now?"

"We need to establish contact before SWAT executes their dynamic entry."

"Is there time to check on Syrone, first?" She glanced around the dark, ominously silent store as they moved farther inside. If he were okay, wouldn't he call out? "I'm worried sick about him."

He consulted his watch. "Me, too. But we've only got four minutes. Listen up. I want you to talk to the suspects."

"Me?" Nausea rolled in her stomach. "Why me?"

"As far as they're concerned, they're chasing a frightened, but surprisingly resourceful bookstore clerk. I don't want to clue them in unless they force my hand."

"Wh—what do I say?"

"Ask for their demands. No matter what they request—unless it's to turn yourself in to them—hesitate, then bargain. See if you can gain concessions. Tell 'em you'll do your best to acquire it. Be careful not to give away any intel."

She sank her teeth into her lip and fidgeted with the cold metal handle on the wardrobe looming beside her. "If I mess up?"

He tugged her close and enfolded her in his embrace. "You can do it. You're great at handling people."

She inhaled his scent. It wrapped around her, as warm and re-assuring as a fleece blanket. Normally, she *was* good with peo-ple, even cranky customers and scared, sick kids. Nothing about tonight was normal. "What if I say something wrong?" She swal-lowed hard. "What if I get our friends hurt?"

"Don't worry, darlin', your sharp brain will handle everything just fine. And I'll be right here." He cupped her face and planted a soft, confident kiss on her mouth, then looked her squarely in the eye. "We're out of time, with no options."

Her friends needed her. She firmed her chin, stepped back and tugged a tablet and marker from her pack. She handed them to him. "For coaching."

"Great idea." He looked at her. "Ready?"

She swallowed again. Nodded. "How will you let the robbers know about the walkie-talkie you stashed in Santa's sleigh?"

He grinned. "Like this." He switched on the blue unit and began to whistle.

It took her a second before she recognized the tune. "Here Comes Santa Claus." Impressed by Con's agile imagination, she waited for a response.

A long, too-silent minute passed. He checked his watch and held up three fingers. Three minutes.

Another sixty seconds. No response. Oppressive cold and darkness pressed in on her from every side. Anxiety sat in a lead weight on her chest. Con frowned and held up two fingers. Anxiousness turned to dread. Looked like SWAT would have to break in and attempt a perilous rescue.

Con held up his index finger. One minute. She tensed. Then her earpiece hummed. The hard, Bronx-accented voice she recognized as Tony's sounded in her ear. "Hey, Santa's little elf."

Con turned aside and spoke in a low, rapid tone into the red unit. "SWAT Command, this is the Nutcracker. Have established contact with the suspects. Abort entry. Repeat, abort entry." He paused to listen, then turned back and gave her a thumbs up.

Whew. Too close for comfort. Bailey sucked in a shaky breath and strove for a calm demeanor. "Call me the Sugarplum Fairy."

A short, shocked silence later, Tony responded. "Ah. The spider rescue squad."

He knew who she was? Bright panic flared, and she sent a wild, silent plea to Con. *Help!*

He stroked a finger down her cheek, then wrote on his tablet, *Have faith. Work him.*

She straightened her shoulders. Nan, Letty and Mike's welfare was riding on her ability to pull this off. She *could* do it. "I imagine you're ready to get out of here. I sure am."

"Who's with you, cupcake?"

"I'm alone."

Tony guffawed. "No way."

She borrowed a leaf from Syrone's playbook. "I was a Marine."

"And I'm a one-legged ballerina." Tony barked out a gruff laugh. "I'm supposed to believe a dainty bookstore babe not only used to be a Marine, but also took out two of my best men, set off the sprinklers, summoned SWAT, and jury-rigged Molotov cocktails?"

"Listen buster, don't underestimate a woman who reads." She'd wager brains over brawn any day. She sounded composed, even nonchalant. Amazing, considering all the saliva in her mouth had dried up. "So, you want to chitchat all night, or you want to tell me what it will take to be rid of you? I'm ready to go home, *Tony*." She emphasized his name to let him know he wasn't anonymous to either her, or the police. "How about you?"

Con's grin bounced back.

"You're too smart for your own good," the robber growled.

"Maybe, considering I'm not the one giving a not-so-impressive performance of Custer's last stand…in a mall."

Con's grin spread, white and wicked in his stubbled face.

"I can think of a dozen better ways you can put that sassy mouth to good use, cupcake."

A scowl wiped out Con's grin. Uh-oh. He went into guard dog mode whenever anyone disrespected her. She patted his arm. He was right about her doing just fine. She might be useless in a fistfight, but she had plenty of ammo for verbal jousting. "Even with a vault full of money, you couldn't pay me enough. We're wasting time. What do you really want?"

"My missing crew members back. Assuming they're still alive?"

Con wrote on his tablet, *Don't be too agreeable. Keep him off balance.*

"Maybe. I might tell you where to find them after the hostages are safe. Anything else?"

"A chopper. Thirty minutes or less."

Con nodded and wrote, *Multiplex parking lot. More time. Free a hostage.*

"I might be able to arrange that. The multiplex lot is the only place big enough for it to land, but it'll take longer than thirty minutes. Delivering a helicopter is a skosh more complicated than sending out for pizza." She drew on the research she'd conducted about Con's job for the correct terminology. "Show me some good will. Release the pregnant woman."

"*Way* too smart for your own good. No can do."

She looked to Con for guidance. *Chopper big order. Try again.*

"Come on, Tony." She used the soothing tone she applied when her boss went on one of his frequent rampages. "I'm sure you're a reasonable man. Let's compromise, work this out. We're all anxious to get out of here. If I'm going to order up something as big as a chopper, I need a hostage."

"How about a dead hostage, cupcake?"

Fear jabbed, swift and deep. Her startled gaze locked on Con's. His eyes narrowed, the deep brown irises lethal twin lasers. He scribbled, *Futile, no profit.*

She took a deep breath, then slowly released it. "That would be suicide, and I don't think you went to all this trouble to steal that money only to waste it. You don't want to hurt anyone."

"Yeah, I do. Starting with you."

Con's scowl grew black and murderous. She tamped down her fear, even as she watched Con ruthlessly harness his rage. Control, one of his many formidable talents. One hundred and ten percent focused on the job. His resolute focus would save them. And their friends. "Threatening me won't gain you anything."

"Satisfaction, cupcake. Worth almost as much as money. I hope I have a chance to personally demonstrate."

Con's words slashed across the paper, but his hands were rock-solid steady. *Everyone safe, or no chopper.*

Had Tony reaped his diseased brand of satisfaction after Brian O'Rourke's murder…by stealing his victim's watch? If so, he'd already wounded the man she loved. She wasn't about to let him damage anyone else she cared about. Bailey clenched her jaw. "Promise you won't hurt any of the hostages." She adjusted her headset mic with sweaty hands. "Or no dice on the chopper."

A long heart-shaking pause ticked past. Finally, Tony replied, "For now. Get that bird in a hurry, or all bets are off."

She switched the blue walkie-talkie into standby mode. Now that the crisis moment had passed, her knees went wobbly.

Con hugged her to his broad chest. "Great job, slugger. If you ever get tired of the bookstore, you could have a long and lucrative career as a hostage negotiator."

"Thanks, but no thanks." She rested her cheek on the soft cotton of his sweatshirt, drawing strength from the steadfast thud of his heartbeat. "Nobody ever died from reading a book."

"Nobody is going to die tonight, either."

She sent up a fast, fervent prayer that he was right.

Con released Bailey and stepped back. The store was quiet. Too quiet. He should be able to sense the subliminal vibe that accompanied another living presence. Should feel the weight of Syrone's interest focused on them. Instead, the atmosphere felt as sterile and empty as a morgue. Dead. Hair prickled on his neck. Every instinct Con possessed screamed to hurry to his friend.

He battled the urge and accessed the red walkie-talkie. First things first. Subjugate his feelings. Stick to procedure. Adherence to training would tip the odds toward everyone's survival. "Command, this is Nutcracker. Suspects demand a chopper. Thirty minutes, that's three-o minutes. Do you copy? Over."

"Ten-four," Aidan replied. "Stand by."

Con watched Bailey as he waited for his brother to discuss options with the team. Her strawberry-blond curls were rumpled, her complexion rosy from exertion. She'd tied the silver hummingbird charm he'd given her around the outside of her turtleneck. Her intelligent blue eyes held his, as if she could discern his thoughts, hear what Command relayed to him.

Hell, sometimes he thought she *could* read his mind. She always knew what he needed. When to talk and when to remain quiet. When to provide companionship and when to leave him in solitude. When to comfort and when to confront. Her moods and his were almost always in sync, a police officer's dream. A man who dealt with constant conflict on the job needed peace and understanding at home. Bailey was the calm eye in the center of his storm.

Admiration and respect arrowed into him. She'd handled the negotiations well. Proven her mettle under fire again and again. She'd stood her ground, even when Tony had threatened her, and insulted her with crude innuendo. *Satisfaction.* No matter what warped credo he followed, the slimebag better not get anywhere near Bailey. Con's hands tightened into fists. Even if he didn't already owe Tony for Pop, Con would kill him if he put his hands on his woman. He'd give the bastard satisfaction. An AK-47 enema.

"Nutcracker, about that chopper." Uh-oh. The edge in Aidan's voice made Con's shoulders stiffen. While Con had struggled to learn to control a volatile temper, he could count on one hand the number of times his roll-with-the-punches brother had lost his cool. Whatever Aidan was about to relay, he didn't sound happy. "The ice storm has grounded all aircraft. Can you stall? Over."

Con swore. "Maybe. We've got—" he glanced at his watch "—twenty-eight minutes. We might be able to bluff. I'll be in touch. Over."

He looked at Bailey. He didn't have to say anything.

Her eyes widened. "No chopper?"

"The bad weather has everything grounded."

"Tony sounds ruthless and edgy. He might go off the deep end."

"We won't let him." He strode to the store's entrance and executed a fast scan. Dark. Quiet. Empty. Maybe now that the bad guys thought escape was imminent, they'd get busy transporting their money and stop the hunt. He wouldn't count on it.

"Let's check on Syrone." Syrone hadn't made a sound during their communication with the robbers. A former Marine would know better. Man, he hoped that was it, and not the worst-case scenario torturing his mind.

"Syrone? It's Con and Bailey," Con warned in a low, but distinct hail. He wasn't keen on getting shot. No answer. With Bailey beside him, he strode to the makeshift barricade at the rear, and then shoved aside the dresser.

"Oh, no!" Bailey gasped.

Con's gut tightened. The big man had slid from his semi-sitting position, leaving a bloody streak on the wall. His eyes were closed, and he lay slumped on the mattress. The machine gun sat askew across his lap, and his hands hung at his sides. He appeared limp and lifeless.

Con cleared the thickness from his throat. No stranger to death, he would never get used to it. Especially if the Grim Reaper had claimed another friend. He glanced at Bailey, her face white and strained in the gloom. She'd been shocked and horrified by a fight. If Syrone were dead, the discovery would devastate her. "You'd better wait over there, sweetheart."

"He's my friend, too. I'm not going anywhere. We have to help him, Con."

Hoping Syrone wasn't beyond help, Con knelt and eased the

Kevlar hood off him. He pressed two fingers to Syrone's neck. His ebony skin was cool. Too cool. Con didn't feel a pulse. His spirits sank, sorrow and dread hovering over him in a heavy, smothering cloud. "C'mon, big guy. Don't do this. Those rug rats of yours need their daddy."

Bailey stifled a sob. "Is he—?"

He shifted his hand, pressed harder. Ah, there! Weak, thready, barely palpable. "He's alive!"

"Thank God!"

Con briskly patted Syrone's cheek. "Syrone. Hey, wake up." Syrone stirred. Moaned.

Con patted him again. "*Syrone.* C'mon, buddy."

"Wha—?" Syrone mumbled.

"Open those big brown peepers and talk to me."

Syrone's eyelids eased open. "Irish? Why did you hit me?"

Relief weakened Con's limbs. "Sleeping on the job, man."

"Oh, crap."

"My sentiments exactly." He unwrapped the quilts and unbuttoned Syrone's shirt. "Let's have a look at the damages." Blood had soaked through, and the sodden bandages had loosened. He reapplied a thicker, tighter dressing.

Syrone shivered. "I'm cold clear to my bones."

"I know." Frustrated, Con turned to Bailey. There wasn't much they could do. Shock would kill their friend. He required surgery, and probably a transfusion. And he needed warmth. Perhaps the two of them could bundle up with him and share body heat. They couldn't afford the time, but couldn't leave Syrone to die, either. "He's fading fast. We need more quilts."

"I've got something better." Bailey dug in her backpack and tugged out a box of disposable hand warmers. She passed a handful to Con. "From the camping store…they'll last six hours. I have foot-warmer heating pads and a Polarshield blanket, too."

Wonder surged through him. Untrained, scared, she'd risen to the occasion and come to his aid countless times tonight. Her quick thinking and unquenchable spirit awed him. "Baby, what would we do without you?" He kneaded the packets to activate them, tucked the already-warming pads under Syrone's armpits and against his chest, and buttoned him up. He applied the foot warmers to Syrone's socks and then put his boots back on. Finally, he wrapped him in the crinkly Polarshield blanket and two quilts. "Okay, big guy, that's about as personal as I care to get with you."

"Likewise, Irish." Syrone sighed. "Damn, that feels fine."

Con again turned to Bailey. Worry shadowed her delicate features, but she gave him an encouraging smile. Outwardly frail and sensitive, his girl possessed innate strength and fortitude. For years his job had been his first and only love. Now, he wasn't ashamed to admit she was the center of his universe. What would happen to her, to the hostages when the chopper didn't arrive? How would he protect them? From here on, the scenario could unravel at warp speed and spiral out of control. People could die.

He shook his head. *Focus.* One crisis at a time. "Do you have any more of that candy syrup from the toy store?"

"Yes, but I thought he couldn't have anything by mouth."

He whispered in her ear. "If we don't get him stabilized, he won't live long enough for it to matter."

Clearly shaken, she passed him the small wax containers shaped like cartoon characters.

He twisted the ears off the wascally wabbit and poured the thick, grape-scented liquid into Syrone's mouth.

Syrone coughed. "What are you feeding me, Irish? Poison to put me out of my misery?"

"Super-secret healing elixir, brewed by celibate Tibetan monks under a full moon." He urged his friend to swallow the contents of the second container. A duck, cherry, unless he missed his guess.

"Ugh! Those monks need to go low-carb. This stuff would strip the paint off my SUV."

Con laughed. "Probably. But as my darlin' explained to me earlier, it's instant glucose." He encircled Syrone's beefy wrist and took his pulse. "Not bad. Much better than when we found you."

"I owe you my life, Irish. Times two. You, too, Bailey. You're both due for major payback."

Bailey shook her head. "You'd do the same for us."

"Hey." Syrone blinked. "How come you're still here? Weren't you supposed to escape out the access door?"

Con fed Syrone another dose of cherry syrup. "The suspects C-4ed the vault, and the concussion took down Santa's workshop. The access door is blocked. They claim they've wired all the exits."

"Has SWAT been able to contact them? See what they want?"

"They wouldn't accept the throw phone, but I made contact. Oh, if you need to reach me…" Con handed Syrone the extra red walkie-talkie. "My handle is Nutcracker. SWAT's patched in, too, just in case." He didn't elaborate. Didn't need to. Syrone's lowered brows told him the ex-Marine knew Con was providing backup. If the bad guys took Con out, Syrone would know when to call in the cavalry. "Have you seen any action back here?"

"Quiet as the grave, Irish. So, what'd the perps want? Are we gonna blow this gig anytime soon?"

"They've asked for a chopper in the multiplex parking lot in thirty minutes." Frowning, he opened the last wax container—a martian—and administered the odious green lemon-lime liquid. "Not going to happen, because of the ice storm."

Syrone swallowed, shuddered. "What's the plan?"

"Bluff like hell." Con took Syrone's pulse. Stronger and more regular. He'd be okay—for a while. If they didn't get him to a doctor, the hand and foot warmers would outlast him. "I'll check in every thirty minutes. If you don't hear from me, call in SWAT." Again, he didn't elaborate. Syrone read him loud and clear. If Con missed a radio check, he would be either unconscious or dead.

He squeezed Syrone's hand. "My gut says the crap's about to hit the fan. It'll go down fast. Hang in there, Marine."

Syrone nodded. "You may be a wimpy SWAT boy, but you're *semper fi,* Irish."

Bailey kissed Syrone's cheek. "We'll see you soon." Her voice was thick with unshed tears.

Con helped Syrone put on the Kevlar hood. Then, for the second time, they left their wounded friend in his makeshift fortress.

"Always faithful," Bailey said softly as they stood just inside the store entrance. "I agree."

"I try, sweetheart." His wary gaze swept the corridor. He had to be doubly vigilant. If the situation went FUBAR, it would happen during the risky transitional phase. Even if they managed to scramble a chopper, no way would SWAT allow the suspects to board. Especially with hostages. Taking an incident site mobile endangered more lives, both civilians and officers. It was never allowed. At any cost. That was the part that had him worried. "I want to hit the multiplex, do a recon before the suspects move."

The multiplex sat at the back of the mall, eight theaters branching off a central main lobby. There was one mall entrance and one parking lot entrance.

He left Bailey hidden next door while he took a fast visual inside the lobby. Red running lights along the walls outlined the walkways and concession area, with decent visibility about six feet up. The far corners and vast, echoing ceiling were pitch black. The buttery scent of stale popcorn lingered in the air.

Squirt gun at the ready, he swept inside and performed a swift, thorough search. The theater doors were all locked. So far, so good. Limited lobby access would facilitate containment.

He examined the outer glass doors, and swore. Wires snaked the perimeter, and a chunk of C-4 was lodged in the lower corner beside a detonation device. The SOBs *had* wired the exits. He didn't have time to mess with it and didn't dare. If he screwed up and went boom, Bailey *might* escape, but the hostages would be on their own. Outside, glittering freezing rain pounded the darkness in a heavy, drumming rhythm. Visibility was limited to a few feet.

Con determined the site was secure and radioed the intel to SWAT so they could get the bomb squad on it. He went back for Bailey. Inside the theater, her glance traveled over the thick, geometric-patterned carpet, dark, menacing nooks and crannies, and then upward. A wistful smile blossomed on her sweet mouth.

He followed her gaze to the board behind the ticket counter, listing shows and times. They'd been here often, but he knew from her dreamy expression she was remembering their last movie date, to see the final installment of *Lord of the Rings*. The books had been Bailey's favorites for years, and she owned every

DVD version and every soundtrack CD. She had a thing for Aragorn, the sword hunk who would be king. She'd even talked Con into dressing up like the guy to her Eowyn for the precinct's Halloween party. It could have been worse. At least he hadn't had to wear tights. Or heaven forbid, be a Scotchgarded-at-birth elf. "A fond memory. Even if you did go through a package of tissues *and* soak the front of my shirt."

"I get choked up all over again just thinking about it," she whispered. "So poignant. Ordinary people, fighting great evil. Never giving up, no matter the odds. No matter the cost. Courageous, noble. What a triumph."

Yeah, except in the movies, the good guys always won. Real life wasn't as neat and tidy. He tugged her into his arms. He needed to prepare her for what would happen next. "You've been a huge asset. I don't know what I would have done without you."

She stiffened in his embrace. "I feel a 'but' coming on."

"The situation is about to reach critical mass. I've got to play the rest out alone, darlin'."

"No!"

He cupped her face in his hands, looked into her beautiful blue eyes. "This is what I'm trained for, Bailey. You've done great, but you're a civilian. You need to step out of the line of fire."

She wrapped her arms around his neck and hugged him tight. "I'm afraid for you, Con. I don't want anything to happen to you."

"Me, either. I'll be careful." He rubbed her taut, quivering back. "I'll take you upstairs and stash you somewhere safe. Then you have to let me go."

Bailey clung tightly to Con's warm, capable hand. Everything inside her roiled in hot rebellion. *No.* Why did she have to step aside and let him risk his life alone? It wasn't fair. Wasn't right. She wouldn't do it.

As they approached the huge Christmas tree near the escalators, her steps dragged, slowing Con's momentum.

"C'mon, sweetheart. Time's a'wastin'."

She scowled at the towering wooden Nutcracker soldiers, hand-carved by local artisans. At the acres of fake snow batting mounded around the area near the tree's base. Decorative, but serving no real purpose. Was that how Con saw her? Drat the man, she could *help* him, had helped him all night. "Con—"

"Don't argue. I'm in charge here."

Yes, but he didn't have to be so all-fired bossy about it. "Con, dammit! Stop!"

He stopped, pivoted and arched a dark brow. "That's the first time I've heard you swear."

"It won't be the last unless you stop towing me along like luggage on wheels and listen to me."

"We'll talk. Upstairs." Still holding her hand, he bounded up three flights to the top floor. On the way, he instructed her to monitor both walkie-talkies and what to do if Tony called again.

Upstairs, she leaned against the wall, the plaster rough and cool behind her. She tried to catch her breath enough to speak. "You said I was an asset."

He wasn't even breathing hard. "I meant it. But things could get ugly. Dangerous. I won't risk your life." He stepped close and smoothed the frown lines from her forehead. "Baby, you said yourself you weren't sure how you'd react if you had to hurt someone. Mere seconds can cost lives. If you hesitated…"

He didn't need to finish. Bottom line, he couldn't depend on her to come through for him. He *was* better off alone. Her shoulders slumped. "Okay. Where do you want me to hide?"

"The food court. It's circular…if one of the robbers comes looking, you have an escape route." He moved closer, his big, warm body pressing into hers. Solid. Strong. Sustaining. Her traitorous brain superimposed another image—his body slumped, bloody and lifeless. She blinked away the agonizing picture.

He tipped her chin up, forcing her to meet his gaze. "Don't." He lowered his head and kissed her. His tongue stroked sure and deep. She tasted his dark, heady essence mingled with cinnamon. Felt the soul-deep connection shimmering between them. She would never get enough of him. She treasured him more than life. Needed him more than her next breath.

Loved him enough to let him do what he had to.

Her intention to break up had been in his best interests. Yet she was forced to admit her choice then had been born of love *and* fear. Not only for him, but herself. She'd been afraid of getting hurt. Now, her determination to release him was for Con alone. Her first decision had been made in cowardice. This one was forged in conviction. He couldn't afford distractions. She refused to behave like a fool and destroy his focus.

Tears threatened, and she blinked them back. She would not cry. Would not cling. She poured her feelings, her emotions, all her longing into the kiss. Telling him how much he meant to her.

Gently, he broke contact. "I have to go."

"I know." She touched his cheek. Warm skin, bristly stubble, exuding confidence and vitality. So alive. So precious. "I love you. Don't ever forget that."

"I love you, too, darlin'." His mahogany eyes crinkled at the corners. Sorrow, yearning and hope mingled in the warm brown pools. "Wait for me in the pub, in the food court."

She bit the inside of her cheek, fighting the compulsion to beg him to stay. To hold on to him and tug him out of harm's way. Keeping him safe wasn't up to her. Never had been.

He had to choose duty over her. Just like her father. But for the first time in her life, she understood why. She knew he'd made the right choice.

Just like her father.

Heroes had to be heroes. They couldn't be anything else. Countless lives depended on them. The women who loved them had to accept that. And keep on loving them, anyway.

Just the way they were.

Con turned and walked away, and her heart shattered inside her chest.

Chapter 11

10:00 p.m.

Con had taken only five steps when the light attached to the blue walkie-talkie at Bailey's waistband blinked. After speaking to the robbers, both she and Con had set their units on standby. Bailey's nerves jumped. Tony wanted to speak to her again. "Con! We have a transmission from the bad guys."

Con whirled. Both simultaneously activated their units. Con would be setting his to receive only, so as not to alert the robbers to his presence. Bailey flicked the switch for voice activation. She donned the hands-free headset, and then cleared the nervousness from her throat. "This is the Sugarplum Fairy."

"Hello?" a woman's tremulous voice whispered. "Bailey, are you there?"

"Nan?" Bailey couldn't believe her ears. "Is that you?"

"Yes. I've escaped." Nan drew a shuddering breath. "That's the good news."

Foreboding settled, thick and heavy, on Bailey's chest. "What's the bad news?"

"I'm…I…" Nan gulped. "I'm in labor. Heavy labor."

Incredulity slashed Con's face. He didn't move, scarcely breathed for too many tense, thumping heartbeats.

"Con?" Bailey started toward him. "Are you—"

"Of *course* she's in labor," Con muttered between clenched teeth. "If tonight follows true to form, I'll soon have a newborn to protect." He spun and pounded the wall. "Holy freaking hell, who did I piss off? What else could possibly go ass-over-teakettle during this scenario?"

The anguish in his voice made her tremble. Her brave knight

had borne tremendous pressure during these long hours without batting one long, dark eyelash. Fought insurmountable odds without losing hope. Unquestioningly assumed responsibility for everyone's safety. She didn't blame him for being upset at the latest turn of events. Talk about going from bad to worse. The more things that went wrong, the less chance of a timely, safe ending. This awful situation would strain anyone's resources.

But if he lost it, they were all goners.

She rested her hands on his back and kneaded the taut muscles. "We'll handle it. Don't fall apart on me now."

His shoulders hitched, and his body vibrated as he battled for control. "I'll maintain. Just…give me a sec." He ran a hand across the tips of his spiky hair and sucked in a deep breath. "Get her location."

She continued rubbing Con's shoulders, and spoke into the headset mic. "Where are you, Nan?"

"I'm hiding in Office Max, on the other side of Death by Chocolate. I couldn't run any farther."

"How did you get the walkie-talkie? Are you alone?"

"Yes. Tony put it on the desk beside me. Letty pointed it out and helped me form an escape plan. I told Tony unless he let me use the restroom, he'd be dealing with a nasty mess. I slipped the unit into my jumper pocket when I stood up. The robbers were arguing." Nan sounded like she might cry. "They're on edge and fighting because two guys are missing, and they're surrounded and everything is fouled up…Bailey, it's awful!"

Bailey flipped her mic below her chin to talk to Con. "Things have gone wrong for us, but tonight hasn't been a stellar event for the robbers either." Con chuckled, and his bunched muscles slowly relaxed under her ministering hands. She wrapped her arms around his wide chest and rested her cheek against his back, offering comfort. She angled her chin toward the lowered mic. "How did you escape? Where were the robbers?"

"I stuffed paper towels into the toilet inside the bank until it overflowed. One of 'em had to take me out to use the mall restroom. I went in, waited a few minutes, then started moaning. When he poked his head inside, I knocked him cold with the metal trashcan. The rest of the crew are in the bank loading money."

Con turned and kissed Bailey's cheek in a wordless thank you. His body language was once again capable and confident, his tone strong and steady. "Tell her we're on the way."

He strode to the balcony, leaned over and peered downward. He gave a thumbs up, then pointed toward the escalators.

Bailey continued talking to Nan as she followed Con down the three-flight jog. "Con's with me. We'll help you."

"Thank goodness! I wondered how you'd wiped out two gun-toting bank robbers and thwarted Tony all by your lonesome."

If she had been alone, she'd be a captive too, helpless and scared.

Or dead.

She reached for Con's hand. He squeezed gently, and she returned the gesture. Silent support and reassurance flowed between them. "We're double-teaming them."

Con shot a smile at Bailey over his shoulder that arrowed straight to her heart, and asked, "Bad guy head count?"

"Nan, how many bank robbers are there?"

"Not including the one I clobbered, three more. And they talked about drivers outside. Someone named Manny and another name I didn't get." Nan moaned. "Ooh, Bailey, I think the baby's coming fast. Hurry!"

"Hang in there, girlfriend. We're on the way."

At the bottom of the escalator, Con pulled her aside. "As soon as the crew in the bank notices how long she's been gone, they'll come looking. When we reach Office Max, recover the walkie-talkie and deliver it to me. We have to stay in touch with the suspects. Especially as the incident heads toward crisis."

Another crisis? *Wonderful.* Bailey empathized with Con's minor meltdown upstairs. She might blow a gasket any second. This night had been one blasted crisis after another. An endless, nerve-racking emergency, interrupted by moments of sheer terror. When they got out of here, she'd have T-shirts made up for everyone imprinted with the words, *I survived New Year's Eve at the Mall.*

She counted to ten. *Get it together.* The last thing Con needed was for her to freak. He had enough on his plate. "Okay."

As if sensing her need for comfort, he kept one arm around her and switched on the red walkie-talkie. She didn't need to be told how blessed she was that he was always tuned in to her feelings. "Command, be advised. BLO, one or more suspects possibly outside. Wheelman ID'd as Manny. Do you copy?"

"Ten-four," Aidan replied. "What's your ten-twenty-eight? Over."

"One of the hostages has escaped, and she's gone into labor. We're in the process of retrieval and transfer to a more secure location. Over."

"The medic is on site if you need emergency childbirth procedure. Over."

Con scowled. "Pray it doesn't come to that, but thanks. Over and out."

She snuggled closer to his solid warmth. Every moment with him had become precious. The next hour, the next minute could make the unthinkable a reality. "What does BLO mean?"

"Cop talk. Be on the lookout." He consulted his watch, gave her one last hug. "Rendezvous here in ten minutes."

Keeping to the dusky edges of the corridor, they sprinted toward Office Max. Con melted into the shadows out front, and she strode inside the dark store.

She veered right. "Nan, it's Bailey. Where are you?"

"Behind the computer armoires. On the left."

The emergency lights were few, and the ceiling-high shelves and pervasive gloom made it hard to see. The crisp, cottony smell of new paper sliced through the smothering darkness. Bailey switched sides and crept among the aisles. Bulky shapes loomed ahead, warning that she'd reached the office furniture. "Nan?"

"Here," her friend shakily hailed from behind a big bookcase.

Bailey rounded the corner and Nan gasped. "I've never been so relieved in my life as when I heard your voice on the walkie-talkie. I'd been in labor for hours and didn't know what to do."

"Don't worry, I'll get you out of here."

Nan choked off a sob. "I was afraid Tony would kill the baby rather than fuss with moving me to the multiplex. And taking a crying newborn on the helicopter?" She shuddered. "No way."

"Stay calm, sweetie. Everything will be okay." Bailey patted the frightened woman's arm. "I need the walkie-talkie."

"Why?" Nan handed over the unit.

"I have to run it out to Con."

Nan grabbed Bailey's hands. "Don't leave me!"

"We have to communicate with the bad guys so they don't hurt Letty and Mike." She gently extricated herself. Now she knew what Con had experienced earlier in the siege when she'd clung fearfully to him while he focused on survival. "Thirty seconds."

She strode to the front entrance as fast as she could without ramming into anything.

Con slid out of the shadows. "I'll head toward the bank and plant the walkie-talkie in the bathroom. The bad guys will search there first. I'll divert anyone who tries to follow you."

"Where will we take her?"

"Third floor. No way can we keep a woman in labor or—God forbid—a baby, quiet. We'll stash them upstairs, as far away as possible." Con squeezed her hand one last time. "If I don't show, get her upstairs and then call in SWAT. We're out of options." He turned and prowled up the mall.

Bailey ran back inside the dark store. Uneasiness roiled in her stomach. If the robbers had noticed Nan missing, they'd be out in full force. And none too happy. Con was rushing headlong into the jaws of evil. Again. She thrust the nagging worry from her mind. She had a job to do, as did he. He was much better trained for his mission. She couldn't afford to worry about him. She needed to concentrate every resource on the task at hand. If either of them failed, Nan and the baby would pay dearly.

Nan was waiting in front of the bookcase. She awkwardly heaved her burdened body out of an office chair. "If we're caught, they'll kill us." Her eyes widened in terror. "And now that I've escaped, Tony will be livid. He might kill Letty and Mike."

"Surely, he won't be that stupid." *Please.* "Then he wouldn't have any bargaining power."

Nan clutched her stomach. "Ooouch. The contractions are really close together. What a wonky sense of timing this son of mine has, huh?"

Yikes! Bailey squelched a sharp burst of panic. She'd hoped Nan was in the early stages of labor, and would be securely tucked away in the hospital long before the baby arrived. Didn't most labors last hours? She forced herself to remain calm. Panicking was not only useless, it could be fatal. "For sure. Let's get you out of here. We need to hurry."

"I doubt I can walk very far in my condition, much less run."

Bailey mentally inventoried the surroundings. "You won't have to." She pointed at the wheeled office chair Nan had vacated. "Have a seat."

Nan clutched the chair's arms as Bailey rolled her friend to the front of the store. Bailey poked her head out and cased both ends of the mall. So far, so good. Though she would have liked to see Con heading their way, the absence of gun-toting maniacs was somewhat encouraging. "All clear. Let's move."

She ran through the cold, spooky corridor as fast as possible while pushing Nan in the chair. The wheels clacked along the floor, and she cringed. Any robbers hanging around couldn't fail to hear the racket. Hopefully, Con would keep the bad guys away.

She bulldozed Nan past Harry's Fine Cigars, Toys Galore and the Bedroom Furniture Emporium. Her nine months pregnant friend was no flyweight, and Bailey's boots slipped on the wet floor. Her arms and legs screamed in protest. Ignoring her wailing muscles, she forged ahead. The sooner she and Con hustled Nan upstairs, the sooner mom and baby would be safe. Well, safer. Until the bank robbers were behind bars, no place was a hundred percent secure.

Almost there. Just when she thought she couldn't run another step, they arrived at the escalators. Puffing like a landlocked blowfish, Bailey tucked Nan into a hidden alcove behind one of the massive wooden Nutcracker soldiers. "We're supposed to wait here for Con." She studied Nan's pale face and tried to catch her second wind. "How are you holding up?"

"Ouch!" Nan grimaced. "Another contraction."

"Remember your breathing exercises." Bailey had sat in on

one prenatal class when Nan's husband Brad had been out of town. Too bad the instructor hadn't covered emergency childbirth procedure.

Nan huffed through the contraction. "I guess I'm…okay. Considering I'm having a baby in a deserted mall, while hiding from homicidal thieves. At least I'm out of that bank. I felt awful about leaving Letty and Mike behind."

Bailey crouched and clasped her friend's cold, trembling hands. "Your life and your baby's are at stake. You didn't have any choice." She shrugged off her pack and rummaged inside for the other Polarshield blanket. An ominous chill had crept into every corner of the building. "How are Mike and Letty holding up?"

"Mike's so terrified he's nearly catatonic. Letty, on the other hand, is verbally flaying those criminals alive. She keeps chewing Tony's butt for exposing us to secondhand smoke."

Bailey gave Nan a reassuring smile, careful to hide her distress. If the bad guys had their way, secondhand smoke would be the least of the hostages' concerns. She checked her watch. Two minutes until she had to take Nan upstairs alone. A muffled scrape caught her ear. Con? She pivoted and squinted down the murky hallway, but saw only shadows. What was taking him so long? Had he been captured? Was he hurt? She tensed and her stomach flip-flopped. Was he… *No! Don't go there.*

She covered Nan. "Is Letty staying warm enough?"

"She seems fine." Nan drew the crinkly blanket around her shoulders. "Her righteous indignation has her pretty hot under the collar…" Nan's horrified gaze froze in midair over Bailey's left shoulder. *"Oh, no!"*

"Look what I found," a man's deep rumble growled behind Bailey. "The Sugarplum Fairy."

Not Con's voice. Not Tony's, either. Her already jittery stomach pitched, and then bottomed out somewhere near her boots. Slowly, she turned, keeping her body between Nan and the stranger.

A rangy, sandy-haired man stepped out from behind the base of the three-story Christmas tree. He appeared to be in his mid-thirties, with an angular face and oddly pale eyes. He pointed a handgun at her. Big. Black. With a long cylinder stuck in the barrel. *A silencer.* "Keep your hands where I can see them."

She held herself very, very still while her heart pistoned in her chest like a jackhammer. She wasn't even sure she was still breathing. "Don't hurt us."

The man's lips twisted in a terrifying smile. "Tony wants to handle that detail personally."

Bailey's thoughts whirled. *Trapped! Doomed! Need a plan!* "Let's talk. Maybe…maybe we can make a deal."

"What kind of deal?"

What would appeal to him the most? "If you let us go, I'll put in a good word for you with the D.A. Perhaps get the charges against you reduced."

His glacier eyes narrowed as he appeared to consider the idea. A small flicker of hope lit the cold black void inside her.

He shifted his stance, bringing him nearer. She took a step back. He again moved forward. "Nah. Only worthwhile if we're caught. Which won't happen. Especially after we erase you from the picture."

The flicker snuffed out as hope died an agonizing death. *Stall!* "Don't be so sure."

He edged closer. She took another step backward. A cruel taunt curled his lip. He was stalking her. And enjoying it. "I like a woman with a strong spine."

Her spine didn't feel all that sturdy as it collided with something—one of the Nutcrackers—and the wooden soldier wobbled. Her terrified gaze spun down the mall. Where was Con? She wanted him to charge to the rescue. No, wait. Maybe not. She wanted him to stay safe. She bit the inside of her cheek, fought not to give in to smothering fear. She wanted this threatening predator out of her face. Gone.

He leaned closer, so close she smelled onions on his breath. He stroked her cheek with the cold gun barrel, and she shuddered. "There is something else you can offer me."

"Wh-what?"

He stroked the gun barrel downward, along her neck and over her breast. "You're a smart chick. Figure it out."

Oh, God! Help! Bailey swallowed a bitter surge of revulsion. "Not a snowball's chance in hell, mister."

"I wasn't asking." He pressed the full length of his body against hers.

"Get off me!" She tried to push him away. It was like trying to move Mount Hood. The Nutcracker at her back wobbled again, but her attacker didn't budge.

Nan shoved to her feet. "Leave her alone!"

Iceberg Eyes pointed the gun at Nan. "Sit, mama."

Her face pinched with fury, Nan obeyed.

The robber's cold, merciless gaze locked on Bailey. He smiled his monster's smile. "Now, where were we?"

He reveled in her fear, toying with her like a feral cat tormenting a baby bird. She'd be damned if she'd give him the satisfaction. She tamped down terror and made herself stare him in the eye. "You were proving the only way you can get a date is at gunpoint."

"Tony's right. You've got a sassy mouth. I want a taste." His face loomed in her vision, and his hot, fetid breath assaulted her lips.

She wrenched her head to the side, avoiding the violation. He fisted her hair in his hand and brutally yanked her head back. Her abused scalp burned. She could not move. Could not stop him from taking what he wanted. She ground her teeth together to trap the scream bubbling in her throat.

Suddenly, her attacker's body rammed into hers. He arched like a bow and the gun went flying. Then he dropped to the floor, landing on his hands and knees.

Nan stood behind him, brandishing the dented office chair. "If you think *mama* will sit there like a trained poodle while you attack my friend," she panted. "You've got another think coming, *creepazoid.*"

Stunned, the robber swayed on all fours. He fought to gain his footing, and Bailey grabbed Nan's hand and tugged. "Nan, run!"

Nan bent over, immobilized by another contraction. "Oooh. Not now." She moaned. "Can't. Bailey, go!"

No way was she leaving Nan and the baby. She pushed her friend behind the Christmas tree. She had to stop the criminal from coming after them! Her frantic gaze careened around the area. *Ah! There!* So, he liked women with a strong spine, did he? She'd show him a strong spine.

She sprinted toward the Nutcracker. Running full out, she slammed her shoulder into it. The big soldier swayed. She planted her boot soles against the faux marble floor and shoved with all her might. The Nutcracker rocked on its platform.

The robber rose on his knees, looked wildly around for the gun. "I'll kill you bitches."

A fireball of resolve exploded inside her. She could not let him gain his feet! She shoved harder. Screeching nails rent the air, lumber cracked, and the soldier toppled onto the robber. Her combatant lay facedown in the snow batting, motionless under the heavy wooden figure.

Panting, Bailey dropped to her knees. Resting her elbows on the broken wooden base, she cradled her spinning head in her hands. He wasn't dead. She wasn't sure how she knew, but she did. He was unconscious, but menace still shivered in the air. He was still breathing. If she'd learned anything tonight, it was the human body's resilience.

She felt no regret. No shame. Just numb relief. She'd done what she had to. Heavy, silent moments passed, broken only by her raspy breathing.

"Bailey!" Con's arms wrapped around her waist. He turned her as carefully as if she were one of the fragile glass ornaments broken in pieces at her feet. "Are you all right? Did he hurt you?"

She burrowed her face in his shoulder. Inhaled his familiar, reassuring scent. "N-no."

He drew back slightly and cupped her face in his hands. "Let me see, baby." His dark, concerned gaze traveled over her.

The implications of what she'd narrowly escaped walloped her with hurricane force. She started to tremble. Fought the urge to vomit. "He had a gun. He touched me… He tried to—"

Con spat out a curse. He seethed with fury, a volcano about to erupt. "I'll feed the SOB his own liver." His taut muscles quivered, giving away his inner war to subdue his rage—even as he lovingly rocked her in his arms.

Finally his harsh, rapid breaths slowed, and he tenderly

brushed back her hair. "Look at me." He held her gaze and she drew comfort from the steady warmth flickering in his eyes. From the respect stamped on his face. "You beat him, darlin'. You won."

She ached everywhere. The battle had left bruises on her body. On her soul. She didn't want a rematch any time this millennium. "If this is what winning feels like, I'd hate to lose."

He kissed her temple. "I should have been here to protect you. It's my job to keep you safe."

She *despised* the thought of being another burden for him to bear. "Con, no. This is not your fault. Don't—"

"I'm sorry, baby." A muscle twitched in his clenched jaw. "I got delayed neutralizing the suspect Nan left in the restroom. He came to and wanted a scuffle before he decided to take another nap. Then I had to secure him in the bookstore's storeroom."

"Nan!" Abashed, she jumped to her feet. "Oh, no, how could I forget about her?"

With Con at her heels, she sprinted to the Christmas tree and circled the base.

Propped against a giant package, Nan squatted on the floor. One hand clutched her abdomen. The other brandished the broken chair arm. When she saw them, she dropped the makeshift weapon. "Thank God! Batman and Robin."

Bailey's heart stuttered. She'd shoved her friend pretty forcefully. "Nan, are you hurt?"

"No. The contractions…are…ouch! Way close together, though."

Con's assessing glance swept the perimeter. "Where's the gun?"

"I don't know. When Nan hit him, it flew into the mounds of batting."

"Was it an Uzi?"

"No, a pistol. Huge. Black. Long cylinder attached to the barrel."

He frowned. "Get Nan upstairs. I'll restrain and contain the suspect, and locate the weapon." His frown deepened. "Too bad there's no dentist office in this mall. We might need running water, towels and scissors."

Nan groaned. "Curl up…and die."

Con helped Nan to her feet, and the puffing woman leaned against him. His arms tightened in a quick hug. "I know you're feeling rocky, but nobody will die. I promise."

Nan's laugh was ragged. "Upstairs. Beauty salon. Curl Up and D-Y-E. Water, towels, scissors."

Con nodded at Bailey. "Go. I'll meet you there."

"Um, *guys?*" Nan's voice rose. "My water just broke." She doubled over and would have fallen if not for Con's support.

After the contraction eased, Bailey managed to urge Nan up several stairs while Con riffled through mounds of batting. He came up empty-handed. "Damn, we need that weapon."

Nan groaned again and had to rest. "This kid isn't waiting."

Bailey bit her lip. "I doubt I can get her up three flights alone."

Con forcefully exhaled, strode to meet them, and then swept Nan into his arms. "I'll get her situated and double back."

As the group climbed, the unconscious man came into view. Nan grinned. "Smack down! Go, Bailey!"

Bailey looked at her fallen assailant. No triumph sang in her veins. She hadn't wanted to hurt him, and took no joy in it. Sadly, he'd pushed her to that decision. The bank robber had forced her to chose. She'd chosen survival. Chosen to save Nan and the baby. She would do it again, without hesitation.

They continued the long ascent and Con shot a concerned look over his shoulder. She held his gaze, mutely assuring him she was maintaining. A shimmer of understanding passed between them. She'd received a crash course about living in his world. About standing between evil and the innocent. Her dragon had roared in outrage and helped her protect Nan and the baby.

Not such a tough moral dilemma after all.

Upstairs, Bailey quickly detoured into Outdoor Outfitters to grab a camping stove. With Con still carrying Nan, the trio arrived at the beauty salon.

Con deposited Nan in a gray vinyl shampoo chair and covered her with the Polarshield blanket. He tugged the lever to raise the footrest, so she could semi-recline. "I've got to return to the scene and secure the perp."

Nan clutched his sleeve. "No! Don't go! The baby's coming!"

That was all he needed. "Listen to me." Desperate, he grasped her shoulders. "You cannot have that baby. Not here. Not now."

The pretty brunette scowled. "Don't think there's much choice."

He wrestled down a tsunami of panic. "Tell the kid this is not a good time to show up."

"You think I haven't? He's not paying attention," Nan moaned. "Not born yet…and already disobeying his mother."

Bailey touched Con's forearm. "Everything will be fine. You're trained in first aid." Her anxious expression said, *Please assure me I'm right.*

He wished to hell he could neutralize her fears. Along with his own. He was out of his element…by a galaxy. Or six. "*Combat* first aid. Bullet holes. Burns. Missing limbs." He scrubbed an unsteady hand over his bristly jaw. "SWAT teams deliver high-risk warrants. Not babies!"

Bailey gnawed her lip. A habit she employed when upset. Well, he didn't feel like the king of the world, either. She squared her shoulders. "Guess there's a first time for everything."

Right. But why did his first time have to be here? Tonight?

He accessed the red walkie-talkie. "Command, this is the Nutcracker. Get the medic, *stat.* Over." His heart pounded so loudly in his ears, he hoped he could hear the response.

Bailey draped the Polarshield blanket more securely over Nan. "You need to remove your undergarments. I'll find towels and scissors."

"Hey, Nutcracker." His brother Grady's amiable voice spoke in his ear. "Doc Holliday, here. About to have yourself a little peanut, huh?"

"This is *so* not funny, Doc," Con murmured.

"I know it isn't." Grady's voice grew serious. "There's a buttload of things that can go wrong. So pay attention."

Watching Bailey light the stove and assemble equipment, Con digested Grady's instructions. He stared at Nan in disbelief. "Say again, Doc? You want me to look *where?* And do *what?*"

Grady repeated his tutorial. *Good Lord.*

Con washed his hands in the sink beside Nan. He returned to

the foot of the chair and gingerly raised the blanket. "Sorry, Nan, but I have to…uh…"

"Like I give a flying fig." Nan was grunting now, straining to push. "Just get this kid out of me."

More queasy than he cared to admit, Con did what had to be done. *Hoo boy.* If he passed out, the team would never let him live it down. "Doc, we definitely have a head in sight."

Bailey set a stack of clean towels on the chair next to him. "I put the scissors on to boil. Anything else?"

Con consulted Grady. "Medic says to find something to tie the cord with."

Bailey found some hair ribbons in a drawer. She handed them to Con as she moved beside Nan and took her hand. "Breathe, Nan. Remember the pattern."

"My son, wearing hair ribbons." Nan panted in rhythm.

"He won't mind." Con patted Nan's foot. "Doing good."

"You *man!*" Nan hollered in a guttural tone, kicking out at him. "What would you know about it? This is all your fault!"

"Whoa!" He dodged just in time. "Uh, Doc? Is her head gonna spin all the way around and spew pea soup?"

Grady chuckled. "Even I heard that. She's getting close."

Nan yelped, and Con winced. "How can I ease her suffering?"

"Afraid you can't. Childbirth isn't for sissies, bro. That's why women get the privilege. Encourage her. Tell her to relax and do her birth exercises."

Con's throat was so constricted he could barely swallow. Relax. *Sure.* And panting in rhythm while squeezing something the approximate size of a Thanksgiving turkey out a keyhole. Definitely helpful pain relief. *Not.* If it were him…he shuddered…not enough drugs in the freaking universe.

Nan screamed, a high, inhuman keen, and the head emerged. *Holy Mary, mother of God.* And some men thought women were the weaker sex?

Kneeling at the foot of the chair, Con supported the baby's head. "Good job, Nan." As Grady coached him, Con concentrated on easing out the tiny shoulders.

Finally, the baby slid into Con's hands. He carefully cleaned the infant's nose and mouth with a dry towel. The baby was supposed to start breathing now. "Doc." He turned his face aside and spoke quietly, so as not to alarm Nan. "It's blue. Not breathing."

"They're all slightly blue when they're first born. Support its body with your hands. Turn it facedown, with the head angled slightly downward and slap the soles of the feet to make it cry."

"He's out. Why isn't he crying?" Nan asked, her voice quivering. "Con?"

"Just a sec, Nan." Con followed Grady's instructions. Whispered desperately into his mic. "Still not breathing."

Nan tried to sit up. "Why isn't my baby crying?"

Bailey shot a horrified glance at him and then moved between them, blocking Nan's view.

Thank heaven for his smart, quick-thinking helpmate. He would never have survived this night without her. Without her, he wouldn't have a reason to.

Grady's calm tone urged Con, "Try rubbing its back. Slap the feet again."

He did. No response from the tiny human. His pulse thundered in his veins. Sweat trickled down his back. "Nothing. Dammit, Doc, help me!"

"Okay, stay calm, bro. You can do this. You're going to have to give it a couple breaths. Two quick, tiny puffs. Be careful."

"My baby's not breathing," Nan sobbed. "Is he…"

Bailey held her friend and crooned in a soothing voice. Her scared blue eyes begged Con to succeed.

He wanted to—more than he wanted his heart to continue beating. More careful than he'd ever been in his life, he gave the unresponsive infant two small breaths. *Please, God, if you're listening…*

The baby sputtered, coughed, and then began to cry lustily.

"Yee-haw!" Grady shouted over the headset. "Yeah, that's the bomb! You did it, bro!"

Everybody was crying. Nan. Bailey. The baby. Tears of gratitude streamed down Con's cheeks. Thank the Lord, the baby was wailing!

"Can I hold him now?" Nan begged.

"I need to tie and cut the cord first." He propped the pink, wriggling infant gingerly on a clean towel. The simple but terrifying procedure was rendered much more difficult by the fact that his hands were shaking uncontrollably.

Nan sniffled. "You saved my baby's life. I'm sure Brad will agree he should be named after you." She wiped her eyes. "You *and* Bailey. Well, Bailey's dad." She stretched out her arms. "Hand over Conall David Thompson."

Bailey smiled at Con through her tears, and his heart turned over. She nodded at Nan. "Has a lovely ring to it."

"That's quite an honor." Con swaddled the infant in towels and placed the tiny, wiggly bundle into Nan's waiting arms. "I'm afraid she's gonna get teased on the playground, though."

Nan stared at him, her dancing brown eyes incredulous. "*She?* It's a *girl?*"

"I'm pretty sure." Con grinned at Nan, then Bailey. "Unless I broke something."

Nan hastily unwrapped the towels to verify his claim. "Well, I'll be! The ultrasound was wrong. A girl, how fun!" She laughed, tears streaming down her face.

"Guess you'll have to rethink that name."

Nan kissed the top of the baby's fuzzy head. "Constance Bailey Thompson. Welcome to the world." She arched her brows at Con. "What time is it?"

As sweaty and exhausted as if he'd run the Boston Marathon with his leg shackled to an armored car, he consulted his watch. "Eleven fifty-nine, and counting."

Chapter 12

12:00 Midnight

"*Happy New Year!*" Bailey whispered along with Con and Nan. Grady echoed the sentiment over the headset.

Bailey hugged Con and gave him a kiss. "To new beginnings."

A wondering expression crossed his face. "Excuse us, Nan. Cover wee Constance's eyes." He turned Bailey, bent her over his arm and kissed her. His warm, silky tongue teased and tantalized. Caressed and plundered. He staked a possessive claim, consuming her. Branding her as his. Her breath evaporated and her head spun. Her bones melted. Bright spots danced before her eyes.

He eased back and flashed her a wicked grin. "Have to kiss my girl properly, and start the new year right."

"Looked kind of improper to me." Nan chuckled and bussed her newborn daughter's cheek. The baby gurgled and waved her fists in the air like a miniature prizefighter. "The best kind."

"Absolutely," Bailey woozily agreed. She couldn't have felt fizzier and warmer had she consumed too much celebratory champagne. High on the miracle of life. High on Con.

"Party's over." Con clapped his hands. "We need to get these ladies hidden and wrap up this incident so we can all go home."

Bailey crashed to earth. They had a lot more work to do before the miracle of life could triumph over evil and death.

Con propped open the door to the employee lounge. "I'll carry Nan to the sofa."

Nan offered Constance to Bailey. "Want to hold your namesake?"

Bailey accepted the precious bundle. The baby was much

lighter than she'd expected. Fragile and helpless. Dependent on them to protect her. "She's so small."

Nan laughed. "Yeah, *now!* She didn't feel small a while ago!"

Constance stared up at Bailey with wide, dark eyes spiked with long lashes, and her alert expression asked, *Who are you?*

Bailey caught her breath in awe. "She's beautiful."

Con winked at Nan. "In a few years, she'll have the boys eating out of her hand." He carried Nan into the lounge.

Bailey followed with slow, careful steps, and then handed Constance to Nan. Nan hugged the infant close. "Her daddy might have a thing or two to say about that."

Bailey straightened. Her gaze locked with Con's, and her heart flipped over.

Emotions shimmered between them. Hope. Love. A thousand unspoken promises. His gorgeous brown eyes glowed with visions of the future. "The first time I saw you," he whispered, "I saw my unborn children in your eyes."

Her heart ached with longing. Con's babies. Would she have the chance to rock them in her arms? Nurture them as they grew. Shower them with the love she and Con shared.

He held her gaze a moment longer. Between one breath and the next, the shimmering connection dissolved. Regret shadowed his handsome face before he turned away. "I'll scout around and figure out how to secure this place."

Bailey tucked away the beautiful memory. One of the most important lessons she'd learned tonight was to savor every moment. You never knew when—or if—you'd get another chance. The time had come for her and Con to separate. Not knowing if they'd see one another again.

Just as she'd tucked away the pleasure, she set aside the pain. Both would wait for later. She needed a clear head and uncluttered focus. "Are you leaving me with Nan and Constance?"

"No. I've modified the plan. Since Nan escaped, the suspects will be furious, their reactions unpredictable. I'll station you with Syrone. He has a weapon, and you'll be my eyes and ears on the first floor as the incident comes to a head."

Surprise, mingled with validation, washed over Bailey. In-

stead of stuffing her into a hidey-hole as if she were a timid little rabbit, he was keeping her in action. He might not want her
on the front line, but he *did* trust her to back him up. She nodded, smiled at him. She would not let him down.

Con used the red walkie-talkie to update Syrone. "Syrone
says you can't beat that woman-power." Grinning, Con hurried
out front.

Bailey plumped pillows behind Nan's back and tucked hand-
warmer heating pads around mother and baby. She covered them
with a purple knitted afghan she'd found draped over the sofa and
the Polarshield blanket. "Warm and cozy. Anything else I can do?"

"I'm super thirsty. And starving." Her face radiant, Nan
grinned. "Having a baby is hard work!"

"Especially without anesthesia. Yikes!"

"I've already forgotten the pain."

"If you say so." Brows arched in disbelief, Bailey raided a
small refrigerator. "You're in luck. Bottled water, and a fast-
food salad one of the stylists must have left behind."

Once Nan had sustenance, Bailey scrounged hand towels and
hair clips to function as makeshift diapers. Who knew how long
the siege would drag on, and Constance needed to be kept warm
and dry. Thank heaven they didn't have to worry about feeding her.

Bailey also gave Nan a squirt bottle of bleach, a straight razor
and big, sharp scissors. "I hope you won't need weapons, but just
in case…" She added scissors and a razor to her own backpack,
and tallied the recent acquisitions in her notebook.

Nan's expression grew lethal. "Anybody who tries to lay a finger on my daughter will lose it."

"After your attack on the robber with the office chair, I have
no doubts." She and Nan exchanged silent communication, friend
to friend. "Thank you."

Nan's dark eyes conveyed her empathy over Bailey's close escape from a woman's ultimate horror. "Anytime, girlfriend." She
shuddered. "For a while, I was beginning to wonder if I would
escape from that bank alive. To make an awful situation worse,
the robbers are fighting amongst themselves."

"About stuff going wrong. Yes, you mentioned that before."

"Well, they're also arguing because one of the guys accused Tony of working in cahoots with you to get rid of them."

Bailey's jaw dropped. "Why on earth would they think that?"

"Letty's egging them on. She's the one who brought it up." Nan's grin bounced back. "She said, 'Interesting how every time he sends someone out, they don't come back. How nice for Tony. Less ways to divide the money.' Tony was gnashing his teeth."

"Hmm." Bailey tapped her chin with a forefinger. "Wonder if there's a way to use that against him?"

"Oh, and maybe this will help, too. Tony's men have orders to bring you in alive, if possible. He's boiling mad over the accusations. He wants to prove that he's not in league with you." Her eyes widened. "And exact his revenge in person."

More of Tony's brutal brand of *satisfaction?* Shivers crawled up Bailey's spine. "I'm glad you told me. I'll fill Con in. If there's a way to turn it around on the robbers, he'll know."

"Be careful, girlfriend. Tony is dangerous, and you've been messing with his head." Nan's brows creased in worry. "They're all dangerous. The one who attacked you…he won't care if Tony wants you alive. In fact, most of them probably won't. You've kept them from taking the money and splitting."

"Don't worry. Just take care of yourself and Constance."

Con returned. "Time for 'Auld Lang Syne.'" He and Bailey said reluctant farewells to Nan and Constance, and headed out.

Outside the beauty shop, Con jumped up and grabbed the security gate. With the computerized system out of commission, only brute force could budge it. Hanging from the edge, he dragged the gate partially down.

Bailey added her weight. Gears grinding, the cage lowered slowly to the floor. He smashed the control panel and upper tracks with the baseball bat, and then wedged the bat in the lower track. "Should do the trick. Anyone on the hunt will assume the cage descended on its own like some of the others. Even if they suspect someone is inside, they'd have to expend a buttload of time and energy to wrestle it back up."

"Which will warn Nan and give her the opportunity to fight."

"That's the plan." He grabbed her hand and they strode down the mall.

She hid inside an electronics store while he headed downstairs to find the pistol and restrain the man who had assaulted her. They planned to contact Tony afterward and use Con's latest brainstorm to stall him about the chopper.

Shivering in the dark, she waited between shoulder-high shelves lined with computers. The hair rose on the back of her neck with the creepy feeling that someone was watching her. She whirled. The blank-eyed monitors stared menacingly. *Put a lid on that wild and crazy imagination, girlfriend.* Her imagination had been a comfort during her lonely adolescence, and come to Con's aid a number of times tonight. But right now, it could take a nap.

For distraction, she fantasized about what would happen after the ordeal was over, and she and Con went back to his apartment. She imagined a lovely, endless night of tender lovemaking. Thought about how incredible it would feel to wake up in his arms.

Con possessed innate athletic confidence and grace, which made him superb at anything physical. He was also tuned in to constant awareness of her moods and feelings. The combination would surely make him a spectacular lover. Goose bumps of anticipation tingled over her skin. She sighed in longing. Both her body and her heart would be safe in his keeping.

"Heads up, cupcake!" The furious growl had her spinning around again.

A long, heart-shaking moment of ice-cold horror crawled by before she realized the voice had spoken over her headset. She flipped the switch to transmit. "T-Tony?"

"Who were you expecting, jolly old Saint Nick? Where's my friggin' chopper?"

"On the way," she lied. Too bad Con hadn't shared his stalling idea with her before he left. He'd thought they had plenty of time. "The storm caused a slight delay, but it will be there. They're…deicing it now."

"It better be. Where's my hostage?"

She feigned innocence. "What hostage?"

"I'm getting real tired of this game, cupcake. The missing hostage. The pregnant one. Where is she?"

"Sorry, I don't know anything about a renegade hostage. But, hey, look at it as one less problem to deal with."

"Yeah, right. And I want my missing crew!"

"Did you misplace some men, too? Careless of you." She forced her words to ooze nonchalance, though she felt anything but. "Another silver lining. Fewer ways to split the money."

"You bitch," he growled savagely. "When I get my hands on you, and whoever you're working with—"

"Let's not go there, because it won't happen."

"Unless my chopper and missing crew show up at the multiplex, and soon…" Tony sounded ready to chew the furniture. "I am going to start shooting."

She covered her gasp by clearing her throat. "You don't want to do that. You'll lose the ground you've gained. Listen, how about I tell the police you willingly released the hostage? Gain you some goodwill." Of course, she'd do no such thing. But the lie might chill him out some. "Nobody will give you anything, including a chopper, if you kill—"

"I don't have to shoot to kill. Taking out Grandma's kneecap would cripple her, though. And it might finally shut her up."

She closed her eyes, fighting nausea. He was just a threatening voice on the headset. Con had everything under control. SWAT was outside, ready to storm in on a moment's notice. "If you hurt anyone, the police will—"

Her words broke off mid-sentence as wide, masculine hands settled on her shoulders. The low, male voice rumbled, "Who are you talking to?"

Her eyelids flew open. She knew that voice. Recognized the familiar scent.

Onions.

Her stomach flip-flopped in terror. She didn't want to turn around. Didn't want to see him, and make the nightmare a reality.

Because *if* he was here, that meant Con was… *Oh, my God! Con!* Her shattered heart cried out in agony.

Her thoughts whirling, body numb, she slowly turned.

Scratches marred Glacier Eyes' angular face, and a diagonal cut gashed his right cheek. The greenish black bruises mottling both pale, emotionless eyes made them look even paler. Scarier. The big, black pistol rode in a scarred leather holster across his chest. He smirked. "I'm gonna rip your wings off, Fairy."

Her brain's frantic shouts finally kicked in and her stunned body moved. She took a step back. Then another. She pivoted to run.

"Don't leave." The robber grabbed her by the hair. Searing pain made her eyes water. The sudden jolt tore off her headset, and it dangled from her belt. "The party's just getting started."

Tony will think I hung up on him. The disembodied thought didn't seem to belong to her. Strange how the mind reacted to fear by enhancing insignificant details.

"Where's your friend?"

For a moment, she thought he meant Con. No. He knew where Con was. Anguish stabbed her heart, the only organ in her body with feeling. He meant Nan.

"She had to leave." Even her lips were numb. Good. Then it wouldn't hurt as much when he shot her. "She hates parties."

"So, we're all alone." His harsh mouth twisted, and she read his intent in those bone-chilling eyes.

He was going to kill her. But he was going to hurt and degrade her first. No way could she stop him. She had scissors and a razor in her pack, but he was twice her size. Even if she could reach the weapons, he outweighed her by at least eighty pounds. Even if she knew how to fight, hand-to-hand combat was futile.

Best case scenario: she'd delay the inevitable.

She firmed her chin. But she could, and *would* fight to the death rather than submit to rape. Heat surged into her frozen limbs. As he dragged her toward him, she reached out, snagged a dangling cord and tugged a monitor off the shelf.

The monitor crashed to the floor and imploded, a seventeen-inch bomb spewing plastic and glass shards.

"Dammit!" Her attacker leapt aside to avoid getting his foot broken, and released her hair.

She ran down the aisle toward the front of the store, yanking cords as she went. Fear and her momentum empowered her.

Reach, grab, *pull!* Monitors, keyboards, printers fell and shattered behind her. Pandemonium strewed in her wake. A tangle of glass, plastic and wires for him to hurdle.

He swore and scrabbled behind her. His hands snatched at her clothing. She swerved and sprinted toward the end of the aisle. Reaching her goal, she whirled and shoved over a big screen TV. The deafening explosion probably jolted the dead in the mortuary down the street. Her notebook tally was gonna go into triple columns.

Disoriented by darkness, terror and the fight-or-flight reflex ricocheting through her, she couldn't find the exit. Panting, she hurtled around a corner and crouched behind an entertainment armoire. She tried to slow her rasping breaths and pounding heart enough to hear her pursuer. Where was he?

Footsteps, crunching glass sounded twenty feet behind her. Con was right. Sound was a dead giveaway. *Con.* Crushing pain swamped her, and she fought it. She couldn't, *wouldn't* speculate about Con's fate now. She had to believe he was still alive. Had to get to him. If he was wounded, she was his only hope.

"I like party games, Fairy." The robber's words vibrated with amusement and sick excitement.

Great. A whack job. You didn't have to be psychotic to rob banks, but it probably helped during the killing part. Cold sweat dampened Bailey's skin as she weighed her options. *Hide. Run. Attack.* None seemed particularly feasible. Or likely to succeed.

"Come out, come out," he cajoled in an eerie singsong, sounding closer.

She crawled along the floor, feeling to make sure she wouldn't tread on debris and give away her position.

"Wherever you are…" His boots crunched on the broken glass. *Definitely* closer!

She glanced up. There! Thirty feet ahead, the gloom lessened. The mall exit! Still crawling, she crept forward.

The robber's footsteps followed. She heard his ragged breathing. Imagined she smelled onions. Locked in the deadly game of cat and mouse, fear threatened to strangle her. Render her helpless. She'd used humane traps to deport rodents from the bookstore, but after crawling a scary mile in their little pink feet, sympathy for the critters churned inside her.

"I'll find you, Fairy." Closer still. "And make you pay."

Her fingertips brushed a metal strip, then carpet. *Yes!* The front of the store was carpeted. Hunkered behind another big-screen TV—intact, for now—she eased off the pack. As carefully as if she were disarming a nuclear bomb, she reached inside and lifted out the retractable clothesline from the camping store. One small, revealing noise could get her killed.

"Now I'm bored," the robber complained.

He was about ten feet behind her, but he'd veered to the right. With any luck, she might have enough time. Though her brain screamed, *hurry,* she crawled slowly around the TV. Looping the clothesline, she tied a secure knot.

"I hate being bored." He shoved something and it crashed to the floor.

She flinched. Wonderful. The whacko was now a *really* ticked off whacko.

Trailing the clothesline behind her, she crawled parallel to the exit until she reached the opposite side of the store.

The robber swore again. "Did you somehow sneak past me?" His rapid boot steps crunched toward her.

She quickly pulled the clothesline tight and looped the other end around a heavy metal filing cabinet. Shin high, the tightly strung plastic rope made a perfect tripwire.

Bailey re-shouldered her pack, shoved to her feet and tore into the mall.

The robber shouted. He'd seen her! His running footsteps followed.

She'd sprinted five yards along the railing edge of the balcony when he yelled, cursed and a thud vibrated the floor. She risked a quick look backward. Her pursuer lay spread-eagled on the faux marble like a sacrificial victim staked out on an anthill.

Ha. Never underestimate a woman who reads, indeed! Especially a guy who'd stood in the brawn line twice, and skipped the brains altogether.

She turned and ran toward the escalators. She had to get

downstairs, to Con! *Con.* She stumbled. If the robber had gotten past him, Con was either wounded or…she couldn't bear to finish. Her duty at the moment was survival. Con would want that.

He'd spent the entire night ensuring her survival.

Her exhausted limbs dragged like lead weights. The day had been long, the night even longer, and she was fighting the strain. She forced herself to keep running. Syrone. She'd head for Syrone. He had a machine gun, and knew how to use it. She could access her red walkie-talkie to warn him, and he'd ambush the guy. Then she'd find Con and help him.

Running footsteps pounded behind her, and she shot another look over her shoulder. Glacier Eyes was up and closing the distance. Fast. The fierce scowl creasing his broad forehead told her he was seething.

Her heart thundered. Dread streaked through her veins, and she poured on the speed. If he caught her, there would be no more chances.

The escalator came into sight. *Almost there. Keep going.*

Shockwaves exploded inside her as the robber grabbed the back of her sweatshirt and jerked her to a stop. *No! Oh, no! So close!*

He spun her around to face him. Red-faced, he growled, "Think you're clever?" Iron fingers clamped her shoulders, and he shook her so hard her spine nearly snapped. "I'm going to teach you a lesson you'll never forget." He raised his fist and backhanded her across the face, knocking her to the floor several yards away.

Dazed, gasping, she sprawled on the cold marble. Her head spun, her face throbbed and black spots swam in her vision. She licked her stinging lips and tasted blood. Down and fading fast. As helpless as baby Constance. His face contorted with hate, the robber lunged at her. Her life expectancy was about two minutes.

They would probably seem longer.

A savage war cry rang in her ears, and Con hurtled out of the stairwell. His narrowed gaze touched her briefly, and the rage in it sent her reeling.

"I'll kill you for that, you bastard!" Running full out, Con tackled the robber.

Joy thrummed through her. Con was alive! And looking plenty healthy.

He clocked Glacier Eyes with a powerful punch to the jaw. The robber grunted and staggered. Then he rebounded and slugged Con.

She tried to scramble to her feet as the men battled, but couldn't coordinate her disjointed arms and legs. The blow had stunned her more than she'd realized.

Glacier Eyes' fist rammed into Con's stomach. Con bent double and the robber whipped his gun from the holster.

"Con, gun!" she yelled.

Con's hands shot out and clamped onto the robber's wrist, and the pistol waved wildly between them. The men struggled for possession.

The robber aimed a vicious kick at Con's knee. Con feinted left, deflecting the blow. The robber broke free of Con's hold, whirled, and pointed the gun at her head. "Shut up!"

She stared into the black hole at the end of the cylinder. Stared at her own death. So, this is how her life would end.

Then everything segued into slow motion. Con wheeled into a crouch in front of her, flinging his body between her and the gun.

Three loud pops broke the silence.

Con jerked backward, then lurched sideways.

Her heart leapt into her throat. He'd been shot!

Events rocketed into fast-forward. Panic careened through her. She surged to her feet, her horrified gaze searching for blood on Con's clothing. She didn't see any.

The body armor! Con was okay. The vest had stopped the bullets.

As relief ebbed away her panic, Con's arms shot out, and he dug his fingers into the robber's shirt. Locked in the horrible dance, the men swung on the momentum and slammed into the balcony railing. For an awful moment they hung suspended in midair.

Then they pitched over the balcony and disappeared.

The robber's scream broke off mid-cry. Con didn't make a sound.

She heard thrashing, felt a gust of wind and then a horrendous crash shook the walls.

Silence descended. Dead silence.

She stood paralyzed. Her breath stopped. Her heart stopped. The world stopped.

The three-story fall had to have killed them both.

Chapter 13

Con! Oh, God, *Con!*

Bailey didn't remember running downstairs, but she was standing in front of the ruined Christmas tree. Fake pine boughs, broken decorations and torn garland littered the floor. The grappling men must have collided with the tree and ridden it to the ground. The lofty branches had slowed the descent and cushioned their fall.

The robber lay crumpled in the snow batting. Unconscious, but alive, both legs at awkward angles. Looked like he wasn't going anywhere anytime soon. Her fingers clenched into fists. If he had killed Con, she would personally strangle him with her bare hands.

"Con?" Her frantic gaze scanned the rubble, but she didn't see Con. If the robber had survived the fall, maybe Con had, too. "Can you hear me?"

She prayed harder than ever before as she searched. What would she do if he was as incapacitated as the robber? Her forearm brushed the walkie-talkies at her belt, and she swallowed hard. If he were badly injured, she would call in the SWAT team.

Bailey spotted the pistol near the robber's limp right hand. Her lip curled in loathing. She took a deep breath and picked up the barrel between her thumb and forefinger, pointing it away from her. The gun was much heavier than she'd expected. And deathly cold. Was the safety on? She didn't know where the safety was, or what it looked like. A three-story fall hadn't caused the gun to fire, so it was probably okay in her pack for a short time. As long as she was careful. With a shudder, she eased it inside.

"Con!" she called again, her throat tight and aching. "Where are you?"

A low groan filtered out from beneath huge, twisted boughs twenty feet ahead. She scrambled over a mountain of flattened packages, squelching the urge to claw the debris aside. Exerting supreme control over her screaming emotions, she gently scooped up crushed ornaments and shredded garland. One at an excruciating time, she lifted branches.

Con lay sandwiched between layers of boughs. His beloved face was scratched, bruised and streaked with blood, but he was conscious. Relieved tears stung her eyelids. "You're alive!"

He groaned again. "Yeah. I can tell by the pain."

She wanted to fling her arms around him, but didn't dare. "Did you lose consciousness? How badly are you hurt?"

He hesitated, as if taking stock. "I'm not sure if I went lights out or not. It's all a blur. Nothing seems broken. My chest smarts where the Kevlar absorbed the rounds. That's SOP."

"SOP?"

"Standard operating procedure."

"Okay, anything else?"

"My head hurts like a mother. Oh, and I can't see so hot."

He couldn't see? Panic assailed her before she realized why. "There's a cut above your right eyebrow. Blood is running into your eyes."

"Head wounds do that. Don't freak, darlin'."

"Do I look like I'm freaking?" Other than the fact that she was trembling from forehead to toenails. Avoiding the pistol, she rummaged inside her pack for bandages. Good thing she'd stocked up when she'd scavenged first-aid supplies for Syrone. "For Pete's sake. After tonight, a little thing like a minor head wound will hardly spazz me out." She hoped it was minor. *Please, God, let it be minor.*

He grinned. "That's my slugger. Sexy *and* strong."

"Here." She pressed folded gauze to the wound. "Hold this in place." She gently cleaned his ravaged face with a wet wipe.

"You're still blurry." He reached up with an unsteady hand and his thumb caressed her bottom lip. "He drew blood on my woman. That's a killing offense."

"Easy there, Conall. Don't go all *Clan of the Cave Bear* on me."

"He hit you." His eyes glittered with heated fury. "I wanted to hurt him, baby. Bad."

"I know." Surprisingly, she'd felt the same when she thought the robber had killed Con. Even more surprising, she'd accepted it. Without shame. Without guilt. Con belonged to her, and by heaven, *no one* would deliberately harm him and get away with it.

She gently kissed his warm, bristly cheek. He wasn't the only one who possessed the instinct to protect his mate. "You did what you had to. You saved my life. Given the chance, he would have killed us both."

He blinked, his face etched with amazement. "Glad you understand. Do you know where he landed? What is his condition?"

"In the batting, twenty feet back. He's unconscious and it appears both his legs are broken. He's no longer a threat, and there's nothing we can do for him right now."

"See if you can find the pistol."

"Done. It's in my pack."

"Come again?" He did a double take. "You picked up a *gun?*"

She'd rather eat raw worm pudding than handle a gun, but a girl had to do what a girl had to do. "I could hardly leave it there for him to shoot us with. Can you stand? We should get out of this exposed area."

"Baby, if you can handle a gun, I sure as hell can get upright."

She helped him sit up. Leaning heavily on her, he struggled to his feet. The second he stood, his knees collapsed and he dropped to all fours. "I can do this. Give me a sec."

"Hang on." She sprinted to the office chair she'd used to transport Nan. It was dented and one arm was broken. Thankfully, the wheels still worked. "Take a load off, Officer Sexy."

"I can walk," he insisted.

"I'm sure you can. Indulge me."

He wobbled and staggered as she helped him into the chair. His solidly muscled body weighed a ton, and he was a lot weaker than expected. "I'm fine."

She disposed of the soaked gauze and placed a fresh pad on his bleeding forehead. "I know you are." She cleared a serpentine path through the rubble, skirting objects too heavy or awkward to move. Then she wheeled him through the maze of debris to the end of the mall and into Sears. Jeez, *men*. One arm could be dangling by a tendon, and they'd insist they were perfectly okay. However, a head cold sent them to bed, where they proclaimed incapacitation and imminent death. What was up with that?

She pushed Con to the furniture department, and parked the chair in a corner while she constructed a makeshift fortress out of furniture like he'd made for Syrone.

"Hey." Con tried to get up, but fell back into the chair. "Stop moving all that heavy furniture around. You'll hurt yourself." His words had begun to slur. Maybe getting him up had exacerbated his head injury. Not good. "Let me help you."

"It's okay," she soothed, tearing plastic off a queen-size mattress. "I'm almost done. Keep pressure on your forehead, or the bleeding will never stop."

"I'm good to go."

"And I'm gonna take up target practice," she muttered as she tore open packages and extracted pillows and blankets. "You bet."

"What?"

"I said, hold still while I put blankets on this mattress. Then you can rest."

"Can't rest. No rest for the wicked…" His insistent tone lost momentum, as if he'd forgotten what he was about to say. "I…have things to do."

She hurriedly shook out a madras plaid comforter. He needed to be prone, and kept warm, or he could go into shock. "I know. In a little while." She wheeled him to the bed. "Are you dizzy?"

"No." She helped him stand and he swayed like a palm tree in a hurricane. "Maybe a little."

"Do you feel sick to your stomach?"

"Don't fuss. I'm fine."

Mr. "Fine" probably had a concussion. She got him on the

bed, propped a down pillow under his head, and then covered him with two blankets and a comforter. "Let's have a look at that cut."

"It's nothing. A scratch. Slap on a butterfly bandage, and it will be…"

She chimed in, making a wry face. *"Fine."*

"No need to get snarky."

Her wounded knight looked so indignant she couldn't help but chuckle. "Sorry. You're just so cute when you're in macho mode."

"Cute?" He made a gagging sound. *"Now* I'm nauseated."

"I'm calling your brother." She accessed the red walkie-talkie and switched it to voice activated. "Hello? I need the medic, please."

"Oh no, you don't." Con struggled upright, and the gauze pad fell to his lap.

She planted her palms on his chest. Only his weakened condition enabled her to push him back down. "Conall Patrick O'Rourke, you stay right where I put you." She replaced the pad. "Do *not* move. Or else."

"Bossy little thing in the bedroom, aren't you?" He chuckled and pressed the bandage to his forehead. "I have handcuffs at home, if you want 'em later."

Though not enunciating clearly, he was lucid enough to tease her. Good sign. Some of her anxiety trickled away, and she wrinkled her nose at him. "Stop griping about my bedside manner, you pervert."

Grady's puzzled voice in her ear said, "Huh?"

A hot flush crept up her neck and into her cheeks. "Um…not you."

"Drat, there goes my rep." Grady laughed. "What do you need?"

"Tell me the danger signs for concussion."

Grady's tone sobered. "Who sustained a concussion?"

"Co—I mean, the Nutcracker."

"Did he lose consciousness?" The question was sharp, all business.

"Not sure. If so, not for very long. He was awake when I found him."

"Stiff neck or vomiting?" Grady's voice was lethally calm.

She replied in the negative, and he continued. "Good. Any severe confusion, difficulty speaking or convulsions?"

"No, but his words are a bit slurred, his vision is blurry, and he's bleeding from a cut on the forehead."

"Can you control the bleeding with pressure? Is it slowing?"

"Yes."

"So far, so good. Use a flashlight to see if his pupils are evenly dilated and reactive."

Con's beautiful brown eyes held hers in a wordless embrace while she checked his pupils. The moment she withdrew the light, his eyelids floated down. He grunted and opened them again. He looked like a little boy stubbornly fighting sleep.

Her stomach clenched. She could not stop to think about the fact that she'd nearly lost him. Later. She'd deal with the ramifications later. "They are."

"Is he pale or clammy? How's his pulse?"

"He is pale, not ghostly white, though." She placed two fingers on Con's wrist and counted. "Strong pulse. About seventy."

"A little fast for him, but not bad." Grady sighed, his relief palpable. "If you have supplies, disinfect the laceration and fasten butterfly bandages across it. Place an adhesive bandage over the top. That'll hold it securely. Keep him quiet. Make him rest, or his condition could worsen. Lots of luck with that."

Con yawned, and his long, dark eyelashes again fluttered down. Again, he battled them open.

"Actually, he's sleepy. Is that bad?"

"One hundred percent normal. Plus, he's been running on pure adrenaline. Now that he's down, he's crashing. Usually, he'd handle it without missing a step, but combined with a knock to the noggin, it will temporarily scramble his reflexes. Sleep is the best thing for him."

She watched Con determinedly fighting drowsiness. "Try telling him that."

"I hear ya." She heard the grin in Grady's voice. "Unconscious is the only way to keep him out of trouble. As long as you can easily rouse him, it's okay. Wake him briefly every hour for the

first four, then every two hours. Hopefully, we'll have you out
of there before then. Questions?"

"No. I've got it."

"I don't doubt it. Hang tough, kiddo. I'll turn you over to
Command, now."

"Sugarplum Fairy?" Aidan's smooth, deep voice said. "What
happened?"

"Co—the Nutcracker fought one of the robbers and they went
over the balcony." She squeezed her eyes shut against the terrible sight. Relived the terror. The anguish. She gulped. *Keep it together. Con needs you more than ever.* "From the third floor."

Aidan whistled. "That boy was always damn lucky."

She turned her back on Con and whispered. "He's going down
for the count, though. And the robber boss is getting impatient
about the chopper."

"Don't worry. Con filled me in on his plan while he was securing the beauty shop. We're going to play a recording of a
chopper descending over the loudspeaker, and lower a floodlight
from the roof, wired at the proper angle. With the storm limiting
visibility to a few feet, it should fake 'em out for a while. The
negotiator is patched in, and he'll take over with Tony. Are you
in a secure location?"

"As secure as anywhere in this blasted mall. We have a gun
now, though." Not that Con was in any shape to use it. She pinched
the bridge of her nose. Her stamina was wearing thin. "I almost
forgot. The robbers are moving the hostages to the multiplex."

"Ten-four we're on it. Stay hidden. Send me a radio check
every hour. Take care of yourself and the Nutcracker."

"That's the plan."

Aidan laughed. "You sound exactly like him. Over and out."

Con had finally lost the battle with sleep. His breathing was
slow and even, his skin bleached under the dark beard stubble. The
cut had nearly stopped bleeding, seeping slightly under the pad.

She let him rest while she ran out to the carnage at the tree,
carrying two comforters. The short nap would do him good.
Now that Con was safe, and her rage had faded, she was obli-
gated to give aid to Glacier Eyes. Leaving him to die of shock

was more than her conscience would bear. She couldn't afford to examine too closely what she might have done had Con died. She liked to believe her morals would have overridden her savage, primitive instincts. Instincts she hadn't even realized she possessed.

Bailey jolted to a stop. Yes, she *had* known. On a subconscious level, she'd realized a slumbering dragon lived inside her. She had battled for years to keep it asleep. Because if she couldn't control it…what then? The fear, the memories of her parents screaming at one another, tearing each other apart emotionally, had kept the dragon in chains. Unconsciously, she'd followed her mother's example and enslaved her emotions. Maintained control at all costs. The dragon had always been something to fear, to avoid. To slay.

Con's wise advice to come to terms with it was right on target. If she slew the dragon she would forever kill a vital part of who she was. Her drive. Her confidence.

Her passion.

She would forfeit her happiness. Destroy her future.

The dragon had roared to life and would not be quieted. Bailey opened her arms and embraced it. And if she couldn't control it? She squared her shoulders. She'd learn to deal with the consequences. The former distinct line between black and white was irrevocably smudged, gray and fuzzy. In ashes.

When she reached the fallen robber, she tore open packages containing the blankets and spread the first comforter over him.

He stirred, moaned and opened his eyes. "Help me."

Compassion swirled inside her. In spite of the fact that he'd tried to rape her, and kill both her and Con, he was still a human being. As reprehensible and dangerous as he was, he must be suffering unspeakable pain. "You just tried to kill the only man trained to help you. I can't move you without causing further injury, but I'll try to make you comfortable."

He spat out a filthy epithet before again losing consciousness.

She shuddered. Imagine living with such clawing hatred. Bitter, twisted values. Desire for material possessions that drove him to steal. And kill. None of it could ever make him happy…or remotely satisfied. One of two fates awaited him. Sudden, violent death, or growing old and feeble locked in a steel cage. When he died, he would die alone. A wasted life. But his choice. He deserved to pay for his crimes. Nevertheless, pity swelled inside her. She covered him with the second comforter and tiptoed away.

After a fast detour into the Dollar Store for ibuprofen and bottled water, she ran back to Con. She stood for a moment with the bottles clutched to her chest, watching him sleep. The most important person in her world. Hurt and vulnerable. Her heart turned over. She would not let anything happen to him.

She reined in her tumbling emotions and arranged first-aid supplies on a nearby table. She eased onto the mattress beside him. "Con? Con, wake up."

He moaned and opened his eyes. The deep mahogany pools were cloudy with pain. "Yo. Officer O'Rourke, reporting for duty."

She forced a smile. "You're easily roused. That's a good thing, according to Grady." Of course, he hadn't been asleep very long.

"I knew you were here. I smelled you in my dreams." A sleepy, sensual grin slid across his mouth. "You could arouse the dead, sweetheart."

Her pulse stuttered. *Likewise.* "That's *rouse,* buster. As in awaken."

"I'm awake. Mmm." He drew a deep breath, breathing her in. "Dewy roses, warmed by the morning sun. And swaying in a soft, peppermint-scented breeze."

She swallowed the aching lump lodged in her throat. If the sweet sentiments came from any other guy, she'd worry about his cognitive function. With Con, it wasn't the head wound talking. The fact that her battle-hardened cop wasn't afraid to show her his romantic soul touched her to the core. She'd fallen in love with the poet at first sight, but she hadn't really known the warrior until tonight. Two halves of the whole man. She loved them both.

Bailey gave herself a mental shake. Right now, Con needed first aid, not fantasies. She uncapped the water and then dumped two ibuprofen tablets into her palm. "Here, take these."

He stared suspiciously at the pills. "What's that?"

"Something for the pain." He started to speak, and she shook her head. "Before you insist you don't need it, let me state for the record, Officer Sexy, you *are* taking it. One way or another."

His slow grin gleamed. "You're not giving me much choice."

"Nope." She supported his head while he swallowed the pills.

"Hand me your pack, please." He woozily propped himself on one elbow and the covers fell to his waist. His movements clumsy and sluggish, he palmed the pistol. "Finally, a weapon other than toys and athletic equipment to fight with."

In his condition, fighting wasn't feasible. She squelched a flutter of panic. Maybe it wouldn't come to that. Metal clanged as he opened and examined the chamber, then dislodged the clip. Should he be playing with a deadly weapon when he was incapacitated? She started to say something but clamped her lips together. Disabled or not, he knew what he was doing.

He jammed the clip back into place, and then slid the gun under his pillow. "Not much ammo."

"Better than none." She didn't like touching guns, but sure as heck wasn't opposed to him having one. In fact, she was darned glad he did. It upped his odds for survival exponentially. "On your back again so I can do the Florence Nightingale routine."

He collapsed onto the pillow with a barely concealed sigh of relief. His smoky eyes watched her, caressing her, as she applied antibiotic ointment and butterfly bandages. His skin was warm and smooth under her fingertips. A steady pulse beat at his temples.

Everything could have gone so differently. So wrong. She could be keeping vigil over his cold, broken body, instead of nursing him.

Her earlier insistence on planning her life to the minutest detail now struck her as incredibly foolish. Fate rolled the dice, and you accepted what you got. Looking so far into the future, she'd been blind to the present.

She slid her fingers into his silky hair. Cradling his face, she stared down at him. Every moment he was hers to cherish was precious. She hoped she would have a lifetime to do just that. "There. How does that feel?"

"Pretty damn fine."

"I meant your wound."

"What wound?" His muscular arms wrapped around her waist and tugged her to him, so her upper body was draped across his hard chest. "Lay with me for a while."

"I don't want to hurt you."

"You won't." He held her gaze, their faces a breath apart. "For the record," he purred, "I have no complaints whatsoever about your bedside manner."

Would he, later, if they had the chance finally become lovers? "I—I hope not. You're so good at everything." She worried her lower lip between her teeth. "The total sum of my knowledge comes from reading books."

"Ah, sweetheart." He soothed her lip with the pad of his thumb, making every nerve ending tingle. "You could never disappoint me."

"You don't mind, then?"

"Mind?" His husky chuckle brushed her with delight. "Baby, I love knowing you're my woman. That you belong only to me." He paused. "FYI, I don't have the wild background you think I do. Sex just for the hell of it isn't all that great."

"You're not trying to tell me that you've never..."

"No." He shrugged. "Don't get me wrong, I have. It feels good at the time. But it leaves you empty inside."

Awed, she shook her head. Would this man ever stop amazing her?

He smoothed back her hair. "You look exhausted, and no wonder. Climb under the covers."

"I'm too warm after all that exercise," she lied. She wanted to be able to move fast if the robbers discovered their hiding place. Instead, she snuggled beside him, sharing his pillow. "Con? How did you know I was in trouble? When you didn't come, I...I thought the robber had hurt you, or—" She couldn't finish.

Keeping his arms around her, he rolled to his side, facing her. The awkward movement told her he was in more pain than he was letting on. After the jolt he'd sustained, every inch of his body had to be stiff and aching. "When I got downstairs, the guy was gone. I figured he'd reported in, and the robbers would be pretty steamed. I'd run toward the bank to do a recon on the hostages. When I heard your conversation with Tony break off midstream…" His eyes closed briefly, then he opened them again. "My guts went ice cold. I knew what had happened." He exhaled sharply. "My heart damn near burst out of my chest before I made it back upstairs."

"He would have killed me. He had me in the electronics store." Bile rose in her throat. "He's sick. He was going to—"

Con clenched his jaw, and a muscle jumped in his cheek. "Baby, did he hurt you? Are you all right?"

She shook her head. "I'm okay. I got away."

His big hand cupped her cheek. "How?"

"I threw computers and a big screen TV at him."

His smile was subdued. "Hooray for technology. Good job, darlin'." He stroked her face. "How can I make it better?"

"You already have." She'd probably have nightmares for a while, though. "I'm so glad he didn't find Nan and Constance."

"Yeah. Speaking of courage…" His callused fingers traced the shell of her ear, sending a quiver through her. "You know I hold my mom in high regard, always knew she was strong. But after delivering Constance, I have a new respect for women." His intense gaze darkened. "I can also see why a woman would want to adopt, instead of going through all that."

She smiled in wonder. Aidan thought she was starting to sound like Con, but part of her had also rubbed off on him. Sometime during the night, she'd found her courage, and Con had honed his compassion. They'd shared the best parts of themselves with each other tonight. Making them both stronger, both better.

Bailey shook her head. No way would she pass up the opportunity to have Con's babies. *Please, let me have that chance.* She planted a kiss on his sensual lips. She hoped their children inherited their daddy's beautifully shaped mouth. "Nan said she's already forgotten the pain."

"And you call *me* brave?" He frowned. "I don't know how you women do it."

"This from a guy who eats bullets for a living?"

"Taking down perps and eating bullets is one thing. I still see every face of every man I've killed in the line of duty. I accept it. Live with it." His expression turned more serious than she'd ever seen. But, when—" He faltered. Swallowed hard. "When I held that tiny infant in my arms and she wouldn't breathe…"

He was trembling, and she hugged him close. "It's okay. Constance is okay."

When he spoke, his low voice was graveled. "If that baby had died in my hands, I would *not* have been able to live with it." He sucked in an unsteady breath. "Not for a second."

"It wouldn't have been your fault. You are not responsible for everyone's safety."

"It sure as hell *feels* like my responsibility."

"Which makes you the man you are. The man I love." She drew away slightly and embraced his anguished gaze with hers. "But not everything is within your control, Con."

"Don't I know it. How the hell…" He drew another shaky breath. "How am I gonna keep everyone alive? Including that baby upstairs? How am I gonna get us out of here?"

She'd never seen him unsure. So raw. Exposed and vulnerable. Her chest ached with the need to comfort him. "Everyone is safe for now. Let's stick with what's worked so far and handle one crisis at a time, okay?"

His beautiful mouth twisted. "I can barely stand, much less defend you in another crisis. If anything happens to you, I'll never forgive myself."

Bailey placed gentle fingers against his lips. "You've been protecting me all night. Let me protect you for a change. You need rest."

"I can't rest with so many lives at stake. Everyone is depending on me."

"I'll keep watch. Go to sleep." She brushed a kiss on his bandaged forehead. "You'll feel better and stronger when you wake up, and we'll take it from there."

He gave her a lopsided smile. "I'd never have made it tonight without you."

"Ditto, Officer Sexy. Now shut those gorgeous brown eyes for a while, and take a load off."

Bailey didn't think he would ever give in, but finally, his lashes drifted down, and his breathing slowed. Fierce determination bubbled inside her. He trusted her to take care of him when he wasn't a hundred percent on top of his game. She lay there, listening to the throbbing darkness that surrounded them. She wouldn't fail him.

Con settled into deep slumber. The seconds crawled. Cold. Dark. Silent. She tried to track time in her head. How many minutes had dragged past? She needed to check in with Aidan, and she was thirsty. Also, if an hour had gone by, she had to wake Con. She eased out of his arms and off the bed. His exhaustion was so profound, he didn't even stir.

She was reaching for the water bottle when she heard it. A slight scrape, a rustle that might have been clothing. Carefully, she crept out of hiding and circled to the front of the store. Her heart slammed into her rib cage, and then pounded wildly.

A stocky man with short-cropped dark hair searched the aisles in the gloom near the entrance. Machine gun at the ready, he systematically swept row by row. Before long, he would work his way back to Con.

Every muscle cramped in dread. Her insides turned to jelly. She couldn't wake Con. In his weakened condition, a fight meant a death sentence. Yes, he had a pistol. But a handgun against a machine gun? A few bullets versus…didn't machine guns contain endless rounds of bullets? Con was the team's best shot, but he was groggy, his reflexes slow and muddled, his vision blurred.

She remembered the searing horror, the eviscerating agony that had ripped her apart when she'd thought him dead. If a firefight ensued, instead of choosing the most viable tactical position for himself, Con would do his damnedest to protect her. He'd die trying.

For the first time, Bailey completely understood that compulsion. She would not hesitate to give her life to keep *him* safe.

In fact, she might be about to do just that.

She took several deep breaths, filling her lungs, oxygenating her muscles. Her timing had to be impeccable, her execution flawless. She wasn't stupid enough to embark on a suicide mission. She could and would make it. For Con. For their future.

She watched Mr. No Neck execute another methodical patrol, and stretched her weary muscles. Prepared for the scariest race of her life. Sweat slicked her palms and her nerves jittered. Too bad she didn't dare return for the pack, a weapon might come in handy later. No time, though. She couldn't risk leading the robber to Con. And the extra weight would just slow her down anyway.

The robber started his third sweep, and she swallowed hard. *Ready or not. Ollie, ollie oxen free.* The ludicrous phrase from a childhood game of hide-and-seek popped into her head. Except this was no game. This was a race to the finish, in every sense of the word.

Balanced on the balls of her feet, Bailey took another deep breath, and hit the exit running full out. Irresistible bait. *Catch me if you can.* Unless he was blind, deaf and comatose, No Neck couldn't fail to see her.

He didn't disappoint.

He tore after her, a bull charging the red flag. Her arms and legs pumping, she dashed down the mall. Having raced up and down this stinking hallway fifty times tonight, she knew every inch.

She hurtled past deserted stores, flashes of dimness breaking the pervasive gloom. Her pursuer lagged behind. She didn't stand a chance going head to head with him in a fight. But in a long-distance run, a greyhound would leave a bull in the dust.

Supercharged by adrenaline, she ran. Her plan was to lure the robber into the tree wreckage. With him entangled in debris, she'd follow the maze she'd cleared to wheel Con out. Then she'd circle the escalators, double back and head for the bank end of the mall. Once she got far enough ahead, she could veer into a store.

If No Neck didn't see where she went, he'd have the devil's own time finding her. The hunt would keep him busy—and away from Con—until she radioed SWAT. They'd send in the cavalry, and everyone could finally get the hell out of here and go home. It was a good plan. Not bad for a bookstore clerk.

The escalators lurched into view. Her mistake with Glacier Eyes had taught her not to look back, no matter how tempting. Her pursuer's harsh panting echoed through the corridor about thirty feet behind. She leapt over the first hurdle and rushed headlong into the wreckage. Several moments later, crashing sounded behind her. So far, so good.

She located the path and zigzagged through the ruins. Thrashing and inventive swearing from No Neck—right on schedule. Clearing the carnage, she vaulted the last barrier. The robber tried to bulldoze out of the epicenter, with no luck.

A fierce grin creased her face. Greyhound, one…bull, zero. Now, circle back, and then get the heck outta Dodge. She tore around the bank of immobile escalators. Her pursuer was out of sight, which meant he couldn't see her either.

Keeping her eyes on the corridor ahead, she instinctively skirted the mounded batting. The last leg of the marathon loomed in front of her. One long, last dash for freedom. For Con. Her blood pumped hot with resolve. With victory.

Something snagged her right ankle. She stumbled, flailed and tried to extricate her foot. For a moment, she teetered in midair. Then gravity caught hold and slammed her to the floor.

She lay stunned, trying to find her bearings. *Up. She had to get up.* Panting, she pushed to her hands and knees.

And came nose to nose with Glacier Eyes' malevolent face.

"What goes around comes around, Fairy," he gritted. He waved a tree branch he'd used to trip her. "Not so smart now, are you?"

She didn't have time for a war of wits with the weaponless. She shoved to her feet and started running.

"Gotcha!" No Neck growled, and she was jerked backward by the hair.

She yelped as the whiplash snapped her neck back.

"Good going, Jace," No Neck gloated.

"I owed the bitch one." Glacier Eyes…she couldn't think of him as anything else…smiled his nasty smile.

No Neck smirked. "If she hadn't covered you up all nice and cozy and left the packages laying around, I would never have known which store to search."

Bailey clenched her teeth on a scream of frustration. She could kick her own butt. Trying to help a fellow human being had backfired, big time. Double backfired. If she hadn't covered

Glacier Eyes, No Neck wouldn't have found her. If Glacier Eyes had gone into shock, he wouldn't have been conscious enough to trip her. She didn't regret covering him. She *did* regret screwing up and leaving behind the blanket packages—emblazoned with the store's name and logo. Exhaustion, worry and her rush to get back to Con had cost her.

Glacier Eyes stared up at her. His face was contorted with pain, but he still found the energy to sneer. "Even with two broken legs, I took you down. What do you think of me now, Fairy?"

She kept her face expressionless. "You're not worth thinking about."

He scowled. "Oh, hey, Rico, watch yourself. There's a—"

Bailey's heart stuttered. He was going to tell No Neck about Con! She nudged his left leg with the tip of her boot and winced when he screamed. Then he passed out. She cringed. Who knew he'd faint? She'd merely intended to stop him from ratting out Con.

"What'd you do that for?" No Neck…what had Glacier Eyes called him? Rico sounded incredulous. Obviously, not the sharpest crayon in the box.

"He got on my last nerve." She hadn't wanted to hurt the man. But protecting Con was her number-one priority. Now, she needed to redirect Rico's attention from his buddy's cryptic message. She tugged against his grasp on her curls. If one more Neanderthal yanked her around by the hair, she would break his fingers. "Let go of my hair, you cretin."

Amazingly, Rico complied. Bailey spun to face him. She wasn't scared. She was heartily sick of being afraid. She was mad. No, mad didn't do how she felt justice. She was livid. Raging. *Breathing fire.*

She planted her hands on her hips and glared at her captor. She was outgunned. Outmaneuvered. Out of options.

"Take me to Tony," she demanded. "Now."

Chapter 14

3:00 a.m.

Con jolted awake, his heart thundering in his chest. Something was wrong. Very wrong.

He struggled to sit up. Where was he? Darkness pressed in from every corner. A hammer clanged inside his skull. Dizziness and nausea broadsided him, making him reel. His instincts were screaming. Bailey's face hovered in his thoughts.

Bailey!

He didn't search. Didn't call out. The vast emptiness, the frozen despair in his guts told him she was gone.

Where?

Loyal to the point of death, Bailey would never desert him. He flung off the blankets, as thick and heavy as the fog muddling his thoughts. Had Syrone radioed for help while Con was out? As much as he'd like to think so, he didn't believe it for a second. Syrone wouldn't endanger Bailey's life. Under any circumstances.

He peered at his watch, the illuminated dial stark blue in the icy gloom, and his queasy stomach pitched. He'd been dead to the world over an hour. Was Bailey with Nan? No. He'd barricaded mother and baby inside the salon. Bailey couldn't get to them.

That left one possibility. One he couldn't bear to consider.

Like an answer from his worst nightmare, the *receiving* light on the blue walkie-talkie blinked. A surge of adrenaline blasted his sluggish reflexes, and he attached the headset with unsteady hands. Dread jittered inside him as he turned on the unit. He didn't have to say anything. The corresponding light on the robbers' unit would show he'd connected.

"About friggin' time," Tony's graveled voice said. "I've got someone here who wants to speak to you."

Con's heart stopped beating. *Oh, Lord. Please, no!*

"C'mon, cupcake. Deliver the message," Tony demanded.

Taut silence hummed over the line. Con held his breath.

"Noncompliance. We're gonna have to do this the hard way." Tony sighed, but he sounded almost pleased.

Without warning, Bailey screamed. A high-pitched blade of pain, slicing Con's skin, drawing blood.

His heart slammed into his rib cage and tried to hammer out of his chest. What had the bastard done to her? His throbbing brain conjured up half a dozen horrifying images, and he squeezed his eyes shut. It didn't help. "You sonofabitch," he snarled into the mic. "Plan on having a closed casket. Because when I get done with you, what's left won't be recognizable."

"Aha. The anonymous thorn in my ass speaks up at last. I want you. Unarmed. In the multiplex. Ten minutes…or the cupcake dies." Tony laughed, low and ugly. "And I'll make sure it hurts." He broke the connection.

Bile surged into Con's throat. He was shaking like a rookie in his first firefight. Bailey must have gone willingly with Tony's men. Even zonked out by the head injury, a struggle would have awakened Con. She had protected him. At great cost to herself. Maybe the ultimate price.

He clenched his fists against the slap of grief. *Hold it together.* Bailey's life depended on his actions in the next few minutes. He sucked in a breath. He had hard choices to make. Fast.

He exchanged walkie-talkies and called Command. Aidan's voice transmitted into his headset. "I was just about to contact you. Alpha Eight snagged a visual on the crew leader through his scope. We've ID'd him. DiMarco, Anthony C. Six foot one, two hundred pounds, age fifty-five. He owns a security company in town. Appears squeaky clean on the surface, no rap sheet. His business trains and supplies guards to banks and armored cars."

"And acquires inside intel to pull bank jobs. Nice setup."

"Ten-four. Unsolved crimes in Denver follow the same MO. When Denver got too hot, he moved to the Pacific Northwest.

Here's another news flash. He joined the army about the same time as Pop. They attended basic together, and were both in the twenty-fifth infantry. They were stationed in Hawaii for three months before Pop was injured and mustered out, and Tony went to Vietnam."

Con's intuition twitched. Their mother had also been in Hawaii, working as a civilian nurse at the army hospital during the war. Coincidence? Not on your life. "There's more to this story."

"A lot more." Aidan paused. "DiMarco did two tours of duty. Black Ops. He's a trained killer."

Con would bet his right arm DiMarco had murdered his father. Now he'd captured Bailey. Hot anger welled in his chest. When Con finished with him, the slimeball's war years would seem like the freaking Mardi Gras. "So am I."

"Not like DiMarco, bro. He did things the military doesn't even want to know about. You've seen the crime-scene photos on those unsolved bank jobs and home invasions. He's a butcher. One who enjoys his work."

"I'm canceling his butcher's license. Now." Con briefed Aidan on the current scenario, and his quickly formed plan.

When Con finished, he didn't have to see his brother's face to know Aidan was scowling. "Going kamikaze won't help anyone."

"I don't intend to crash and burn." *Unless I have to.*

"You're breaking every damn protocol, and you know it. Greene will skewer your ass for shish kebab."

"I don't have a choice."

"Aw, hell." Aidan's gusty exhale oozed frustration. "For what it's worth, I'd do the same."

Con grinned. "I know."

"The weather is hell on wheels out here. We're having trouble getting the equipment situated. If the timing doesn't click, if you don't catch the right break…" Aidan's voice deepened with suppressed emotion. "No. We'll do it. Come back breathing, bro."

"That's the plan." Con ran his hand over his hair. "Listen, if…well… Just tell Mom…" He shook his head. "Tell her I know I was always her favorite."

"You wish." Aidan's chuckle sounded ragged. "Good fortune

be yours." His brother invoked their grandmother's Irish blessing in a not-quite-steady voice. Gran had said the blessing over them each time the family had departed the Emerald Isle after a visit. "May troubles ignore you each step of the way."

Con swallowed the lump in his throat and finished the blessing. "May the saints protect you. And your joys never end." He set his jaw. "I'm glad you've got my back. All of you. Give my regards to Alpha Seven and Doc Holliday." With the final farewell to Aidan, Liam and Grady, Con signed off. "Over and out."

His hands now rock-solid steady, Con removed the blue unit from his belt and stowed it in the pack beside the loaded squirt guns. He wouldn't need to contact the team again. Palming the pistol, he made sure there was a round in the chamber. The clip held twelve more. He released the safety and slid the gun into the pack. Ignoring the pain clamoring for attention in his temples, he tossed a tab of cinnamon gum into his mouth and strode into the mall. A walking weapon.

Locked and loaded.

Keeping to cover, he sprinted toward the multiplex. A frozen, greasy ball churned in his stomach. *Fear.* Not for himself. For Bailey. His woman. His soul mate. He'd never been afraid before a mission. Sure, a part of him always knew he might not come back. Cops died every day in the line of duty. He didn't dwell on it. You couldn't. Not if you were gonna survive.

He made a wide circle around scattered jawbreakers outside Toys Galore. His throat tightened. His girl had fought valiantly beside him. Untrained, she hadn't flagged. Unprepared, she'd never failed. Not one complaint had passed her sweet lips. Not even when she'd been attacked and cruelly beaten. He pressed a fist to his aching chest. Now he knew why surgeons didn't operate on members of their own family. Bailey was being tortured at the hands of the madman who had very possibly brutally murdered his father. Con couldn't stop it. Couldn't help her. The thought razored his insides. His objectivity was shot to hell. A liability he couldn't afford.

He passed Bedroom Furniture Emporium and sent a silent salute toward Syrone. With any luck, the big guy would soon rejoin his family. *Family.* A cop's most valuable asset. Con would have self-destructed without his mom's wise guidance, his brothers' loyal friendship. The awareness that his brothers were outside, backing him up, twisted inside him. They wouldn't let him down. But they also shared his danger. Shared his distress. As he shared theirs.

The knowledge was both comfort and torment. Bittersweet. After Con's dad was murdered, he'd witnessed his mother's anguish, his brothers' suffering. And hadn't been able to stop that, either. He'd hated feeling helpless. Despised his vulnerability. Didn't ever want to feel that way again. Instead, he'd become Super Cop. Putting his body between innocents and the criminals who would tear them apart so other families wouldn't suffer.

The love of his life had just done the same for him.

As he prowled down the dark corridor, the lightbulb in his brain switched on, illuminating his heart with bone-chilling clarity. He finally realized why Bailey had tried to break them up. Finally understood her fears. She'd hit the target dead center.

He *had* wanted to be everybody's damn knight in shining armor.

Bailey had pointed out the chink in his chain mail. He didn't take foolish chances, but he *had* shrugged off what he considered acceptable risks. Only now, from Bailey's viewpoint, those risks didn't look nearly as innocuous.

Con grimaced. Saving the world *wasn't* his responsibility. Wasn't in his control. In spite of what he liked to believe, he was as vulnerable as every other mortal man. He inhaled sharply, filling his lungs. Well, hallelujah. He'd seen the light. Not a great revelation to whammy him with before going into combat.

Counting, he slowly released the breath. He would not go off half-cocked and do anything to jeopardize Bailey's safety. Or his own. Not unless he was forced to. He had brand-new incentive. He wanted to come home to the woman he loved. Every night for the rest of his life.

And if he lost her?

Like an invisible brick wall, the horrible thought slammed him to a stop. He'd lose his perspective. His balance.

His reason to live.

He stood immobile, struggling to master his feelings. He could *not* lose control. Bailey's scared face wavered in his mind's eye. He rolled his taut shoulders and shoved down his emotions. Froze them beneath a layer of icy determination. He stashed the pack in its hiding place. Phase one of the op complete.

The fight of his life was ticking down to the final bell.

Inside the theater lobby, Bailey pressed her spine against the concession counter, determined not to shrink away as Tony again approached her. Instinctively, she realized he respected her—in his own warped way—because she hadn't shown the fear raging inside.

Even when he'd burned her with his cigarette.

Terror crouched inside her, ready to pounce and tear her composure to shreds. She clung to anger, using it as a welcome shield to beat back the fear. She touched trembling fingers to the blister on the side of her neck. Tony hadn't been able to force her to talk to Con and arrange Con's surrender. She'd walk into hell barefoot and naked before letting herself be used as bait.

Tony towered over her, obsidian eyes snapping. The blood-red theater lights creased his rugged face in hard lines. "In spite of your denials, I knew you weren't alone out there. You're a quivering little librarian. You couldn't even kill a bug, much less take out my crew, cupcake."

The burly man named Rico, the one who had captured her, snorted. He and Tony were the only bank robbers left standing. *And then there were two.* She and Con had leveled the odds. "I don't know, boss. You should ask Jace about that."

Tony ignored him and moved closer to Bailey. "Who is it? Who's been helping you?"

She gritted her teeth and remained silent. As she had earlier when Tony had taunted her—and backhanded her across the face. She didn't regret protecting Con by turning herself in. Con had said he'd never trade himself for a hostage; it was stupid and against procedure. She'd bought him over an hour to rest and recover. Time to plan and summon SWAT. One hour that could mean the difference between life and death. For him. For all of them.

She held Tony's gaze. Unlike the man who had attacked her in the mall, Tony's eyes glittered with fervor. A fanatic, dedicated to his cause. Not afraid of anything. There was no compassion in those crackling black orbs. No trace of humanity.

So this was what uncompromising evil looked like.

Bailey bit the inside of her cheek, battling despair. If only she hadn't screamed when he'd burned her! If she'd seen it coming, she could have been prepared, gritted her teeth and held it in. Considering how Con had reacted when Glacier Eyes hit her…she shuddered. Her scream of pain would be the one thing that might make Con ignore his training. Make him burst in, guns blazing. Cause him to react instead of act.

Get him killed.

She raised her chin. *Keep the faith.* Faith in Con's intelligence. His integrity. His love for her, love that would hold him steady. Hold him to his training. It was their only hope.

Tony pinched her cheek, which, judging from the lingering sting, probably bore his handprint. "Let's try another question. Where are my men?"

Bailey shrugged. If she didn't speak at all, no information would slip out by accident. No way could she tell him. If Tony's crew returned, Con would be vastly outnumbered. The SWAT team would face five armed men instead of two.

"You've got more backbone than I thought, I'll give you that. But you're not too bright." He extracted another cigarette from the pack on the counter and lit up. The noxious smoke attacked her sinuses, mingling nauseatingly with the smell of stale popcorn. "Or you like pain. You bent that way, cupcake?"

Bailey's stomach clenched. He was going to hurt her again.

"Oh! You! Leave her alone!" Letty spat out, half rising from her chair by the parking lot door. Tony had positioned the old woman and the cowering, catatonic bank manager between the robbers and the police outside. The wheeled, enclosed metal cart loaded with bags of money sat in front of the concession counter. When Bailey had first arrived, Tony had made her sit with Mike and Letty while he and Rico finished bolting a clear, bulletproof windshield to one side of the cart. She'd overheard them congratulating themselves for being prepared for any eventuality with their specially made armored cart and Kevlar suits with hoods. The robbers were thrilled that the wind and sleeting rain made it impossible for the snipers to shoot accurately. They also planned to use the hostages as temporary protection to get to the chopper and take off. Emphasis on the temporary.

Letty huffed. "You're a toughie, all right. Picking on little girls. You should be ashamed of yourself."

Tony bared his teeth at Letty. "For the last time, shut your mouth!" He held the cigarette close to Bailey's face. Heat prickled her cheek, and she braced herself. She would not make a sound this time. "Once more. Where is my crew?"

"Do you believe in karma, young man?" Letty asked in a falsely pleasant tone. "You've got a bucketload of bad stuff coming your way. You can bet your sorry buns it won't be pretty."

Tony growled. "I've had it with you, Grandma! One more word, and you're next." He paused, half turned. "In fact…" He slanted a sly look at Bailey. "Maybe there's more than one way to make this hummingbird sing." He pivoted and strode toward Letty.

Trembling, Bailey gripped the charm at her throat. *Oh no!* He was going to burn Letty! "Wait! Don't hurt her."

Tony stopped in his tracks. "So, you can speak. I was beginning to wonder."

"Hummingbirds don't sing. Don't say a darned word." Letty scowled at the robber, but her voice quavered slightly, revealing the fear undercoating her brave stand. "I'm a lot tougher than him. Had five babies, at home, with nothing but my own grit for the pain."

"Your men are all dead," Bailey declared.

Letty flinched as Tony lowered the glowing cigarette tip toward her wrinkled arm, and a tremor rippled over her. Tony snorted. "Try again." He dangled the cigarette millimeters from Letty's skin. A small gasp escaped, then she pressed her lips determinedly together.

"Stop!" Bailey shook her head. She could not let him hurt her friend. Perhaps it could serve a double purpose. Tony would send Rico to free the others. *And then there was one.* One less armed bad guy for Con and SWAT to handle. "Two are in the rest-rooms down by the main entrance. The other is…" Alarm jangled her nerve endings. Where had Con said he put the guy Nan had knocked out? "He's…uh…" Her memory flashed, wrenching her heart. Con rocking her in his arms, soothing her, while holding back his anger over the attack. Would he ever have the chance to hold her again? "In the bookstore storeroom."

"Rico, go fetch." Tony ordered. "And pick up Jace after you're done."

"You got it. Don't give away my share of the dough while I'm gone. Ha, ha." The burly man who had captured her trotted out.

Letty frowned. "You shouldn't have told him."

"It will be okay." Con had jammed the doors, and getting the men out and unbound would take a while. Hopefully, long enough. She couldn't wait to see SWAT burst inside. She peered expectantly into the stormy darkness beyond the front door, empathizing with every hostage Con and his team had saved over the years. How many people were alive and rejoicing? How many criminals behind bars, thanks to them? Heroes? You bet. Every single one. Every single day. *C'mon, guys. Now would be good.*

An answer to her silent plea came almost immediately, as the blue walkie-talkie at Tony's belt crackled. *Not* the response she'd expected. Tony didn't have a headset, so Con's voice echoed inside the theater. "I'm ready to turn myself in."

The air froze in Bailey's lungs. She couldn't breathe. *No!* Impossible! He'd said he would never do that!

"Sign in, Mr. Mystery Guest," Tony replied, his smile wide and triumphant. "Join the game. It's just getting interesting."

"Release the hostages, first. Me for them. A one-shot deal. Take it or leave it."

Dizziness washed over Bailey and she gripped the edge of the counter to keep from falling. She would rather die right here, right now, than see Con hand himself over to Tony. The grisly trophy of Brian O'Rourke's watch told her the robber would not release Con alive. The man carried a grudge to deadly extremes. Every instinct she possessed cried out in horror.

"Why would I accept those terms? What's to stop me from

offing them right now?" Tony gestured at Bailey with his cigarette. "Starting with cupcake, here?"

Do it. I dare you. She bit back the words. If Tony killed her,
Con would lose his head and charge in, running on blind rage.
And probably get shot.

"Go ahead. You'll die, too." Con paused just long enough to
ramp up the tension. "I'm betting that watch on your wrist says
you want the *satisfaction* of meeting me before you go, DiMarco."

Tony went absolutely still for a moment. Slowly, he nodded.
"I'll be damned. Isn't fate a wily bitch?" Amusement creased his
craggy face. "Satisfaction comes full circle, at last. To which
O'Rourke do I have the honor of speaking?"

Tightly controlled rage simmered in Con's voice. "Conall."

"Ah, the number two son."

"Do we have a deal, DiMarco, or do I storm in there and blow
you to hell?"

"And if you miss?"

"I don't miss." This time, Con's reply was icy calm. "On the
chance I'm having an off night, my brothers will transport your
cold, dead body to the morgue. Makes no difference to me."

Bailey bit her lip. Since Con was speaking over the blue
walkie-talkie, the SWAT team couldn't hear the conversation.
Con must have conveyed his plan before contacting DiMarco.
The fact that his brothers were outside backing him up ignited a
flicker of hope. Aidan, Liam and Grady were as good at their jobs
as Con. If the O'Rourke brothers couldn't get them out of here,
nobody could.

A long, wrenching pause ticked past. Tony flicked ashes from
his cigarette into a dish on the counter. Finally, he spoke. "Deal."

No, no, no! Bailey's mind shrieked as Tony herded the trio of
hostages into the main hallway at gunpoint.

Con sauntered down the opposite side of the corridor, exuding courage, strength and command. Though his posture appeared casual, the planes of his handsome face might have been
cast in granite. His muscles were tense, his lean body alert.
Power and grace, a tiger on the hunt. Sharp resolve glinted in his
dark eyes. His taut jaw worked rhythmically—chewing gum.

Her warrior was in full battle mode.

"Get them moving," he demanded.

"Hands on your head," Tony shouted back.

Con complied, and Tony waved his pistol at Bailey. "Go." Then he trained his gun on Con.

Ensnared in the icy shroud of her most horrifying nightmare, Bailey slowly walked forward. Letty followed, leading a stumbling Mike by the arm. With each step, Bailey walked farther from danger. With each step, the man she loved walked toward it. The man who would sacrifice everything for her. Even his own life.

She couldn't blame him. She understood exactly how he felt. As she passed him, he held her gaze. Across the distance separating them, his dark eyes conveyed love. Sorrow. And something he'd gone to extreme lengths to control. Fear. Not for himself. For her.

"You said you'd never do this," she whispered.

He smiled, a wealth of love shimmering in his gaze. "My heart chooses you."

Her heart broke on a sob. "Turn around. Run!"

"Don't worry, baby. Go hide out till it's all over. It's gonna be a pleasure cruise." He emphasized the last word slightly, and his gaze quickly flickered to the left.

She couldn't dissuade him. Perhaps she could tip the odds somewhat in his favor. "The money cart is armored," she whispered.

"Stop flapping your jaws and keep walking," Tony ordered.

When Bailey reached the bend in the corridor, she turned around. Con shot a glance over his shoulder. His gaze drank her in…one last, lingering look. His face softened with compassion. "I love you," he mouthed. "Be strong." He turned and strode into the theater at the point of Tony's gun.

Inside the theater, DiMarco shoved Con against the wall next to the concession stand and patted him down, then spun him face front. "No weapons. Good boy. Daddy would be proud."

"I stuck to the terms." Con was armed only with his wits and training. The man who had spent the entire night trying to kill him packed a 9mm, and was bulked up, hard and fit. Despite the fact that Con had twenty-plus years on the guy, he would be a formidable combatant.

"You can keep the Kevlar vest, for all the good it will do." DiMarco pressed his weapon to Con's temple. "A head shot followed by a five-mile freefall from the chopper will do the job right."

Con kept his face expressionless. Let the bastard gloat. The freefall wasn't gonna happen, because there was no real chopper. The SWAT team planned to lure the robbers outside and take them down, away from the civilians inside the mall. No chance of stray bullets or escaping bad guys hurting the ex-hostages. It was gonna be close-quarters battle because the snipers couldn't get an accurate shot in this weather. A 9mm point blank to the skull would do the job, though.

DiMarco was combat-honed and battle savvy. If he squeezed off a shot before the team could neutralize him, Con's brains would be spattered all over the parking lot. Con had to take his chances on the ambush distracting DiMarco enough for Con to disarm him and take him down. He refused to consider the not-so-hot odds of survival. He'd saved Bailey, his top priority. He also planned on living through the night. On going home.

DiMarco's dark, contemptuous eyes locked on Con's face. "You look just like your old man."

Con nodded. All the O'Rourke boys resembled their father. "So, you did know him." A man who wore a worthless watch as a trophy for years after the fact had a lot of hatred simmering inside. Con was bargaining DiMarco would want to brag about what he'd done to Con's father before he killed Con.

In fact, he'd bet his life on it.

"Yeah, to my everlasting regret." DiMarco lit up a cigarette and took a deep drag.

Con shuffled the cards and opened the highest stakes poker game of his life. "What does that twisted mind of yours think he did to you?"

"You can't begin to imagine, kid." DiMarco exhaled smoke. "You know, you could have been my son."

Red-hot rage boiled through Con's veins. "My mother wouldn't get near you without a biohazard suit, you freak."

Tony set his cigarette in a dish on the counter beside him. His movements deliberate, he drew back his arm and belted Con across the face. "You'd be surprised what your sainted mother did, back in the day."

Con swiped blood from his mouth with the back of his hand and fought down his rage. Tony's willingness to chat played right into his plan. Many standoffs ended after the suspect aired their grievances with the hostage negotiator. Sometimes, all they wanted was someone to listen. Sometimes, they killed the hostages and/or themselves without anyone learning their motives. DiMarco would never surrender, but he obviously had things he wanted Con to know. All Con had to do was rein in his temper long enough to win the game. He could do that. "What the hell are you insinuating?"

"The truth hurts, kid."

"Yeah?" Con mentally counted minutes. DiMarco was a wild card. If the "chopper" didn't arrive soon, he could blow a gasket and decide to shoot him here and now. Every minute Con kept him talking was another minute he stayed alive. "What's your warped version of the truth?"

"Your dad, mom and I were best friends. Until Maureen chose Brian over me."

"Mom's always been a supremely good judge of character." DiMarco clubbed him again. Con shook off the blow. "So, what happened?"

"I'll tell you. But only because I want you to die with the truth about your 'perfect' parents gnawing at your guts." DiMarco's eyes blazed with righteous indignation, and cold chills shivered up Con's spine. Wild card? The guy was a buttload of fries short of a Happy Meal. A certifiable lunatic. Which made him totally unpredictable. But crazy like a fox. DiMarco had ripped off banks and evaded the cops for nearly a decade—in two different cities. Nuts, but not stupid…a highly lethal combination. Thank God Con had bargained Bailey out of his clutches.

"I can live with that." When all you have is a pair of deuces, bluff like hell.

"Not for long." DiMarco's smile was slow…and nasty. "Maureen and I were an item. I wanted to marry her before I went to war, but didn't figure she would have me without any money. Broads love their diamonds. When we were out on the town, she mentioned a load of medical supplies the hospital had received by accident. That stuff brought big bucks on the black market. Brian borrowed a truck from the motor pool, and loaded up the swag."

"Mom and Pop wouldn't have gone along with that scheme."

"Maureen didn't realize she'd passed on valuable intel. I told Brian that she had arranged for us to deliver the supplies to the airfield for transport to another hospital. I knew he was hot after my girl. He would have done anything for her. To make a long story short…and your life as well…" DiMarco's smiled widened into a chilling grin. "The MPs caught up with us, and I rolled the truck. I told Brian to run, and took off on foot, assuming he would do the same. Only he couldn't, on account of a broken leg."

Con nodded. He knew Pop had broken his leg once upon a time, but had never heard the details. "He got caught."

"Yeah. And didn't rat me out. Big of him, huh? When confronted, he took responsibility rather than implicate Maureen or me."

"You've carried a grudge against Pop for over twenty years for not squealing on you? Color me confused."

Tony hit him again, and Con swore. "I am not your personal punching bag, maggot."

"Just having a little fun before the main event." Tony wiped his knuckles on his shirt. "Nothing happened to Private Goody Two-shoes. The CO was a broad." Tony sneered.

Ah, DiMarco, your cards are marked, and I just figured out how to read 'em. "You have a problem with women in authority?"

"Yeah, Nancy boy, I do. Broads don't know squat about leadership. Even when lives are on the line, they're too friggin' soft-hearted to do what needs to be done."

"Is that right?" Too bad he hadn't seen Bailey flattening his crew member with the Nutcracker.

"Maureen didn't hesitate to bring my name up and proclaim her beloved friend Brian's innocence, but I kept my mouth shut. So Maureen insisted it was a mix-up with the paperwork, and tried to take the blame. The CO knew something was fishy, but couldn't prove a thing. She didn't want to lose a top-notch nurse like Maureen, and she went easy on Brian because she liked him. He'd always been a good little soldier. No black marks on his record. Not to mention that Irish charm. They got the loot back, no harm, no foul." He raised his cigarette, inhaled, and again parked it in the dish. "No laws had actually been broken, so they couldn't press charges. Brian went into the hospital, where Maureen nursed him through recovery and rehab." Tony sneered. "While I went to 'Nam and came back a walking cliché."

Con scowled. DiMarco was bent long before he marched off to war. Millions of men, men like Con's commanding officer, Captain Green, and Syrone served active duty without turning into whack jobs. Every crook Con arrested trotted out the Big Excuse, and whined about it in court. Something to blame for their downfall. Everything but themselves and poor choices. "I still fail to see how this is my father's fault."

"Are you blind, kid? He got caught red-handed, and was rewarded. He turned my woman against me, the only person I've ever loved. Then stole her out from under my nose. He got the gorgeous wife, four sons and a big-shot career as a hero. Me? Nobody ever caught me with my hand in the cookie jar, but I got shipped off to hell. When I came back, instead of being hailed the hero I was, I got spit on. I lost everything. Including my dignity."

"Maybe you should have done the right thing, instead of slinking away. You could have admitted your culpability and taken what was coming to you like he did. Like a man."

"I'm more of a man than he could have ever dreamed of being."

"A legend in your own mind." Con did a covert visual sweep of the exit. No signs of the "chopper." Keep him talking. Raise the stakes. Buy a few more minutes. "Did you follow him to Riverside after Denver fell through?"

"I tracked his whereabouts. Keep your friends close and your enemies closer. Brian finally got what was coming to him. So will you. I'll retire with all this beautiful money, and live the high life. The life I deserve."

"You'll get what you deserve all right." Con stared DiMarco in the eye. Dammit, the slimebag was dancing all around the edge of an outright admission, never tipping his hand. Con hadn't heard any viable evidence, and DiMarco knew it. Crazy, not stupid. "Did you frame and kill my father?"

"I know a rotten apple in the high-and-mighty O'Rourke family tree is unthinkable. It eats at you, doesn't it? Not knowing."

Con gritted his teeth. *Play the game. Ignore the pain.* "I *do* know. I want you to confirm it."

"How does it feel every time you visit that empty grave? Not knowing where his body is? Bet it rips Maureen's heart out." Triple aces on the table.

Agony arrowed into Con's chest. "No, it doesn't," he lied. He'd be damned if he'd give DiMarco the *satisfaction* of losing it. DiMarco hadn't told him a thing he could take to the D.A. All the evidence was circumstantial. All the "testimony" hearsay. Without a body, the murder was impossible to prove, and the bastard knew it. "We know where his soul is. We'll see him again. You won't. You think you went to hell before? Eternity's hottest wiener roast has a standing reservation with your name on the books."

"You hang together pretty good, kid. I've kept my eye on your family all these years. Yep, Daddy *would* be proud. You want more?" He held up his beefy wrist. "See this watch?" The watch Con and his brothers had worked so hard to buy and fix up. The watch he had seen his father wearing on the last day of his life. DiMarco laughed, and bet the pot. "The hands stopped at twelve-forty-nine and thirty seconds. The second I saw Brian O'Rourke depart this world…screaming like a woman."

Con clenched his fists so hard his short nails cut into his palms. He shook with the desire to wrap his fingers around DiMarco's throat and squeeze the breath out of him. *Hold the line, Officer O'Rourke. Stay in the game. For your honor. Your family. For Bailey.* See you and raise you one. "You wouldn't know the truth if it was tattooed on your forehead."

Outside, the sound of whirring blades filled the air. Bright lights cut a swath through the darkness. Con risked a quick glance at the front door. Showtime.

DiMarco patted Con's cheek. *Raise and call.* "The chopper is here. Time to die, kid."

Outside the theater, Bailey watched as Tony tugged a remote from a vest pocket and pointed it at the door. "Explosives disarmed." His lips curled in an evil smile. "As soon as my crew shows up, we're outta here. In case I forget later, be sure to say hello to your father for me. Maybe I'll give my condolences to your mother personally. The lonely widow might be glad to see me."

Terror's sharp talons sunk into Bailey's chest. Once DiMarco's crew returned, she'd be vastly outnumbered. Time to execute her hastily formed plan. What had Con called it earlier? Improvise, modify, adapt, overcome. And pray it worked. She whirled inside and pointed the gun at DiMarco. "Freeze. Drop the weapon."

Con's startled gaze locked on her. His eyes widened and he swore.

DiMarco froze for an instant, then turned his head to stare at her. He grinned and kept the gun pointed at Con's temple. "Look who it is. Charlie's Angel. This isn't the movies, cupcake."

"I'm not acting. Drop it."

"Sure thing. I'm gonna drop my gun for a broad who doesn't even have the heart to kill a spider." DiMarco peered at her. "What the hell is that in your hand?" He squinted. "A toy? A friggin' water gun?" He started to laugh. "What are you gonna do, cupcake, dribble me to death?"

The real gun was tucked into her front waistband, under her sweatshirt. She didn't know how to aim or shoot it, and Con was safer with her bearing the squirt gun. At least if she accidentally shot him with acetic acid, he wouldn't die. He'd left the pack containing the weapons stashed behind a life-size cutout of Tom Cruise at the end of the hallway. Thus, his "pleasure cruise" hint. She knew how his mind worked. He meant for her to take the weapons, hole up with Letty and Mike and hide.

"Are you so sure it's a toy?" Bailey risked a glanced at Con. Once Tony got him outside, he'd kill him. DiMarco would go psycho when he found out the chopper was a decoy and he wasn't escaping with his precious money. He and Rico had claimed the snipers couldn't shoot in this weather. Con was unarmed and unprotected. At the mercy of a madman who would gladly die before surrendering to the police. As Con had said, SBC—suicide by cop.

"Give me a break. I was Black Ops for years. That sorry imitation doesn't fool me."

The gun might not, but she was about to. Good thing Tony didn't know about her and Con. A huge advantage. In his wildest dreams, DiMarco would never have guessed she'd come back for Con. He had another think coming.

She'd be damned if she'd hide and cower while her man died.

"Maybe it's loaded with deadly poison."

"Yeah, right. And I wear women's underwear for thrills."

"What you do for jollies doesn't concern me." Her hands were shaking like leaves in a windstorm, and she sucked in a breath. "Let the officer go and we all walk away with what we want. Your chopper is here, you've got your money. Grab it and leave."

Tony's eyes gleamed with avarice. "Wrong, cupcake. I don't have my satisfaction."

Whatever twisted philosophy he followed, he followed it to the max. A zealot. Her throat had turned into the Sahara, and she tried to moisten her mouth. Zealots did not hesitate to die for their beliefs. And take innocents with them. "If you kill a police officer, they will hunt you to the ends of the earth. You'll never get a chance to spend one dollar of your haul." She attempted to swallow. "Is your satisfaction worth that?"

"Yeah. It is." His obsidian gaze crawled over her body, making her long for a shower. With Lysol bodywash. "You're a real hot number, aren't you?" DiMarco nodded. "Yeah. You really do remind me of that special someone. Instead of killing you both, cupcake and I will get better acquainted."

"Don't touch her, maggot," Con snapped, drawing Tony's attention back to him.

"So, it's like that is it?" Tony smirked. "I've already touched her, and she liked it."

A low growl rumbled in Con's throat, and Tony winked at Bailey, clearly enjoying Con's anger. "You know what kind of piddly ass wages cops make, cupcake? We could have a lot of fun. Bet you've never partied on a tropical island with a rich man."

Con's entire body tensed, and Bailey's heart galloped in her chest. She could not look at him with that big, lethal gun pointed at his head and consider the possibility that he would again put himself between her and the bad guy. There was no Kevlar between the bullets and his brain.

"I'm sorry, Tony. I cannot let you walk out of this theater with him."

"Damn, you are cute when you're riled." Tony's words were playful, his demeanor dead serious. "Okay. I'll shoot him now. I only need one hostage, and you'll be a hell of a lot more fun." She didn't doubt him. He meant to murder Con in cold blood.

Her pulse hammered in her ears so loudly she could barely hear. She was trembling all over. She'd done plenty of things tonight she hadn't thought herself capable of. But looking into Tony's eyes and making a cold, calculated decision was different. Hurting, possibly killing another human being, even a vile criminal, was much harder when done in chilling reality. Without the fight-or-flight instinct thrumming in her veins. Without her immediate survival at stake. Con made this decision every day. Then lived with the consequences. How did he do it?

"Bailey." Con's low hail was soft, and deathly quiet. His glowing mahogany gaze caressed her, cherished her, his most treasured possession. "It's okay, baby. I love you for who you are. Always."

Tears stung her eyes and a lump swelled in her throat. Con was staring into the jaws of death…and telling her that even if she didn't have the courage to save him, he understood. And loved her anyway.

Bailey blinked back the tears. She'd found her courage hours ago, wrapped in the faith of the man she loved. A man who loved her in return. Unconditionally. Protecting your loved ones wasn't a burden. It was a privilege.

She sent a silent message to Con. *My heart chooses you.*

His full lips wobbled for a brief second, and then he pressed them into a firm line. His gaze embraced her. Message received.

She cocked her head at Tony. She only needed the gun at Con's temple to waver for a moment. "I'll go with you. But I have three conditions." On the word three, she flashed a quick glance at Con.

Con's eyes flickered in recognition. As DiMarco chuckled and again puffed his cigarette, Bailey shifted and brushed her free hand over the front of her sweatshirt. The casual motion looked like she'd merely adjusted her stance. But in reality, she'd signaled Con, telling him where she'd hidden the pistol.

Tony returned his smoldering cigarette to the dish. "I can't wait to hear this."

"One." She did not look at Con, but felt the weight of his intent gaze focused on her. He would do his job. Now, she had to do hers. She watched DiMarco. She wanted, needed his complete attention. "Let the cop go. Alive. We don't need him, and I don't relish becoming a raccoon for the FBI bloodhounds." He wouldn't even consider it, but that didn't matter.

"But he *loves* you," Tony mocked. *"Always."*

"Mom always said it was as easy to love a rich man as a poor one." Ellen Chambers *had* preached that sermon. At least once a week. "I guess she was right." *Not.* Bailey shrugged. Though she feigned nonchalance, every nerve in her body shrieked and cold sweat dampened her skin.

"Typical broad." DiMarco snorted at Con. "What'd I tell ya? They never come through in the clinch. She's throwing you to the wolves for the money, kid. Dying should come as a relief."

"Two." *Broad?* She'd show DiMarco a broad who came through for her man. Bailey swallowed hard and tried to stop shaking. *Stay balanced. Hit the target the very first time.* If she missed, Con died. "About the money. We leave your crew, and split the take."

Tony grinned. "Enterprising little hummingbird, aren't you? That point is negotiable…we'll discuss it later. What's your third condition, cupcake?"

Bailey shifted the water gun from her right hand to her left.

Her fingers tightened on the grip. Her stomach rolled and nausea rose in her throat.

Con's heightened state of alertness hummed in the silence, like a live wire connecting him to her. She had the eerie sensation she could read his thoughts and he, hers. As if they were one person, sharing one mind.

Their survival in the next few seconds depended on it.

She knew the power of the weapon she held. The primal, instinctive fear it inspired. A fear that overrode reason. She knew its ability to maim, to kill.

To scar.

She harnessed the dragon and rode it into battle.

"Three." Before the word completely cleared her mouth, she aimed the water gun at the cigarette and pumped the trigger. Fire exploded from the dish and crackled up Tony's arm. He screamed and flailed. An instant later, she yanked the pistol from her waistband with her right hand and tossed it to Con.

He caught the weapon on the fly, and barked, "Down!" She hit the floor facedown. Two gunshots roared in fast succession.

Then all hell broke loose.

Tony's crew tore into the theater, weapons drawn. Con shoved the money cart in front of her, then his body slammed on top of hers, sheltering her. All eight theater doors imploded with a huge crash and the SWAT team stormed inside. A brilliant light flashed, blinding her. A deafening boom shook the building. Choking, sulfurous smoke roiled, burning her throat and making her gag. She couldn't see, couldn't breathe. Could only listen and pray.

Boot steps thundered, vibrating the floor. Men's deep voices shouted. "Down! Get on the floor! Everybody on the floor!"

Gunshots exploded, bullets whined.

On top of her, Con fired his gun. A series of clicks sounded in fast succession, and his weight settled more firmly. He must be out of ammo. Suddenly, his body jerked. Thick, warm liquid soaked her sweatshirt. The coppery tang of blood assaulted her nostrils.

Con's blood.

Chapter 15

"Con!" Bailey's scream was lost in the turmoil. She struggled to roll over, but his body pinned her to the floor. In the thundering, smoky melee, she couldn't tell if he was purposely holding her down, or if he was merely dead weight on top of her.

Her throat closed up in horror. Dead weight. *Dear Lord.*

"Clear!" Eight different deep male voices boomed. "Clear!"

Boot steps trampled the carpet. More shouting. Con's weight lifted. Seconds later, a man's strong arms scooped her up and carried her through the thick, swirling haze. She coughed and gagged, battling to catch her breath. Involuntary tears streamed down her face, and she couldn't see who held her.

Every shrieking instinct proclaimed it wasn't Con.

She had to find him! Bailey beat her fists against the man's Kevlar vest and struggled to escape. One big hand captured hers and his hold tightened, immobilizing her. She blinked rapidly and squinted up at him. He wore a black helmet, with the faceplate lowered against the smoggy gloom. A blue-and-gold patch rode on the upper arm of his black uniform. SWAT. One of the good guys.

Where was Con?

Her rescuer swept her outside, and sharp, cold air slapped her face. Stinging pellets of freezing rain struck her skin. She sucked in desperate breaths, exhaling the noxious smoke. The man whisked her past a row of lit ambulances. Raised stretchers inside the open vehicles held bleeding bank robbers and police officers, surrounded by gun-wielding cops and busy paramedics. Uniformed police and SWAT team members shouted and sprinted past in the swirling sleet. In the wet, white pandemonium, everywhere she looked, she saw the red gleam of blood.

She caught a brief glimpse of Liam and Aidan bent over a cop on a stretcher. Grady leaned close to the patient, his face grave, his movements rapid and precise. Her rescuer quickly turned aside, his body blocking her view.

"Con!" She fought the man's iron hold. "Put me down!"

He shifted, holding her more securely. "Medic," he roared. He strode to the last ambulance in line and stepped inside, then laid her on a stretcher.

Bailey sat up. "Let me go!"

"Easy." One big hand tugged off his helmet, while the other urged her back down. Hunter Garrett's tawny mane spilled to his shoulders as he leaned over her. "I'm not gonna hurt you." He stuck his head out the door and again shouted for a medic. None came, and he muttered under his breath.

She fought his restraining hold. "I need to get to Con!"

"His brothers have him." His soft Carolina drawl was kind, his blue-gray eyes implacable. "Stay still. You're bleeding."

A sob caught in her burning throat. "It's Con's blood."

"All right." He grabbed a pair of scissors and cut off her shirts, leaving her in the lacy camisole. "Just let me check."

Chilly air washed over her and she shivered. Couldn't stop shivering. "How badly wounded is he? Tell me!"

"I don't know, honey. Sorry." He wiped her arm and shoulder with a damp cloth. The white cotton came away streaked with red. Con's blood. Hot anguish balled in her chest. Hunter set the cloth aside. He cupped her chin in his broad palm. "Look at me. Con will get the best possible medical attention." He studied her eyes, her face. "Now calm down and talk to me. Do you hurt anywhere?"

Yes. My heart has been ripped out. She shook her head.

His quick, impersonal hands skimmed her limbs, her ribs, before tucking a blanket around her trembling body. His gentle fingers brushed aside her hair. "DiMarco burned you."

Con! Please be all right. "It doesn't matter."

Hunter's square jaw tightened. "It does to me." He applied soothing ointment, followed by a bandage. "There. Is that better?"

She sat up, shoving aside the blanket. "You have to let me go to Con!"

"I can't do that. The best thing for him right now is for you to stay calm and let me take care of you." He encircled her wrist to check her pulse.

"Hunter." She gripped his vest straps in both hands and yanked, bringing the surprised cop nose-to-nose. "Take me to Con this instant, or I will—"

"Playing doctor with my woman, Garrett?" Con's deep voice asked from outside.

Bailey's heart stuttered on a surge of wild relief. "Con!" She scrambled past Hunter.

Con stood outside, his arms spread wide. "Come here, darlin'."

She leaped out of the ambulance, into his waiting arms. Tangled emotions—held at bay too long—slammed against the battered wall of her composure. Overwhelmed, she burst into tears.

Warm, vital, alive, Con held her tight. "Easy, baby. It's all right. I'm here."

Clinging to him, she sobbed. "You were shot. There was b-blood all over. I th—thought you w-were dead!"

"I'm sorry, darlin'. I tried to get to you." He stroked her hair. "A round ricocheted off the cart and grazed my scalp. Dazed me for a second. Liam and Aidan grabbed me and hauled me to the ambulance. They held me down while Grady checked me out and bandaged the wound. Took both of 'em to do it, too, the swine. I have to stop in at the ER for stitches on the way home."

"Your poor head." He was all right! Why couldn't she stop crying? Tears streaming down her face, she tried to pull away. "L-let go, I'll hurt you."

Con wouldn't release her. "It's nothing. A scratch."

"A scratch that b-bled all over? Th—that's what you always s-say."

"That's all it is. Hey, now. You're shaking so hard, your bones are rattling." He swept her off her feet and stepped into the ambulance. Sometime in the last few minutes, Hunter had faded into the storm. Con eased her down on the edge of the stretcher and wrapped the blanket around her shoulders. He sat and again took her into his embrace. "Are you all right?"

"N-no. Y-yes," she sobbed. "I don't k-know."

He rubbed her back in slow circles. "You've had a rough time. Just let it out. Let go. I'm here."

She rested her cheek on his wide chest and the night's trauma poured out of her in wracking sobs. She cried for all she'd lost. For what she'd gained. For what she'd done, and everything she'd left undone. "I—I'm s-sorry. I—I'm such a w-wimp."

"You're anything but. It's a natural reaction after all you've been through." Con held her close, murmuring comfort. "Crying will make you feel better."

"Y-you d-don't c-cry."

He chuckled. "No, but I'll probably go a hundred rounds with the punching bag tomorrow. Everybody has to purge strong emotions, sweetheart. Even cops. Well...wise cops."

Con gently rocked Bailey as she cried. He calmed and soothed, while fighting growing dread. Her sobs didn't worry him; tears were a healthy response after a crisis. He'd be far more concerned if she acted cool and detached. What had him on the ropes were the long-term consequences. Bailey had held her own during an ordeal that would have wigged out most people. Without her intelligence and courage, he might be going home in a body bag. He didn't doubt she loved him—enough to sacrifice her own life.

But tonight, she'd lived through combat. Waded knee-deep in bullets, blood and death. His tenderhearted girl had been forced to hurt another human being with cold, premeditated violence. If that wasn't enough horror, she'd seen him get shot, and had thought he was dead. Even if the other events hadn't traumatized her beyond bearing, that could be the final nail in the coffin of their relationship. He couldn't blame his brothers, they hadn't known how badly he was hurt. But in trying to save his life, they might have snatched away everything that mattered.

Bailey shuddered, and he held her tighter, continuing to rock. She wouldn't stay with him if he resigned from the team, she'd made that perfectly clear. Every time he donned his uniform, holstered his weapon…every time he walked out the door, she would remember. She would know. She didn't have to imagine the hazards of his job anymore, hell, she'd experienced them up close and personal. Could she live with that?

His stomach clenched. Would she want to?

He patted her back. Her sobs were slowing, becoming quieter. "C'mon, darlin'. I'll take you home."

She sniffed, and wiped away tears with the back of her hand. "Don't you have to do paperwork or something?"

He smiled in spite of his inner turmoil. Leave it to his practical girl to remember duty in the midst of mayhem. She must be feeling more stable. "Yeah, reams of it. You'll have to give a statement, too." He wrapped the blanket more snugly around her slender shoulders as they climbed out of the ambulance and cold sleet smacked them in the face. A thick layer of ice crunched under his boots and coated everything with a silver sheen. "But not tonight. I doubt any of us are coherent enough." His grin widened. "Except Letty. I heard her bending Wyatt's ear about DiMarco outside the ambulance when Grady was doing his doctor impersonation. Good thing Wyatt has negotiator training."

Bailey jerked to an abrupt halt in the center of the melee. Several ambulances had departed. Others lingered while medics stabilized casualties. Police officers and SWAT teams swarmed the parking lot and adjacent mall. Yellow crime scene tape around the perimeter flapped in the bitter wind. She hugged the blanket tighter. "DiMarco…" She hesitated. "Is he…did we kill him?"

"I don't know. I can check once we get home, if you want." He glanced at her pale profile, as white and translucent as the snow drifting against the building, and a band of pain constricted his chest. How would she react if they *had* killed DiMarco? Would she be able to recover? Post-traumatic stress took good cops out of action. Men who were trained to deal with violence and death. Bailey didn't have the resources to deal with that enemy.

"Yes." He could barely hear her low reply. "I need to know."

"Yo! Irish!" Syrone's shout hailed Con from inside an ambulance.

Con kept one arm around Bailey as they hurried over. Syrone

was propped up on a stretcher. IV tubing snaked from one arm, and a BP cuff dangled from the other. Con patted the big man's leg. "Hey, buddy! How's it hanging?" He didn't bother to disguise the deep emotion simmering beneath the lighthearted greeting.

"Low and mighty, thanks to both of you." Syrone's gaze held Con's and the men exchanged unspoken respect. Each knew the night had brought them both too close to the Grim Reaper. "Considering."

"You need me to contact Jazelle?"

"Nah, she's meeting me at the hospital. Liam sent a squad car for her. He and Murphy found me. Man, I have never been so glad to see that hound dog. And the German Shepherd, too." Chuckling, Syrone gestured at the leather jacket draped over the stretcher. "Couldn't let them haul me off without delivering this."

Con picked up the coat, his heartbeat thundering in his ears. Hours ago, Bailey hadn't wanted the ring tucked in the pocket. Tonight's events had probably massacred any chance he'd had of changing her mind. "Thanks. I appreciate it."

"Hey, Bailey." Syrone's wide smile flashed. "You're look-ing fine."

"Ha." She self-consciously smoothed her tousled curls. "What's in that IV, Ecstasy?" Weariness tugged at her wan smile. "Get well quickly. The mall won't be the same without you."

"Aw, go on." Syrone waved a broad hand at Con. "Get your woman outta this dump. Take her someplace warm and friendly."

"That's the plan." He hoped.

Con draped his jacket over the blanket covering Bailey's shoulders. They turned and walked down the row of occupied ambulances. Bailey kept her face averted. As they reached the last ambulance, Con gave her a gentle squeeze. "Look, sweetheart."

She turned. A stretcher bearing Nan was being loaded into the back. Nan's husband Brad hovered protectively alongside, cra-dling his daughter in his arms. Nan waved and blew them a kiss.

Con glanced at Brad, cuddling the baby, and then at Bailey. Purple bruises in the shape of a handprint marred her pale cheek. His throat tightened. He hadn't noticed that before. He leaned over and brushed a soft kiss on the marks. She glanced up, her eyes wide and wounded, and his throat closed up completely. He'd imagined himself by her side as she brought their children into the world. With each passing moment, his hopes and dreams seemed to fade farther from the realm of possibility. His hands fisted. DiMarco had not only murdered his father, he might also have succeeded in killing Con's future.

They continued the slippery journey across the dark parking lot. He'd parked his truck on the outer perimeter so she wouldn't spot him when she left work. Her shoulders sagged beneath his supporting arm, and she stumbled several times. His poor darlin' had to be running on fumes.

They'd just reached the crime scene tape when running boot steps sounded behind them. "Hey, bro!" Aidan yelled.

Con stopped, turned. "What's up?"

Aidan skidded to a halt. He had Bailey's purse in one hand and the pitcher of pink roses in the other. "Liam and Murphy found these in the bookstore during their sweep. The mall will be closed for days while CSI does their thing, and Bailey needs her stuff."

Con resisted the urge to groan as Bailey tucked her purse under her arm. Subtlety wasn't an outstanding trait in the O'Rourke family. Aidan and Liam must have discussed Con's dilemma and the resulting flower purchase. Hell, Grady was probably in on it, too. He should be grateful his brothers thought Bailey was perfect for him and had embraced her as one of their own. But their matchmaking efforts were nearly as zealous as Letty's.

Aidan offered Bailey the roses. "A shame to let these wilt and die in a deserted mall."

Bailey's hands shook as she accepted the bouquet. The fragile petals trembled in the wind's icy bite before she tucked them under the blanket. Bailey looked as frail and easy to destroy as the flowers, and Con's heart ached. Their relationship might have withered and died in that mall. He shook off the thought. Not the time or the place. He had to shove aside his anxiety and focus on Bailey's needs. She wouldn't be up to a discussion for several days, at least.

Aidan hesitated. "Bailey, your mom is in the command center across the street. She wants to see you. This incident shook her up pretty badly."

Bailey nodded. "I imagine it did."

"I'll take Bailey over before I head to the hospital." Con drew her close, sheltering her against his body. "Aidan, what's DiMarco's status?"

"Second-degree burns and gunshot wounds. He's on the way to Mercy Hospital." Aidan's gaze assessed Bailey. "How are you holding up?"

"Okay, thanks."

Aidan nodded, a gesture of respect. "Incredible job in there."

Her subdued reply was barely discernable. "I just did what I had to."

"Don't kid yourself." Aidan's face grew serious. "Because of you, my brother walked out instead of being carried out."

Bailey stiffened. "He did the same for me."

Con narrowed his eyes at Aidan in warning. Him dying was the last thing he wanted her to think about. He attempted to steer the conversation to safer ground. "If I recall, you and Liam dragged me out. In fact, one of you apes had ahold of my hair." He grimaced. "What's left of it that Grady didn't shave off."

The brother in question suddenly appeared out of the swirling storm. "Taking my name in vain again, I see. Think you're getting away with driving yourself to the hospital? Think again."

"I'm fine." Con frowned. So that's why Aidan was stalling him. It *was* a conspiracy. "I wouldn't risk it, otherwise."

"The E.R. doc will be the judge of that. Until you get his okay, you're not driving."

"Yes, Mom." Con rolled his eyes. "Remember, bro, paybacks are hell."

Grady smirked. "Looking forward to it. Get your butt in the truck."

Aidan's grin flashed. "Now that your chauffeur has arrived, I've gotta run." With a final wave, he sprinted away. As commanding officer, he'd be on-site the rest of the night and most of the following day.

Con lifted the yellow tape so Bailey could duck underneath. Followed by Grady, they finally climbed into his pickup.

Several hours later, they walked out of the hospital, with Con the disgusted owner of six stitches. His CAT scan and vitals were good, and he'd refused pain meds, so he was cleared to drive. Bailey had checked out fine.

Ellen Chambers had insisted on following them to the hospital. She and Bailey had engaged in a heated discussion in the waiting area while he had his scan. By the time it was over, Ellen was gone and Bailey was even paler than before.

Inside the truck, Con started the engine and turned the heater on full blast. "The windshield will take a minute or two to clear." He touched Bailey's arm, offering comfort. "Uh…everything go okay with your mom?"

"Surprisingly, after the first few hairy minutes, yes. She actually admitted she was grateful to you for keeping me alive." She slumped in the seat, both her fatigue and her relief palpable. "She wanted to stay, but respected my need for you and I to have privacy, and agreed to wait until tomorrow to talk."

Not sure what to make of that development, he stared out the frost-patched window at the dark, icy landscape. "Maybe she's coming around." He tried to ignore the other possibility clanging painfully inside his skull. If Bailey planned to break up with him for good, maybe Dr. Chambers's willingness to leave simply meant Mommy dearest would get what she wanted sooner.

"Maybe. I hope so. I'm glad she didn't kick up more of a fuss. I honestly expected her to." Bailey sighed. "I'm too beat to even begin to decipher her sudden about-face tonight." She leaned her head back against the seat. "What was that explosion when the SWAT team burst inside the theater? I thought DiMarco disarmed the doors."

"He did. It was a flash-bang grenade. SOP for dynamic entry." The windshield had finally cleared, and he reached across and buckled her seat belt. "The brilliant light and loud kaboom scrambles the senses. The shock factor gives SWAT time to neutralize the bad guys. And the smoke provides cover."

"Oh," she replied in a listless tone.

He glanced at her in concern. He needed to get her home ASAP. He'd tried to send her home with her mother, but she'd refused. "I'm sorry you worried about me, sweetheart. My brothers were just looking out for my welfare. They didn't know how bad of a hit I'd sustained. Sometimes mortally wounded people don't even realize they're injured. Adrenaline blocks the pain."

He released the emergency brake, and slowly drove out of the parking lot and onto the icy street. "Aidan and Liam knew you'd be taken care of. We're briefed on the situation before going in, and each team member is assigned a specific duty."

"Hunter took good care of me. Even if he wouldn't let me go to you," she added in a grievous tone.

"You looked like you were about to hurt him."

"Darned right. I was afraid you were…" She choked.

Yeah, and it wouldn't tilt the odds in his favor. His hands tightened on the steering wheel. "Don't dwell on that. We're both okay, and that's what matters." The moment of reckoning would arrive all too soon.

She didn't say another word all the way to her place. Con parked in the small lot behind her building. Had she fallen asleep? He grabbed his nylon gym bag from behind the seat before striding around to the passenger side and opening the door. He'd planned on the two of them spending the night together at the Ambassador Hotel and had packed accordingly.

She stared straight ahead, her expression dazed, and he touched her arm. "Let's get you inside."

He tried to carry her, but she refused. He supported most of her weight as he helped her to the top-floor apartment of the converted Victorian house. He held the vase of roses while she fumbled in her purse for the key. Good thing Liam and Aidan had been on the ball or he would have had to kick in the door. And wouldn't that have gone over well?

Inside, she flicked the light switch. Nothing happened. She groaned. "The electricity is out. I'm glad I have gas appliances, because I am not waiting one more minute for a hot shower."

"Is that the best idea? You're nearly out on your feet—" He

broke off at her cranky scowl. "On second thought, it will probably make you feel better."

She trudged toward the bathroom, then turned back. "Con? Don't leave."

He wasn't about to leave her in this condition. "I'm not going anywhere."

Her teeth worried her lower lip. "We need to talk."

The emotions he'd been stonewalling whammed him in a rush of dread. "I know." Heart sinking, he headed into her bedroom. They *would* talk. But not before she had a chance to rest.

Luckily, Bailey the romantic had candles all over the apartment. Even better, there was a fireplace in her bedroom. Bless the Victorians and their lack of technology. He set the roses on the nightstand alongside a stack of books, dropped his bag beside it, and then built a roaring blaze.

Firelight washed the pearl gray walls, and the chilly room warmed. Bailey floated out of the attached bathroom in a cloud of rose-petal-scented vapor. Carrying his leather jacket in one hand, she wore a long, cream silk nightgown that left her arms bare. Damp, golden-red curls, brighter than the crackling flames, spilled over her shoulders. Her sleepy blue eyes reflected the glowing light. His breath jammed in his lungs. His goddess. Aphrodite rising from the misty sea.

She draped his jacket over a gray upholstered chair beside the queen-size bed, and said something. He saw her sweet mouth move, heard her low, musical voice, but the words did not compute. She cocked her head. "Con?"

He blinked away the sensual haze. "Sorry, what did you say?"

Her tired smile was patient. "I left you plenty of hot water."

Along with stonewalling his emotions, he'd been ignoring the aches and pains stabbing his fatigued muscles. He was operating on adrenaline dregs and stubborn Irish determination. When he finally crashed, he was gonna hit hard and fast. Not to mention, he probably smelled like Letty's bulldog, Jean Claude. A shower wasn't a bad idea. He turned down the pale gray comforter on the bed and patted the inviting mauve satin sheets. "Hop in. I'll just be a couple minutes. Then I'll fix you something to eat."

Con carried his bag into the bathroom. A huge, old-fashioned claw-footed tub sat in an alcove surrounded on three sides by a glass block partition. Dozens of candles on a shelf behind the tub flickered pinpoints of light along the mauve walls. He made quick use of the separate shower on the other side of the partition. After checking the stitches on his scalp in the mirror—crap, he now had a distinctive part in his hair—he replaced the bandage on his forehead. Then he brushed his teeth and shaved.

When he strode out of the bathroom and into the bedroom, the bed was empty. Barefoot, he tugged the hem of his dark green cotton shirt over his clean jeans and followed muffled sounds to the kitchen. Candles on the counter shone with soft, muted light. Bailey glanced up from stirring a pan of scrambled eggs at the gas stove, and he frowned. "Hey, I was going to do that."

"You're wiped out, too." Her fingertips brushed the bandage on his forehead. "Not to mention injured."

He opened his mouth to speak. She pressed her fingers to his lips, and his muscles tightened with the urge to kiss her fingertips, the soft skin on the back of her hand, her warm palm. He fought down his need. He could not touch her unless she told him she was his. Exhausted and vulnerable, they could easily start out seeking comfort and end up doing something she would regret.

"If you're about to say, 'it's just a scratch,' be warned. I'll clobber you with the frying pan." She didn't look like she was kidding. Con bit back the words. He made toast and put on the teakettle so she could have peppermint tea.

When the eggs were done, they dished up two plates. She steeped tea, he poured orange juice for himself. They moved in perfect tandem in the small kitchen, as smoothly as if they'd lived and worked side-by-side for years.

Bailey exhaled softly. "I don't have enough energy to sit at the table."

They walked into the bedroom. She set her plate and mug on the nightstand and slid into bed. Con put his food on the opposite nightstand, and started to remove his jacket from the chair. Bailey patted the sheets. "No way. You're as tired as I am."

He climbed into bed, careful to keep his distance. She wanted reassurance, nothing more. Even so, his pulse kicked up. And he'd thought working so close to her in the cozy kitchen was torture.

They consumed their meals in silence, too hungry and exhausted for conversation. Bailey started to get up with the empty dishes, but he blocked her with his forearm. "Let me."

She fell back against the pillows. "All right. But when you get back, we talk. We need this settled. Once and for all."

His stomach flip-flopped. "Right." He'd wanted her to rest first, but she seemed determined to have her say. He gritted his teeth against a backlash of pain. *Once and for all.* He prayed all the way to the kitchen her words weren't prophetic.

Nerves jittering, he cat-footed back to the bedroom. Outside the door, he braced himself. No matter what she'd decided, he had to accept it. He didn't have any arguments left. She'd seen and experienced the violence, the pain of his world firsthand. If she didn't want to share it, he couldn't blame her.

Braced for the worst, he walked through the door. "I'm ready—" He jolted to a stop. She was curled on her side...sound asleep.

So this was what death-row inmates felt like when the warden called at the last minute. Relief warred with disappointment. Had impending doom been merely forestalled? Or had he just missed out on receiving his heart's desire?

He stripped off his clothes and changed into a pair of black cotton drawstring pants. Yes or no? Heartbreak or joy? Hearing the verdict had to wait.

He briefly considered sacking out on the couch, and dismissed it. If bad dreams assaulted her, he wanted to be nearby. The chair? Every exhausted, aching cell in his body protested. And she *had* invited him into her bed. To rest.

Con slipped under the covers beside the woman who owned him, body and soul. He could not keep from curving himself protectively around her. He draped a careful arm across her waist. Holding her close, pain slammed into him as he breathed in her rose-petal and peppermint scent.

Maybe for the very last time.

Chapter 16

Con lay propped on one elbow, watching Bailey slumber. Bad dreams had disturbed her several times during the past few hours. He'd comforted her cries, and she'd finally succumbed to deep, dreamless sleep.

He'd awakened thirty minutes ago and slipped out of bed to stoke the fire. When he'd returned, Bailey had rolled onto her back, but continued sleeping. Her shiny curls glowed in the firelight. Long eyelashes curved in coppery crescents on her sleep-warmed cheeks. Slow breaths sighed from her softly parted pink lips. The bruises on her cheek had darkened, and the bandage on her neck looked harshly out of place on her creamy skin. Stark evidence of DiMarco's cruelty to the most gentle, loving woman on the planet.

Con fought down a hot surge of anger. He needed to stay cool and levelheaded. Needed every cylinder firing at full capacity for the looming discussion. Needed all his strength to walk away from her if she demanded he leave forever. He drank in the sight of her sleeping beside him, barricading the memory deep in his heart. For now, for a stolen moment in time, she was his to love. To cherish.

All too soon, she stirred, and her long eyelashes floated up. Apprehension jittered up his spine. *Reprieve over, pal.*

Her puzzled blue eyes stared at him. She blinked. "Am I dreaming?"

He swallowed the lump in his throat. "No. I'm here." For the moment.

She glanced at the gloom crowding the lace-curtained windows. "I went to sleep."

"Yeah, that happens." Especially when you'd been hunted down like an animal for fifteen hours by gun-wielding killers.

She stretched, and her silky calf slid over his foot. A mere innocent brush of skin on skin, but his body instantly went rock hard. He jerked his foot away like she'd burned him. So much for cool and levelheaded. She yawned. "How long have we been asleep?"

"A couple hours." Outside, the wind howled and sleet pattered the windowpanes. "It's still storming."

"Mmm." She turned on her side facing him and snuggled against him. "It's nice. Like being in a safe, cozy nest."

She wasn't nearly as safe as she thought, with her soft, sweet smelling body snuggled so close. Battling the overwhelming urge to kiss her, touch her, to make her his, he eased away.

"Where are you going?" She again moved close.

"Sorry, darlin', my self-control only extends so far." And raging hunger was rapidly consuming what little he had left.

The slow, trusting curve of her lips was as tempting as a banquet to a starving beggar. She chuckled. "That's a bad thing?"

He didn't respond, and she studied his somber face. "What's wrong?"

"Nothing is settled between us."

She frowned, her expression confused. "What?" Her eyes widened. "Oh! I fell asleep too fast." She flung her arms around him. "I love you!"

"I love you, too, baby. We've already established that." The consolation prize before the big bad news. She'd told him she loved him in the diner. Then broken up with him. He seemed to have forgotten how to breathe. He inhaled sharply. Since when did breathing hurt? "It didn't stop you from breaking up with me yesterday morning."

"Oh, Con." Tears pooled in her eyes. "I never wanted to hurt you. I'm sorry."

Agony slashed through him. The moment of reckoning. The thought of never seeing her again shredded his insides worse then he'd ever imagined, as if he'd eaten ground glass. "Sorry because you have to tell me to leave?"

She gasped. "No! Stay!" Her arms tightened. "Don't go."

Stay? Temporarily, to help her deal with the trauma...or for the long haul? "Be honest with me, darlin', I can take it. After last night, can you be with me?"

"After last night, I can't be without you." She tenderly cupped his face. "You belong to me, and I belong to you."

Pressure burned behind his eyes. His throat felt tight, raw, and he swallowed hard, not yet able to believe. "Will it eventually drive a wedge between us? Will you resent me, because you had to hurt someone on my behalf?"

She shook her head. "Absolutely not. I'm sorry it happened, and I'll never forget what I had to do. But if DiMarco had let you go and walked away, he wouldn't have been hurt. He chose his own fate." She stroked Con's face. "If I hadn't stopped him, he would have killed you. It's impossible to bargain with evil or compromise with corruption. I can live with my decision."

A tiny spiral of hope glittered to life. "You can live with it, but will it haunt you?"

"Remember when you said you still see the face of every man you've killed in the line of duty?" He nodded, and she continued. "That's the difference between us and them. It's easy for criminals to kill; they don't think twice about taking a life." Her smile was gentle. "When it haunts you...that's how you know you're one of the good guys."

The constriction in his chest loosened. She understood the choices he faced every day. She had no doubts they'd both done the right thing. What an amazingly generous, intelligent woman.

Breathe. One more hurdle to jump. "What about seeing me shot, thinking I was dead? Can you live with that, day after day?"

"It's an awful feeling I never want to experience again." Bailey bit her lip. "However, you were right all along. All my planning was my way of trying to maintain control." She snorted. "Ha! There's no such thing. From now on, I will live in the moment. Live every moment. Every second with you is precious." She drew a shaky breath. "I won't waste any more energy worrying. If you're hurt...or worse...on the job, *then* I'll deal with it."

He held her gaze. "I promise, Bailey, I will do my damnedest to come home to you every night. I won't try to be a hero."

"You already are. And you know what?" She touched the bandage on his forehead. "The world needs heroes."

Hope soared into joy. He feathered his fingers through her silky curls. "No scars, darlin'?" he whispered.

Her smile widened. "Not a one." She pointed at a thick volume on the nightstand. "There's a quote in there by Noela Evans. 'Challenge is a dragon with a gift in its mouth. Tame the dragon, and the gift is yours.'" She paused. "I didn't understand it before, but I do now. I faced down my worst fears…and conquered them. The privilege of sharing one day with you is worth risking the pain of a lifetime without you." Firelight flickered in her eyes. Within the warm blue depths he saw wisdom. Resolve. Complete peace. "Con…you're my gift."

His heart melted. He'd waited, longed for the moment when she would completely accept him for who and what he was. Once upon a time, he'd thought her as delicate as his mother's porcelain dolls. But this woman possessed strength and fortitude beyond imagining. He would never doubt, never underestimate her again.

She studied him, her gaze somber. "So, are we okay?"

He grinned, relief and happiness making him feel like he was floating. "Better than okay, baby."

"Good." Her copper brows arched. "Because I think it's about time you made love to me."

Air exploded from his lungs. "Whoa! Where did that come from?"

She trailed a fingertip along his jaw, down his throat. He shivered under the sensual torture. "From the depths of my heart."

His body thought it was a damn fine idea. His brain wondered if she was well enough. She'd been through the wringer tonight. "Don't you want to wait until you're feeling better? Until—"

She stopped him with gentle fingers on his mouth. "I'm tired of waiting. We've waited long enough." She grinned impishly. "Who knows? There could be a giant, fiery meteor headed our way this very minute." She replaced her fingers with her lips and kissed him, as hungry for his taste as he was for hers.

Brilliant stars burst inside his head. "Well, when you put it that way…" He kicked off the comforter. Between the fire crackling in the fireplace and the sparks crackling in his blood, it was plenty hot. And he wanted lots of room to maneuver.

"Oh!" She gasped, and he followed her horrified gaze downward, to the three black-and-purple bruises mottling his chest. "What happened?"

"It's where the Kevlar vest absorbed the rounds. No biggie."

"Thank God for Kevlar." She bent and tenderly kissed each bruise. "My poor baby."

Wherever her soft, moist mouth touched, his skin jumped and quivered in reaction. "On second thought, it kinda hurts here, too." He pointed to his forehead, and she brushed her lips along his dark brow. "And here." He touched his bottom lip.

She giggled. "There's nothing wrong with your lips." But she bestowed a kiss there, anyway.

"Mmm. I like your lips, too." He slid his fingers into her hair and deepened the kiss, drinking in warm, willing woman and peppermint.

She caressed his shoulders, chest, then moved lower to his abs and stomach. He rolled to his back and let her explore. In spite of her lack of experience, she'd never been timid about touching him. Knowing her, she'd conducted meticulous research. His girl was thorough with every detail.

Hoo boy! He hissed in delight. Whatever books she'd been reading, he highly recommended them. His pulse kicked up and he fisted his hands. He wanted to pounce and devour her. Instead, he slowly released his breath. Forced himself to lie still. *Don't go all caveman and scare her. Go slow. Be careful.*

The snap and sizzle of the flames faded as his world narrowed to only her. Her lovely face swam in his vision. Her uneven breathing sighed in his ears. Her intoxicating scent dizzied his senses. *Heaven.*

"I love your body." She sighed, planting tiny kisses all over his chest. Her hair trailed over his torso, cool silk teasing his fevered skin. "So different from mine. All fascinating planes and angles. So strong, so hard."

Con laughed. "Yeah, and getting harder by the minute."

"I also love knowing I turn you on." She grinned. "It makes me drunk with power."

"You should be staggering, then." He returned her grin. "By all means, have another round on me, darlin'."

Bailey slid her palms up Con's broad chest, reveling in his response. His body was a thrilling playground of contrasting sensation. Smooth, hot skin. Sinewy muscles. Crisp hair that tickled her fingertips. She kissed a meandering path from his ridged abs to his neck. His skin rippled under her touch, and his muscles bunched everywhere her lips touched. She nuzzled into his throat and inhaled his scent...fresh soap and warm, aroused man. Yum. She nibbled his earlobe, then blew softly into his ear.

He arched and groaned. The room spun, and without warning, she found herself on her back beneath him. His passion-dilated brown eyes danced. He grinned, white and wicked, and her stomach flip-flopped. "My turn to play."

Embracing her with his gaze, he lowered his head, and their breaths met, mingled. Whisper-soft, his lips touched hers. He nibbled on her lower lip, kissed the corners of her mouth, the bow of her upper lip. Fleeting kisses, sweet with promise.

He moved closer, increasing the delicious contact. His tongue flirted with hers, withdrew. She sighed in disappointment. Twice more he enticed her with brief, unsatisfying forays until she emitted a frustrated moan. Immediately, he answered her need, cradling her head in his palm as his tongue glided inside her mouth. His taste rocketed through her, cinnamon and spice, dangerously arousing. Her body was alive with the taste of him, the scent of him.

His muscles taut with ruthless control, Con's tongue stroked the inside of her mouth and dallied in intimate play. Slow and patient, his talented tongue teased and coaxed.

Desire built, need grew, and she gripped his shoulders. His body heat radiated through the thin fabric of her gown and his heartbeat slammed against hers. She drank in his potent, intoxicating kisses, craving more. So much more. Her breasts tingled, tight with need, and she rubbed against the hard planes of his chest. He groaned into her mouth.

Panting, he broke the kiss and eased back. "You're shaking," he whispered.

"So are you."

"Nerves?" he asked, his expression gentle.

"Passion," she breathed. "You?"

"Same here. Passion." He chuckled, a low rumble in his chest that vibrated inside her. "The word is hardly adequate to describe what I'm feeling. Whew!" He exhaled and rubbed his hand over his hair. "Before I lose *all* ability to think, I need my coat." He leaned over and tugged his leather jacket off the chair.

"What?" Confused, she shook her head. "I never figured you for the shy type. A bit late for an attack of modesty, don't you think?"

He laughed. "Baby, I've got condoms in the pocket."

She arched her brows. "Pretty sure of yourself, aren't you?"

"I'd hoped." He dumped a handful of bright gold wrappers on the bed. "So I came prepared."

"Holy cow." She goggled at the stack. "I guess so!"

His mischievous grin flashed. "Hope we don't run out before the storm is over."

"I dunno. I've got quite a list of activities for later."

"And 'later' just arrived." He kissed her, long and lingeringly. "Now that's a 'honey-do' list I can get into."

"Your honey appreciates your enthusiasm." She tugged on the drawstring at his waist. "Can I help you out of those pants, Officer Sexy?"

Con's grin widened. "You can debrief me any time."

Her giggles dissolved as he knelt and his pants slid low on his hips. With quick, efficient movements, he stripped them off. He was perfect. Male beauty and grace, strong and powerful. She blinked in awe. "Wow."

His fingers flirted with her ankle, stroked her calf and then glided along her thigh, sliding up her nightgown. "Now, let's get this off."

Con supported her with a hand behind her back, and she sat up. He eased the gown over her head and tossed it on the chair. Her cream-lace panties quickly followed. Naked, she lay back, smiling as his smoky gaze roamed over her. She'd expected to feel shy and awkward. Instead, rightness and peace filled her— as if she'd been born for this moment, this man. Indeed, she had. Her body knew she belonged wholly to him, as did her heart.

Con inhaled raggedly. "You are so beautiful." He reached over and plucked a pink rose from the pitcher on the nightstand. Holding the stem, he brushed her lips with the soft, cool petals. She breathed in the sweet fragrance.

Holding her gaze, he slowly, gently trailed the silky blossom along her throat, and she shivered under the erotic sensation.

As light as a butterfly's wing, he stroked the velvety rose in a straight line down the center of her body, just skimming the surface of her curls. From her thighs to the tips of her toes, he treated each leg to the sensual caress. Then each arm, from fin- gertips to shoulders. The rose wandered in a leisurely, languid journey over every inch of her, melting her bones.

Con's glowing eyes told her without words that she was pre- cious. Cherished. Loved. The heart connection shimmered be- tween them, and she silently returned his love. His eyes darkened. Message received.

If she lived to be a hundred, she would never lose the sense of wonder, the feeling of privilege to share his life.

He trailed the rose upward and circled her breasts with feath- ery strokes. Though he didn't touch her nipples, they pebbled, and she arched her back. He continued the delicious torment until her skin was so sensitized every nerve ending sang. Until she yearned to feel his hands on her.

"Con," she begged. "Touch me."

He set aside the blossom and moved over her, his weight propped on his arms. He bent his head to her breasts. "You smell sweeter than any flower," he murmured. His husky whisper bathed her skin in warmth. "A rose by any other name..." He leaned down and took her nipple into his mouth.

"Oh!" Her inner muscles clenched. A sweet, burning ache flowed through her and settled heavily at the juncture of her thighs.

He gave each breast his undivided attention, and with every

flick of his warm, textured tongue, the fiery ache inside her grew. His hands skimmed her curves, followed by his mouth. He tasted and tantalized like a man sampling desserts at a banquet, learning her secrets, telling her his.

Clinging to him, she panted for air, her limbs taut and trembling. This was a different kind of fire…vital, alive and almost too exciting to bear.

Seeking relief, she rocked her hips into his hardness, but the molten friction only increased her need. Con had ignited the inferno and only he could satisfy the hungry, licking flames. She gripped his wide shoulders in desperation. "Con, please!"

He covered her mound with his broad palm, and then his thumb brushed an exquisitely sensitive spot that had her nearly leaping off the bed. "Easy, sweetheart." His thumb stroked in a steady rhythm that set off bright, hot flares in every cell of her body.

She was shaking uncontrollably, couldn't remember how to breathe. She gasped. "I could die any second."

Con's tender, amused gaze captured hers. "You won't die."

Neon ribbons of pleasure streamed through her. "It's okay. I…don't care. As…long…as you don't stop doing…that."

His laugh was uneven. "I'm just getting started, baby."

Her belly tensed in anticipation as a thousand different sensations blazed to life at his touch. One long finger slid inside her, and she moaned at the unfamiliar, but amazing feeling.

His face inches from hers, Con pressed a soft kiss to her mouth. "Okay?"

"Better than…okay."

He stroked, slow and deep, wringing another moan from her. His clever fingers moved in a devastating rhythm, sending shimmers up her spine. Another finger joined the first. A moment of pressure, a slight twinge, and then the delicious sensations swirled again.

Con studied her face. "Did I hurt you?"

"No." The moment had quickly passed, was quickly forgotten. Wrapped in a sensual haze, she struggled to form a coherent thought. "Why?"

He withdrew his fingers, but his thumb continued the spiraling pleasure. "I just…made it easier for you later."

"Oh." Talking was becoming extremely difficult. As was thinking. "You're so sweet."

"Sweet?" Her hips rocked involuntarily under his hand, and a slow smile curved his sensual mouth. "What happened to sexy?"

What he was doing felt incredible. Her limbs trembled, and her breath rasped in short, hard gasps. "Sexy? Definitely. Yes."

He increased the pace, and her entire body went rigid, suspended on the verge of something wonderful.

"Go over for me, baby," Con murmured.

"Yes." She wanted to. Her body shuddered with wave after wave of sweet release. Con kissed her, giving her his essence, his breath. His hand slowed, drawing out the sensations. Like a warm, tropical ocean, desire retreated, advanced, never completely disappearing.

Con's hand teased and coaxed, and passion again spiraled. An intolerable emptiness inside her begged for fulfillment. The need for him thrummed in her blood. "I want you," she demanded against his mouth. "All of you."

"Milady's wish is my command." His knee parted her thighs, the slight rasp of hair sending a thrill through her nerve endings. The length of him slid tantalizingly along her center. His blunt heat pressed against her, then slowly pushed inward. Filling her with himself. Filling her with awe. Wonder. Happiness. "I didn't know," she gasped.

His hands clasped hers on the pillow beside her head and he linked his fingers with hers. They lay joined, palm to palm, heartbeat to heartbeat, soul to soul. "What, darlin'?"

"I never guessed. I never could have imagined how complete in every way I would feel with you inside me." Physically and emotionally.

He groaned. "I imagined it. But the fantasy didn't even come close to reality." He kissed her. "I love you, Bailey."

"I love you, too, Con."

He began to move and she lost all ability to reason.

She held his gaze, wrapped in the miraculous cloak of his love. He took her up, higher than she ever thought possible. Together, they danced on the sun's fiery surface. Flames blazed inside her, hot and bright. The flames grew stronger and more powerful with each rhythmic thrust, until they burst into an inferno inside her. With Con's glowing brown gaze embracing hers, she exploded into a thousand brilliant particles of light.

Con's fingers tightened on hers, his gaze dark, intense. He hastened the rhythm, spinning her even higher. "Again, darlin'."

The second peak hit her almost instantaneously. Swamped in ecstasy, she was dimly aware of Con's body shuddering on top of hers, of him shouting her name in completion. She didn't know where her joy ended and his began. They were one body. One spirit.

Forged into an inseparable bond.

Con lurched back to awareness. Or maybe regained consciousness, he wasn't sure which. He was still inside Bailey, with his face buried in her neck. Still gasping for breath. Still tingling from forehead to toenails.

Her dazed blue eyes blinked up at him. He brushed damp, tangled curls from her temple. "Are you all right?"

"Mmm. Absolutely. You?"

"I think I levitated off the bed at one point, but yeah."

Holding her gently, he kissed her, murmuring words of praise and endearment. She belonged to him, now. For all eternity. She slid her arms around his neck, and they rested, not speaking, but connected in the most elemental way. Forever united.

After a while, Bailey stirred. "Con?" A question shimmered in her low voice. She looked up at him, her face open and trusting in the flickering firelight.

God, he loved her so much. If she asked him to chop off an arm, he'd head for the knife drawer in the kitchen. "Yes, sweetheart?"

"Um. I…about that list…" She whispered in his ear.

The part of him that he'd thought down for the count eagerly rose to the occasion with a leap of exhilaration. He grinned at her. "Milady, your *every* wish is *definitely* my command!"

Sometime later—a long time later if he wagered a guess—he gently disengaged and rolled to one side, taking Bailey with him. Her luscious lips tilted, a slow lazy smile of perfect contentment, and his heart fisted. He wanted to see her this happy every day for the rest of his life.

The rest of his life. The thought slammed into him. Argh! He'd done everything ass-backwards. He'd meant to ask Bailey to marry him *before* making love to her. But when she'd propositioned him—both times—he'd completely lost it.

He gave himself a mental head slap. Okay, so he was a guy. Sometimes, the wrong part of his anatomy did the thinking. He'd make it up to her, here and now. He sat up and dragged his coat from the bottom of the bed. Fumbled in the pocket for the ring box. Once more, the atmosphere wasn't exactly moonlight and roses, but his proposal was way overdue. And a hundred percent from the heart.

He returned to her side. "Bailey—" The words evaporated in his mouth.

She was curled on her side, sound asleep. Again.

Bailey floated awake. Outside, the storm still sputtered, scattering sleet over the slate-gray morning. Con's attentive lovemaking had sizzled into her system, until everything inside her sparkled. She stretched and sighed. Every cell in her body was sated. She turned her head, and his mahogany gaze ensnared hers.

He grinned, his eyes crinkling at the corners. "Hi, there, Sleeping Beauty."

Her stomach clenched in wonder and appreciation. Draped in her mauve silk sheets, his hard, tanned body looked even more gorgeous, more potently male than she'd imagined. "Hi yourself, Officer Sexy."

"How do you feel?"

She smiled. "Glorious." She lowered her brows. "Don't you ever sleep?"

"Not when I can watch you, instead." His penetrating brown eyes studied her, his expression far more alert than the occasion warranted. What was he up to now?

He tweaked a curl. "How does a nice hot bath for two sound?"

Hmm. So much for conspiracy theories. Maybe she was imagining the undercurrent of intensity. "Heavenly."

"Be right back."

He strolled into the bathroom naked, at home in his body. She watched him, admiring his lean, athletic build, bronzed by firelight. She'd learned to appreciate exactly *how* athletic during the past—she glanced at the clock—three and a half hours. Con made love the way he did everything else. With thorough, utter commitment and contagious joie de vivre. He'd coaxed her dragon out to play, and it would never again retreat back into the cage. Not that she wanted it to. Now that she and the dragon understood one another, she *liked* the bolder aspects of her personality.

Water splashed into the tub, and then Con returned. He scooped her off the bed before she could rise. She giggled. "Hey! I can walk."

He wiggled his eyebrows at her. "We're a full-service establishment."

Whoo baby, he wasn't kidding. She didn't have the nerve to inventory the scattered condom wrappers as he carried her into the bathroom.

The pitcher of roses sat on the shelf behind the tub, along with replenished lit candles. Another pitcher of orange juice and two fluted champagne glasses completed the romantic ensemble. Con must have arranged them while she was sleeping. He left the door open so they had a view of the fireplace, and lowered her into the hot water, brimming with rose-scented bubbles.

He climbed in and sat facing her, their limbs entwined. She slid her hand along his calf, the sinewy muscles slick and soapy. "You'll smell all girly. Like me." She rather liked the primitive notion of branding him with her scent.

He inhaled, and passion glittered in his dark eyes. "I don't mind if you don't."

"The guys at the station will razz you up the wazoo."

"I don't intend on going back…" She narrowed her eyes, and he held up a dripping hand. "For a while. I'm taking some time off."

She cocked her head. "Right. To recover from your injuries before you accept the team leader position."

"No." He lifted a lone rosebud that was lying beside the tub and handed it to her. "To ensure you believe in the realm of mysteries."

Puzzled, she accepted the flower. "After the past twenty-four hours, I'm a faithful believer." Watching Con, who was again regarding her with that odd, smoldering intensity, she automatically lifted the blossom to her nose.

Anticipation stamped his handsome features. He looked like he was waiting for something. "What, Con? What is it?"

He merely grinned. Still bewildered, she lowered her gaze to the rose. A sparkling jewel—something that looked suspiciously like a diamond ring—was tucked inside the folded pink petals.

Her breath jammed in her throat. With trembling fingers, she withdrew an exquisite engagement ring from the rose.

"Bailey." Con's expression sobered. He clasped her left hand in both of his. "I love you with all my heart. With all my soul. With every breath I take. Will you marry me?"

Her heart leaped with joy. Tears filled her eyes and she flung her arms around his neck, sending bubbles flying. "Yes!"

He was shaking now, too. Holding her on his lap, he slid the ring onto the third finger of her left hand. A perfect fit. Just like the two of them.

Overflowing with happiness, she smiled through her tears. "You do realize I will never be able to tell our children and grandchildren exactly how you proposed?"

His grin bounced back. "We'll lie."

She feigned mock outrage. "Why, Conall Patrick O'Rourke. You want me to fib to our daughters and granddaughters?"

Laughing, he brushed bubbles off her nose. "Aphrodite, my goddess, rising from the foamy sea. You were right. You are like water."

She paused. She hadn't exactly been flattering herself with that description. Hesitantly she asked, "I am?"

"You bet. Water is one of the most powerful forces in nature. Ask anyone who has ever experienced a tsunami. But it can also quench thirst. Grow living things." He scooped up a handful of hot water and poured it over her shoulders. "Water cleanses, refreshes and restores."

She smiled into his dancing eyes, reflecting the golden firelight. Her joy was boundless. Her happiness complete. "I was also right about you. You are fire. Fire that warms, that banishes darkness with energy and light. Fire that sustains life."

He kissed her, long and deep, then drew back. Misty white vapor curled around them, enveloping them in a cozy, rose-scented cocoon. He stroked a wet finger down her cheek. "And together, they make…"

Grinning at each other, they spoke as one.

"Steam!"

* * * * *

Don't miss the next story in
Diana Duncan's thrilling new miniseries
FOREVER IN A DAY
TRUTH OR CONSEQUENCES
The story of Aidan O'Rourke and the persistent—
but beautiful—journalist
whose search for the truth wins Aidan's trust—
and his heart!

Coming in June 2005
Available wherever Silhouette Books are sold.

Coming in May from

 Silhouette®

INTIMATE MOMENTS™

and author

LORETH
ANNE WHITE

The Sheik Who Loved Me
IM #1368

When a deadly storm washes a beautiful
amnesiac onto the shores of the private
Red Sea island owned by Sheik David Rashid,
the life of the handsome businessman is
thrown into turmoil. The mysterious woman
awakens David's soul, stirring in him a
powerful passion he never dreamed possible.
But as her memory begins to return, the secrets
buried inside her threaten to destroy them all.
Because she is Jayde Ashton, a British secret
agent sent to betray the man she is falling for.

***Don't miss this thrilling new book...only from
Silhouette Intimate Moments.***

Available at your favorite retail outlet.

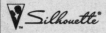

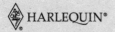

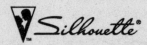

COMING NEXT MONTH